"When the killing ____ ____, Spear, then what?" Her question struck a ____ in him.

"Then something that will ease the pain."

"You mean liquor and women?"

"They help, sometimes."

"Spear," Carlotta whispered, "I need a man, right now, to make me feel alive. Lie down with me."

She was like a jewel, hard and precious. It seemed to him he could hold her in one hand, tiny and turning, someone remarkable just to behold. She was magnificent, too difficult to get close to, too compelling to avoid. If nothing else, he had to trust her.

He stood and took her in his arms, lifting her from the ground as he did so. Carlotta wrapped her arms around his neck and pulled him to her, their mouths open, greedy for one another, propelled not so much by urgency as longing. They kissed, deeply and long, her small body pressing against his. Brad set her down and she took his hand, walking toward the crude tent he'd made . . .

# The Silver MISTRESS

by Chet Cunningham

**API** Books

ISBN: 1-55547-310-5

Printed in Canada

# Chapter 1

Sam Eagleton looked like a fidgeting cowboy gussied up for church. A quick glance told anyone who cared to notice that the big, rawboned man worked long and hard out-of-doors. His broad, tanned face was roughened by the wind and sun. And the little finger of his left hand was missing, torn away years before as he tried to hold a cow down for branding. So, dressed like a gambler in a ruffled shirt, starched cuffs and a ridiculously tailed coat, the rancher looked awkward, or uncomfortable, but certainly foolish.

Still, his grin indicated that he was filled with pride. Sitting in Silver City's most elaborate hotel suite, surveying the table set before him, Sam nodded to himself. A man who could work and think too was unbeatable, he mused. And this, he was sure, was the winning.

Sterling silver candlesticks and goblets, fruit and wine, cream for your coffee and a rug under your feet. The Silver Crown Hotel had set him up with the perfect dinner with which to celebrate. Yes sir, when Sam Eagleton decided to do something, he did it with style. He glanced at the brand-new, shining Mexican boots on his feet that were perched on the dining table and then picked up a large silver tray that sat next to them.

He studied himself in the tray, using it like a mirror, admiring his oiled and well-combed hair. No bumpkin, not me, he thought as he straightened his scarlet tie.

Eagleton's feet clomped to the floor and he rose from his chair. Time to celebrate. There were only a few two-room suites in the Silver Crown and the management had obliged Sam with one of them. The connecting door between the parlor and bedroom was closed and he opened it quickly, without knocking. Everything here was his, he thought, so no need to stand on ceremony.

The woman who stood before him in the bedroom made the rancher exhale with appreciation. She was more than pretty and available, she was beautiful. Sam had seen her around town many times, had watched her walk down the street the way polite ladies don't. He had seen her stride into saloons all alone and had noticed that she didn't pay for the single whiskey and beer chaser she generally drank. He had never spoken to her, never dreamed of it. But riding the range or relaxing by a fire at night he had thought of her, often. Incredibly, on this the best day he'd had in months, he'd bumped into her in the Silver Crown's lobby, quite by accident, and they'd taken to talking.

"Like my dress?" Bunny West asked.

Sam didn't say a thing, smiling and trying to decide if he had ever seen anything like the straight, sheer gown she was wearing. Unlike most western dresses, it was simple and dark. It covered her completely, from the neck to the ankle, but, since its fabric was thin and Bunny wore nothing beneath it, the dress concealed nothing.

"Blue or black?" Eagleton asked.

"Huh?"

"Is the dress blue or black? I can't tell in this light."

"Blue. Do you like it?"

"Almost as much as I like the way you fill it," Eagleton replied.

Bunny laughed softly, neither embarrassed by the compliment nor surprised by it. Her trim, five-foot-three body was spectacular and she knew it. Her breasts weren't large but seemed so on her small frame and her hips flared dramatically from her tiny waist. Staring at Eagleton invitingly, she turned sideways to him and watched the rancher's eyes race over her.

"But I don't like the buttons," Sam said. Her dress was fastened in the back by a row of small, white buttons that extended from her neck to her waist. "Let's get rid of those damn buttons."

Eagleton took her by the shoulders and turned Bunny around. Immediately he began parting the back of her dress, one button at a time. Halfway through the chore, and impatient, he broke one and it went skittering to the floor.

"Damn," the man complained.

"No loss, I've lots," Bunny shrugged, closing her eyes in frustration. "Why don't you slow up on that and let me take care of it?" she added, turning to face him.

Sam couldn't stand all this much longer, but, resigned to sitting and watching her undress, he reached for her breasts eagerly, roughly.

"Whoa there, big fella, easy now. One thing at a time." Bunny waved him to a chair, a kind of mock scowl on her face and a twinkle in her eye. She reached behind and slowly unbuttoned her dress. The action sent her breasts jutting toward the rancher and forced her buttocks back.

"God. What a day." Eagleton mumbled, more to himself than Bunny.

Finished unfastening her dress, Bunny didn't remove it, but instead turned and walked back into the dining room. As she went, Sam watched the huge, deep V at the back of her opened dress disappear through the door and concentrated hard on the remarkable sway of her rump and thighs. Bunny popped a grape into her mouth and looked at the remains of their meal. Brown-sugar-glazed carrots still swam in a serving dish and the remains of a standing rib roast lay on its platter. She lifted a nearly empty bottle of wine out of a sterling silver stand and took two, long-stemmed glasses with her back into the bedroom. Placing the glasses on a bedside table, she began pouring a toast for the two of them.

Sam stood, walked up behind her and then slid his hands under her dress. He felt his way around her waist and then let his fingers glide up her ribs to the soft, full mounds he was seeking. He teased her nipples, gently this time, and bent at the waist to kiss her neck. Bunny shuddered at the thought of his nine rough fingers kneading her, but forced a low moan to encourage Sam.

"I swear," Sam whispered, "you're the prettiest thing in Nevada."

"I'll drink to that," Bunny laughed, standing and handing a glass to the rancher. She then quietly walked to the bed and sat, her legs crossed, her wine glass held to her lips.

Draining his glass in an instant, Eagleton turned to the woman who seemed to be waiting for him but keeping him waiting at the same time. He was a bit perplexed and almost irritated by all the prancing around and walking away that was going on. Sam had had his way all day and was damned if he wasn't going to get what he wanted now.

"Now, my dear," his voice deeper, more serious, "let's get on with dessert."

Bunny smiled and put her wine down, but didn't

move to undress or lie down on the comforter that lay across the featherbed. Sam sat down next to her and pulled the fine fabric of her gown first from one shoulder and then the other. Her breasts, firm and white, seemed to rise to him as she breathed deeply. Sam ran his four-fingered hand from her neck to her navel and then forced Bunny backward. Bending over her, he kissed her lips impatiently. Bunny answered him, her mouth opening and her left leg easing between his legs.

Bunny was surprised. She had endured the man up to this point because she had a job to do. He was a hick, though a rich hick, and rough. His hand was grotesque and his manner crude, she was sickened by him. Pinned beneath his broad shoulders, her arms half-bound by her dress, she gasped as his fingers slid across her skin.

"Thinking about finishing with you has me bothered, Sam," she whispered. "You're so huge."

He chuckled confidently, kissed her lips again and raised his massive frame so that he could study her. He moved his hand slowly across her body, brushing her stiffened nipples, then kissing them.

"Let me finish my wine, please, Sam. I want to savor you," she said.

"Huh? Now?"

"Please?" Bunny pleaded in a little girl's voice, her deep brown eyes searching Sam's.

Bunny sat up, pulling her dress back to her shoulders, and reached for her wine. Sam watched as she sipped, her fine, long fingers clasping the stem of the glass as though it would break at the slightest pressure. Bunny drank slowly, calming herself.

"We celebrating your visit to town or your clever way with land?" Bunny asked, trying to seem solicitous but not interested.

"My clever ways, Bunny, my very clever ways."

"Those certificates of yours are really something then?"

Eagleton grinned. "Damn right, little sweetheart. Sam Eagleton gets what he wants, every time, and what I wanted today was those certificates. I come after 'em and I got 'em."

"Tell me about it so I can celebrate with you," Bunny urged softly. "Otherwise, I might be celebrating you, not your success."

Sam leaned back, smug and self-satisfied. "What the hell, we've got all night," he began. "And you might as well know what this grin of mine is all about. I just picked up six sections of land, real cheap. Six sections of prime grazing property just west of my spread. Dumb railroad folks don't know what they've got to sell most of the time and so they peddled the property for a lousy five hundred dollars a section. Those certificates are Land Grant Certificates, straight from the government. They're worth a thousand or more apiece. And to me they're worth even more. They make me the largest cattleman north of the river."

Bunny's eyes sparkled and she let a slow smile spread across her face. It was her own hand that now moved to slip her dress off her shoulder. With two tantalizingly slow movements she was bare to the waist. She then stood, facing Sam, and her dress fell away, a small, shimmering pile of fabric at her feet.

"I know what a man wants when he's winning," she announced, her tongue playing over her lips, wetting them. Bunny walked to the seated man, her breasts bobbing slightly as she came. Sam reached around her as he sat on the bed, his knees spread, her hips pushing against him. He opened his mouth and nearly inhaled her breast. As he tasted her, his fingers roamed across her buttocks and down her hips. Then, pulling her down next to him, his fingers searched for her dark, waiting mound. His hand threaded through the curled hairs that hid what he was seeking and Sam felt Bunny's lips and tongue in his ear. Suddenly, she was off the bed and gliding naked through the door, back into the dining room.

"Christ, woman! What the blazes are you up to this time?"

"If we're going to celebrate, Sam, we'll need more wine." She winked at him, poking her head around the door. "And just to save time, why don't you get out of your pants while I pour? I never saw a man yet who was much good with his britches on."

Eagleton grumbled under his breath and quickly began wrestling with his belt.

At the table, Bunny took the last bottle of wine from the sterling silver stand and filled Sam's glass. She then removed a vial from her purse on the table and with swift, sure movements removed the cap and emptied the container's contents into his wine.

Returning to the bedroom she found Sam naked from the waist down and she stared at his powerful legs and half-erect organ. Sam didn't notice her. Ever the cowboy, no matter how clever, he was struggling with the elaborate cuff links that held his new shirt together. He was beginning to think he might never get this woman on her back.

"Let me," Bunny offered, handing him his glass and turning to his shirt.

Sam took the glass of wine in one hand and extended his other toward her. "Thanks, but it wouldn't pay to get drunk."

"Drunk?" she laughed. "This is your third glass of wine. You mean you're not man enough to drink with little me?"

Sam sipped his wine.

Bunny, finally finished releasing Sam from his ruffled

sleeves, stared at the man. "Come on, Sam," she urged. "I'm getting wilder and wilder as I wait for you. Just move along with that wine and I'll treat you to a New Orleans Grinder. Ever hear of it?"

The man's eyes widened, aching in their sockets. "Gal, I've heard of it but never been blessed with a woman crazy enough to give it a try." Sam took a swift gulp of wine, emptying his glass. "Let's have at it."

"Comin' up, Sam. Twice if you're man enough to stand it."

Eagleton didn't hesitate. He dropped his empty glass to the carpet and rolled into the bed. Bunny watched him as he lay in the deep folds of feathers and comforter, naked, smiling and erect. She smiled.

"Better lock the door and hide your prize certificates," she suggested. "No sense your worrying over them while I'm working you over."

"Okay, okay," he replied. "Shove my saddlebags under the bed and let's get on with it."

Bunny lifted the saddlebags from the desk opposite the bed and held them just beyond Sam's reach. As he raised himself to grab the bags, his face flushed and his eyes rolled. "That's funny," he said. "Everything got fuzzy there for a minute. Damn, that was strange." He lay back in the bed and closed his eyes, his hands pressing firmly on his forehead.

Bunny then moved to the bed and dropped the saddlebags beside Sam's feet. She stared at him, watching his erection fade in his confusion. Gently, slowly, she reached across the bed and fondled him.

"What the hell . . . ," Eagleton moaned, annoyed.

"Ready, big fella?"

Sam moaned again, dizzy and feeling a touch of fever.

"What's the matter, lover? Too much to drink?" she teased.

As she taunted him, the fuzzy fires in his temples grew warmer and a burning started in his belly. He shook his head once more and let out a roar that was part pain and part anger. Knives seemed to be working in his middle, but when he raised his head to see what was happening, the world spun around him, out of focus. Sam's face contorted in agony and, involuntarily, his knees came to his chest, turning his huge frame into a pathetic ball.

"What the hell?" he groaned, the pains sweeping over him again. He lay bunched on the bed, his mouth hanging open, his jaw stiff.

Bunny backed away from the man, picked up her dress from the floor and hung it neatly over the back of a chair. She then stood and stared at the trembling, half-naked man on the bed.

Eagleton made one last, feeble attempt to sit up. But as he did so, a spasm racked the length of his six-foot frame and he screamed, or at least thought he did. The sound that rasped from his mouth was little more than a furious burbling. His knees rose and fell, apparently trying to smother the pain in his midsection. Then a violent convulsion ripped through him, jerking and flopping him up and down on the bed. His face twitched and his mouth made bizarre chewing movements.

Bunny West, naked, standing with her hands on her hips, became radiant. Rapt, fascinated, unable to turn from her victim, she cautiously approached the suffering man. Her eyes bore into his agony, concentrating on his face, then moving to the tormented fists that beat against the bed. As she watched him struggle, her nipples grew erect and she felt the simultaneous chill of her skin and growing warmth within her body.

Bunny simply whispered, "Ahhh!"

She moved to the far side of the bed, never once

taking her eyes off Sam. Once well beyond his thrashing, she climbed into the featherbed beside him, lying on her side, one hand propped beneath her head to witness his death. Her other hand wandered downward, fondly stroking first her breasts and then the soft wetness between her legs. Her thighs spread slowly and she fingered herself.

Each time Eagleton arched his back or lifted his knees, whenever his throat would groan or his eyes open in panic, Bunny moaned. Unable to take her eyes off the dying rancher, she rubbed herself with faster and faster strokes. The jolting of the body next to her seemed to echo deep within as she played on the sensitive point of all her pleasure. Finally, as Sam Eagleton quivered and became still, her building tension burst to the surface in a violent, exhausting orgasm.

She lay there for a moment, perspiring. The man was completely still save for the faintest sign of shallow breathing. Bunny then rose and looked at him. Her eyes dry and hard, her face without emotion, she walked deliberately to her dress, slipped it on and began to re-button it, never taking her eyes from the almost-dead rancher. Once dressed, she picked up the saddlebags from the bed and groped through them until she found a long envelope holding six Land Grant Certificates.

Bunny didn't smile. Her catch was assured hours before. Her face did not betray a hint of satisfaction. All business, she stopped in front of a mirror and touched her hair, fluffing it back into place. She rinsed her hands and face with water poured from a large china pitcher into a heavy china washbowl and then dried her beautiful face with a small towel.

Lifting Eagleton's pants from the floor, she searched his pockets. The wallet she found there contained two ten dollar bills, two fifties and six gold double eagles. She took the coins and the fifties and left the smaller bills. After replacing the wallet in the pants, she entered the dining room.

Bunny retrieved her black shawl from a sofa and her purse from the dining table. Quickly, she exited the suite and, taking the stairs slowly, walked into the lobby of the hotel as though she were a proper society dame.

That same night, just down the street from the Silver Crown, in a private gaming room at the Sundown Saloon, Wyoming Jones looked over the tops of his cards at the mark across the table. Jones appeared to be a drifter. His hair hung blond, a little too long about his ears, and his full mustache drooped at the corners of his mouth. But his casual appearance was a guise. His piercing blue eyes and rock-steady hands told the appreciative observer that the man was a professional.

Wyoming Jones was, in fact, a magician. A master of sleight of hand and the inventor of several remarkably ingenious machines all dedicated to mystifying people from a stage. The West, though, had little need for gifted magicians. So Jones used his skills to play cards. It bothered him sometimes, since the arts of misdirection and illusion were so much more challenging to him. Still, dealing cards paid better.

Jones was waiting for the next player to bet or toss in his hand. A friendly sort, the town's hardware store owner and a sharp card player as well, the older man peered at Jones. He was trying to figure out whether Wyoming was cheating or bluffing. The shopkeeper decided it was a bad bet. He threw in his cards.

Jones turned his attention to the third man and allowed his eyes to soften a bit. The next player was Dr.

Paul Brockington, a sometime physician who more often concentrated on real estate. He secretly owned the Sundown Saloon, one of many shadow operations he ran in Silver City. About five and a half feet tall, with the paunch of a wealthy and secure man, Brockington loved black cigars, the clink of glass and the fall of cards. Wyoming Jones knew that with old Doc Brock, playing cards wasn't really gambling. He was a masterful calculator of odds, a shrewd judge of character and an able cheat as well.

"Jones," the doctor offered almost offhandedly, with an affected air of casualness, "I'll see your five hundred and raise you, oh, fifteen hundred." The good doctor dropped a Land Grant Certificate into the pot. "We set the price on these things at two thousand dollars when the game started—right?"

Jones nodded and looked toward the man who called himself Willard Martin. Martin was visibly nervous and held his five cards so tightly it seemed the ink would squeeze out of them and drip onto the table. He looked at his hand—an ace of clubs. A thin line of sweat slowly appeared across his forehead.

Martin didn't know what to do. He was there from Humboldt, looking into silver mining holes near town. He was no stranger to high stakes poker, but this game had him puzzled. He couldn't put his finger on any cheating, but something was strange. No watchers ringed the table and no mirrors loomed overhead. Yet something was awry.

But what a hand he held! It was all he could think about. He saw in his mind's eye the two queens he'd been dealt in this game of draw poker. He'd discarded the other three cards and stayed in. The dealer had then slid him another beautiful queen, the ace of clubs and then that last one, a fourth queen! His queens spoiled anyone else's hopes for a royal flush and the lone ace in his hand made a foursome of the game's highest markers impossible. The chances of a better hand being held were slim, very slim.

Still, Martin hesitated. He pondered the doctor, who he reasoned, could hardly be a cardsharp. And it didn't seem likely that the drifter would slip a reputable citizen like Brockington a bum deal. Martin sweated. He was more than five hundred behind already. The bet was two thousand to him and he didn't have that kind of cash. His only real assets were the two Land Grant Certificates he possessed. But they were reserved for the purchase of a promising silver mine. He ran his sleeve across the band of forehead sweat that reappeared more frequently as the hand went on.

"Two thousand to me?"

Dr. Brockington nodded.

"Hell, I'll give it a shot," Martin decided. He reached inside his coat and extracted a folded certificate. With a weak smile and trembling hand, he tossed it in the pot.

The certificate was a curiously plain document, with a small engraving of horses pulling a plow at one top corner. Following the plow, in sturdy block letters, were the words "THE UNITED STATES OF AMERICA," and in script "To all to whom these presents shall come, Greetings." A red, official seal appeared at the bottom of the page, and the legal description and the township and range number of the section of land in question were included. It was simply eight by ten inches of fairly stiff paper. But its possession entitled the holder to a substantial piece of American frontier.

The next man in the game quietly dropped out, leaving the dealer, Wyoming Jones, to make the next move. He met the fifteen hundred raises to his five hundred bet and jumped the ante by another fifty dollars. It wasn't time to let it die. When all eyes moved to Dr. Brockington, he didn't make them wait. He glanced briefly at his cards and threw in another Land Grant Certificate plus the necessary fifty dollars. With a flourish he then added yet another fifty.

Willard Martin shook his head, leaned back and gazed at the ceiling. It was filthy, coated with dust and the grime of cigars. Its roughhewn timbers supported a small menagerie of spiders.

"Somebody at this table is crazy," Martin observed, apparently consulting with an imagined friend floating among the rafters.

The stakes were too rich for Martin, he was sure. But what a hand he held. The odds had to be at least a thousand to one either man still in the game was holding four kings or a straight flush, and those alone could beat him. It just didn't figure! He tapped his cards on the table and wondered if it were he who was crazy. The pot was unbelievable, his hand nearly perfect. Without a word he dropped his last Land Grant Certificate into the pot and added the required hundred dollars to meet the previous bets.

Jones looked at the pot and called, pushing in stacks of bills to cover the two thousand fifty to him.

The hardware store owner, no longer playing, couldn't help but comment. "Now we come to it," he said, thrilled by the game.

"Let's see what you're so proud of, Sawbones," Jones eyed the doctor.

Dr. Brockington turned his cards over, one at time, revealing a full house, aces over jacks. "Read 'em and pay up," he replied with satisfaction.

"Sorry, Doctor!" The excited words leapt from Martin's throat as he jubilantly laid down his cards. "But my four ladies beat your house into the ground." He reached hungrily for the pot.

Jones touched Martin's hand. "Mr. Martin," he drawled, "you don't know what I'm holding."

Martin nodded, the lines of his face sagging and his fingers retreating across the table. His faith punctured, he knew the outcome. Wyoming Jones confirmed it by spreading four kings across the table.

Martin exploded. "Goddamnit!" he thundered, knocking his chair over backward as he jumped to his feet and reached for the gun at his hip.

The doctor waved a pudgy hand across the table. "Don't do it, boy."

"Jones is a cheat," Martin roared. "It's obvious."

"Not to me," offered the doctor. "And if he is, he must surely be quick with his gun to have survived this long."

Martin took his hand from his still-holstered .44 and gazed at Jones stacking his winnings. The cardsharp didn't seem to be paying attention to the frustrated man.

"You're wearing on me," Jones finally stated. His money and certificates counted and folded in his vest, Wyoming Jones stood up, his hand hovering just above his side arm.

"Now, now, Mr. Jones," Dr. Brockington intervened. "I don't want any trouble here. We don't want anything to spoil this little game. Now you just calm down, the both of you. All the money here isn't worth getting killed over."

"It ain't me that's doing the dying here," Jones retorted, an obvious and irrevocable truth.

Martin glanced at Jones and decided the gambler had the edge. What's more, in a strange town, with no money, Martin knew he'd find nothing but trouble even if he survived a draw against the card player. Dr. Brockington nodded to the frightened hardware store owner who was slowly but steadily inching his chair away from the table.

"Show this young man the door, for his own sake," the doctor ordered. With that the room emptied, save for Brockington and Jones. On his way to the street, Willard Martin bought a bottle of whiskey. He went to his hotel room $4,500 poorer, but alive. He thought about riding north in the morning to study the three silver holes he was interested in. Maybe one of them would pack a rich vein that would return his losses before too long. He swore off cards. And strangers. The whiskey had no taste.

In the back room of the Sundown Saloon, Dr. Brockington and Wyoming Jones sat finishing their drinks. The physician rose, locked the door and held out his hand for the winnings. Jones gave him more than seven thousand dollars, including the Land Grant Certificates.

"A masterful performance, Mr. Jones, if I do say so. You played beautifully tonight. Your technique is impeccable. Not once did I notice you dealing from the bottom, and I was looking for it. You didn't seem to even glance at the cards."

Wyoming Jones stood expressionless. "Thanks, Doc. A craftsman is worthy of his hire."

"Well, true. But an artist shouldn't be overworked. I think you ought to stay in your hotel for a few days. Practice your prestidigitation. We can't have you winning too much money all at once in a town this small."

"Whatever you say, Doc. You're the boss."

The doctor-turned-realtor waved as Wyoming Jones went out a back door into the alley. Damn right, he was the boss, Dr. Brockington mused.

The Right Honorable Ramsey Stuart Rogers' hand cradled a huge snifter of dark brandy. The burgundy leather of his chair creaked as his tall body stood up, surveying the small gathering in his private study. The smell of fine cigars, the company of powerful men and the conspiratorial purpose of the meeting pleased him. A United States Senator, Rogers was at home in any arena where polite collusion was the rule.

"Fine brandy, Ted," a guest noted.

"Difficult to acquire here, I must say," the senator responded. "To ship a case, unopened, across both the Atlantic and the better part of this country demands the logistical skill of a truly gifted freight agent. Finding one is a chore."

"But worth it."

"At least to your guests."

"It is my mission in life to bring this state the cooperation of Washington, the financing of New York and the brandy of France," the senator offered with a smile. He was leading to his favorite subject, the purpose of the evening's entertainment. His guests, the four most influential men in the state, were fed and comfortable, surrounded by the high style of his home and engulfed in the reassuring tone of his deep voice.

Nicknamed Ted because no young man could ever be called Ramsey, the senator was interested in money more than in anything on earth. He was from a silver-rich state, handsome, articulate, well-married and greedy. But to those who knew him he appeared a visionary.

Louis Kingswood, a banker from Aurora, distrusted the zeal of this visionary. "Now that the brandy is warming in my hand, but before too much of it seeps into my skull, let's get to the business at hand." Kingswood had traveled from Aurora to Silver City's "Heights" district solely to attend this dinner. A staunch financial conservative, he could ill-afford the state's elite discussing their future without his being present.

"Yes, Ted, what's on your mind?" the state treasurer asked.

"Gentlemen, Washington wants to know what we're *doing* out here. They see us as the temporary silver capital of the world. And because they know, just as surely as we do, that the silver will one day be gone, they conclude we are childish not to plan for that day."

"Plans are cheap," interrupted the banker.

"Washington understands that. They've funded the railroad with public land sales, asking nothing from the state. But now they expect us to grow, to develop, to produce more than we consume. They want our population to double in the next ten years. They want us to absorb the human flood at their shores and turn this continent into something. The bonanza from silver will end, soon. When it does, Silver City and Eureka and the other mining towns may well disappear. While we're rich we must invest, invest in the future."

"That's easy for you to say, Ted. But I don't see you putting millions into irrigation or fronting hundreds of thousands to ranchers who need breeding cattle," the banker argued, sure of his facts.

"Ted, the risks of state projects are far greater than those of mining. You can't expect private investors to sink their money into the public welfare."

"You folks in Washington can expect anything you damn well please, but that won't get the job done."

"He's right, Ted."

"Gentlemen," the senator continued. "You know that I'm not a wealthy man. But I can assure you that every penny I possess is invested in Nevada real estate—every penny. My purpose is to benefit all, myself included, by developing the ground we all live on."

"How?" the blunt banker inquired.

"As I see it, the key men in the U.S. Senate and House are looking to help us. But they want an organized effort, and some commitments. That means that Carson City is the key. Our state government, both the legislature and the governor, has to come up with some enabling legislation. Some state cooperation is necessary. Then we must marshal our forces and contribute, invest, what we can. I'm convinced that Washington will see us through once we've begun."

The senator sat down in his chair and sipped his brandy.

"You want us to go first, basically."

"You'll profit first, actually."

"Or lose everything on our own, finally."

"Correct."

"Then, Senator, perhaps you can explain why there is so much activity in Land Grant Certificates, especially around Silver City. If our wonderful state is in so much trouble, why are people gobbling up land so fast?"

"It's true," the senator replied. "There does seem to be a minor flurry of activity in the certificates, but it's strictly local. Probably blow over in a week or two. They tell me it happens whenever the railroad opens its doors to buyers."

"Then you think this is a passing thing?"

"I do. However, if any of you happen to own a certificate or two from the Silver City area . . ." The senator smiled, an apparent jokester, and the men laughed. One guest, though, glanced at Senator Rogers and nodded.

"A splash more of this stuff?" Rogers asked to no one in particular.

"Certainly."

"And why not? It seems our host will see to it we pay for the bottle, one way or another," the banker frowned. He knew that if the governor and state senate moved on the issue, he must follow. And he was certain, now, that the tide of events would force them to gamble in order to be re-elected. It was that simple. Rogers would win.

Over their second drinks the men talked of women and horses, the likelihood that gold might soon be discovered and the weather. In an hour their wives called them to their carriages and the guests bid their host a good evening.

As the mahogany doors of the Rogers' home closed behind the last of the evening's guests, Rebecca Rogers sank into a large chair and sighed. She was a handsome woman, tall and energetic. Even though exhausted from the prattle of country conversation with the wives of important men, she looked alert. Her darting green eyes shone in the warm light of candles and tall-chimneyed kerosene lamps.

"That was a pleasant enough party, Ted, considering. I hope you found out what you wanted to."

The senator loosened his tie with one hand while sloshing his brandy about the snifter in the other hand. "I beg your pardon, my love."

"Ted. Really. I'm your wife, remember," she sighed. "I've been married to you too long not to see the signs. I simply hope it all worked out the way you intended it to."

"You, my dear, are a predator of the most delicious sort."

"Nothing, really."

"No, no. You're too modest. There isn't one woman in the state who can understand the politics of money as well as you."

"Learned at my daddy's knee."

"Ahhh. Boston's legendary thief. That old son-of-a-bitch should have been hung."

"They shot my father, remember?" she corrected with a strange smile.

Senator Rogers shook his head. He had been married to Rebecca for twenty-two years and yet she continued to amaze him. Outrageously wealthy, she had wed a handsome, educated nobody. And today, in her late forties, her long hair piled high on her head, her flawless complexion and aquiline features made her a beauty still. Especially in the glow of candles, brandy and a successful meeting.

Rebecca Rogers peeled her shoes from her feet and lifted them to an embroidered hassock. "Will much of my money be required?" she asked.

"Am I that transparent to you?" he wondered aloud.

"Oh, God, no. I just understand your problem, and want to help, if I can."

The senator knew from her posture, from her lazing head and flashing eyes, that his wife had but one thing on her mind. Not money or power or politics. Content with himself and his performance, the meal and his prospects, it seemed to him to be a perfect idea. He looked fondly on her outstretched form and thought to himself that a man who married wealth didn't also deserve such a mate.

"Sleepy?" he asked.

She rose and walked to him, unbinding the dark, straight hair above her head and letting it fall to her shoulders. It cascaded around her neck and down her full bosom. While sipping his brandy, Ted Rogers watched Rebecca as she knelt beside him on the floor. Her hand glided to his thigh and then slowly wandered to his stiffening member.

"Not sleepy, but ready for bed," she whispered.

"If I can walk the stairs . . ."

"I'll help," she offered, her mischievous eyes gazing up at him.

Ted Rogers chuckled. He was relieved. He had won. Not only would his wife support the next stage of his plan with generous contributions from her inheritance, but she would exact a most pleasant price for her involvement. She would worm the details from him, even counsel him on the scheme, but she would lend him the money. The additional Land Grant Certificates would be his. Now he need only enjoy his wife's beauty and insatiable lust.

In their bedroom, Rogers undressed quickly, shedding his clothes as though they were meant to be discarded once he had worn them. He then settled into the massive four-posted bed that stood in the very center of the room. Half-seated, half-lying down, he continued to swirl the last bit of brandy in his snifter.

While watching him, his wife removed the stiff bodice of her dress, followed by her full skirt and several petticoats. Inhaling, she unhooked the girdle around her waist. Only then, thought Rogers, could one understand the sublime vanity of his wife. Not thin, she was tall and full-breasted. But though a woman who had not been a girl for twenty years, Rebecca Rogers kept her figure under careful control. Her narrow waist hardly required a girdle, under any circumstances, and the gentle curves of her thighs could not be more inviting.

Naked, except for the pearls around her neck, Rebecca turned down the wick of the lamp beside their bed. She then rolled beside him, smelling of perfume, and lifted the glass from his hand.

"Sleepy?" she asked.

"Tired."

"Relax."

Her hands began at his chest, her long nails leaving faint white lines. She bent and kissed his shoulder and Rogers' hands settled behind his head. He sighed as her hands moved across his belly to his crotch, and one knee lifted as she continued down its thigh. He felt himself hardening, rising, as Rebecca played with him, touching too lightly, too quickly to satisfy. As his heat grew, he moved one hand from behind his head and stroked the breast that floated before him.

Rebecca's pale skin felt as smooth as silk. He contemplated its sweet touch often, but never quite imagined her as she really was. In bed, trailing over her, he was always surprised by the delicacy of her. Large, soft breasts yielded to his touch, conforming to him, and her skin glistened with her growing excitement.

"Yes," she said, holding herself perfectly still. "Yes."

But Rogers didn't want her to stop. So he reached for her hand and replaced it on his thick member. She stroked him, running her fingers through the dark hair of his groin and along his shaft.

He then settled into a lazy play, massaging the rich hemispheres before him. Rebecca's eyes closed and her head fell, sending shivers through his body as her hair brushed across his chest.

Her hand finally reached for his and guided it to the silken mound between her legs. He slid a finger into her, finding a moist welcome. Her full hips shuddered and strained toward him as he played with her.

Rebecca lowered her mouth to his, pressing against him, and quickly lifted herself until she straddled him. Moving her lips from his, she watched him, her eyes narrowed, her arms straight, her breasts hanging full and soft.

On her knees, she lowered herself. His tip worked

against her, touching, easing. She rotated against him, gently, and then raised herself with a moan.

Rogers moved his hands to his wife's waist. He was fascinated by her rapture. The touch of her skin and the bliss of her expression suspended him, or distracted him, from his own desire. And so he watched her.

Finally, Rebecca lowered her hand and steadied his organ beneath her. Then, she descended. Slowly, so slowly he thought he might scream, she consumed him. And as she lowered her soft buttocks to his thighs, he found himself deep within her.

The patient rotating of her hips grew quicker only gradually. But as he watched her, feeling her breasts and belly, running his hands along her thighs, he saw Rebecca's eyes widen and felt her movements grow more intense, more frenzied. Listening to the liquid music of her movements, he felt the growing weight of her desire. She pressed him eagerly, so steadily he thought she might explode, and then came release. Her head shook from side to side and her hips surged against him as his wife hung her head, tapping the last of her strength before she collapsed on him, motionless.

She settled to his chest, limp, slick with perspiration, and kissed his neck.

"Wonderful," Rogers said.

"Mmmmm."

"Lie quietly, my love." He unclasped the pearls that now lay pressed between them and dropped the strand to the floor. Still beneath her, he held her quietly a moment and then lowered his hands to her buttocks. In an instant he was moving in her, deeply.

"Yes, please, more," she whispered.

Burning, he forced her hips into the air with each thrust and pulled them to him as she fell back into the soft bed.

"God, more," she moaned. "Now."

In seconds Rebecca came again, this time screaming her delight and Rogers spurted into her, groaning with the release. His energy kept her moving, though, and she lingered over him, sliding her hips from side to side until he slept.

# Chapter 2

The late morning sun threw crisp shadows across the railroad siding in Silver City. While the sky was clear, bright and dry, the air failed to warm very much and it was bitter cold in the shadows. No wind blew, but the chill worked its way into the stationmaster's bones as he stood waiting for the 11:04 to arrive.

"At last," he muttered as the telltale line of smoke appeared in the distance, "the thing's gonna be an hour late getting out of here."

Within minutes the unholy clatter and wheezing breath of the engine pulled to a stop beside the station. A tired and dirty engineer smiled down at the stationmaster.

"Blowing like crazy back there, Jim. Couldn't keep the grit out of my eyes. And raised hell with two packer boxes."

"Terrific," the stationmaster responded, shaking his head.

As the two men continued to console each other over the perils of rail transportation in the West, a tall man carrying a carpetbag stepped from inside the train onto its platform. His eyes were shaded by a tan Stetson hat pulled low over his brow. He studied the nearly empty station as he stood waiting for the stationmaster to place a step stool on the siding. But the harried, chilled attendant continued to talk with the engineer, ignoring the passenger.

With a disgusted glance at the duo and an irritated scratch of his black, close-trimmed beard, Brad Spear jumped from the train. A thin layer of brown dust clung to his beard and coated the shoulders of his topcoat. He had the look of a hard man made harder by a long, sleepless trip.

Nor did the surroundings seem to improve his disposition. Spear looked at the railroad station, the jabbering stationmaster and the filthy train, then reached into his pocket and retrieved a notebook. "Nevada House Hotel" was written on one of its pages.

The Pinkerton Detective Agency, for which Spear worked, had wired reservations, under an assumed name, to the hotel. His immediate superior in San Francisco had explained that the place was "inconspicuous," code for a dump. Mediocre dining and the siege of bedbugs were virtually guaranteed. And, thought Spear, it was cold.

The hotel was only a few blocks from the train station, so Spear's long strides, quickened by the cold, brought him there in minutes. Once inside, the warmth of a potbelly stove comforted him as the agent approached the desk clerk. A tall, gaunt man, wearing mittens and a scarf, greeted him. "Welcome, sir, to the Nevada House."

"Reservation for Streib."

"Yes sir, best room in the place," he said, handing Spear the key and turning the register for his signature. The agent logged himself in as Brad Streib.

"Yours, Mr. Streib, is number 312, top floor, on your right. Can I carry your bag?" the clerk asked, clearly wishing not to.

"No, thanks, not much in it anyway," Spear said.

Brad Spear climbed the stairs of the hotel with an

athletic sureness, moving swiftly up two flights. He paused a moment at the last landing and surveyed the grim walls and threadbare carpet of the narrow hallway. He wondered where the nearest hot tub could be found.

Spear's strides were light and easy along the carpet runner. As he moved down the hall to the last door on the right, marked 312, he thought he heard a faint noise from within.

Brad stopped, listening, and drew his six-gun. With one motion he turned the knob of the door leading to his room and tossed the carpetbag into the air. At the same moment he dove to the floor, his weapon rolling with him, taking dead aim at the man inside. Spear didn't fire, however. Once prone, his gun leveled, he found a rotund little man sitting in a rocking chair in the corner. He was wide-eyed, his large fists white-knuckled as he gripped the chair's arms in panic.

"Allow me to introduce myself," Spear said.

"What?" croaked the uninvited guest.

"My name is Brad Streib. May I ask yours?"

"Loftin. Loftin. The banker."

"Ah yes," muttered Spear. "Sorry if I startled you, but in my line of work folks usually knock before settling in my room. Damn near blew your head off, Mr. Loftin. A bad way to start off a business relationship."

"God," was all Loftin could manage.

Brad eased the hammer of his side arm down on the empty chamber and sat on the sagging, coarse-blanketed bed against the wall.

"I came here to talk to you, Mr. Spear," Loftin spoke in a rush. "It's important we get on with it as soon as possible. I'm sorry I didn't wait in the lobby, but the desk clerk is an idiot. His talking drives me crazy. I . . ."

Brad raised a hand, interrupting Loftin. He then told the man to relax.

Loftin rose and shook Brad's hand. His grip indicated that the fidgety, balding man had done something in life other than run a bank.

"Pleased to meet you, Mr. Spear. I'm grateful that Pinkerton managed to send you on your way so quickly. The local sheriff hasn't uncovered a thing about the robbery and I'm beginning to wonder if he hasn't given up entirely."

"Let's begin at the beginning," Brad suggested, opening his notebook. He watched Lyn Loftin, owner of Silver City's only bank, light a long, thin cigar in an effort to steady himself. "Your bank was broken into and robbed some two weeks ago, correct?"

"Correct."

"And as I understand it," Spear continued, "you're out $15,000 in cash, plus the contents of your safety deposit boxes. Jewels, stocks, bonds, cash, and the like."

"That's right."

"Do you know what the property in the safety deposit boxes was worth?"

"Well, sir, yes and no. I've compiled a list of the material that the owners *claim* was in the boxes, but I've no way of knowing if they're telling me the truth. We don't log things in and out of the boxes."

"We'll get to that list in a while."

"I hope not," Loftin said, almost pleading.

Spear furrowed his brow, the question obvious.

"I hope you don't need the list, is all. Everything on it is, how do you say, confidential. I had a devil of a time getting people to tell even *me* what was stolen."

"Mr. Loftin," Brad lectured. "My role here is as confidential as it can be. We'll look that list over later. Tell me about the break-in."

"Somebody had two keys. They got into the building without breaking anything and didn't have to force the door to the back room, either. They busted up the vault for sure, but just walked in, otherwise."

"Sure sounds like an inside job, sir."

"I know, I know," sighed the banker, pacing the room. Once he stood up, it was clear that Loftin had worked with his hands and back for years before becoming a banker. Overweight, he nevertheless had the sort of barrel-chested, thick-wristed look of a man who worked with a shovel. Brad recalled his background information: Loftin had made his fortune mining coal, then silver and gold during Nevada's earliest boom days. He had hit it big, finally, and sold his share of a silver mine for nearly a half-million dollars. He had set up a bank in his favorite town to hold his earnings and had prospered as other miners sought a place to keep their wealth.

Loftin drew on his cigar and looked straight into Brad's eyes.

"Mr. Spear, you may find this difficult to fathom, but I don't feel that there's the slightest possibility of an inside job. Even though it seems like the whole thing couldn't have been pulled off any other way. The more I think about it, the more sure I am my people weren't involved."

Brad peered at the banker, skeptical.

"I have only five employees. I've known all of them, or their families, for at least ten years. And I'm not so long out of the mines, where you better be able to judge folks, that I can't spot a thief when I see one. I'd trust any of them with my entire stake. You can save yourself some time . . ."

"Mr. Loftin," Brad interrupted, "time I've got. Suspects are harder to come by. The burglars somehow got

their hands on two keys to your bank and until I find
out how, I'm not ruling anyone out. Even you."

The banker sat down. He was out of his league and
smart enough to know it.

"Well, Mr. Spear, you'll want to work in the bank,
then."

"That's right, as planned. If I nose around your
place for a few days, undercover, of course, I may turn
this case quickly. As you can see from the lavish ac-
commodations here, I would consider a quick end to
this investigation a blessing."

Lyn Loftin couldn't help but laugh. The tall, handsome agent had been in worse places, that was obvious,
but he knew enough about better lodgings to dislike the
Nevada House.

"You'll start as a teller trainee, Mr. Spear. We'll call
you Streib, a friend of the Loftin family."

"Sounds fine," Spear agreed.

Loftin pulled a heavy silver chain out of his pocket
and looked at his watch. "It's almost noon. Have some
dinner and stop by the bank at one. I'll pretend not to
know you, only your name, all right . . . Mr., er,
Streib?"

Brad stood and shook the banker's hand. Once his
client had left, Brad thumbed through his notebook. It
contained precious little information at this point. No
solid suspects, absolutely no real evidence that might
lead to any and the very odd question that bothered
him the most: nobody really knew what had been
stolen. Spear pushed the notebook aside. The issue was
the keys.

Spear arrived at the Loftin State Bank a little before
one o'clock. The bank was well-constructed, brick with
impressive stone lintels over the doors and windows. Its
double front doors were solid oak. Inside, a low divider

walled off most of the interior, forming a lobby. One portion of the divider contained two teller cages and the rest blocked customers' views of the vault and offices.

A large table stood outside the barrier and Mr. Loftin loomed around it, looking pleasant and a bit self-important. Brad approached him. "Mr. Loftin?"

The banker greeted Spear, gave a short description of a teller's duties that had clearly been given to new employees before. The banker then turned him over to Alice Carter.

"Alice is our head teller, Mr. Streib. But the title doesn't really explain her job. She's a sort of office manager, running the bank on a day to day basis. Though I own the place, she's the boss."

Spear greeted the woman and thought to himself that Miss Carter was destined to remain a Miss for the rest of her life. Everyone's idea of an old maid, she wore steel-rimmed glasses perched on the bridge of her nose and a tightly wound bun of mousy-brown hair across the nape of her neck. She was nearly as tall as Mr. Loftin and her grey dress concealed completely any womanly curves that might lie far below the heavy fabric.

Alice Carter wasted no time putting Brad in his place. "Mr. Streib, you may come as a friend of the Loftin family, but there are no favorites here. Mr. Loftin's daughter toes the mark the same as the other bookkeeper. I will expect no less from you."

"Of course, Miss Carter," Brad offered in his politest tone. He wondered if his feigned reserve was at all convincing.

"You look more like an outdoorsman than a banker, Mr. Streib," Miss Carter observed. "I do hope you have a more conservative coat to wear during business hours. Corduroy won't do. Something in grey or black would be more acceptable. And we frown on fancy ties."

"Yes, ma'am."

"All right, then. Stand behind me at the window for the rest of the afternoon. I'll close at three and teach you how to balance the day's activity. We balance out each teller every night, regardless of how long it takes to reconcile every cent in or out. Shortages and overages are unacceptable."

"Yes, Miss Carter," Brad replied with what he hoped was the proper amount of respect. He was impressed with her rigidity, even her officiousness. Her personality struck him as decidedly unpleasant, yet ideal for her job.

Once Alice Carter had closed her window and balanced her cash drawer, a chore requiring only fifteen minutes of alarmingly efficient counting and totaling, Brad was introduced to the other employees. Phil Gregory, the bank's number two man, had been there since the day it opened. Gregory, a man with scholarly grey hair, eyebrows and whiskers, had been a banker for twenty-seven of his forty-five years and had helped Loftin plan, organize and start the bank. In return for his expertise and ongoing counsel, Gregory had been given ten percent of the bank's stock. Brad pegged him as a company man, solid, pleased with his work and well-paid.

Gregory's position, though, made Brad wonder about the safety deposit boxes. While stealing from the bank vault injured the establishment's position, the emptying of the boxes had no real impact on the bank's financial position. They neither insured nor guaranteed the contents. Gregory, any other trusted employee, even Loftin himself, could benefit from such a heist. Brad made a mental note to inquire into the financial condition of the employees, Loftin and the major borrowers of the bank.

Fred Parker, the bank's second teller, was a nervous sort. Upon meeting Brad, the investigator thought he'd blown his cover or, at the very least, found one of the culprits. It turned out that Parker simply feared for his job. A profoundly insecure man, Parker viewed Brad's introduction to the bank as a direct threat. Though an excellent teller, he was sure that no one liked him. And so the thin, pale, stammering man saw Brad as his fated replacement. Finally, Brad explained that he was only training at the bank and would soon disappear, but the point didn't get across to Parker. His worry, etched on his face, convinced Brad that the teller didn't have the gumption to walk into a darkened building alone, much less cooperate in a robbery.

Having dismissed Parker, Brad realized he had eliminated four of his six potential suspects. These folks were either terminally dull or honest. Or both. Perhaps Loftin was right, none of his people were involved.

Feeling discouraged and dirty from his train ride, Brad was wondering when he would find a bath and a moment's rest when he heard Miss Carter suggest a visit to the bookkeeping department.

In that partitioned corner he found Wanda Loftin, the banker's daughter, and her fellow bookkeeper, Virginia Mahon. Upon being introduced, Brad nodded to the pair of women, noting that Virginia had the reddest hair he'd ever seen. She was a small, pleasant, quiet woman who looked up for only a moment as Brad stood in the doorway. Wanda, on the other hand, had the face of a child but the batting lashes of a barmaid.

The sixteen-year-old girl stood to greet him as Brad walked into the room. "Oh, Mr. Streib," Wanda gushed, looking brightly at Brad as he approached her. "You don't look like the man I expected."

"Sorry to disappoint you."

"Well, uh, no. I mean, I've been meaning to talk with you."

"Well, I'm here, teller-in-training, meeting you all. So what can I do for you?"

Asked a simple question, Wanda offered a complicated expression. She had a sassy sparkle to her eyes and a coy way of tossing her chestnut hair. The girl seemed to be trapped in a woman's body, confused by her allure, brazen and unsure at the same time. She was, to put it simply, a torrid young woman.

"May I speak with you alone?" she asked.

"Of course," Brad responded, curious and wary.

Wanda led him to a small room lined with shelves, file cabinets and mounds of ledgers. She gestured to him to enter first and then closed the door behind them.

Spear suddenly felt, or sensed, the heat of confined quarters. Before him stood an employee of the bank, its owner's daughter, a child. But at the same time, he cast his eyes on a splendid young lady, her hand on her hip.

"So," she began, "you've come to save Daddy from his woes."

"What?" Brad asked, understanding in an instant what the tart meant.

"You're a Pinkerton. I know. I overheard my father talking about you with Mother."

"Are you sure?"

"Positive."

"Then I've nothing to hide, you think?"

"Not from me, Brad, or whatever your name is. And I've nothing to hide from you."

Spear looked at the girl and cursed to himself. This mess grew worse every moment. Now he had to contend with the childish, flirtatious, sexy daughter of his employer. A fellow worker, a suspect, a possible source of information, and, he thought again, lovely. Whatever his inclination, Brad felt certain this temptation wasn't to be indulged in.

"I'm a teller-in-training, Wanda. I'm trying to figure out the banking business, that's all. If you can help me, I'd appreciate it."

"I can help, in my way." Wanda moved slowly toward him and the tired, slightly bewildered Pinkerton agent backed away from her like a frightened boy.

"Thanks," he said, trying to figure a way out of the tiny room.

"Listen," Wanda hushed, looking around.

As Spear looked to the door, following her gaze, she stood on her toes and planted a furious kiss on his lips, her arms wrapped tightly around his neck. Brad looked down at her closed eyes and ample body. Oh, Lord, he thought. She finally let him go, wiggling her way out of the storage closet in a straightforward, overstated way that left his temples throbbing just a bit.

Moments after Brad emerged from the storage room Virginia Mahon, the other bookkeeper, approached him. Her eyes scanned the floor and her hands fussed with the knot of tightly braided red hair atop her head.

"My apologies, Mr. Streib. That girl is an outrage."

"What?" Brad asked.

"Wanda Loftin, for heaven's sake. She corners every pair of pants that comes in this place. She usually has the decency to prowl around for a day or two, though."

"It's nothing, really, Miss Mahon. It is Miss, isn't it?" Brad was trying hard to change the subject.

"No, no. It's Missus," she blushed. "Or it was. I'm a widow. My husband was killed in the War, charging up a hill in Pennsylvania. He fought for the South."

"I'm sorry."

"Oh, it's all right. At least I have a healthy son to keep me company. Donny's a wonderful boy, sharp as a tack and happy to stay with my mother here in town while I'm working. He's only three, you see."

"That's a nice arrangement."

"How would you know?" Virginia Mahon shot back, chilled somehow by his remark.

"Good for you and for your son, that's all," Brad explained.

"Not so good," the woman observed, an inexplicable bitterness creeping into her voice. "But enough, I've books to balance and you can be sure the boss's daughter isn't likely to be much use this late in the day."

Virginia Mahon turned and left Brad standing near a teller's cage. All of a sudden Mr. Loftin's tidy little group of faithful employees were developing quirks. Jealousies, bitterness, perhaps frustration churned through their veins. Nothing, not even a sleepy institution like the Loftin State Bank, was ever quite what it seemed.

As Brad thought about the staff that Lyn Loftin had assembled, the banker interrupted his reverie. "Stay awhile, will you?" he asked.

"Sure," Brad agreed.

Later, a little after five, only the bank president and the Pinkerton agent remained. Both moved to Loftin's private office.

Incredibly, it was filled with mining souvenirs. A worn pick hung, crossed by a dented shovel, on the wall behind Loftin's desk. Renderings of mines and miners, maps, a canceled certificate of claim and even an oil lamp were strewn about the room. Loftin's desk was polished and cluttered, the chair surrounding it gleaming but piled with papers, coats and other debris.

"What can I show you?" the banker asked.

"Walk me through the burglary."

Loftin nodded and led Brad to a back door which exited onto an alley between the bank and the building beside it.

"They came in this outside door with a key," Loftin explained. "That's one of the strongest locks made and it wasn't damaged at all during the break-in. The burglars kicked in the door to the vault room and used the other key to unlock the master door. The boxes were fair game after that."

Loftin led Spear inside the vault, a small, walk-in type. It wasn't new, but it was probably the best that a banker like Loftin could afford. The customer safe deposit boxes were ranged along one wall, with the shelves on the other side reserved for the teller drawers.

Loftin sighed as he spoke. "Every bank robber in the West knows we keep about fifteen thousand dollars on hand. Round numbers like that get to be public knowledge around here—God only knows how. Wish they didn't."

Brad glanced around, walked the route from the vault to the rear door and returned.

"Your people aren't involved, Loftin," commented Spear, keeping his eye on the banker for his reaction. "I know. I've talked to the lot of them and, I must say, I've never seen a more timid collection of clerical types."

Loftin grinned, obviously delighted at the news.

"But there are a couple of stories that don't add up," Spear continued. "I'll do some more adding later. But I'd better warn you—sometimes an investigation like this strikes pretty close to home."

Loftin winced and Spear took note of the expression.

"All right. I need to know more about those safe deposit boxes. It's time I took a look at those inventories we talked about."

"I'm sorry, Brad, but those lists are private . . ."

"You want me to stay on this case?"

"Absolutely."

"Then you're going to have to show me the lists. I'm not going to advertise their contents. I just want to see if I can turn up a lead. We can't be sure that the cash in those boxes was the only target of the burglary. In fact, the cash may have been an afterthought. Or a smoke screen."

Loftin nodded, still reluctant, and went to his desk. He unlocked a drawer and removed a thin file. "Here you go. Have a seat and look them over. There's a summary on the first page."

It didn't take Brad long to detect a pattern in the summary sheet. "What about all these Land Grant Certificates? Last I heard, those things were issued by the U.S. Government to raise money for building rail lines. Seems to have been a mess of them in your bank."

The banker nodded. "There's quite a few of them around here and most for local land."

Spear stared at Loftin, hoping that the man had more to add. But Loftin seemed to have dismissed the documents as yet another sort of currency kept in his bank.

"I've worked on a dozen bank robberies," Spear remarked, "but I've never seen so few clues."

Impassively, Loftin put the papers back in the drawer and locked it. He blew out the lamp on his desk and the two men left the darkened bank. Brad took careful note as the banker methodically locked the building.

The November sun had long since set and winter darkness gathered in the mountains surrounding Silver

City. The town had no street lights and the cold evening air made Brad realize that they were at a high elevation. Winter, he thought, would hit hard when it finally arrived. Brad said goodnight to Lyn Loftin and watched the banker as he walked slowly up the hill toward the town's finest houses.

Although most of the town had closed up, light spilled from an occasional saloon and gambling hall. Brad stopped and leaned against the side of a saloon, listening to the talk and the tinkle of piano keys. He had to start some place, and this one, with its out-of-tune piano, would be as good as any.

But after one glance through the window, Spear turned away. It wasn't the classiest bar in town and couldn't hold a candle to Lady Jane's in Cheyenne, Wyoming. Brad had been thinking about Lady Jane lately and he wondered what else she was up to. Up to almost anything, he thought with a smile. Then his growling stomach reminded him: he needed food, not memories. He turned down the dusty street and headed for the Nevada House Hotel.

The hotel proved to have a fair meat and potatoes eatery. A young waitress warmed him with a smile.

"You're new around here, right?"

"Must be, 'cause I don't seem to remember your name."

"Pattie," the waitress replied.

She took his order and served up a meal which disappeared in slightly less than fifteen minutes. But when it came time for the custard, she paused by his table.

"You're staying here at the hotel, ain't cha?"

Brad nodded.

"You got a name?"

"Brad."

"I like that name," Pattie said, sliding an extra dish

of custard onto his table. She winked and when she came back to retrieve his plates, Brad felt her deliberately brush herself against him. The pressure of her warm breast lingered awhile on his right shoulder.

"I bet I can guess which room you're in," she said. "If I'm right, do I get the prize?" Brad allowed as how she would and the girl quickly replied, "I guess three-twelve, right?"

"That's right, Pattie, I guess you win." Brad's attention returned to his custard.

Pattie grinned and walked lightly away from the table. "Good, Brad, because you're the trophy."

Brad finished his custard, trying to put waitresses and saucy bookkeepers out of his mind, and walked out of the Nevada House. He was thinking mostly of Virginia Mahon, bookkeeper. Virginia was bitter about something, perhaps bitter enough to take part in a robbery. It might not be too tough for her. She might not have even been directly involved. All she'd have to do was pass on a pair of keys to an accomplice with a strong pair of boots. Unlock two doors and kick in the rest.

Brad had purposefully avoided pressing Loftin for details on bank keys, expecting all along that the man would give him the information without any prodding. But he had told the banker he took nothing for granted, so he knew he'd have to raise the issue first thing in the morning. Maybe Loftin had misplaced a set and was concealing the fact simply out of pride. Maybe Loftin's personal life was involved, somehow. It was impossible that the man was as orderly and decent as he seemed.

Brad thought about the redhead again. Virginia Mahon was angry about something. Perhaps she was mad at the whole world. A widow left with a young child to raise? Suddenly a curious thought occurred to Brad

Spear. Virginia had said that her husband was killed in the War. But her son was only three years old. Any son fathered by a soldier would have to be at least four or four and a half. Spear chuckled to himself. Virginia Mahon, new to the game of lying, couldn't even keep her dates straight. And the angry woman's lie might be just the thread to follow through this case.

# Chapter 3

In the evening, after dinner, Silver City changed its character. While mercantile stores and laundries, hardware outlets, granaries and warehouses shut down at dusk, saloons and dancing halls were open, full-blast. Hack-running and auctioneering went on late into the night. Arguments were everywhere. And ladies, feigning loneliness, patrolled the streets.

Spear, well-fed, was curious about the city. He knew Silver City by reputation as the "cussedest town in the states." But, strolling its streets that night, he discovered a kind of split personality to the place. Unlike so many mining towns, this one kept its gambling private, behind closed doors. Its streets were wide and straight, and many of the buildings were brick, as though their owners expected them to outlive the few gold and silver mines still producing well.

Silver City suggested permanence. But it was peopled by miners and cowboys, prospectors and gamblers, the lost, the unlucky and the desperate. Not surprisingly, such folks made a lot of noise after dark.

Walking down a wooden sidewalk, sometimes covered by storefront awnings, sometimes not, Spear noticed a sign hanging half into the street. It advertised a brightly lit saloon known as The Mammoth.

Choice liquors, wines, lager beer & cigars, served by pretty girls, who understand their business and attend to it. Votaries of Bacchus or Venus can spend an evening agreeably at The Mammoth.

Inside The Mammoth Saloon, Spear slid a nickel across the polished bar and asked for a beer. It was quickly delivered, with ice floating in it.

In one corner of the room a small group of men talked and laughed around a bottle of whiskey. From their heavy accents, Brad knew they were Irish miners. From their conversation, it was clear they were unemployed for the winter and outspoken in their hatred of the cold. Elsewhere men sat playing cards or pawed at the women who trafficked pitchers of beer between the tables and the bar. A piano hugged the corner, with a bugle resting atop it, but both instruments were quiet.

Over the general hubbub of the large room, Brad asked the bartender if he knew Lyn Loftin.

"Loftin, hell yes. Known him for years. Fact is, I used to swing a pick with him back when the Lucky Lode was working. Man was strong as an ox."

"And no fool," Spear added.

"Dumb as a fox is more like it. And honest, too. He once owed me five dollars for more than a year. Ran up the debt in a poker game. I'd forgotten all about it, but a year later he looked me up and gave me that half eagle and forty cents interest. Can you beat that?"

The barkeep smiled, somehow proud to know such a man, and pushed a second beer toward Brad, who pushed another nickel back at him.

"Lyn went out on his own not long after that. Finally struck it big with his own hole. Made a bundle from what I gather. Don't seem to have changed him much."

Brad asked if the bartender still spoke with Loftin.

"One beer a day, every day. And two on the Sabbath. Comes in here after dinner, plunks down his nickel and drinks his beer."

The agent shook his head. Loftin was as regular a guy as you could imagine. Rich and friendly, honest, strong and fair. It wouldn't have surprised Brad if the man ran a charity for Nevada's orphans and infirm.

The barkeep leaned forward and lowered his voice. " 'Course, Loftin ain't without an occasional lapse of character. He has an eye for a pretty girl, same as the rest of us. Always was quick to jump in the bushes. Fact is, one time I stumbled on him with two whores at once, all three of 'em bare-assed as can be, not fifty feet from the Lucky Lode mine." The bartender chuckled at the memory. "Makes him just that much better to my eyes anyway."

"Guess so," Brad agreed, trying to imagine the nervous, balding banker involved with two whores.

"Do me another, would ya?" the rough-looking man standing at the bar next to Brad asked.

"Sure," the barkeep slid him a beer.

"Name's 'Elephant' Osborne, what's yours?" the man questioned Brad.

"Streib, Brad Streib."

"Couldn't help but hear you talkin' about Lyn Loftin with Sandy. Fine fella, just like he says."

"Everybody in town seems to agree on that score."

"Well, you see, he's pretty admired. Looked up to, really. 'Specially by the likes of me."

"How's that?" Brad inquired.

"Well, back when this town was a-boomin', going crazy with people and women and new strikes every week or so, loads of fellas like me went out prospecting or digging for somebody that had a dollar a day to spend. Those that found somethin', like me, hardly ever ended up with it. 'Cept Lyn. He got most of what was comin' to him."

"And you?" Brad prodded, enjoying the crusty man's yellow-toothed smile and the wag of his head as he spoke.

"Huh," the man snorted. "Mine's a different tale all right."

There was a pause, one that Brad understood, and he slid two more nickels across the bar to Sandy, who had already drawn two more beers for the men.

"There's them that's honest and there's them that ain't. That's all," Elephant said, shaking his long, tangled hair. "In '60 I fell in with a fella from Montana selling salt. He was making a pile off the rush around here and needed someone to ride with him 'tween San Francisco and the mines. For a bit of an interest I went along.

"Well, worked good, sure 'nuff. Made three hundred dollars one trip and outfitted myself for prospecting. Went out along the ridge there," he pointed west, "for 'bout a hundred miles. Damn near went blind hunting and looking for quartz a-sticking up out of the ground. Found nothin', though. Leastwise 'til I come upon Adler Gulch. There, to beat all, was a young punk who'd run away from the Yellowrock Band & Gymnastic Troupe. Could play the fiddle, do handstands and flips, and was a hell of a drinker, that kid.

"Well, anyway, he and I went north and started digging. Wasn't long before we came upon a mire of black ground. And were we laughin'. Not a foot below ground we had nuggets of gold as big as your thumb and we were sittin' there, heftin' and running our fingers through it like it was flour dough.

"Next thing you know there's a fella standin' over us, starin' right at our claim. And what's he say but we're trespassin' on his ranch. Ranch! You couldn't graze goats up there!

"But me and the kid, Moses he called himself, weren't fools. We'd seen the broken-down quartz for sure and we'd posted our claim, proper. We'd three hundred feet for each of us and another three hundred for staking the claim, just like we was entitled. But that guy went on a-hollering and a-wavin' his arms—gonna stir up trouble, he was, gonna take the whole claim from us.

"Well, friend," the storyteller paused, tipping his empty beer glass to his lips, "it seemed trouble all right."

Spear ordered and paid for two more beers.

"So we talked it over, Moses and me, and decided to give him a hundred feet for his ranch and another hundred feet for what he called the water rights to the place and the three of us was partners. We laid in three holes and hit big with one, takin' hunks out as big as your fist. We was winnin' sure as could be.

" 'Bout then my wife took off, sick of wonderin' and waitin' and ol' Moses was sick of diggin' and anxious to do some spendin'. So we went to Jim Knight, the fella who's our partner, and wondered would he buy us out. Well, nope, he said, but he'd lease what was ours, with one thousand dollars down and the rest to come from the diggings. Moses was to get one-tenth of the profits and so was I. Plus which we're to receive one hundred dollars a month no matter what.

"So off I go, a thousand dollars richer and set for life, little knowing the rascality of civilized sorts. I left my papers with a judge in Carson City and headed out to find my wife and her wanderin' friend so's I could show her my money and kill the son-of-a-bitch.

"Got caught up, though, in some French joint in a town I don't recall and ended up goin' to New York with a lady named Belle. She and me actually took to the traveling and we allowed as how we was doin' good headed east so we might as well go on with it. We took a steamer, Paris-bound and actually got to Cairo in the end. She died there.

"Running low on money, I headed on back to check on my interest in the mine. Figured I'd have a pile comin' to me by then, two years it'd been. But when I got back the judge had got robbed, or something, and was nowhere to be found. So's I had no papers to prove my lease.

"Sad thing about it all is I went back to the spot where Moses and me had found the mine. It was called the Lost Ranch Bonanza by then and the fella runnin' it wasn't the one we leased to. So there was nothin' for it. And the place was buzzin', too. They worked it to 1,500 feet, takin' out ore worth one hundred and fifty dollars a ton. Some said that for one year the spot yielded a *million* dollars a *month*. And all I got out of it was my nickname from Cairo: Elephant."

Spear ordered another beer for each of them. "Did you dig again, Elephant?" he asked.

"Nope," the old man replied. "Mind if I chase some whiskey with this beer?"

"Be my guest," Brad muttered, wondering over the easy way that the miner told his tale and perplexed by his good humor. Brad ordered a shot of whiskey for the man. "It's a bit of a surprise to me that you're not more low down on the world."

"Why bother?" Elephant smiled. "After all, could'a been worse. Take my wife, for instance. Got killed makin' her way as a whore in New Orleans."

Brad could sense another story, bought with whiskey and beer, on its way. And he thought that the old lunatic probably could go on for hours, drinking the saloon dry if he tried and Brad paid. But not this night.

"You're as smooth and easy as a dime novel, Elephant. But there's only so much I can listen to while standing at a bar, so, if you don't mind, I think I'm going to search for a bath."

"No search required," Sandy, the bartender, said. "We've got one in the back and all the hot water you want."

"A remarkable place you have here," Brad observed. "How much for the tub?"

"Tub's free. Girl with the water is twenty cents."

"Fair enough. Show me the way."

Brad headed in the direction of Sandy's outstretched finger, through a back door into a small room. In it he found a huge, square, wooden tub, hooks to hang clothes on and a rough grey towel. On the door was a sign that said "Empty" on one side and "Water, please" on the other. He turned it over, requesting water, and closed the door behind him.

One side of the tub room contained a very small wood stove, sufficient only for heating the tiny room. A low fire burned in it and so Brad piled on a few additional logs. As he was doing so, someone knocked on the door.

"Yup," Brad responded.

Opening the door and sticking her head inside, a young woman with freckled cheeks announced, simply, "Hot water on the way."

"Terrific," the agent commented with genuine pleasure. Brad sat on the edge of the tub, looking at its tin liner and feeling the room warm quickly. The tin, he thought, was cold. He'd wait for the first few buckets of water.

In a matter of minutes the freckled young attendant returned with a large bucket filled with cold water and a steaming kettle. She poured first the bucket, then the kettle's contents into the tub and disappeared. Brad glanced at the inch and a half of water at the bottom of the tub and hoped more was on its way. Within minutes the girl returned and repeated her performance. And after four trips it seemed to Brad that the room and tub were comfortable enough to bathe in.

He stripped quickly, groaning over boots that simply didn't want to let go of his feet.

"Now, isn't that better," the pert little creature bubbled as she returned to pour more water on the agent.

"Much," noted Brad, sitting, soaking, his eyes closed. The room now was hot, steam and sweat warming him. "Is there soap?"

"I'll bring it," she said, "next trip."

Spear soaked, finally warm, feeling the easy glow of the beer, recalling the strange tale Elephant had spun, waiting for his soap. Within minutes his water carrier returned again and, pouring yet more gallons over him, Brad found himself submerged up to his navel.

"I'm Janice, sir, and here's your soap."

"Thanks, Janice."

She then rolled up a sleeve and submerged her empty kettle in the tub, filling it with water. Once it had stopped gurgling air, she lifted it and placed it on top of the tiny stove to heat. She then turned to Spear and asked for her twenty cents.

"In my trousers," he directed, pointing.

The room was lit only by a tin wall sconce burning some sort of oil, but Brad could clearly see the girl rummage through his pants until she found her payment. She placed the coins carefully in a small purse, walked to the door and bolted it. Without a word she approached the tub and took the soap from Brad's hand.

"Ready for a scrub?" she asked.

Spear was half-mesmerized by the warm water and

air, half-asleep from his trip and the rigors of his first day on a new case. "Mmmmm," was all he could manage.

Janice's white frock had short, puffy sleeves and a drawstring neckline that was tied loosely at the front. Her skirt, too, was white and simple, extending to her ankles. Still, one could see that this cute girl with a bar of soap in her hand was attractive, even sexy in a way. As she knelt beside the tub, even the semiconscious Spear noticed the soft, round breasts that peeked at him over her neckline.

Janice lathered her hands, dipping them in the warm water and rubbing the soap. She then began massaging the day's tension from Brad's shoulders and neck, moving her hands over his upper arms and chest.

Speak exhaled, the long, low puff of exhaustion.

The girl continued her ministrations, applying the rough bar of soap directly to his hairy chest and then spreading the lather over his upper body. After a while she held him by the back of the neck, pushing him forward and scrubbing his back. Periodically she would stand, shake her hands dry and walk to the small stove. The water there then would be poured into the tub, reheating the bath immediately. And she would refill the kettle from the tub, return it to the stove and kneel once again before the agent.

After several such trips, an unavoidable amount of splashing and dripping and reaching about, the front of her blouse became soaked. Spear watched her as she washed his hair, her arms upraised, the cotton material of her blouse clinging to her firm breasts, outlining her nipples as she worked.

"Mmmmmm," he mumbled.

"Dunk your head," she ordered once his hair and beard were white with soap. She pushed down on him gently and Brad slid under water. Coming up for air he found her moving, then sitting on the edge of the tub, her bare feet beside him. Without hesitation, she reached into the soapy water and felt for his organ. Finding it, she ran her hands across him, up his belly and down his thighs. She rubbed his legs to his ankles and massaged her way up again, tantalizing, touching, pulling on him.

Brad looked at her, felt himself growing harder and lifted a hand to touch her breast.

"Don't touch, sir."

"What?"

"Don't touch, not allowed."

"Jesus," he grumbled and slid almost under water again.

Janice continued her work, scrubbing and massaging Brad, fingering his erection, washing his thighs for what seemed like hours. Brad kept his eyes closed most of the time, moaned and moved and several times thought he would explode. But whenever he would open his eyes to watch her pleasant face, splendid body and expert hands bring him closer to oblivion, she would move those devilish fingers to his belly or hands or feet.

"Woman," he finally said, "either get in here with me or get the hell out of the place."

"*I'm* leaving," she said, simply, "but The Mammoth Saloon employs a number of fine ladies who can help you with that problem of yours." She then wrapped a shawl around her shoulders, covering her dripping blouse, tossed Brad the soap and disappeared.

"Goddamn," Brad swore, "that's the finest bit of advertising I ever saw. Talk about creating a demand for your product . . ." Spear rose from the tub, clean, wet and hard. He toweled himself off, dressed and walked out through the saloon. Two overly-made-up women smiled willingly at him as he did so, but the agent proceeded straight to the street.

Once back at his hotel, Spear climbed the three flights of stairs, paused outside the door to room 312 and listened. He tried the doorknob. For the second time that day it opened without benefit of a key. Spear sighed. It seemed as if his room had open visiting hours. Brad drew his .45 and edged the door open. A coal oil lamp burned brightly on the dresser, throwing a glow on the recumbent figure sprawled across the bed.

Sound asleep, Pattie the waitress had her arms spread wide on the bed. One knee was raised, bunching her skirt almost to her crotch, showing just about all of one white leg. Brad smiled and shook his head. If ever he were to be receptive to a brazen young waitress, this, indeed, was the evening. She obviously had bribed the night manager, with what Brad could only imagine, and had been waiting for him. The agent clicked the hammer of his .45 back in place and holstered the gun.

Pattie sat up sleepily, rubbed a hand across her face and patted the bed beside her. "Where the hell have you been? Out funnin'? I've been waiting here since eight-thirty, just like I promised."

Brad glanced down at her, noting the dimples in her soft, pink cheeks. She ran a hand through her short, brown hair and fluffed it back into position.

"Sit down," the girl commanded. "You make me nervous standing there, looking like a thirsty man in need of a drink."

Spear sat down but didn't make a move toward her.

"You locked the door, didn't you?" Pattie jumped up and ran to the door where the key hung in the lock. She twisted it and then hopped back in the bed.

Brad, silent, felt himself hardening as he watched her unbutton her blouse.

The girl looked at Brad skeptically.

"You act as if you didn't know why I was here."

"I know all right," he replied, as he unbuckled his gunbelt and hung it on a peg. "I just don't want to miss any of you by being hasty."

"What ya can't find on the first go around will be here for the second."

That, it seemed to Brad, covered the issue adequately. He thought, very briefly, that she might have a gun or knife concealed beneath her clothing, that she could be involved with the bank robbery somehow. But he didn't have long to consider those suspicions. By the time he had hung up his gunbelt, she was already out of her blouse and peeling her skirt away.

"Come here," she urged. Her eyes were fixed on the area just below his waist. He had to admit, he was pleased to have found such a hot-blooded creature on such a cold night. He crossed to her and her hands flew to his trousers, working at a set of difficult buttons down their front. He felt her cool fingers grope their way along his hips as she dropped his pants and drawers, and by the time his clothes were out of the way, he was all ready for the kiss that was coming.

But she wasn't. Not quite. She hissed in wonder as she looked at him and drew back for just a second, letting her eyes fly up to his. Then she leaned forward, and took him between her lips. As Brad's eyes closed, he had the vague impression of a beautiful young woman, naked to the waist, clinging to him, with a delicate part of his body mysteriously and totally possessed by the beautiful creature whose head bobbed slowly, gently caressing him. His hands reached out, grasped her silky hair and for a few more blissful moments, while the tempo increased, he was aware of nothing beyond the sensations of her lips and tongue on his body. She was taking him in, completely possessing him and the sensations were too much to bear. If he made any sound at all, he wasn't aware of it, but suddenly he was exploding and she was perfectly still, holding him until the end.

She leaned back and looked up. Brad grinned.

"Guess I better take off my boots," he said.

Some short time later, reclining on the big, uneven hotel bed, she began talking while her fingers strayed up and down the lean, taut muscles of his groin. The coal oil lamp had already been snuffed out, and the only light in the room came from a sliver of moon that was just easing its way out of the corner of the window.

"It's funny the way a girl like me learns her way around," she said, her fingers working out a circular pattern on his chest. "I'm supposed to be a quiet farm girl, according to my upbringing. Supposed to learn about love from watching the hogs mount up and the horses go to stud."

"You didn't learn *that* from . . ." Brad began.

"No, no!" she interrupted, laughing. "I learned *that* from a person of my acquaintance, and you won't ask who. Anyhow, he only stayed in town a few days and he was from foreign parts.

"Anyway . . ." she stretched and rolled on her back, pointing her toes toward the bedposts. "It was an auntie of mine who taught me the facts. Just the facts, mind you. She was only six or seven years older than me. She took me out behind the granary and opened my blouse. She touched me all over and told me that's what the boys would be wanting to do pretty soon. She got me so wild and excited she thought she'd hurt me. I don't know why I reached out for her, but I did, and that was the first time I understood how excited a person could get. Auntie spent the night at our house and since we were so crowded, we had to sleep in the same bed. Well, I swear, the rubbing we did to each other's private parts was a wonder."

Brad would have happily dropped off to sleep while listening to Pattie share her life story, but something about the way she searched the middle of his anatomy kept him alert. "When did you graduate from girls to boys?" he asked.

"About a year later. A boy from two farms down was out searching for his daddy's prize heifer one day and the looking for it brought him all the way to our place. I offered to help him find the cow and we went walking through the fields. Well, I finally cornered that boy. Took some doing since he was especially bashful, but I managed it. And after a little tickling and some fooling around with each other, we took our clothes off and were humping like crazy in minutes. When I was seventeen I moved to town—there's just not enough men in the country."

Ever the investigator, Brad had one more question. "You say you're nineteen?"

"Just over," she said and ran her hand down his beard.

Brad brushed her hand away and pinned her wrist to the bed with a firm grasp.

"Oh," she cried, as if the wind had been knocked out of her. And Pattie wasn't quite so cheerful anymore. She even looked a little scared.

"That's right," said Spear. "My way this time."

He twisted her body until she lay face down on the bed. Up to now, everything had seemed like a lot of fun to her, but she suddenly wasn't so sure what was going to happen next. And the insecurity made her thighs tighten involuntarily. His muscular body was on top of her now, controlling her every movement as if she were some kind of limp rag doll. And then she felt him begin to invade her, the muscular groin pressing against her from behind, seeking the opening.

"What . . . ?" she began.

"Shut up."

His voice hissed in her ear and suddenly she knew he was teasing—but it wasn't quite a game, either, not her kind of game. And still his body was seeking for her, probing. She tightened again, trying to close him out, but now her own body was disobeying. She could feel herself becoming moist, could feel the energy escape from her thighs as they relaxed and her legs spread.

"Oh!"

She wriggled under him, but there was no escape, and the pleasure was almost overwhelming. He thrust into her, again and again, and with each thrust she felt compelled to reply, raising up to meet his thrusts and grasp him more tightly with the arching of her body. And finally there was no thought in what she did. The deep throb of his body pressing against her, urging her on, caught her in his rhythm and the pleasure dictated her every movement. She felt a ripple of attentiveness run like a warm wave from the tips of her down-pressed breasts to her belly and thighs, and suddenly all her concentration was directed toward the point of her own body where he was lodged, insisting, driving into her. She gasped, feeling a strange, wonderful shuddering begin to emanate from that single point of contact, and as the spasm traveled through her body, she felt him moving inside her, spilling into her. For a moment longer they were locked by the quiver of response that passed from his body into hers, and then she fell, relaxed, her face in the pillow, gasping.

"Nice. Oh, awful nice."

She sounded so surprised that Spear had to laugh. He withdrew from her and rolled onto his back. Her hand rested gently on his chest and her breath hissed in his ear.

"I had no idea . . ." Pattie murmured.

"Well . . ." He moved somewhat painfully, accommodating his back to the interesting contours of the hotel bed. "I guess you've got some idea now."

She didn't reply immediately and Spear filled the lag in conversation by falling into a very deep and contented sleep.

When he awoke she was gone, leaving behind a note that looked as though it had been scrawled by a schoolgirl.

"You're swell. I'll be around to collect my prize again tonight. How come you registered as Streib instead of Spear?"

The paper on which the note was written had been torn out of Brad's own notebook. It made him wonder if she'd gone through its pages and whether he'd taken a chance he shouldn't have by falling asleep with her. Brad crumpled the note and rammed his fist into a pillow. It might be all right and, then again, it might not. On a case as strange as this one, he didn't need anything complicating the situation. At any rate, he'd have to reconsider his cover. He decided to have breakfast up the street at another hotel.

As Spear walked down the last flight of stairs into the Nevada House's lobby, he couldn't help but notice the desk clerk. Though the potbelly stove nearby had taken the chill from the morning air, the man stood clapping his hands against his upper arms, apparently trying to warm them. He still wore grey, knitted mittens and a long scarf wrapped around his neck. Spear thought he must be either terribly ill or completely insane.

"M-M-Morning," the clerk called to him, a huge smile cracking from his lips.

"You too," Brad responded, nodding.

"Have a good evening?" A strange, lascivious grin appeared on the man's face.

"Yup," Brad replied, thinking to himself that the entire hotel was populated by bizarre sorts, fugitives from mental institutions, or funny houses, or both. Throughout this short conversation, Brad kept a steady pace toward the door and, to his pleasure, was through it before the strangely mittened clerk could say another word.

The slow, hollow drumbeat of Brad's boots on the raised wooden sidewalk echoed down one side of the street. It disturbed few, however, as the city was only beginning to stir. Two miners sat on a bench in front of a hardware store, smoking and talking, and a lumber company wagon, pulled by a brace of horses, stood nearby. The horses' breath was visible in the cold air. Brad strode along the east side of Main Street, looking for a place serving steak and eggs.

As he passed the two miners, he overheard one complain of the Comstock Lode's "borrasca," or cloudy weather. Spear knew the man wasn't referring to actual cloud formations, but instead was talking about the ever-slowing silver production of Nevada's richest mine. That once extraordinary hole in the ground had produced progressively less ore since 1865 and showed no signs of recovering.

Two doors past the unemployed miners, Brad stopped to study a hardware store's display through its front window. Unlike such establishments in smaller towns, this one sold neither rifles, bridles nor saddles. Instead it specialized in mining and prospecting equipment. Tables were piled high with rough, red blankets and the walls were draped with calico in loads of colors. Various tins of tack, the rough, almost tasteless food carried into the mountains, were stacked on shelves. Rusty bacon and jerky sat in clear glass jars. Blue cotton overalls were folded and piled in three groups, one for each size. Fancy boots were rare inside, but the indestructible "nigger" shoes of the day were plentiful and the pungent chew that was so popular, "dog-leg" tobacco, was available. Pick handles and hardware, shovels, flat pans, spoons, string and nails were everywhere.

Staring into the store, Brad thought about the way in which most men lived. Though often poor and old by the time they were forty, the vast majority of Silver City's residents were hopeful, sensible folks. They lived in a world that revolved around the simple necessities to be found in the hardware store. Few, except during the War, had ever killed a man, virtually none had been in jail. Unlike the Pinkerton, they'd known their fathers well, worked in peace for a living and never wondered about unseen enemies. Brad tried to imagine what such a life was like.

As Spear stood, still gazing into the store's window, a pane of glass exploded beside him. An instant later he heard the telltale report of a large-caliber rifle. He spun on one heel, drawing his specially-made, long-barreled .45 as he did so. Quickly scanning the west side of the street, its doors, windows and roof tops, he saw nothing. The two horses hitched to the wagon filled with lumber raised their heads and stamped their hooves, alarmed by the single shot. The casual, bored miners up the street had disappeared.

"Shit," Brad muttered.

A man appeared on the street more than one hundred and fifty feet north of him. And then another strolled from the sidewalk one hundred and fifty feet to the south. Each carried gleaming rifles with jet-black stocks. The weapons were clearly tools of their trade. Polished nickel, immaculately cared for and deftly handled, they were being used by men who didn't dig mines for a living.

Brad knelt in the deep shadows on his side of the street. He knew that though the high, bright sky made him visible, the low sun at his back would be distracting to his attackers. If he could find an alley or open door filled with real darkness, he had a chance.

The marksman to Brad's right shielded his eyes from the sun. He then raised his rifle and held it level for what seemed an eternity. Brad rolled, almost tumbling on one shoulder, and heard the crack of splintering wood behind him, then the explosion of the high-powered rifle from up the street.

These guys are pros, Brad thought, tumbling once more and turning onto his belly. They were too far from him for any standard .44 handgun to fell. They'd taken their positions carefully and neither had panicked as Spear strolled down the sidewalk. He had centered himself, dropped into each man's sight, and had waited, studying the calico in the storefront. It was amazing, he thought, that he was alive.

There was little Spear could do, and he knew it. Even his remarkable side arm was chancy, at best, from this distance. But no other option seemed available. He was lying on a sidewalk, alone, while two very cool, very professional killers zeroed in on him. As yet another slug slammed into the door behind him, Brad grasped his right wrist with his left hand. He planted both elbows firmly and spread his legs. For only a moment, he raised his head and aimed.

The featherlight spring of his gun's trigger mechanism served him well. In less than three seconds he emptied five chambers of his gun, aiming above, below, to the right and left, then finally directly at one rifleman. One slug found its mark. The man's head turned crimson in an instant, blood flowing like a fountain from what once was an eye as he fell back.

Spear rolled once more, turning as he did so in order to present the other killer with the smallest possible target, and reloaded.

He was gone. Spear froze. He watched for the bright glint of sunlight off the man's rifle. Listened for the hurry of feet in the dirt of the street. Nothing.

Crawling on his belly, elbows and knees, Brad inched his way down the street. He was headed in the direction of the vanished rifleman, his eyes straining as he watched the brightly lit storefronts opposite him. Twice the sun ricocheted off uneven panes of glass as he moved and each time he leveled his pistol at the would-be target.

But no one appeared, no further shots were fired. Once behind a horse trough, Brad raised himself on one knee and scratched his beard. Whoever this newfound enemy was, he'd disappeared.

Within minutes three men, followed by the town's sheriff, appeared on the scene. One of the men, a mountainous creature fully six inches taller than Spear, carried a double-barreled shotgun and aimed it straight at Brad's head as he approached. The sheriff walked behind him, his pistol drawn.

Brad stood, holstering his gun.

"Okay, mister, hand over that side arm," the sheriff ordered, his head craning to see around the shoulder of the man with the shotgun.

"Kindly point that somewhere else," Brad requested. "I'm a little worried about your nerves so early in the morning."

"The side arm," repeated the sheriff.

Spear handed his Colt to the man with the shotgun, pushing the rifle toward the ground after having done so. "Mind?" he asked as he reached for his wallet.

"Go on," the sheriff replied.

Spear pulled his small, stiff Pinkerton identification card from his wallet and handed it to the sheriff. As the lawman looked it over, the brooding, well-armed giant of a man fingered Brad's six-gun.

"Never seen nothin' like this," he boomed, òbviously impressed with the weapon. "Look at the barrel on the thing and that handwork on the butt. Jeez!"

"Made special for me in San Francisco. Only one like it in the world."

"No kidding. Well, sure is a beauty," the man grinned.

"Give him back his gun, Ben," the sheriff directed. "He's Pinkerton."

"Gosh, sure, Sheriff. Sorry about aimin' this thing at ya," Ben apologized, raising the rifle again only to have Brad lower it once more to the street.

"Thanks," Brad said, taking his pistol and identification. "But, Ben, if you want to see a really beautiful weapon, come with me. That bushwhacker lying in the street up there has my rifle. Stole it last night and then set out to kill me with it this morning. I don't know him, but he must have been a nasty sort."

Brad turned immediately, smiling to himself, and walked toward the body in the street. He'd just acquired a new rifle. But within moments it became clear that Spear's ploy to claim the remarkable weapon wasn't going to work. His assailant lay face up on the street, a thick, broad pool of blood spreading behind his head, seeping into the sand. His mouth was agape, a scream frozen in his throat. His one remaining eye stared skyward into the cruel, empty blue of Nevada's approaching winter.

But there was no rifle near him, nor any to be found even after a considerable search.

Spear felt certain no one had approached the body while he had talked with the sheriff and his ragtag trio of vigilantes. But clearly he was wrong.

Ben lumbered across the street, pushing a wheelbarrow in front of him. The sheriff, obviously paled by the gruesome sight of the body, searched uncomfortably through the pockets of the dead man. Brad knew he'd find nothing. Neither identification nor money. It was unlikely that the killer had even registered in one of the city's hotels and it was certain that no one could recognize him now.

"Sheriff," Brad half-whispered as he watched Ben dump the corpse into the wheelbarrow and push it off down the street, "I'd appreciate it if you'd keep my identity quiet for a day or two. I have a few more folks to talk to undercover before I go public."

"Sure, got cha," the sheriff said. Brad looked into the man's small blue eyes and realized the whole city would know his identity within hours.

# Chapter 4

Jane Harrington sat alone in her husband's office, her eyes welling with tears, her fist pounding slowly, over and over, against the green blotter in front of her. Staring blankly out the window, she looked at nothing. Her blonde hair, touched with the color of wheat in the early morning light, fell softly across her shoulders and then dropped like a veil over her face as she lowered her forehead to the desk and sobbed.

Jane Harrington was the principal stockholder and chief officer of the Silver Lady mine. The business had been left to her by her husband, who had died two months before. Mrs. Harrington ran the mine successfully, maintaining the methods established by her husband, altering and improving a few, taking counsel from the most experienced people around her. But even the weight of the work, the intolerably long hours, the pressure to keep production up and the difficulties of managing hundreds of miners didn't always distract her from her grief. Now and then, in the quiet of his office, she wept. Exhausted. Alone.

But she kept such emotion private. To those who worked for Mrs. Harrington she seemed a woman possessed. Wealthy beyond most people's dreams, she operated the mine as though it were a clock to be put straight. She was unusually concerned with safety and preoccupied with efficiency. A singularly relentless

woman, she expected her mine to run better than anyone else's. It must produce more and with fewer in-
juries than any in Nevada. It was that simple.

And Mrs. Harrington dressed the part of a perfec-
tionist. On this day she wore a light-brown, tailor-made
suit of wool chevoit serge. The elegant jacket was
handsomely cut and her skirt swept the floor. But
beneath her businesslike garb there was clearly a beautiful woman. Her broad, rounded shoulders, full
breasts, straight back and long legs were unmistakably
lovely. Were it not for her forbidding British accent
and regal manner, she would surely have been the most
eligible woman in Silver City.

Raising her head from the desk, Jane Harrington
dabbed at the tears that ran down her cheeks. As she
did so, her face was transformed. The beautiful lady,
the delicate and emotional woman, disappeared, only
to be replaced by a shrewd and practiced street-fighter.
Her keen eyes narrowed and her lips pressed together.
Looking out the window, Mrs. Harrington stared down
at the tailings from the mine and stamping plant. Her
gaze wandered up the narrow gauge tracks that vanished in the dark hole dug in the mountain side. She
watched, counting to herself as an ore-laden car
emerged from the main tunnel. She continued counting
the seconds as the car skidded down a slight incline,
depositing its load as it clanged to a halt.

Karl Oppenheimer, the mine's general manager,
waved his arms and bellowed at the workers around
him. Two men fell in behind the car and a third
harnessed a mule to it. Within minutes the emptied car
moved once again into the mine and Oppenheimer
stood watching, his arms folded.

Jane had learned to trust Karl during the first weeks
after her husband's funeral. He had been with the Silver Lady from its first hard days and Randolph Har-

rington had always relied upon him. He was fifty years old and a family man, comfortable with his duties and pleased with the way his boss's widow had handled herself. He cared about the mine. Karl had struggled right along with Randy to create miles of tunnels on borrowed money and many times had suffered disappointment, exhaustion and despair. And now that the payoff had come, he was saddened only that his friend had died before he could fully enjoy it.

As Jane sat thinking about Karl and her husband's early days, there was a soft knock at the door.

"Come in," Jane answered.

Mary Dabrowski entered the office. She had worked as Mr. Harrington's secretary for nearly ten years before his death and she now proved herself indispensable to Jane. The woman's understanding of the entire operation was extraordinary.

Mary was a plain, aging woman who wore her heart on her sleeve. She was shy, reluctant to demand anything from anyone, but quick to give. She seemed forever concerned that her friends might be injured, as though they were made of the most delicate porcelain. Even now, two months after Randolph Harrington's death, she approached Jane with overwhelming sympathy, not wanting to intrude upon or upset the woman.

"Mrs. Harrington, I've those letters for your signature."

"Oh, yes, I forgot," Jane said.

Mary shuffled around the desk to Jane's side and placed the first of the letters in front of her.

"Mary," Jane continued, turning to face her secretary, "why did you never remarry?"

The question struck the woman like a slap across the face. "I . . . Mrs. Harrington . . . I . . . don't you see . . . I mean, you must understand . . ."

"But I don't understand, Mary. Please try to explain to me."

"Well, you see," the woman paused, still taken aback by her employer. She shuffled the papers in her hand, trying to decide what exactly was being expected of her. "Well, you know, I'm not much of a looker, as they say. And I just didn't find too many fellas knocking down my door. A couple, but not many. And I wasn't real comfortable with them, the ones, I mean, that were my own age. I just felt like a fool, a grown woman trying to be a girl again. I just couldn't."

"But weren't you lonely? Aren't you still?"

"Yes," she whispered, her voice trailing away.

"How do you stand it? It seems I'll never get the knack."

"Ma'am, there is no standing it. You just unlearn the hurt somehow. It goes away."

"And while you're waiting?"

"There's only the remembering to keep you company. Recalling the good times, the happy things, what there was of it all that makes the losing of it hurt. Just settle, ma'am, on that. And wish, now and then, or dream. It helps, for me, in the night."

"It is the nights, you're right, Mary. There's nothing so black as the night that closes in on a widow."

"Yes, ma'am," Mary nodded. The woman now stood staring at the unsigned letters in her hand, not seeing them.

"I'm sorry," Jane apologized with a start. "I didn't mean to make you feel low. I've plenty of that for the two of us." Mrs. Harrington smiled at her secretary, hoping to ease her back into the work of the day. "And call me Jane, would you please, Mary? This Mrs. Harrington business really seems too formal. And no 'ma'ams' either."

"If you say so, ma'am, I mean . . . Jane." Mrs. Dabrowski pushed the still unsigned letter on Jane's desk toward her. She seemed to be praying that her employer would turn her attention to business matters rather than persist in this personal conversation.

"Thank you, Mary. I don't need lots of friends, but one or two good ones would certainly help." Jane then began signing her letters, patiently swirling out the elaborate signature that ended with the name she was so proud of.

"Mornin', Mrs. Harrington," Karl Oppenheimer nodded, closing the door to her office behind him. Karl never knocked. In fact, he rarely closed the door behind him. Jane thought to herself that he treated her with the same sort of hearty good humor and straightforward boisterousness that he had reserved for her husband. He treated her as an equal, almost like a man, and she was grateful to him for it.

"Mornin', Karl," she chimed, mimicking his casualness.

Karl Oppenheimer was a little thicker at the waist than he was when he first lifted a pick twenty years before in California. But there was considerable spring to his step. He took off his hat and sat down.

"How is everything going this morning?" Jane asked.

"Production is fine. We got the track repaired on the lower level and the hoists are all working well again." Karl cleared his throat. "If you don't mind, Mrs. Harrington, it's something else."

"Yes?"

"You know that fella, Jeb Engle?"

"I do. He came on board with us a month or two before Randy and I came back from Cheyenne."

"That's right. Well, he's from Pennsylvania, had lots of experience in the coal mines there. And he's a strong back, too. But there's a problem with him."

Jane tilted an eyebrow and nodded.

"Seems he was chased out of the East for trying to organize a labor union out there. And he's started pulling the same stunt here, telling the men wild tales about how great things are for the miners in Pennsylvania."

"That's absurd. Everyone knows there's nothing but death in the black clouds that fill those holes."

"Not everyone knows it, ma'am. To begin with, I didn't think Engle had any chance at all with our men. Your giving them a raise and hiring the doctor to treat them seemed more than enough to keep every pick in the place happy. I didn't think five drunk men would sign up. But they have, and more than five. Engle's a fancy talker, and you know our men aren't the quickest thinkers alive. The man's going at it smart, real smart."

"How?"

"He's sweet-talking a shift, just one, and only in special sections of the mine. Seems to hope he can take one vital section out on strike and shut us down."

"What's he telling them, exactly?" Jane's voice turned harder and harder as the discussion continued.

"I'm not too sure, Mrs. Harrington. But I've got a man, a good man, who's going to join up tomorrow so he can find out what Engle is up to and just what he's promising."

"Then don't fire Engle, yet." The mine owner was anticipating Karl's inclination, knowing he'd probably prefer shooting the organizer, if the truth were known. "The last thing we need is a martyr wandering around."

"Yes, ma'am."

"And let me know precisely what he's proposing to the men before you take any action at all."

"I will. So far I only know that he's talked twenty or so of 'em into paying a quarter a week in dues. Another twenty and he'll have enough to shut down a shift."

"Our only weak links are the ore hoists and the rail cars."

"That's right, Mrs. Harrington. But if he can stop either, the ore will pile up in a hurry. We'd have to stop digging within an hour or two."

"We'll see."

"Yes, we will." Karl got to his feet, then hesitated.

"What else, Karl?"

"Well, I just thought to ask about that other fella, Young. He givin' you any trouble?"

The night shift manager had been a little forward since Jane had become a widow. He was a handsome and capable man, but simply not Jane's cup of tea.

"No, it's all right. He hasn't come courting, if that's what you'd call it, for a week or more. I think he understands I'm not particularly interested in him. Don't worry, Karl."

"Not worried, ma'am. Just wasn't proper, that's all." Karl grumbled a bit, knowing Jane was able to handle the man herself, yet wanting to protect her just the same.

Jane Harrington nodded to her general manager and returned to her letters. Karl collected his hat and left.

Jane Harrington completed her calculations on October's production just before noon. The mine was producing twelve hundred dollars worth of ore for seven hundred and twenty dollars in costs. Since she had raised wages and hired a full-time physician, her weekly expenses had risen but production was up more than enough to cover the added overhead. She was pleased. Her mine would certainly be mined out more rapidly this way, but that didn't concern her. When the silver was gone she could leave. But she had to see the mine through to its end.

As she was replacing her ledger on a shelf filled with others, Mary Dabrowski knocked on the door. "There's a messenger from Mr. Loftin's bank here. He has a new safety deposit box to replace the one that was robbed. I asked him to leave it with me, but he said that he needed to talk to you for a moment. He insists. Shall I let him in?"

"Show him in. I'm finished with the books."

Mary turned, "Come in, Mr. Streib."

Brad walked through the door holding a small tin box. His close-cropped beard had been trimmed by a barber only hours before and his new black suit fit his shoulders like a glove.

A startled Jane Harrington looked at him and her hand flew to her mouth. "Brad!"

Spear laughed aloud, his interesting morning growing more so by the minute.

"Brad, I can't believe it's you."

"Jane, I could say the same."

Jane Harrington waved Mary from the office, bewildering her secretary, who closed the door wondering aloud what could possibly be going on.

Jane stood her ground, her fists on her hips, her heart pounding, her eyes fiery. "What, may I ask, is this Streib moniker? And where did you get that ridiculous suit?"

"The suit comes to me from your fair city's only tailor, a dry goods clerk with a scissors and needle. I came by the name less simply."

"Wipe that silly smile off your face," ordered the agitated woman. "And for God's sake, put that box down."

He did so, leaving his arms free to embrace the mine owner who, without comment, reached around his neck, drew his head down and pressed her lips to his. A few hushed, incoherent expressions of intimacy could be heard in the still office and it was several moments before they separated.

"Mrs. Harrington?" Brad questioned, moving slowly away from Jane.

"I'm a widow, Brad. He died two months ago."

"I'm sorry. I didn't know. I didn't even know you were married."

Jane shook her head nervously, trying to speak but fearing the attempt might end in tears. She fell into a chair as though burdened and tired.

"You are the most beautiful widow alive, more so than when we said our farewells in Cheyenne. Pardon me for my eyes, but I can't take them off you."

"Oh, blarney," she puffed. "Such rubbish. For a quiet man, you can damn near fill a room with nonsense."

"Jane. Shut up."

"I know. It's been six months of tornados, Brad, and now you walk in here, calling yourself Streib, flustering me, carrying an empty tin box, dressed like an undertaker. Good God, man."

"What's happened, since Cheyenne? Tell me all of it."

Jane closed her eyes. Finally, she thought, someone she could tell it all to. "Ahh, Cheyenne. It's a fine place today, I'd wager. After you left, the town settled down. Cy Frisco was elected mayor, complaining all the while that he wasn't fit for the job. He was wrong though, as usual. The old codger really set things moving, built a library and a school, Russ James was elected sheriff, and even the gunfights were kept to a minimum."

"And my outhouse?" Brad asked with a grin.

"Fanciest three-holer in the West. Sits behind the

school with a sign on it saying 'The Brad Spear Memorial Relief Station.' "

Spear scratched his head, warmed by the pure orneriness of Cy Frisco.

"And what about Harrington. Did you meet him there?"

"Yes, Brad. About three weeks after you left, he came into the Lady Jane for a drink. I'd never seen anyone like him, really. I think I turned into a bit of an idiot for a while, a long while. I just had to have that man.

"He'd come through Cheyenne for a look at the famous Lady Jane Saloon, he claimed. But I think he was more interested in the view of Lady Jane."

"No false modesty from you yet, I see."

"None, thank you," she acknowledged. "Regardless of Randy's real intentions, a few drinks and a long chat turned his short stopover in Cheyenne into an extended visit. Between buggy rides and dinner, long talks and . . . and wonderful nights, we became a pair. I've never wanted to be around a man so much.

"Before I knew it he was courting me. He was at the saloon all day, every day. I was never so happy. We ate and drank and talked endlessly. And after eight days I couldn't stand it anymore, so I asked him."

"Asked him?"

"To marry me."

"You're kidding!"

"No. Not at all."

"A perfect gentleman and no fool, he obviously accepted."

"Yes. In fact, he had a ring with him. A splendid show."

"You're amazing, Jane."

"Anyway, we were married within the week, and

what a wingding it was! Half the damn territory showed up for the party."

"I had no idea, or I'd have been there, too."

"I contacted your office, Brad, but they said you were off on a case somewhere. But you'd have loved it, the biggest, grandest bash you can imagine. Champagne everywhere. Even Russ James got drunk. Two weeks later we were here, at Randy's mine." Lady Jane paused and looked aside. "It seemed then that nothing could go wrong. Nothing."

Spear took her hand, regretting he had never met the man who could bring Lady Jane such happiness.

"I think Randy knew it was too good to last. Something drove him. Drove him to teach me all about the mine. He'd joke about wanting me around and kid me about my 'business' experience, but there was something desperate about the way we poured over the books and worked nights on tunnel designs. He died two months ago."

"What happened?" Brad asked gently.

"It was an accident. A car broke loose in the main tunnel while Randy was supervising a shoring crew below. They say he heard the rumble above, but I'll never know. . . . For two weeks I wanted them to shoot me. I had nothing. The saloon had been sold and I owned a mine I didn't want." Spear embraced her, not comforting so much as surrounding her.

She sat up and wiped away the tears. "Damn you, Spear."

"Easy, Lady. Time will help."

"God knows I've had plenty of that. The mine fills the days well enough, but the nights are unbearable. I've tried working 'til I drop, but it doesn't help. The memories find their way into my bed."

There was nothing to say, nothing that either of

them could add, so the conversation stopped, silence marking the moment.

"I'm all right now, though! Thank God for Allan Pinkerton."

"If you knew him, you might not say so."

"He sent you here, that's all I care about. You must be investigating the bank robbery."

"Yup."

"That's sensible enough, but why the assumed name? You getting to be famous or are you just hiding from some woman?" She laughed at the thought of a pursued Spear.

"Not so well-known, actually, and I can handle the ladies, thank you." Brad was relieved that the tone of the conversation had changed. "I'm playing an undercover game here. But it doesn't seem to be working very well. I'm supposed to be a teller trainee at the Loftin bank, but I can't imagine why hired guns would want to blow such a fella's head away."

"Again?"

"Always, I'm afraid. The belligerence of some folks is enough to downright disappoint you." Brad's eyes narrowed almost impishly and Lady Jane pushed him away from her, annoyed he could joke about the very real peril of his work. Then she drew him toward her and they embraced. She moaned softly as she looked at her Pinkerton and sent her tongue darting about inside his mouth. She pressed hard against him for just a moment, then pulled away.

"Lord, you're wonderful." Spear kissed her again. Losing control, in her own office and so recently a widow, Lady Jane began to think this scene could become very awkward very quickly. "Mary!" she shouted, easing away from Brad. "I think I should introduce you to my family here," she explained to Brad.

Mary entered looking more sheepish than ever, but

with a trace of glee on her face. It was obvious, even to the secretary, that Brad was more than an old acquaintance come to visit.

"Mary, the nicest thing has happened. Mr. Streib and I knew each other in Cheyenne and, by chance, his business has brought him to Silver City. Brad, this is Mary Dabrowski, the real controller of the place. I couldn't live without her."

Mary shook Brad's hand warmly. "Pleased to meet you, sir. Anyone who can cheer this lady up is a blessing to me."

"I'll do what I can, Mary."

# Chapter 5

"Loftin!"

The banker looked up from his desk at the Pinkerton agent, startled by the raised voice in his bank.

"Hell of a town you got here," Brad bellowed, raising the down-turned heads of the bank's tellers.

"Mr. Spear, please," Loftin said, his voice a panicked whisper. "Please lower your voice. That's no way for a teller trainee to behave."

"Mr. Loftin," Brad continued, still loud enough to be heard throughout the bank, "that teller-in-training foolishness proved about as useful as your locked doors. Everyone who matters knows who I am."

"Are you sure?" The banker looked disconsolate, as though his hopes had been crushed.

"As sure as I am that your thieves are still in town. They know what I'm doing here, know who I am and are making their best efforts to perforate this Pinkerton."

"I heard about the shooting."

"Congratulations. Your nose for news means nothing to me. But what does interest me is the folks you've got working in this place. I'd like to horsewhip the one who fingered me on the street this morning. And I'll do it yet. One of your loyal little weasels is an informer and a thief."

The entire staff of the bank had, by then, risen from

their plain oak chairs and desks and formed a pathetic circle around their employer. Each looked both curious and alarmed at Spear's outburst.

"Let's talk," Brad ordered, walking immediately toward the banker's office. Once inside the room, with the door closed, Brad spoke, his voice low, "That ought to shake somebody up."

"Jesus," the banker muttered, obviously confused.

"Talk to me about those keys of yours."

"As I explained, there are only two sets. I have one and Mr. Gregory the other. But surely . . ."

"Loftin, don't try to pour oil on these waves. Someone in this town has been thinking very clearly, very quickly and with a lot of professional help. I'm riled and haven't time for your reassuring ways. Tell me about those keys."

"Mine are always at the other end of my watch chain. Always. Mr. Gregory keeps his in the top drawer of his desk during working hours. They are available to the tellers if both he and I are busy when they're needed. Only the tellers are authorized to touch them."

"But it's common knowledge that they sit in that desk."

"Yes."

"Then anybody in the bank can borrow those keys, correct."

"I suppose so."

"Terrific." Brad thought a moment, setting the sequence of his interrogation in his own mind, knowing that timing more than incisiveness mattered now.

"Was Alice Carter ever married?"

"Mr. Spear . . ." The banker grew more disoriented by the minute.

"Was she ever married?"

"No. Never. She's a wonderful woman, though,

clever, loyal, a little cold it seems, but a noble woman."

"And Virginia Mahon, what about her?"

"She married, of course, a soldier, I think. She has a son." Brad noticed a tightening around Loftin's mouth as he spoke. "She's worked hard to raise him well, powerful hard."

"Do you know anything about her husband? How he died? If he died? If he ever existed?"

"Good God, Spear, no, I don't know anything about him. She almost never speaks of her married life. I don't even know the man's name."

Loftin paced the room, avoiding Brad's stare, waiting for the next question. "Tragic loss for such a pretty young woman, don't you think so?"

"Sure, tragic," Loftin responded a little too offhandedly, a little too callously, a little out of character.

"Tell me about Brockington," Brad demanded, keeping the banker off balance.

"He's got money, that's for certain. So much that he doesn't practice medicine anymore. He only doctors when there's a real emergency. Rumor has it that his fingers are deep in a lot of pies around town."

"Does he know Virginia?"

"What?" Loftin exploded. "That cheat! A fine lady like Virginia wouldn't, couldn't, be involved. Even know the man. Never. She's a lady, I tell you." Loftin seemed genuinely upset, as though the mere suggestion of an association between the doctor and his bookkeeper offended him deeply.

"Suppose I ought to ask the good doctor himself about that." Spear marched from the bank, a safety deposit box under his arm.

Dr. Brockington's office had once been a house. It was set back from the street ten feet or so, and flanked

by the false facades of more traditional storefronts.
Spear climbed its steps slowly, eyeing the clean, freshly
painted white trim. He crossed the deep front porch
and rapped on the front door. A sign posted beside the
door read: "Knock and Come In."

Spear stepped into an unusually impressive front
hall, its staircase winding around three sides of the
room as it ascended to the upper floor. The hall contained a large, patterned rug surrounded by two
benches and a few chairs. It must once have been a
busy waiting area for patients, but was empty now.

Through the open double doors in the hall Brad
could see a converted dining room. Its walls were lined
with shelves containing tins and bottles, boxes and rolls
of bandages. It appeared to be a small apothecary,
complete with porcelain mortars and pestles, diagrams
of the human body's inner organs and a dusty skeleton
hanging in the corner. Dr. Brockington had once both
prescribed and filled his remedies.

"Might as well come on back here. I'd as soon not
get up," a voice called from the other side of the house.

Brad walked through a narrow door off the hall into
the doctor's office. A large, roll-top desk dominated the
ten-foot-square room. A few pictures and a framed
medical certificate hung on the walls. Dr. Brockington
sat behind the desk in a leather-covered swivel chair
which he spun deftly to greet his visitor.

"Dr. Brockington?"

"Yes, yes. But if you're ailing, you've come to the
wrong place. I don't do much doctoring these days.
There's a fine doctor out near the Silver Lady mine . . ."

"I'm not sick," Brad interrupted. "My name is Brad
Streib and I've been sent by Mr. Loftin with a new
safety deposit box." Brad studied the doctor intently,
trying to discern a twinge of doubt on his face. The
sheriff or someone at the bank or an unknown enemy

might have revealed his true identity. There was no way to know.

"Well, I hope this one's stronger than the last," Brockington frowned. "I lost a stack of gold coins in that burglary." The doctor seemed to be taking Brad's story at face value.

"The bank knows you lost heavily, Doctor. That's why I'm here. Mr. Loftin would like a detailed list of everything in your box when it was stolen. Anything special it might have contained and your estimate of each item's value. It seems that a new insurance policy which the bank took out shortly before the break-in might cover some of your losses."

Brockington's eyebrows rose high on his forehead at the mention of insurance. "Hell, I already gave Loftin a list. What more does he need?"

"I've been sent, Doctor, to ask if you omitted anything from your accounting. Stocks, bonds, anything traceable that you should be reimbursed for. Just in case your earlier list was incomplete."

"I see."

"Good."

"But I can't say I believe much of what you're saying, young man. Your employer is inviting me to lie about what I've lost and offering to pay me for doing so. Worse, he sends you, Mr. uh . . . Streib, with the offer. And you don't much look like an errand boy to me. What sort of craziness is this?"

"Don't know, Doctor. I'm a teller-trainee, that's all. Doing what I'm told, learning about the banking business."

"Horseshit."

Brad pondered the situation, then tried another approach. "To tell you the truth, my father owns several banks on the Coast and sent me here to learn what I could about a boom town. He thinks there's a great deal of money to be made financing and selling shares in new gold or silver strikes. He expects me to discover just how much money."

"I knew you weren't any damned errand boy!" He leaned back in his chair and squinted through his glasses. "Is it true about the insurance thing?"

"Yes. There's a chance. If your first accounting suits you, that's fine. But if you would like to amend your list . . ."

"Mmmmmmmmm. Never hurts to try, does it?"

"No, sir."

"I'll drop the box and my new list off at the bank this afternoon, Streib. Tell Loftin I appreciate his efforts on my behalf."

Brad turned and left, convinced Brockington knew far more than he let on.


"You can come out now, Senator," Brockington called.

With that simple demand, Senator Ramsey Stuart Rogers walked through the side door of the doctor's office into the room. "You sure he's gone?" the man inquired.

"Gone," the doctor nodded.

"He's not going to admit his identity, Brockington."

"It doesn't matter, I tell you. Relax. So long as we know where he's probing, we can control him. Now, down to business."

Dr. Brockington unrolled a huge sheet of paper across the top of his desk. On it was marked the route of the Central Pacific Railroad across Nevada. The thin red line was gridded with sections of land deeded to the railroad by the government as subsidies for finishing the transcontinental line. Each numbered square on the map represented the property owned by the holder of a Land Grant Certificate.

"We're concentrating here, Senator. This gap, try to remember that. Don't go wild buying up every section you hear about. Copy the numbers of these sections and buy only those."

"I have them somewhere," Rogers responded. In his excitement over becoming part of the fantastically lucrative scheme, he seemed to be misplacing important things lately. It bothered him. "But, Doctor, there are plenty of other sections that can turn a tidy profit. I can swing state and federal funding for all kinds of improvements: dams, spur rail lines, you name it. There's a fortune to be made developing this state."

"Rogers, don't feed me any of your Washington, D.C. mule muffins. We're not 'opening the West,' we're buying specific sections of Nevada. You can flimflam bankers and representatives of the state, you can even bamboozle a lawyer or two if you like, but don't speculate in land. Buy *only* the plots I tell you. Got it?"

Hurriedly writing down the numbers indicated on the map, Rogers bobbed his head absent-mindedly. He didn't like being treated like a child. He liked the implication that he was a two-bit politician even less. Still, he would do as he was told. This was his chance. However odious the company he was forced to keep, no matter how demeaning the chores he was assigned, he was resolved to go on with it. Somewhere in the back of his mind, he imagined that his share of the riches could be invested in huge tracts of land that one day would be developed. He would connive his way to wealth and help his country, too. But first, the wealth.

Bunny West wandered into Dr. Brockington's office, a glazed stare in her eyes. Her otherwise striking face, dark and exquisitely chiseled, appeared flaccid, drawn, vacant.

"Doctor, doctor," she mumbled, struggling to focus on the two men.

"Bunny, what are you doing here?" Brockington asked, irritated.

"Doctor, I've dreamed again. Make it stop. I'm dreaming those awful things . . ."

Senator Rogers couldn't believe his eyes. Before him stood a young woman dressed only in a man's shirt, wandering asleep or drunk through the doctor's office. "Can she recognize me?" he asked, worry showing on his face.

"No, thank God, she can't. I doubt she can see the nose in front of her face."

Rogers stared at the woman, unable to take his eyes from the gentle, firm curves of her legs. The shirt Bunny wore draped around her loosely, half-buttoned, revealing the dark, smooth skin of her thighs and the firm tops of her breasts. Even almost unconscious, she was a striking beauty.

"What's the matter with her?" Rogers queried the doctor.

"Plenty. She's a sick woman, haunted, I'd say. Or possessed. But I manage her, control her, and she's useful to us."

"It's frightening . . ."

"Fascinating is more like it, Senator."

Bunny lowered herself into a huge, overstuffed chair in the corner of the room, murmuring softly. As she did so, the dark, silken triangle between her legs became uncovered and the slim turn of one thigh transfixed Rogers. The doctor looked at him and smiled. The pompous, self-deluding, self-righteous son-of-a-bitch liked the ladies well enough, he thought. Even the well-married senator had his weakness.

"Excuse me, Senator," said Dr. Brockington, unctuous apology oozing through his voice. "I'll just give her a quick ministration and then she'll be out of our way."

"Beg pardon?"

Rogers' mind was on other matters.

"She needs rest, Senator. Tranquillity."

At Brockington's words, Rogers shuddered, somehow terrified by the ghostly woman before him, but at the same time attracted, both by her beauty and her condition. Before he could answer, Brockington pulled a syringe from a compartment high in his roll-top desk. He busied himself with powders and a clear vial of liquid, filling the syringe with a milky substance. Then he walked to Bunny, whose head lolled from side to side, and injected her with the drug.

For a moment she sat perfectly still, her eyes closed tightly, her hands rising slowly to her head.

"What was that?" Rogers asked.

"Never mind," the doctor dismissed him with a wave, never taking his eyes from the figure slouching before him.

Through the growing haze, Bunny West saw her mother's face. It smiled warmly at the girl, affection pouring on the innocent. Her mother lifted her, a girl of thirteen, and stroked her hair. Bunny moaned in the doctor's chair, comforted, her knees rising to her chest.

Bunny's mother whispered to her. It would be all right. It would be all right. But the noise was beginning, the screech of distant anger, the terrifying wail of her drunken father filled her skull.

Her mother fell away from her, bloodied. Large, relentless fists beat against the woman and the sound of cracking bone sent a frozen knife through her. There was screaming, the helpless cry of a woman beaten, the roar of an angry man, the sobs of defeat. Bunny's heart spun. Her arms wrapped around her head, her shoulders shaking.

Then it passed. In Bunny's dream, her mother lay

moaning. She was lying on the floor before the girl, bleeding, weeping. Her father stood over his wife, drinking from a bottle, undressing himself clumsily, then standing huge and naked over Bunny's mother. The girl watched as he pulled at her dress, tearing it. She stared at the cotton bloomers her mother wore, and whimpered as they were torn away. Bunny wailed, then and now, as the man plunged into the bleeding woman, battering himself against her, clawing at her and moaning.

The sound in Bunny's head was shrill as her father stood and drank, whiskey pouring down his chin. She watched her mother roll to her side, heard her cry, quietly, fear and hatred smothering her voice. And then Bunny saw her father's half-toothless grin and she saw the rough, dark hair of his beard pressing toward her.

Bunny's father pierced her, huge and vicious. She clawed at him, tearing at his eyes, but his fist pounded against her face and her hands were quickly pinioned above her head. For what seemed hours he moved against her, tearing, bruising, hurting something, somewhere deep inside her.

And then he disappeared. The rough chafe of his beard against her forehead and the wrenching strain at her arms stopped, but the burning between her legs remained. And in a moment the battered face of her mother appeared, hovering over her, whispering, "It'll be all right, it'll be all right."

Bunny felt as if she were staring into some inner sun, her eyes burning, her lips drying, and then a cool breeze blew through the kitchen window of her youth. The thin white curtains billowed across a crude wooden counter and the scent of flowers filled the room. The girl whistled to herself, softly, drying dishes in a deep basin.

Her mother was dead. They had taken her away and

put her in a box. And they had buried the box, that morning, throwing dirt on it. A man had droned from a book. Her father had worn his hat to protect his eyes from the sun. And Bunny, thirteen years old, had not shed a tear.

Now, she finished the dishes. The coffee made, the bread sliced, waiting for her father. He would come, drunk, feigning sorrow. Soon.

His eyes are red, she dreamed. Running red.

Her father lifted her, the smell of whiskey on his breath and in his clothes, and carried Bunny to the bed. He set her down without a word, took the bottle, the green bottle, from his hip pocket and drained it. Bunny looked up at him, silent, as he unbuckled his belt and let his trousers fall to the floor. She turned her head and watched the curtains billowing in the kitchen. He had taken her now many times, the door locked, her mother pounding on it from the kitchen. And she had struggled, bit him, kicked until he beat her into submission or tied her wrists to the bed, the ropes blistering her arms. He had taken her many times.

In the swim of her dream, Bunny saw herself calm. She heard her father cough and stand, hairy and hideous before her and she watched herself unbutton the small, plain, childish corset that covered her young body. He groaned into her, sweating, pumping until it surged from him. And she heard him say it: "Ahhh, my lovely, we're alone now forever." He rolled off her, the sickening sound of him leaving her echoing in her mind, and she stood, kissing him.

As Bunny dreamed, her hand trailed slowly down her neck to her breast, circling her nipple. It wandered there, outlining the clear, round shape, then brushing lightly across the tip of her. The nipple hardened as her hand then slid, only finger tips touching her skin, across her chest, stopping, for a moment, teasing and then slipping to her stomach. The fingers played at the perimeter of her silken mound, glancing over the low ridges of her hips, caressing her thighs.

And the terrible images swept over her again. Bunny's father lay on his back, his organ drooping to one side, his hands behind his head. The girl, still naked, walked from the kitchen with a glass filled with whiskey. The warm air and thick smell of the drink filled her head, leaving her dizzy, but she managed to reach him and ran one hand across his chest as he drank.

Her father shook his head. "Can't drink all this," he laughed, guffawing at the girl. Then he lifted himself on one elbow and ran his free hand across Bunny's small breasts. Roughly, he cupped a buttock, his fingers digging into her, and pulled the girl toward him. Smiling, he emptied his glass. Suddenly, with a horrible noise, he turned and spat across the room, fell back into the pillow, groaning.

Bunny's dream was filled with the growing screams of her father. Her ears rang with the yowling of the tortured man. The poison made his eyes roll back, those bloodshot orbs staring at her as he groped the air trying to find the girl. His stomach wrenched and his legs buckled while she watched the pain rack his face and the panic drive his outstretched arms and fingers high into the air.

Bunny's hands now raced across her body, her knees spread wide, the center of her glistening as she probed herself. She turned, straining after a vision of profound suffering. Exhilarated, freed, she seized the image of her revenge, that death as tantalizingly close as the release she anticipated at her shuddering center. Witnessing the end of her confusing, endless abuse, she arched, her mouth open. Her thighs pressed hard against her hand and she opened, her hips rising, her buttocks tight. She felt the sure, relentless pouring of balm across her and the building urgency of her desire held her spellbound. For a moment, at the lip of this vessel, she paused and then cried "YES, YES, YES," coming violently. Her father was dead! Dead, at last! Secure in that blissful knowledge, Bunny felt the ache between her legs quiet and her mind once again floated in the warm ease of darkening oblivion. She slept.

Long after Bunny's passion had subsided, Senator Rogers' mouth hung agape. He had watched Bunny struggle with herself, the twisting and turning of her body. He had witnessed her weeping, the violent pain that seemed to rack her as she shook with terrible tremors.

His mouth closed. His lips were dry. He could not take his eyes from her. Her full, firm breasts were flattened against her chest, the dress torn open, exposing a soft expanse of heaving breast, now flushed with the dying fire of her emotion. Her skirt was pulled up around her waist. One moist finger, now still, rested in the soft gash that it had probed so relentlessly only moments before.

Senator Rogers looked up, the blood drained from his face.

"Is it over?"

His voice was hoarse.

"Yes, Senator," Dr. Brockington replied.

He stood almost solemnly and walked to Bunny's side. Her neck, her breasts and the tortured thighs sparkled with perspiration. Gently, the doctor pulled her hand away from the soft mound of hair where it rested, laying her palm demurely on her abdomen. Bunny moaned softly. The doctor ran the back of his hand gently across her cheek and covered the woman with a thick comforter. Turning to a baffled, awestruck Rogers, Brockington tilted his head toward the door, wordlessly inviting his guest to leave. Rogers obeyed.

Long after Rogers had departed, Brockington sat alone at his desk, strangely comfortable with the unconscious woman only an arm's length from his work. He contemplated his map, checking its colored sections against his inventory of Land Grant Certificates. Finally, after nearly half an hour of mindless rest, he rolled the map into a tube, tied it securely and hid his plan from view.

Sitting, staring at Bunny, the doctor didn't hear the visitor enter the room until the faint click of his inner office door interrupted his reverie. Brockington turned, hearing another click, and was stunned to see the black muzzle of a .44 staring at him, held by a suntanned man in his early forties.

"Easy there, Doc," the gunman barked. "Hands flat on the desk. I'm a nervous man, nervous as hell."

"What do you want?" Brockington demanded with all the cold authority he could muster.

"Just you. I been huntin' you for six years now. All I want is you."

"What?"

"I said I been hunting an old army doctor friend of mine for six years, waitin' to settle with him. And now I've found you, you bastard!"

At the mention of the army, Brockington recoiled. Holding his ground, nevertheless, he calmly stated, "You must be mistaken. I don't know you." The stranger's face was hidden by a soiled brown hat and two or three days' worth of beard stubble and riding grit. The simple filth of the man made it difficult for the doctor to ascertain his feelings. But the steady .44 aimed at him was threatening enough. Brockington bided his time.

"Hell's fire, Doc, you just don't want to remember me. We didn't exchange what you might call formal good-byes, but leastwise you could recall a body you faced death with. For sure you can recall a few of the fellas that used to call you 'Captain'."

Army days. The thought sent a shiver through Brockington. Somewhere in the quagmire of his military duty he'd crossed this man. When? What double-cross?

"I'm not sure what your game is, mister, but I never argue with a loaded six-gun." The doctor was beginning to get himself under control. "Yes, I was in the army, most of us doctors were. And I was a Captain, along with hundreds of other physicians. What does that prove?"

"Six years ago, Doc. Think about it. Remember the 314th out of Prescott?"

Brockington stiffened at the mention of the 314th, thinking to himself that it was impossible anyone knew.

"I'm sorry, sir. I spent my army time in Chicago and Omaha. I was never in Prescott."

"That's a lie, Captain. I know it, you know it and this pistol knows it. Don't weasel around. Ten of us left Yuma bright and early, headed into Prescott. But only you and I survived them Injuns. They killed most of the horses and men, leavin' just you and me and the gold. Comin' back to you now?"

Brockington knew he was in trouble. The dead man was alive. Corporal Pat Doolan, left to die in the desert after the doctor made off with $40,000 in gold coin, was alive.

"A man can walk farther without water than you thought," Doolan said. "I lived, Doc, and I've found you at last." The man with the gun then scanned the room, finally noticing Bunny. He moved to her and, never really taking his eyes off Brockington, lifted the comforter from her body.

"Sweet, Doc," he said, admiring the nude, sleeping woman.

"She's drugged, leave her alone."

"Sick, huh?"

"Not exactly, Doolan, but ill, in a way."

"No matter. All I want is my share of that $40,000 you made off with. Just hand over my share."

"I can't give it to you now. It'll take me two or three days to raise that kind of cash. But I'll put you up until I manage it and then pay you everything you've got coming. You can even take my friend here to bed if you'd like. She's a pleasure on a cold night."

Doolan lifted the comforter again and feasted his eyes on the beautiful woman before him. "Deal," he announced and threw the blanket from the woman, leaving her uncovered. Bunny curled into a tighter ball at the rush of cold air against her skin.

"This way," Brockington said, raising an arm and standing.

Doolan slipped his gun hand under Bunny's arm, around her back, and worked his other arm under her thighs. With one grunt he lifted her, the light from the single high window in the office reflecting off her breasts and thighs. Held in his arms, warm, Bunny snuggled against the cowboy, wrapping her arms around his neck. A low gurgling came from her throat and Doolan bent his head to kiss her shoulder.

As he did so, Bunny stirred and the armed man planted a kiss on her lips. It was his last. Brockington, standing at the door, grasped an unused scalpel, one that had been on his shelf for years, and rammed it into Doolan's back. It struck a rib and the man turned, releasing Bunny to fall to the floor in a heap. But as Doolan swung his gun toward the doctor, hurried surgery was performed on his side. The scalpel's second assault slid deep into the man's chest and cut across his side quickly. Blood flowed in a torrent as Brockington reached for the gun, missed it and then rolled behind his desk.

Doolan staggered, holding himself together with one hand, waving his now unsteady six-gun in the other. "Bastard!" he screamed. He stumbled around the desk in search of his prey, blood pouring down his chaps. As he rounded the tall desk, a look of panicked bewilderment came over his face. The doctor had vanished. But as he turned to search for him, Brockington leapt from beneath the desk, plunging the blade deep into Doolan's back.

The sound of air rushing from the man's body hushed the room as Brockington stood, watching Doolan take a single step before falling over Bunny's unconscious form. Blood ebbed from him, soaking her, for nearly fifteen minutes before the doctor had gathered his wits.

# Chapter 6

Brad Spear's day had been unproductive. He had walked the streets of Silver City, delivering one new safety deposit box after another. An upset school-teacher had bemoaned the loss of treasured, if value-less, mementoes. A bristling hardware store owner threatened Brad with a pick handle for no other reason than representing the bank. Nearly everyone was annoyed with his loss, but not ruined by it. Having now met all thirty box owners, Spear couldn't help concluding that only Brockington had the nerve and resources to mastermind the burglary.

Brad stood outside the Loftin bank, leafing through the pages of his notebook. As hard as he tried, he couldn't imagine a connection between Virginia Mahon, the bank's pretty, quiet bookkeeper and Dr. Brockington. It was time to push Virginia.

As the agent entered the bookkeeping area of the bank, he felt Wanda Loftin's eyes on him. The girl sat straight in her chair, her shoulders pushed unnaturally back to emphasize her breasts. "Good morning, Bradley," she cooed. "I was hoping you'd find the time to drop by."

"I found the time, Wanda, but I'm afraid I'm going to have to ask you to leave." He pointed toward the door. "Why don't you go powder your nose or something?"

"Drat," the girl said and fumed from the room.

Virginia Mahon became obviously uncomfortable as Brad closed the door behind Wanda.

"Mrs. Mahon?" Brad said, approaching her desk.

"Yes, what is it?" she replied. Then, her voice nearly cracking, she made a feeble effort to avoid the confrontation. "Can't you see I'm busy?"

Brad sighed, slipped his Pinkerton identification card from his pocket and sat next to her. "All right, Mrs. Mahon, let's get one thing straight. I'm not a teller-trainee. I'm here to investigate a bank robbery. I think you know what I'm talking about . . ."

"What could the robbery have to do with me?"

"Mrs. Mahon, someone who had access to the keys used in the break-in is responsible for the theft. I suspect you played a part in it."

"Me?" she sputtered. "Why that's impossible. I'd never do anything to hurt Mr. Loftin, never . . ."

"It's not a question of loyalty, Virginia," Brad soothed. There was no need to cross-examine her into a frenzy to find the truth. Her lie was the key. "I suspect you because you lied to me and I think a great deal of grief forced that lie. If someone found out your secret, he could make you do just about anything . . ."

Mrs. Mahon gasped.

". . . even steal from Mr. Loftin."

"But I didn't, honestly."

"Mrs. Mahon, it's clear from the age of your child that his father wasn't killed in the War. If I can figure the simple adding and subtracting it takes to work that out, so can someone else." The woman began to weep, tears forming in her eyes, her shoulders shaking.

"Please, Mr. Spear. I didn't have anything to do with the robbery."

The door to the office opened abruptly and Lyn Loftin walked in looking very much more like an angry miner than a banker. "Is something wrong here?" he asked Virginia.

"Mr. Loftin," Brad answered, "I'm sounding out Mrs. Mahon on a sensitive matter and I don't think I need your help right now. She and I have to discuss something that's none of your business." Virginia looked up at her employer, wordlessly shaking her head.

The bank president didn't move. "My God, Spear, surely you don't suspect Mrs. Mahon."

"Yes, I do. She had access to the keys and she's lied to me at least once."

"I'll vouch for her honesty, Mr. Spear. Absolutely."

"Loftin, back off." Brad's voice grew more cutting by the minute.

"Spear," the banker spoke with the tone of a man accustomed to final decisions, "either stop grilling this woman or you're fired."

"You're an idiot, Loftin."

"No," Virginia shouted. "I've had enough."

Both men looked at her.

"You can't send him away, Lyn. You can't. I'll tell him the truth. Mr. Spear, I was pregnant when I left town years ago. I went away to have my baby and his father paid all the bills. He wasn't killed in the War. In fact, he's alive today."

"Virginia," the banker interjected, "you don't have to say another word."

"Hush, Lyn. The father lives here in town and takes very good care of both of us. I have no money problems and no one knows what I'm telling you now. I didn't give anybody the keys and I don't know who did. I'd never steal from this bank . . . I swear it."

"Mrs. Mahon, I don't believe you," Brad stated. "Your secret was discovered by someone, you feared for your son's reputation, for your job, for something . . ."

"Spear! I'm the father," Loftin disclosed. "She wasn't involved in the burglary."

Brad stepped away from the pair, baffled for a moment.

"Mrs. Loftin is a drunk, Mr. Spear," Virginia whispered, "a falling-down drunk. She doesn't deserve a man like Lyn." Loftin moved his hand to her cheek, softly stroking her as he watched the agent.

"Virginia, why don't you take the rest of the day off and go home? We'll see you tomorrow morning," the banker suggested.

She nodded and quietly put away her pens and account book. After she'd left, Loftin turned to Brad. "I really didn't count on your learning about this."

"Mr. Loftin, I'm here about a bank robbery and nothing else. As far as I'm concerned, I've one less suspect, that's all."

"Thank you."

"Forget it. I can think of a time or two when I've done what I shouldn't have. Seems to me you're doing what any decent man would, maybe better. We'll leave it at that."

Loftin stood, surrounded by the workings of a bank he'd built himself, his face drawn with years of hard work and worry. He could think of nothing to say. He didn't want to offer any explanations and he was sure Spear wasn't interested in them.

"Good day, Mr. Loftin," Brad said quietly as he left the man alone with his thoughts.

The mittened hand of the front desk clerk poked a pale blue envelope toward Brad's face. He was shivering still, his hand quaking inches from the agent's nose.

"Thank you," Brad said, his eyebrows rising wryly

on his forehead as he looked down on the strange thin man.

The note was characteristically intriguing: "Brad, we must dine with friends first. See you at seven o'clock." Though the message was unsigned, the swirling flourishes of the handwriting told him that Lady Jane was, in her way, inviting him to her home for the evening. He chuckled to himself, hoping dinner would be served promptly and consumed quickly.

He sponged himself briefly in his room, washing the dust that constantly rose from Silver City's streets from his face. With the small brush he carried everywhere, Brad removed the grit from his new, black suit. He dressed quickly, knotting a fancy striped tie around his neck instead of the dull grey one preferred by Alice Carter. He arrived at the Harrington mansion a little early.

Lady Jane greeted him at the door, flushed with excitement. Her wheat-blonde hair was drawn into a large, brilliant chignon at the back of her neck and was held there by a black net decorated with tiny ribbons. Her dress, long and flowing, plunged slightly, revealing only a suggestion of cleavage. As she moved toward Brad, the rustle of taffeta petticoats hushed the imposing front hall.

Like a schoolgirl she swept toward him, stopped, raised her arms and pirouetted for his inspection. "Yes?" she asked.

"Yes," came the only conceivable answer.

"Do you like the house? It took Randy years to build it."

"It's as large as any in San Francisco. And beautiful, really."

"Come see," she urged, hurrying him along by the arm.

The living room was nearly fifty feet long and half

as wide. It contained three separate groups of finely upholstered furniture, each surrounding a separate fireplace. In one corner stood a harpsichord, constructed of inlaid woods and intricately carved legs. Here and there the rich oranges and deep reds of Japanese and Chinese cabinetwork shined below lamps, and three patterned red rugs, similar but not identical, covered the floor.

"Downright intimate," Brad noted with a grin.

"There's more," she said, disappearing ahead of him.

The dining room was nearly as large as the living room. But it was dominated by a single, immense cherrywood table circled by matching, high-backed chairs. One end of the table was set for four, the silver gleaming below tall, white candles.

"Be it ever so humble . . ." Lady Jane smiled, proud to the point of being giddy.

Brad took her in his arms and the faint scent of lilac surrounded him.

"Now Bradley, don't muss me up before the judge arrives," she giggled, pushing him away.

"A judge?"

"Judge Roscoe Thorpe and his wife. He sits on the county bench here and travels around the territory from time to time, hearing cases. Anyway, Lucy's a delight and I invited them weeks ago. Fortunately, the judge leaves town on his circuit tomorrow, so I think they'll say goodnight early."

"How early?"

"Stop it, Bradley. And remember, you must call me Mrs. Harrington."

"No remarks about your pickpocket days in London allowed?" Brad recalled Jane's past, her parents thrown in debtors' prison, leaving her alone on the streets. Her urchin days of scrounging for scraps, her inevitable life of crime and the spectacular con that took her to the most sacred bastions of wealth in London. If they hadn't caught and hanged the man who taught her so well, she might be there still, lifting valuables at formal balls.

"No, that life is gone. Forgotten."

"What a shame that your old skills are lost."

"Ooooooh, I wouldn't say that, love," she cooed, sporting a thick cockney accent. "Give me a fortnight and I'd be as quick as ever." As she spoke she approached him and gave Brad the gentlest kiss. "See," she said, handing him the wallet that only moments before nestled safely inside his jacket.

Lady Jane was forced to suppress her laughter when she heard a knock at the door. "It's them. Now behave yourself." Brad straightened his jacket while she hurried to greet her guests. He could hear the mutter of idle talk from the front hall as the two women complimented each other on their dresses. Then, after only a moment, Jane returned with the couple.

"Judge and Mrs. Thorpe, this is Brad Streib. Brad's in town working with Mr. Loftin at the bank. He's an old family friend of mine from Cheyenne, Wyoming."

Judge Thorpe extended a firm hand and Brad shook it. Mrs. Thorpe nodded politely and then turned to Jane. Thorpe was a rather solid man, with a thick mustache and mutton-chop sideburns that met the handlebars above his lip at each side. The flowered vest beneath his black suitcoat showed off a heavy gold watch chain. He gazed soberly through steel-rimmed glasses.

"Glad to have you here, Streib. Hope you get that bank whipped into shape."

"It's me that's being put into shape, Judge. I'm a trainee of sorts, evaluating the business, you might say."

"That's what the sheriff tells me," Thorpe offered with a wink. "Good luck to you, whatever you're doing."

"Thank you," Brad replied. Word of Brad's identity was clearly spreading fast. Still, the less said the better. The agent and judge had apparently agreed to ignore the truth of the situation for the sake of a pleasant meal.

"I do believe our food is ready," Jane announced.

They sat themselves at the end of the long table and Brad enjoyed a sumptuous meal and endured some of the most boring conversation he'd ever heard. After nearly forty-five minutes of municipal titter and social gossip, he poured himself a third glass of wine.

Sipping his drink he glanced at Jane, who was staring at him despite the more or less constant prattle coming from Mrs. Thorpe. Jane's eyes sparkled as she watched him, thrilled and impatient but containing herself. Finally, there was a lull in the conversation.

"Mrs. Harrington," Brad remarked, "there are few meals more delicious than a well-turned leg of lamb resting on a bed of rice."

"I'm glad you so appreciate our efforts, Mr. Streib."

"I do, really."

"Preparing such a feast is simply a question of patience."

"Oh?"

"Yes. The meat you find at this table is delicious only because it is fresh and was carefully, patiently cooked. The heat came to it slowly, building, for hours."

"Nerve-racking business."

"For some," she said, a napkin concealing her smile. "But others, gourmets of the first rank, enjoy the waiting nearly as much as the feast itself. Basting and seasoning a fine leg until its aroma fills the kitchen and it shines above the fire is a considerable skill. Most men haven't the temperament for it."

"Well, I've always thought myself a patient man. But I think that the anticipation of sinking my teeth into such a meal might overcome me, that is, if hours are really required to serve such a perfectly pink slice of lamb."

"Ahhh. Just like a man," she observed. "The teeth, sir, are crude devices. It is the lips and tongue that truly savor and appreciate a proper dinner."

"Of course," Brad said. "You're right."

The talk then returned to Nevada politics, the judge's unschooled but shrewd sense of public opinion and his hopes for higher office. Brad tried, twice, to inquire about Judge Thorpe's duties on the circuit, hoping he would consider a good night's sleep a prerequisite to a long trip. The ploy failed. The man held forth for nearly an hour on the shortcomings of the present administration and its management of state affairs.

Inevitably, the cheery Mrs. Thorpe noticed that Jane made no effort to spur the conversation along. The hostess nodded agreement to almost everything, but never asked a question. When the woman finally noticed the faint smile that crossed Lady Jane's lips when she looked at Brad, it occurred to her that the judge was outstaying his welcome. Mercifully, Mrs. Thorpe immediately acquired a headache. Within minutes the judge's buggy pulled away from the mansion.

Jane leaned on the closed front door of her home, listening to the clop of hooves in the distance. "God, are they *boring!*" she said.

"Not really, if you concentrate on them."

"Can you recall *anything* he had to say? Anything?"

"Absolutely nothing."

"Boring."

She pushed herself from the door and hurried to
Brad. His arms were around her quickly, her narrow
waist firm beneath his touch, and they kissed. The evening had provoked in Jane a deep, abiding greed for
him that ached in her.

At the top of the circular stairs, a landing opened
onto a long, carpeted hall. Unlike the first floor of the
home, its walls decorated with large, ornately framed
paintings of ships, mountains and animals, the hallway
contained a more personal sort of memorabilia. A
worn hat hung on a simple hook. Two rifles were
crossed on the wall beyond. A framed deed, the first
page of a newspaper announcing the Silver Lady strike
and a portrait of Mrs. Harrington could be seen. One
hand on Brad's shoulder, Jane reached down and
peeled a black, patent-leather shoe from one foot.
Without saying a word, she removed the other. At last
she had left the public spaces below for the retreat of
her home's second floor.

Jane handed Brad her shoes and opened the paneled
double doors that led into her bedroom. In it stood the
largest double bed he had ever seen. Its four posts supported a creamy-white, laced canopy that hovered
above a puffy down comforter. Great, knotted tassels
hung from the bedspread, nearly touching the floor.

Lady Jane walked toward the bed and, with a small
skip, dove into it. The plentiful billows of down,
feathers and springs collected her silently, surrounding
her body.

"Your bed is a playground," Spear admired.

"And a refuge, a place to hide, the smallest room in
the house."

Brad lifted her shoes to his shoulder, tilting his head
to ask her where they belonged.

"Anywhere," she said, disinterested. He dropped them.

Brad walked to the bed, loosening his tie. As he sat on it beside her, he felt the almost mysterious support that only a featherbed offers. He was suspended on it, but couldn't feel the thing beneath him. He was floating. His eyes closed for a moment, the tension flowing from his body.

Lady Jane watched him, her man in black, as he stretched his neck. Then the pure white fingers of her hand slid bristling through his beard. She turned his head and, rising, kissed him. They fell into the expanse of white and pink she called a bed, their mouths open, drinking each other. She felt his hands at her sides as she held his face captive, and shuddered as his broad, hungry weight eased down on her. She reached around him, tugging at the hair which hung over his collar, pulling Brad into her kiss. Her lips danced across him, open, soft, moist, more sensuous and probing than any woman he had ever known.

As she held him, caught in the softness of her bed and the lusty, moving desire of her arms, his hands searched. He played across one breast, his fingers rustling against the lace which bound them, molding her with his palm. That strong touch sent a chill through her and she drew her hand quickly down his chest.

Their lips parted and Jane busied herself with the buttons of his shirt. Successful, she drew her fingers through the dark hairs on his chest and then circled his waist, her cheek pressing against his side. Brad stroked her hair, slowly pulling away the pins that held it in a ball. Then, cautious and gentle, he released the netting from her hair and watched it cascade across her shoulders. He eased her from him and stopped, pondering the intricate maze of buttons, hooks and ties which wrapped her.

"First, the hooks," she said, rolling on her stomach. He peered at her in the dim light, his hands separating one hidden hook after another. Finished at last, she stood and let the gown fall in a heap of color on the floor. Brad removed his jacket, tie and shirt and threw them on a chair next to the bed.

"Now the buttons," she said, pointing to the front of her corset. He struggled with the tiny white buttons lining the front of the embroidered garment, each spaced a fraction of an inch from the next.

"Help," he pleaded in a kind of mock desperation.

"No," she responded, running her hands through his hair, down his neck and across his shoulders.

Brad worked at her clothing, feeling her distracting touch, trying hard to concentrate on the infinitesimal barriers before him. Gradually, the garment parted and the soft, round globes of her breasts stood before him, only a thin chemise covering her. He ran his hands against it, the fine fabric skimming her skin, her nipples rising at his touch. Suddenly, Jane backed away and lifted over her head the last bit of cloth covering her body.

Naked, she nearly ran to him, collapsing against him, pushing him back into the bed. Her moist lips slid across his neck and wandered to the nipples on his chest. She toyed with him, running her hand across his belly to the hardness at his groin. Reaching beneath his belt, she gathered clusters of hair between her fingers, then searched gently and found him, pulling tenderly.

"God, woman, let me up."

"No," she insisted, kneading him, cupping him, tormenting him with her teasing.

"Help," he pleaded again, his hands lightly touching her back.

"Yes."

She unbuckled his belt and unbuttoned his fly. Jane's

full breasts swayed slightly as she moved, her nipples dark against the pale skin of her arms and bosom. Brad reached out and traced her silhouette, running his hand across the upturned outline of her breasts, meandering toward her neck. She stood in front of him in an instant, straining at his boots, pulling his trousers to the floor. Directly behind her, a lamp cast a soft glow across her skin, her perfect, full shape highlighted by the warm yellow light.

Jane crawled through the comforter toward him, pausing to toy with his member, one hand cradling him, the other racing along his length. Brad lifted his head from the bed, took great showers of her wheat-blonde hair in his hands and pulled her to him.

"You're trying my patience, Jane."

"I'm trying, Brad," she smiled.

He rolled her on her back and, his fingers following his eyes, watched the rise and fall of her belly, hips and thighs. Her long, white legs seemed to stretch endlessly into the dim light and soft folds of the bed. Her breasts were large, their firm, tight slopes rising to him, their soft sides billowing under their own weight. He cupped her, softer than he remembered, and opened his mouth against hers.

Jane sank, feeling his leg pressed across hers, as his hands playing against her thigh, easing slowly into her glistening, moist triangle of blonde hair. His fingers approached her and she lifted one knee, turning to him, open, spread. Then Brad touched the silken edge of her, running a finger tip along the slippery folds of her body. She moaned, holding him, touching his tip over and over.

She reached for, found and guided his shaft against her. Her hands teased his swollen member lightly across her core, shivers of delight rushing through her body. Then she stopped, grabbed almost frantically at his shoulders and pulled him onto her. Jane's legs lifted, opening wide below him, her heels wrapped around his legs. He slid into her as she seized his back, pulling, and he plunged deep inside her.

"Yes." The word seemed to escape from her like the last breath from a messenger. But "Yes" followed, and "Yes" again, as she felt him moving over her, pressing into her, forcing the sublime sensation of total contact to spread through her. His powerful body seemed to roar over hers and she held him tighter, panting.

It came at her like a wave, a distant swell at first, growing gradually. Then, too soon, it crashed over her, white, churning and loud as she came. Her hips pressed him and her fingernails clawed across his back as she moaned, "Now, now!"

Brad lifted his upper body with his arms, his face hovering above hers in her passion. Jane's hands slid from him and reached into her hair as, her mouth wide and eyes closed tightly, her face formed the wracked grimace of bliss. As he watched her breasts stretch and back arch, he felt the buckling within him. His release came hot, pulsing, flowing into her open, willing body. And he fell to her, feeling her arms lightly on his back, her legs relaxing and lying still.

They lay quietly, neither wishing to move or change their hold on one another. He nibbled her ear, finally, and Jane touched his side.

"You sweat," she said.

"Are you sure that I'm to blame?"

"Of course! *I* glow, *you* sweat."

Brad moved his body on hers, sliding on their moist, slick skin.

"Mmmm. Don't go," Jane whispered. She held him tightly.

"You'll catch a chill."

"Not down here, I won't."

"Then I will, shivering and shrinking all at once."

She laughed, kissed him and let him roll to his side. "Oh," she exclaimed as he left her. Brad sat in the bed, gathered the comforter in his arms and threw it across them. Jane snuggled down, peeking out at him.

"I have a plan," she announced. "We'll sell the mine, find a bedroom in Boston and live in it."

"Jane . . . ," Brad appealed, almost sternly, to her better judgment.

"San Francisco? Chicago?" she suggested, kidding.

"Stop." He was amused, a bit, but saddened at the same time. Jane could never support him, his sense of himself wouldn't allow it. And she couldn't travel with him, the risk too great.

"I'm sorry."

"You should be," he said, not smiling.

"We could marry and you could visit, now and then."

"Jane, damnit, stop it. I need a drink. Where's your liquor?"

"I'll get it," she jumped from the bed, buoyant again, her soft, full body bouncing across the room. Jane poured wine from a carafe into two long-stemmed crystal glasses and climbed back into bed, making a show of balancing the drinks as she did so.

They drank silently, leaving the earlier conversation behind them.

"Tell me about the case you're working on," she spoke.

Brad told her that it was pretty obvious how the robbery had been accomplished, but that his best lead turned into a dead end. "I figured Virginia Mahon might have been blackmailed into turning over a set of keys. But we had it out today and she's clean."

"What about that shifty-looking one, what's his name?"

"Parker."

"What about him?"

"No guts. Can't be him."

"Hmmm," she muttered, a furrow appearing on her brow.

"Sorry I messed up your hair," he said, touching the wheat-blonde curls that spread across the pillow toward him.

"Alice will fix it."

"Alice Carter, from the bank?"

"Yes, from the bank. She's the best hairdresser in town, and sort of a nice person when you get to know her." Something in Jane's voice troubled Brad.

"And you know her well, I take it."

"I used to think so. But she's been distant lately."

"Since the bank was robbed?"

"No, even before that."

"Tell me." He leaned on one elbow now, studying her, his eyes narrowed slightly, sipping his drink absent-mindedly.

"Don't you ever stop working?"

"Sometimes. Tell me about her."

"It probably doesn't mean anything at all, but Alice has been acting strangely, at least for Alice. Anyway, about a month ago, five or six weeks maybe, she came in here just about bursting at the seams. She was so happy she was humming."

"A man?"

"Exactly."

"Go on."

"She told me she'd found herself a bona fide boyfriend. A sudden thing, a stranger in town. And she sounded serious about him. She asked me about men, about the way they are, about kissing and touching and the like. It was almost sad how little she understood.

But I was happy for her and we had some funny talks. I'm sure she planned on marrying him."

"What happened?"

"One Friday she came in here heartbroken. While she was fixing my hair, she literally broke down, crying and carrying on. She told me he'd left her, gone back to San Francisco. It was over."

"And that was just about the time the bank was robbed." Brad wasn't guessing, it wasn't a question.

"Why, yes, that's right. But . . ."

Brad was grinning. "It's just like Mr. Pinkerton always tells us. If you get out there and wear out some shoe leather, pump a few hands, ask the right questions, sooner or later the hard work pays off. Well, it looks like this night's hard work was worth the effort."

"You bastard," she yelled, dropping her drink and pommeling him with her little fists.

"Hey!" He lifted his drink away from her and set it on a bedside table. "Look at that mess," he said, pointing at the deep-red wine stain on the bedclothes.

She came at him in a rush, throwing one leg over his body and pinning his shoulders to the featherbed with the palms of her hands. She looked at his sharp, clear eyes and the neat trim of his black beard. Whatever it was to this man that she couldn't control thrilled her. She wanted him. Slowly, she lowered one white, round, pendent breast to his lips. Brad's tongue darted across her nipple and his lips wandered about her flesh. A gutteral, almost rasping moan escaped from her throat. Then she felt his beard against her skin, rough, moving, hard, and a spark went through her.

Sitting up, she slowly slid her hips down his belly until his tip touched her. Jane could feel herself growing soft and moist, feel the churning begin, opening to him. She wanted him in her. She raised her hips and with one hand reached for him, guiding his engorged member to her. Brad raised his knees and thrust his hips to her, she lowered herself, feeling his thighs against her buttocks, the great shaft of him deep inside her.

His fingers lightly teased the skin along her flanks, rippling across her rib cage to her thighs. He moved under her, pressing upward, then turning, rotating, filling her with a thousand sensations. She tried to hurry his pace, grinding him into her, pressing her knees against his sides but he moved relentlessly, if too slow, maddening the growing need in her.

The sound of their lovemaking filled the room. Jane listened to it and moaned. "More." She thrust at him, her head swimming with the constant touch of his hands on her and the overwhelming sense of him in her, deeply, moving constantly. She felt it begin in her and, once started, grow more quickly than she could imagine. She exploded in waves of intense excitement, which spread through her suddenly and completely.

As she came, Brad's thrusts grew urgent, desperate. He pounded up at her, jolting her hips. And then the huge, throbbing being inside her seemed to seize itself, pouring into her again and again.

For a long time, neither slept. Her breasts pressing against his chest, her lips brushing his neck, his hand moving gently across her back.

# Chapter 7

Brad rose from the bed at 6:00 a.m. Jane was sleeping on her stomach, one smooth, bare shoulder shining in the morning chill. He covered her and she stirred in her sleep.

A little bleary-eyed, he walked to the railroad station and purchased a copy of the *San Francisco Chronicle*. Over coffee in his hotel's dining room, Brad scanned the news, interested only in the crime stories, wondering where he might be sent next by the Chicago headquarters. About the only crime the journal alerted him to was that by the end of 1870 some 154 colleges in the United States would be co-educational. Brad wondered how young men and women expected to learn anything in such close proximity to one another.

Brad went to the bank shortly after it opened. He walked stiffly up to Lyn Loftin and asked to be shown the back door once again. The pretense raised no eyebrows among the bank's employees and, once outside, the agent told Loftin he suspected Alice Carter was involved in the robbery.

"A man, even a weak-kneed one like Parker, can be pushed around, cowed, even beat up some. But if the going really got tough, he could always move on, leave town. A woman has a harder time moving. And that makes her vulnerable. Alice seems to have been vulnerable to the charms of her first boyfriend, a fella who happened to leave town only a few days before the robbery."

Loftin nodded soberly. "Perhaps I'll join you when you talk to Miss Carter."

The two men returned to the bank and Loftin motioned Brad to the vault room. He then fetched Alice Carter. The woman wore a grey skirt and matching blouse. A small pearl hung on a thin gold chain around her neck.

"Alice, Bradley here is not a teller-trainee, as you may have figured out by now. He's here to try to catch the bank robbers and we need your help. He has some questions . . ."

"I understand," Alice said, unnerved, looking cornered.

"Alice, six or seven weeks ago you had a boyfriend. I wonder if you would tell me his name?" Brad asked gently.

Alice seemed embarrassed by the question, her cheeks flushed and she glanced at Mr. Loftin. "Mr. Loftin, it seems to me my friends are a personal matter. Why is he asking me about him?"

"Just answer the question, Alice," Brad interposed. "You have access to the vault. Like everyone, you're under suspicion."

Alice looked at the bank president in a silent appeal for help. His icy stare frightened her even more.

"And if I refuse to say?"

Mr. Loftin cleared his throat. "Miss Carter, I don't want anyone working here whom I can't trust. If you don't tell Mr. Spear what he wants to know, I'm afraid you'll be worthless to me."

"Oh, all right, then." It seemed odd to Brad that the woman was more angry than defensive. "My friend's name is David Fritsch and he said he had to go to

San Francisco suddenly. I'm sure he'll be back. I'm sure . . ."

"That wasn't so bad, now was it?" Loftin soothed.

"Is there anything else? I have a lot of work to do," she snapped.

Brad looked at Loftin. "That should do it," he concluded.

The agent left the bank and went straight to the sheriff's office in the county courthouse. There he looked through several hundred wanted posters before he found the right one. The flyer on David Fritsch was less than a year old. Brad read it over. The man was described as smooth, an expert on locks and vaults. He was wanted in five different places for bank robbery: three southern states, the Territory of Colorado and in Missouri. Fritsch was so cocksure of himself this far West he didn't even bother to use an assumed name.

Back at the bank, Brad waited while Loftin finished with a customer. "Mr. Loftin," he said, "I think I know who broke into your bank. To wrap this case in a really tidy sort of bundle I need to know more about the Land Grant Certificates being traded in these parts. In some states they're almost worthless."

Loftin nodded.

"Then why is it so many were in your safety deposit boxes?"

" 'Cause they're worth a lot around here. Their value has gone way up in the last two or three months."

"Why is that?" Spear asked.

"Beats me. The government gave them to the railroad as a subsidy to help finance the laying of track. It gave the rail line alternate sections along the route, usually six to ten miles deep. Sometimes even more."

"So the spike drivers are paid from the sale of the land, right?" Brad asked.

"Right."

"Seems like the land isn't worth what people are paying for it, though."

"Right again, Brad. But you know what happens when speculation starts. I'd bet there were dozens of those certificates in my bank when it was robbed."

"More than the eight or so listed in your inventory?"

"Yes, I imagine so. And they're not recorded or registered anywhere. Except for the section number and legal description of the land, they're identical." Loftin paused and scratched his head. "Actually, they are recorded. Like any piece of land, the certificate is the title deed. It's the record. Whoever has it owns the land. It's that simple."

"So you can spend them, like double eagles."

"Yes," the banker agreed, "they're negotiable, just like cash. But they have no fixed value. Just depends on what a fella thinks they're worth."

"If there were twenty to forty of those things in your bank when it was robbed, even if they were worth one thousand dollars apiece, that's a tidy sum."

"They're worth more than one thousand dollars each these days."

"A very tidy sum, then."

"Makes you stop and think about what the Jaspers who broke into this place were after, doesn't it, Brad?"

"Yup." Spear left the banker and wandered, as casually as he could, toward Alice Carter. "Do you have a moment, Miss Carter?" he asked.

"Not now, I have a customer," she replied curtly, counting coins at her window.

"Then when? I've got to talk to you. After work? Tonight after supper?"

Brad's insistence was drawing a lot of attention from the customers waiting in front of Alice's window.

"I've got choir practice."

"Before it, then. It's important. It's about David Fritsch."

"Did you learn something about David?" She was suddenly more interested in the man at her elbow. "You come by about six o'clock. But I won't have long."

Alice Carter's home was a dreary, unpainted structure nearly a quarter of a mile outside the center of town. Its front stoop stood only feet from the side street on which she lived and plain, white curtains hung in the windows.

Brad rapped on the door and waited. Alice fumbled with the lock and opened the door a crack, peering through the slender opening into the darkness.

"We need to talk," Spear said. "May I come inside?"

"No, it wouldn't be proper. You just stand your ground and I'll hear you out."

"You want your neighbors to hear all this, I gather."

The door closed, a chain was released and Alice permitted Brad into her sparsely furnished living room. The interior of the house was immaculate, plain but comfortable and impeccably clean.

"May I sit down?" Brad asked.

"If you must, but I don't have much time."

Spear sat in a rocker obviously reserved for guests and Alice positioned herself in a chair at the opposite side of the room. After a few awkward moments, he explained the colorful career of David Fritsch. She didn't believe him until he handed her the wanted poster. She confirmed its accuracy by tearing the thing to shreds, sobbing as she did so.

"The liar, the cheat, the thief," she cried. "Men are terrible, they take and take and take . . ."

"Do you want to talk about it?" Brad asked, afraid she might become hysterical.

"Talk? You mean tell you what an absolute dumbbell I was? I don't think so. I'm ruined, don't you know that? Don't make fun of me on top of it."

"I need to know about him. Tell me and have an end to it."

"I'm ashamed."

"Did he seduce you?"

She gasped. "How could you say such a thing?"

"You're a woman, Alice. A lonely woman, I'd guess. If I had his job to do, I think I'd have tried to seduce you. And I think you would have reacted the way most women would."

"No . . . No . . . he didn't, I didn't."

The explosion blew the front door across the room. It cartwheeled between them, slamming into a mirror and splintering as it fell. A roar echoed in the room, blinding light filled the small space. A hot, driving wind blew unnaturally through the door.

Brad bolted from his seat, rolling behind an oak table that had been overturned in the blast. He drew his six-gun and looked for Alice. She sat on the floor, her dress torn, blood streaming from her nose as she shrieked hysterically.

"Get down, get down," Brad ordered, but she sat, her legs spread, screaming.

The shotgun blast pounded against the table protecting Brad. He saw the flash of a weapon through what was once a front door and heard the rattle of stray pellets around the room, but he could see nothing. He fired into the night, taking aim at the spot where the flare of a shotgun muzzle had been only seconds before. No sooner had he let loose a single round than a rifle crashed through a side window, directly above Al-

ice's head. She screamed again as the weapon fired
over her head, barely missing Spear.

Then another blast rocked the room and Brad was
pinned against a wall, the heavy oak table broken, lying across one of his legs. Pain shot through his shoulder and he could feel the warmth of his own blood
spreading down the side of his head. The single lamp
in the room had fallen to the floor, its kerosene alight
on the rug. Flames lapped at the walls, consuming curtains, tickling the ceiling. Then another rifle muzzle,
this one shining, gleaming in the night, slammed
through a pane of glass and fired three quick shots into
the room.

Brad raised his pistol and emptied it into the window. Glass flew everywhere, the sound of his firing and
the yowling of the wounded man outside turning the
scene into bedlam. Spear dropped his pistol, its chambers empty, and tried to lift the table off his leg. Working against it sent rivers of pain through his upper arm
and, looking down, he saw the growing stain of his
own blood coating his jacket and shirt.

His head spun as he peered into the smoke-filled
room. Men and women shouted outside, flames burned
brightly all around him and he could feel his lungs
struggling for breath. As his eyes squinted, tears blur-
ring his view of the burning room, he saw Alice walking toward him. She came through the smoke in a
daze, bent at the waist and groped for him. Finally, she
touched the boot that was trapped by the table.

"Mr. Spear?"

"Get out of here," he ordered.

The frail little woman wiped blood from her mouth
with the back of her hand, bent and lifted the table off
the agent.

"Jesus!" he blared, the pain wrenching him. Then,

as he felt her hands grabbing his ankles, pulling him across the room, he passed out.

Brad awoke in Lady Jane's bed. She was dozing in a chair beside him. He struggled to recall the calamity that brought him there, his shoulder bandaged and his leg aching, but didn't remember very much. He could only picture a weird vision of Alice Carter walking through smoke and flames.

"Mornin', ma'am."

Lady Jane stirred, then woke with a start.

"Bradley! You're awake!"

"Barely. What happened?"

"Let me fix some coffee," she said and disappeared. Brad tried to sit up, but discovered a throbbing in his temple and decided to stay where he was for a moment. Jane soon returned carrying a tray with cups, coffee, sugar and cream. "Here," she directed, handing him a steaming cup.

"Thanks." Brad rose, his left arm nearly useless in the effort. "This arm shot?"

"No, Bradley. Your head and shoulder were gashed by flying glass. It took the doctor an hour to get the stuff out of your arm."

"Ruin my suit?"

"Ruined your suit."

"Damn. How's Alice?"

"She'll be all right. She's sleeping down the hall. Her house burned to the ground, so I took her in. They tell me she pulled you out of the fire."

"I think I remember that."

"I thought I'd die from the sight of you when Loftin brought you to the doctor. Brad, it was terrible . . ."

"Spare me a description."

"Okay." They were silent for quite a while as Spear drank his coffee. His head was clearing and he began to wonder how a simple bank robbery had grown so complicated. It was obvious that Alice Carter's boyfriend was only a bit player, a cog in the machine. If he'd robbed the bank on his own, he'd simply have disappeared. But there were several men involved, and at least one professional gun. This whole case was going to take some thought.

Brad rose from the bed, over Jane's protests, and tested his leg. It was stiff, but only stiff. He could move his left arm, but not much.

"Can I tell you about Alice?" Jane inquired gently.

"Please."

"I don't have to tell you about the courtship. She fell head over heels in love. The con was simple. He came to her one night, apparently frightened. He told her two men had threatened to kill him if he didn't steal Alice's keys to the bank. He swore he couldn't steal from her, said he'd rather they killed him. Naturally, she gave him the keys. He made beeswax impressions of them and she returned them to the bank. And it was done. She was afraid if she told anyone he'd be hanged."

"Whoever is behind all this is an ornery sort of cuss, don't you think?" Brad smiled, then winced.

# Chapter 8

The field office for the Silver Lady mine was a ramshackle shanty about one hundred feet from the mine's main entrance, with a single window that looked out on the main tunnel opening. The daytime domain of Karl Oppenheimer, it belonged to Richard Young during the night shift. A handsome man of about thirty, Young, like Oppenheimer, had worked up through the ranks, proving himself at every job in hard rock—from the hammer drill at the tunnel face to the shovel down below. He had shown up at the Silver Lady a year before with good recommendations after the mine he was working in California had run through its vein.

Young stood looking sternly out the window. There had been a small accident in Shaft #2 and he was not at all pleased. A man had fallen and was lucky to get away with a broken leg. Young didn't give a hoot about the miner. But he'd had to send a man to fetch the doctor at Mrs. Harrington's mansion and then wait for him to arrive. Production had slowed while they brought the worker to the surface. The fall disrupted ore flow and it would mean a drop in his shift's output. Young didn't want anything to mar his record.

Dick Young spent many of his waking hours trying to figure out ways to make himself appear exceptional. He wanted, more than anything, to control the Silver Lady mine. When Mr. Harrington got killed, it looked easy. He'd simply marry the widow and pick up a fortune. Only it hadn't worked out that way.

He started coming around to Mrs. Harrington's office every day before the night shift began. He's strike up a conversation with her on some pretext or another, trying to seem as helpful and cooperative as he could. He dressed carefully, shaved close and even brushed his curly hair for the lady.

He had waited a whole month after the funeral before he began his campaign in earnest. At first she seemed polite, but distant. And in her widow's weeds she was more provocative than ever. But she changed from polite to cool the day he asked her to go to a traveling drama show that was coming to the city. She quickly refused him. He asked why.

"Because, Mr. Young, you're not the kind of man I run with. I don't mean to be insulting, you're a good night manager, but don't push it beyond that."

Undaunted, if thick-headed and arrogant, Young had walked up to her and taken her in his arms. He tried kissing her and she pulled away. Young honestly believed himself irresistible and so blundered ahead, putting a hand over one of Jane's breasts and squeezing it gently. Her knee rocketed to his groin and while he was doubled over in pain, she slammed a vase over his head, dazing him and splashing the two of them with water and fragments of pottery.

"Get out," she screamed. "I don't want to see you in this office again."

It was shortly after he departed from her office for the last time that Young began working on a plan to take over the Silver Lady. Jeb Engle could be put to good use, if a fella was smart.

Young had known Engle in the Pennsylvania mines, but they hadn't been real friendly. Now Young sought him out. Engle's union organizing plans could fit into his. At first he considered becoming the company's negotiator in the inevitable strike, pulling off a settlement that would thrill the lady. She'd be so grateful she'd fall in love with him. Then he decided it'd be easier to side with the union and close down the mine—take it over from within. A little violence and chaos. Young smiled just thinking about how a shrewd operator could profit hugely from just a little chaos underground.

Jeb Engle reported to the night shift manager each evening. Young heard a knock on the door and called Engle in.

"Well, Jeb, how does it go? Got any new members?"

"Seven this week. I'm averaging one a day and I'd say that's damn good in these parts. Most of these hicks never heard of a union. 'Least they believe any damn thing I tell 'em. Course, most of 'em won't be around to see the truth of it anyway . . ." Engle pushed a blue stocking cap back on his forehead and grinned.

"How long before you can take out the day shift?" Young asked.

"You said I got a month."

"Well, word comes to me we got a week. Plan's changed."

"Boy, I don't know." Engle rubbed his forehead with the back of a dirty hand. "I'm working on the hoist men and the ore car crew. If we shut down the lift crew and the cars, she's stoppered up tight, like the neck of a bottle."

"You got it."

"Well, let's see. . . . I got twenty-four of 'em now. 'Nother dozen from the two crews should do it. Say, a week-and-a-half?"

"A week, that's it. But, to grease the skids you can start telling the men they'll get a dollar a day strike pay when we go out, for doing nothing at all. That should help."

"Help. Jesus, it'll help. But where we gonna get that kinda money?"

"Just don't worry about that. My backer has it. No problem at all."

"You know what I'm worried about? I'm scared that bridge structure at the six-hundred-foot level's gonna go," Engle said. "I want to make damn sure I'm on the right side of that thing when it drops. I still don't like the idea of using dynamite at all down there. It could collapse a dozen tunnels."

"Not with one stick it won't. You've used powder in mines before. It's tricky, but you can do it. And with all the evidence, everyone will think it was a gas explosion or maybe a dust blowup. Just relax."

"Yeah, sure," Engle responded curtly. "You won't be down there sweatin' it. You're gonna be sittin' up here when that damn thing blows."

"I'll be doing my part, Engle. You be sure you're doing yours. You just get the men signed up and then get them on the shaft side of the bridge. And make sure it looks like a gas explosion. Hey, would you like a snort?"

Engle suddenly was wearing his smile again. "I never turn down a free drink." Young opened a small foot-locker, reached in and pulled out a pint of whiskey. He tossed the bottle to Engle, who tipped it and took a quick swallow. Jeb wheezed and smacked his lips. "Damn, that tastes so good it hurts!" He handed the bottle back to Young and the night manager hid it away again.

"What about Oppenheimer?" Engle asked.

"I've taken care of that. Lead poisoning. And it's no concern of yours how, so don't ask."

"What about the lady, then?"

Young grinned. "You never can tell. With all the accidents around here, she just might have one herself."

"And then we take over?"

"No, dummy," Young said. "Then our man moves in. We can't do a damn thing except get this place in such a mess that the selling price goes to rock bottom. A desperation sale. Start-up costs on a mine that's not operating are always high. The buyer yells 'start-up costs' and a judge is likely to listen."

The way the vein was holding up, the Silver Lady was probably worth a million and a half or two million dollars, Young thought. "If it brings a half million at court auction, I'll be mightily surprised. It'll be a jinx hole by the time we're through. Anyone'll be able to see that and my man will make a killing."

"All right," Engle agreed. "So he has the money and we do the dirty deed. Does that mean a three-way split?"

"Not quite. We get ten per cent each. If the mine clears a million, we get one hundred thousand . . . in cash."

Engle couldn't actually grasp such large figures. The idea of a hundred thousand dollars was a completely unimaginable thing to him. He wondered how big a pile of double eagles that was. He couldn't picture it. "I get to be the day manager, right?"

"Sure, Jeb, if that's what you want," Young laughed. "Unless you'd rather be president of the union . . ."

"Won't tolerate no unions in my mine."

The two men looked at each other, self-satisfied, amused. "Oh, Dick," Engle said, "just who is this guy with all the money?"

"Now, Jeb, you know I can't tell you that. You wait till someone hands you a bag of money that weighs more than you do, then you'll know. Now finish your shift and then get down to the saloon and hoist a few with the boys. Promise them anything. I want this mine closed in a week."

Young watched through the window as Jeb Engle walked slowly to the tunnel entrance. Then he put on his jacket and walked down there himself. It didn't seem like the ore cars had been coming out as often as they had been before the man broke his leg. Shovel men must be spooked. Dick Young was all for shutting down the mine, bankrupting it if he could, but until it closed he had to stay on the job. Keep the lady happy. He was determined to maintain his production record for at least another week.

# Chapter 9

It was Saturday and so Lyn Loftin was dressed casually. He wore the clothes a miner might wear, dark corduroy trousers, a heavy, tan shirt open at the collar and a lambskin jacket complete with a thick fur collar. His boots fell heavily on the varnished floor of Lady Jane's bedroom.

Brad thought that Loftin appeared much more comfortable when he wasn't playing the banker. Though his clothes weren't worn and dirty from the work of digging underground, there was no mistaking how Loftin felt in them. He seemed at ease. Sure of himself for the first time since the agent had met him.

"Mornin', Brad."

"Good morning, Lyn."

"Feeling better, I hope."

"Between you and me, I could leave anytime but the service around here is too good to pass up." Loftin laughed, thinking to himself that he was actually glad Spear knew about his relationship with Virginia. For some reason, Brad had become more relaxed around the banker since discovering the secret. Or maybe it was just Loftin's imagination. At any rate, Lyn felt better. He didn't like hiding things. Too complicated.

"Spear, I think I've discovered something."

"What?"

"Well, last night I worked late. Cleaning up some

accounts that had either been closed or moved or changed. Stuff that can be put off. I came onto a real peculiar one. Thought you'd better know."

"I'm all ears," Brad replied, walking around the room looking for his other boot.

"A fella named Eagleton got killed here just before you arrived. Poisoned, the doc said. Well, he banked with me and so I was going through his records, cleaning up the account so I could give his widow a complete tally. Seems he withdrew three thousand dollars the day before he got killed."

"Carrying that kind of money around sure proved unhealthy for him," Brad had found his boot and was pulling it on.

"Nope, don't think so. Same day, one of the lawyers here in town deposited three thousand into his account. Told Alice he'd sold some Land Grant Certificates."

"Same three thousand, you think?"

"Can't know for sure, but I'd bet. That kind of cash doesn't float around every day, even in Silver City."

"So somebody poisoned this fella . . ."

"Eagleton."

"Eagleton, to get his three thousand dollars or to lift his Land Grant Certificates."

"Could be. At least I thought you should know."

Lady Jane knocked on the door to the bedroom and walked in, not waiting for a reply. She was dressed in a plain blouse, simple skirt and wore no make-up.

"Mr. Loftin, if you're talking business with this man, I'm going to horsewhip you."

"Sorry, Mrs. Harrington. Can't help it."

Jane picked up the tray that sat beside the bed and cast a decidedly unfriendly scowl in Brad's direction.

"Seen my gun, Jane?" Brad asked, ignoring her.

The early morning light shined through the small,

high windows of Dr. Brockington's office. The man sat, puffing on a stogie, sending billows of smoke into the air. The hard winter sun formed a shaft of light, a beam of illuminated smoke above his head. Brockington studied it. His head back, he blew a plume of white into the air that drifted toward the ceiling. As the smoke passed through the sunlight, the doctor watched it swirl, then disappear. It occurred to him that though the smoke moved about the room, the shaft of sunlight remained stationary.

Brockington liked the idea. The players change, but the game's always the same, he thought. The doctor considered himself a manipulator of the first rank. He was sure he knew the rules and so could make the players do what he wanted. His mind, he knew, had been trained in the best scientific tradition. It observed the world relentlessly, without color or sympathy or bias.

As he sat thinking about his current dilemma, he recalled the wizened old professor who had lectured a first-year medical student so many years before. "Prejudice and faith make lousy observers, Brockington," the teacher had said. "When you search for a solution to a problem, put your beliefs aside."

Brockington had honed that lesson, turned it into a way of life. He was, he thought, a realist, a pragmatic man who believed in absolutely nothing. He watched the world and concluded that it was peopled by the weak, the stupid and the greedy. His task in life, he felt, was to prosper among such players.

Brockington frowned at the knock on his door. He hated to be interrupted while planning his next move. "Who is it?" he shouted.

"Me, Bunny."

"Now what?" he muttered. "Come in, come in." He was impatient to be rid of her.

Bunny West walked meekly into the room, knowing she was intruding. The jumble of books and papers that filled the shelves in the doctor's office, the littered tables and overflowing desk gave the room a cramped air. Bunny thought of the place as a terribly bizarre hideaway, a room jammed with secrets she would never understand.

On this bright, sunny Saturday morning, Bunny West looked very much like a girl. Her shining hair was pulled back and hung in a loose ponytail behind her. She wore a checkered dress, with a high lacy collar, that might blend easily into a church social.

"Dr. Brockington?"

"Yes, Bunny, what can I do for you?"

"I don't want to do it anymore." It was said, she'd managed to say it. Bunny had rehearsed the line a thousand times, wondering if she dared utter those few words. Now she'd done it.

"Do what?" Brockington asked, anger creeping into his voice.

"You know, with those men."

"Those men don't hurt you, do they?" Brockington oozed calm now, his voice a comforting, paternal drone.

"I don't like them. I don't like the way they touch me. I don't like looking at them."

"But you can't hide from men, Bunny. They're everywhere. You know that."

"I don't like poisoning them, though. If they wouldn't touch me, if you wouldn't let them touch me, I wouldn't do it. And I don't like it, Doctor. I don't want to anymore."

Brockington sat back in his swivel chair, its spring creaking under his weight. "Come here," he said quietly. She walked toward him with tiny, silent steps. At last she stood beside him and Brockington slapped her face with the back of his hand. She reeled, her cheek burning, tears filling her eyes.

"Come here, Bunny," he ordered, waving his short, fat fingers in the air. Brockington reached out to her and began kneading the girl's breasts through her light dress. "You don't like this, do you Bunny?" he whispered.

"Stop . . ."

"You don't, do you?"

"No, please . . ."

Bunny began to back away from him and he slapped her again, this blow ringing in the room. Then he pulled her by the wrists until she stood between his knees. With both hands he ripped the front of her dress apart and rubbed her bared breasts roughly.

"Please . . . ," she begged him, sobbing.

Brockington's face grew crimson with rage. The beautiful young woman in front of him hunched her naked shoulders, raising them against her neck, and sobbed. Furious, he pulled her dress down, tearing it until the cloth lay at her feet. His hand shot between her legs and began stroking her crotch. With a small cry she fell to the floor.

"You'll do what I tell you to, when I tell you to."

"No, please . . . ," Bunny whimpered. She was nearly hysterical, her eyes closed, her head shaking. "I can't do it anymore. I can't kill those men. I'm not crazy, I want to be well. Let me stop . . ."

"Arnie," Brockington hollered. A voice answered from another part of the house. "Come here, will you please?" The doctor glared at Bunny. Still in shock, she had not moved from his feet and sat trying to cover herself with the torn dress. Arnie was the doctor's hired hand, a wiry little man with crooked teeth and a pockmarked face. He was good with horses and wore a dirty-white cowboy hat propped back on his forehead. He stared at Bunny as he came into the room.

"Yes, Dr. Brockington?"

"Arnie, hitch up the buggy. We're taking a little ride."

Arnie leered at the girl and Brockington shouted, "Move it."

"I don't want to go for a ride," Bunny said.

"Get dressed."

Brockington's buggy bounced along Main Street, headed north. The doctor turned a heavy wool scarf against the cold, wrapping it a third time around his neck. He tilted his head against the wind and pulled his hat low to his ears as the magnificent chestnut gelding in front of him puffed clouds of cold breath. Bunny shivered next to him, her hands in the pockets of her bright red jacket.

It was the season in Nevada's elevated regions when afternoons sometimes brought bitter cold rains. When the weather turned wet, the region's roads became rutted, muddy and nearly impassable. And then, with nightfall, the avenues and trails froze, turning the ruts into solid ridges and mounds. This morning the narrow wheels of the buggy clattered across still-frozen dirt roads and bucked from side to side as a rut captured and then released the vehicle. By afternoon the road would be a swamp, mud nearly a foot deep dragging against horses' hooves and wagon wheels.

Bunny sat in a daze. The road wound along one side of the valley for nearly a mile, then forked. The more traveled route descended, wandered north along the valley floor and then turned west into San Francisco. The nearly unused path they followed went up into the hills. Grey-brown rock and tortured pines stood on either side of the road and the tall grasses that grew in clumps everywhere bent in the wind.

Six miles from Silver City, Brockington brought the buggy to a halt near a faint track that led across a barely passable wagon road. "Remember this, Bunny?" The girl shivered as he turned down into a canyon. Soon they came upon a gate which barred the way. On it was a sign, crudely lettered: "Fetterman's Institution for the Criminally Insane, J.W. Fetterman, Prop."

Brockington climbed from the buggy, opened the gate and then clattered on toward the roughhewn log stockade in the distance. Poles, buried deep in the ground, reached twelve feet into the air, completely enclosing the dead-end walls of the canyon. A cabin that had once been a mine office stood just outside the boundary, near a wagon-sized gate in the fence.

Brockington called out, his voice directed at the shack. A man soon appeared, carrying a shotgun.

"Oh, it's you, Doctor." The man was Jim Fetterman. "Just the man I want to see. Got some interesting developments 'round here since you last poked your nose in this stinking hole." Brockington reached into the buggy and pulled out a bottle of whiskey. Without a word, he tossed it to Fetterman.

"Come on inside and warm yerself, Doc," Fetterman invited. "We can talk a bit."

"On my way out we'll talk."

"Sure 'nuff, whatever you say. See you brought my favorite little sweetheart along with ya. Hope you're putting her back in here for a spell."

"Never can tell," Brockington answered, "you never can tell." Brockington grabbed Bunny's hand, pulled her out of the buggy and dragged her toward the gate. Fetterman raised the beam that locked it and swung the entrance open. It groaned on its rusty hinges.

"Now, Doc," Fetterman said, "you just bellow when-

ever you want to git out of there." He calmly reached
toward Bunny's jacket and started grabbing at her. She
reacted quickly, kicking him in the shin and he yelped
in pain, hopping around on one foot. "Hey, what is
this? You damned bitch, gettin' uppity?"

"She's not feeling herself today, Jim," the doctor
explained. "That's why I brought her out here. I
thought a look at the old homestead might bring her
out of it."

Brockington pulled Bunny inside the stockade. But
the scene within held no surprises for her. The high
fence was so smooth that no one could climb out. The
wall extended nearly seventy-five yards from one side
of the steep canyon walls to the other. At the very end
of the canyon there was nothing but a sheer rock wall.
She'd seen several men die trying to scale it to get out.

A trickle of a stream splashed down the rock and
wandered across one corner of the enclosure, providing
the only water for the inmates. A pair of old buildings
that had once been miners' barracks served as bunk-
houses for the residents. Most of their windows were
broken and crudely patched with wood. Smoke poured
from the metal stovepipe above one building, but the
other contained no stove and so had no heat.

Behind the buildings stood the gaping hole of an old
mine tunnel. It had been a silver strike that worked itself out in less than six months. Fetterman then bought
the place and contracted with the state to house the
criminally insane. People were housed at Fetterman's
for a variety of reasons. Alcoholics without families
were admitted. Women diagnosed as suffering from
"faulty menstruation," "uncontrolled grief" and "hysterical trauma" were sent to him. Men gone mad
during the brutal winters of these mountains were
incarcerated. Homosexuals, mutes and a wide variety
of misfits ended up behind the stockade.

This collection of the emotionally disturbed, brain damaged or socially inconvenient men and women roamed the compound. Crimes of every kind went on among them as each, in his own way, battled the conditions of the asylum and the rage in his skull in an effort to survive.

Brockington didn't like the place any more than Bunny did. At any one time, there were about sixty inmates spread across the enclosure. Winter usually lowered the population some, but the courts replenished it constantly. With Brockington's assistance, Fetterman managed to convince the state that nearly one hundred souls were kept in his institution.

Brockington kicked a woman who grabbed his foot as they walked toward the mine shaft. At his side, eyes wide with terror, Bunny West gripped his arm in desperation, nauseated by the smell of the place, struck dumb by the memories of her life there.

Two women appeared in the open window of one building. They wore dirty, tattered shirts and screamed at Dr. Brockington as he marched along. A guard standing nearby waved a gun at them and they disappeared, cackling. Two men sat on a rock, holding hands, swaying back and forth, staring at nothing. A woman squatted by the stream, washing some clothes in the murky water and a man ran to her waving his arms. She ignored him and he ran away, flapping like a bird in a feeble attempt to fly. A shot rang out somewhere in the compound, followed by an anguished, mournful cry and Bunny began to weep uncontrollably.

"Remember all this, Bunny? Remember the guards and good old Jim Fetterman?"

Tears rolled down Bunny's cheeks. Her fingers dug deeply into Brockington's arm and she nodded blankly. He smiled, but his self-satisfaction was interrupted when a heavily built woman walked up to him, fol-

lowed by a group of ten or so other women. They were
obviously an organized gang, well-clothed and quiet. A
guard ran quickly to the doctor's side, his rifle leveled
at the group.

"Well, if it isn't Dr. Brockington," the leader said.
"You slimy bastard, you monster! You here to gloat
over us animals again? You're dead when I get out of
here, Brockington. I'm coming after you . . ."

Brockington led Bunny away from the ranting
woman, toward the tunnel entrance. It had not been
boarded up, and when an inmate disappeared inside it,
no one bothered searching for him. Ahead of the pair
two men chased a third. The target was tackled from
behind, beaten briefly and then stripped of his jacket.
He was left shivering on the ground.

"Seen enough?" the doctor asked his ward.

"Yes," she meekly replied, her eyes red, her nose
running in the cold.

Bunny was so weak at this point that Brockington
practically had to carry her to the gate. Near the main
entrance an old woman with matted grey hair ran up
and grabbed Bunny's jacket from behind. With a
screech of glee she gave a surprisingly rough pull on it
and the girl fell backward to the ground. Bunny
scrambled to her feet and ran to the exit. Brockington
kicked the old woman, sending her limping away,
caterwauling randomly, a lunatic.

Brockington reached the gate, where Bunny stood,
and yelled for Fetterman. Within seconds the door
creaked open and they were outside.

"Doc, if you got a minute, I got one here you ought
to see," Fetterman said, gesturing with the half-empty
whiskey bottle toward the cabin.

"Okay, Jim. But I have only a minute." Bunny sat
in the buggy, the plaid lap robe wrapped around her.
"Want to come inside with Jim and get warm?" the

doctor shouted. Bunny shook her head and Brockington shrugged, walking toward the cabin.

The cabin was warm and clean, if sparsely decorated. Two bunk beds stood at one end of the large room, a small pine table between them. There was a square table at the center of the room, surrounded by straight-back chairs, and a large, black kitchen stove at one end. A tall, thin man with a holstered side arm was kneeling, feeding the stove wood when the doctor walked in.

"Good mornin', sir," he said, standing up as Brockington entered. "Care for some coffee?"

"Don't mind if I do," Brockington responded. The doctor looked around the room, searching for the "interesting development" Fetterman promised. He quickly found it. A thin, short man, sitting on a stool near the stove, was washing dishes in a basin at his feet. He wore several layers of clothes, all ill-fitting. His heavy, blue overcoat covered a tattered shirt that covered yet another shirt. From his cuffs Brockington could tell the man had two pairs of pants on. His boots, old and worn, didn't match. The man's matted hair fell stringy and wild to his shoulders, his filthy hat lying nearby.

"Your idea of 'interesting' is growing more and more dull, Jim. From the look of him, he's got consumption. Probably a drunk, too. I'm leaving." Brockington turned to go.

"I beg your pardon, Doctor," the slight man at the stool said. "I have not contracted tuberculosis and I am extremely sober."

Brockington turned back to the wretched little creature in the corner to see if he were hearing things.

"My name, sir, is Pierre Dufond. I was once a man of the cloth, but found the profession impossible to pursue. For reasons which would certainly bore you, I find myself confined to this unsavory establishment against my will. Mr. Fetterman here believes I might be of service to you."

Jim Fetterman, now half-drunk, beamed with pride. He considered himself a judge of his charges and was always pleased to deliver one to the doctor. Brockington walked to the stove, where the guard handed him a cup of steaming coffee.

"You drink, I assume," Brockington asked Dufond, his voice expressionless.

"To excess, when available. In fact, it was that very habit of mine that caused the State of Nevada to send me here. They tell me I used a knife on a whore, not killing her, but almost. They tell me I removed her ear and a toe, but I can't recall. I don't remember any of it."

"Dufond, you're disgusting." The doctor was fascinated.

"I agree."

Brockington shook his head. "What is it you think I can do with you?"

"I am a practiced liar, an experienced thief and a reasonably able murderer. Take your pick. I want out of here."

"We'll talk in the buggy," the doctor turned and left the cabin. Dufond bolted to his feet, bumping into the basin and splashing water on the floor. He punched his hat onto his head and, grinning, ran after Brockington.

During the long ride back to Silver City, Bunny sat awkwardly folded into the small stowaway behind the buggy's seat. A beautiful woman, her posture and exhaustion made her seem a sleeping child, a huddled infant.

Brockington walked the buggy slowly away from the asylum, the reins held firmly in one hand, a .44 caliber Tryon derringer in the other. The small weapon rested on his thigh and he fingered it throughout the ride.

"There's a bottle under the seat," the doctor offered. Dufond scurried to the floor, his layers of oversized clothing making every move clumsy, his haste aggravating the situation. Once he'd retrieved the pint, he held it in both hands, inches from his face, then kissed it, his eyes closed. Brockington sat speechless, watching the man drink hurriedly for a few minutes. As the alcohol worked its way into Dufond's mind, wobbling him, the little man receded, slouching, into his voluminous clothing.

"Dufond!" Brockington shouted at the half-sleeping man. With a start the drunk looked at the driver, at his gun and then wiped his mouth with a sleeve.

"At your service."

"How does a man of the cloth end up in such rags?"

Dufond straightened himself, confused. He felt the weakness that real hunger brings to the bones and the blur of drink in his eyes. He struggled, terrified, trying to decide what this doctor wanted. A chameleon, Dufond would become it, a whore, he would perform whatever was required. But he had to discover the man's wishes. And Brockington's blank, cold eyes told him nothing.

"Women, or a woman, I should say."

"And the bottle."

"This?" Dufond inquired, raising the pint. "No, this follows. It comes afterward, when the ruin is complete. This just makes the fool more . . . more . . . obvious."

Brockington pulled back on the reins and the chestnut gelding eased to a halt. Still fingering the palm-sized weapon, he raised it so that Dufond looked straight into the broad, black hole of its muzzle. "Dufond, or whoever you are, I am an impatient man. Especially with the likes of you. I deal in wretches, like yourself. But only when I control the situation, only when I have complete control. You have a choice: answer my questions, do as you're told, or return to Fetterman's wonderful world."

Dufond looked calmly into the short barrel of the derringer aimed at his forehead. The small, quick animal within him felt panic, his mind racing, searching for an escape. But some other voice echoed in his head. It didn't matter to him. In fact, he half-welcomed death. At least it would be over.

"You may use me or kill me, but I'm not going back."

"Tell me how you ended up like this." Brockington replaced the weapon on his lap and, with a click of his tongue the horse walked on.

Dufond's tale began with a church in Mexico. Through the slurred speech of a man growing more and more drunk and the chattering teeth of a waif, a story unfolded. Years before he had comforted a woman, one of his flock, during her hour of sorrow. In that moment both of them had discovered an emotion, or a yearning, that had led the faithful priest to love, or lust, or something. Something that filled a void in him. He had fallen, held her, kissed her, made love with her. Dufond described the woman with reverence, his voice trembling at the thought of her. He wept and drank, his voice so low Brockington had to strain to hear it.

"I tried to pray. I called to Christ, hoping for an answer. But he abandoned me . . . the silence of him . . . the silence . . . was more than I could bear. So I answered what I heard, I lived like a man instead of a priest. Or a coward instead of a man. I loved her, stealing away to her when I could, performing the rituals of the church when I couldn't. And then we were discovered."

"Her husband?"

"Yes, a very powerful man, the governor of the province of Sonora."

"And he killed her?"

"He stole her beauty with a knife. She killed herself waiting for me to save her."

"And you ran, then, hiding from him?"

"I'm running now, always. I'm tired of it, Mon Dieu, I'm tired of it. But," Dufond said with a smile, "warmed by my friend, the demon rum, I manage to survive. I live." Dufond at last emptied the bottle, a hopeless man. Brockington saw him as rudderless, doomed, and knew he would be useful. Dufond closed his eyes and fell asleep as the doctor hurried the buggy into the city.

Brad Spear worked the stiffness from his leg by walking from Lady Jane's home into town. As he approached the center of the city, it was nearly noon, the streets filled with wagons and horses, noise coming from restaurants, saloons and stores. He heard the clang of a blacksmith pounding iron at the livery and the clatter of lumber being stacked.

Spear walked the wooden sidewalks more casually than most of those around him. He winced as a clumsy miner, carrying a sack of flour over his shoulder, banged into his injured arm. Lady Jane had offered steak and brandy for lunch, a warm fire and a game of cards. But he'd turned her down, laughing at the idea that he'd ever consider shuffling a deck with her across the table from him. The proprietor of Cheyenne's Lady Jane Saloon would own his eyeteeth in an hour.

The gaudy red sign of The Mammoth Saloon came into view as he walked along and, remembering the miner who called himself "Elephant," Spear thought it a fine place to sit for a while.

Inside The Mammoth's large main room men milled

about. Winter was beginning in earnest and so prospectors, those who panned for gold and silver in the hills, a few trappers and scores of unemployed miners were traveling into the city. Even reasonably successful mines that found themselves in remote areas were forced to shut down operations in the dead of winter. It was impossible to provision them once the heaviest snows had fallen and so men from all over western California and Nevada were, like the streams that lined the mountains in the spring, flowing toward Silver City.

The center of attention in the saloon was a traveling hawker, a man dressed in a coat fit for an Admiral in the Royal Navy. Its broad lapels and ridiculously long tails were edged in tattered gold piping and he wore a hat festooned with feathers.

"And this," he roared above the din of the room, "is genuine frog sweat, my friends. Guaranteed to cure the rheumatism, bone creak and headache. Derived from the finest oriental frogs, bred special to concoct this here elixir."

Two boys, fresh from San Francisco in search of their fortune, laughed and sipped their beer as he talked. A surly-looking miner, dressed in buckskin and corduroy, grabbed the little bottle the hawker waved about and held it up to the light.

"This here water and vinegar or gin and sugar?" he asked with a laugh.

"None, sir. Not a bit of it. That there's the stuff of emperors, the real stuff. I seen it sweated off them frogs myself."

"Horseshit." The buckskinned miner slapped his hat on the table. The two boys ordered another pitcher of beer from the barmaid standing nearby, and Spear took a seat in the corner of the room.

The hawker smelled a commotion brewing and decided to encourage it. He swiped the bottle from the miner's hand and bounded onto a chair.

"Now see here, my good man. I'm the purveyor of foreign music boxes, the seller of charms and rings, the most famous trader in special ointments Nevada's ever seen. I'm a man of faith and true belief, a pilgrim bringin' the benefits of civilization to you hard-working folks. And, if you can listen close, I'll tell you of a mystery that will thrill you to the bone."

A small crowd gathered around the improbable speaker, several men moving from the bar to listen to him, others leaning against it, disinterested.

"I sailed the great Pacific, at some risk to myself, and went to the strange blue city of Japan. I went there and I saw it. The priests and the temples, the places so wonderful they paint them with gold. And I watched the sacred rituals them heathens understand and learned the ways of curin' frogs."

Several of the onlookers walked away, guffawing.

"Now see here, fellas, hear me out. The way of sweatin' frogs goes like this. They keep 'em in a room, sittin' on rocks, and feed 'em flies and such for days. They get 'em fat and croakin' loud till them frogs are as happy as can be. Then them priests, wearin' dresses, net 'em, one at a time and stick 'em in a box. Inside that box there's nothin' but mirrors, shiny bright mirrors. And folks, I tell ya, them frogs git scared out of their wits. They hop around and croak and get to worryin' till they sweat. Not much, mind ya. But a bit, a drop or so. And them priests, they bottle the sweat for drinkin' purposes, in case of ills to emperors and queens and their like.

"Well, folks, at considerable risk, I brung some back. Some magical fluid for these here states to enjoy. I was knowin' of your troubles in these hard mountains and mindful of your needin' a potion like this here frog sweat so I brought me some back. A hundred little bottles to spread among the needy.

"Yeah, how much?"

"Since you ask, to you, the first enlightened soul, a dollar a bottle. To all that follow, two dollars, and worth its weight in gold."

One man, staggering a little as he reached into his pocket, bought a bottle for a dollar. He quickly opened it, took a sniff and twisted his face into a wrinkled frown. He handed it to a friend, one only slightly more sober, who smelled the bottle cautiously. "Whew!" he exclaimed, "sure smells like frogs." Then, with a grin, he poured it into his companion's beer. "Git well, friend," he laughed. The ice thus broken, the man in the feathered hat sold a dozen or so of his bottles.

Spear waved down a waitress and ordered a beer, steak, potatoes and a slice of bread. The beer appeared quickly. Spear smiled to himself, quietly perplexed by the gullibility of those buying bottles, but pleased the entertainment was available.

Two men sat at the center of the saloon, sprawled in their chairs, pounding, alternately, on the table between them.

"That there bitch ain't no better than a whore, you jackass," the brawnier of the two shouted.

"Stuff that face of yours," the man next to him replied.

"Now don't get ornery on me, friend. We'll be heading out of here soon enough, that hussy far behind."

"Nope, don't think so."

"You can't bring her with ya, she's dead weight, meat not worth the toting."

"She's mine and I'm keeping her."

"You dumb hick," the big, bearded man hooted in disgust as he stood, overturning the table, their mugs and a pitcher of beer tumbling to the floor. Ben, the

huge hulk of a man Spear had met on the street with
the sheriff, edged around the side of the bar, watching
the argument. As the miner who, it seemed, was in
love, bolted headlong into his disgusted partner, Ben
walked over to them.

The ultimate bouncer, Spear thought.

But as Ben walked toward the grappling, stumbling
fight, a ten-inch hunting knife appeared in the smaller
man's hand. He waved it in the air, fury burning in his
eyes. Without saying a word, Ben reached for it, but
the man turned and buried the blade in the bouncer's
stomach. With an expression of muted surprise, he
doubled at the waist, both hands holding the knife's
handle.

Spear's hand reached reflexively for the butt of his
side arm as he watched the giant man back slowly
away from the two men. Ben finally reached the bar
behind him, leaned against it and then slid to the floor,
his back against the bar. Someone ran through the
saloon's doors. The bartender knelt beside the bar. The
room was silent. Ben roared and his head fell forward.
Dead.

"Let's git out of here," the bearded miner yelled to
his companion, grabbing him by the arm. The man
who'd wielded the knife tripped over an overturned
chair as he made his way to the door. His friend hoisted him to his feet and dragged him along.

"Hold it." The order came from the far end of the
bar. A man with a beard reaching nearly to his waist,
his white hair hanging to his shoulders, stood with a
rifle aimed at the retreating pair. The two men turned,
looked at the old man and then ran toward the door.
The shot screamed in the room, the thunderous sound
of a buffalo rifle deafening the crowd.

The man who had killed Ben was lifted off his feet
by the slug as it blasted through him. He crashed to

the floor, a hole the size of a man's fist in his chest where the two-inch-long slug had exited. His friend stared at him, frozen for a moment. But he turned, faced the old man and drew his side arm.

The old man stood at the bar, the smoke from his single-shot Sharps, breech-loading rifle still pungent in the air around him. He settled the weapon on the bar and reached for his beer. Spear watched the old man empty his glass, knowing that the incredibly powerful rifle he'd just fired could only be reloaded slowly.

As the bearded miner drew his pistol, several men dove away from the bar. But, incredibly, the old man stood, calmly setting down his mug. Spear's shot came from his hip, below the table. It whistled through the air and caught the miner in the back of one knee, spinning him like a top and dropping the man, wailing, doubled on the floor. He lay there, swearing, holding his leg as the echo of gunfire began to abate. Brad's ears rang with the sound as he watched the writhing wounded man.

No one spoke. For what seemed an eternity the only sound in the room was the shriek of pain that came from the miner. Gradually, his wails subsided, the shock of his injury deadening his leg, and men moved, shuffling in the room. The bartender appeared, his head poking above the bar, a .44 held uneasily in his hand, his eyes like a ferret's looking around the saloon. One man walked to Ben, knelt sadly beside him and closed his staring eyes. Another righted a chair. And the murmur of men who had recently been afraid grew slowly.

Several of the saloon's customers, the cook, bartender and a boy from the back room hauled the dead body from the place. The boy returned quickly with a mop and pail and began scrubbing blood from the floor. The wounded man, his leg shattered, lay moaning next to a spitoon for quite a while. After some time he was carried, bleeding, into the street.

"I appreciate your aim, stranger," the old man said, approaching Brad.

"Damn near missed him," Brad replied, dropping the spent shell from his gun and refilling the chamber.

"Name's Jebediah Jones and I'm beholdin' to you either way." The old man stood, his hand outstretched, his rifle dangling over one arm. Brad shook his hand and gestured toward an empty chair beside him.

Jebediah Jones worked for the railroad. He had shot buffalo east of the Rockies, feeding the crews as they lay track across the continent. But by the late 1860s, the buffalo had thinned, the vast slaughter of the animals depleting the herds. So he had come West, a guard and scout, variously employed moving payrolls safely and keeping the crews of Chinese workers under control.

Brad thought he was the most striking-looking man he had ever seen. His bright blue eyes glistened, alert. White hair, wavy, hung about his ears and the deep furrows of his face gave him the look of a sage. Despite his obvious age, Jebediah's quick hands and animated expressions revealed a kind of energy that few young men at their prime possess. As he was settling into the chair beside Brad, leaning his carbine against the wall, Spear called the bartender to his table.

"Beer for the gentleman, and another for me," Brad ordered, then, turning, asked his guest, "and a steak?"

"And a steak."

Spear looked at the man, noting his curious dress. His boots were made of lightweight deerskin so supple that it had to be kept from collapsing around his ankles by rawhide drawstrings tied high on his calves. His greatcoat was an ornately stitched combination of beaver and muskrat that reached well below his knees. A rattlesnake belt bound his trousers in place and the shirt he wore was beaded in the style of ceremonial Indian dress. The sheath of a hunting knife hung from his hip. He didn't wear a holster and Brad couldn't find the bulge of a six-gun anywhere on him.

"Seems to me, Jebediah, that if you're going to stand around blasting folks with their friends nearby, you ought to tote a side arm."

"Probably right about that. Never took to the things, though."

"Better learn, old man. You were about to be perforated over there." A girl came with a pitcher of beer and two fresh mugs. She was uneasy about waiting on their table and kept glancing furtively at Jebediah.

"Doubtful he'd of shot me."

"How's that?"

"Jes' doubtful. Man's a miner out of work. Stuck under the cloud and in a hurry to get out. Doubtful he'd fire on an old man in a crowded room."

"You mean the mines are slowing down? That fellas like him with nothing but picks are scattering, looking for other work?"

Jebediah leaned back in his chair, hooked a knee over its arm and sipped his beer. "I mean there's more panic within three hundred miles of here than I've ever seen before."

"How do you know the going's so tough? Papers keep reporting that the mines are, by and large, turning a good profit."

"Papers are a lot of foolishness, if you ask me. Fellas that write 'em never get two miles out of San Francisco. They just sit there and write what they're told and they're not being told what's going on. Truth of it is that there's less ore coming out of the ground and damn near no new strikes of consequence, and all the while those that get laid off keep pouring in here, look-

ing for work. Like any idle crowd, there's a lot of el-
bowing going on."

"You a trapper?" Spear wondered.

"Nope. I work for the railroad, scouting the route
and moving their money around."

"Then, old man, we're in the same sort of work. I'm
a Pinkerton, working on the bank burglary here in
town."

"Young man, I'm beholdin' to you for helpin' out
back there, and I'm enjoying the beer, but it'd please
me if you'd call me Jeb rather than referring to my age
all the time."

"Sorry, Jeb," Brad was genuinely embarrassed. By
the time a man reached sixty in Nevada, he was generally either rich or broken. Though Jebediah Jones was
neither, Spear had been treating him condescendingly,
almost humoring him. "And my name's Brad Spear. I
didn't mean . . ."

"Forget it."

Brad looked around for their steaks and noticed the
cook, still wearing his apron, coming in the front door.
Their meal had been delayed by a visit to the undertaker.

"If you're trackin' those that robbed the bank,
you're sure doin' it in a funny spot," Jeb observed.

"You think so?"

"Yup, no riffraff involved in that one."

"How do you know that?" Brad was slightly stunned
by the old man's observation. He had reached the same
conclusion, convinced that the burglary was a well-
planned, well-financed operation involving very high
stakes. There was more to it than met the eye, he just
wasn't sure what.

"I'm guessin', but the whole thing seems a bit warm
for November. Reminds me, sorta . . ."

"Of what?"

"Of the change that happens anywhere the railroad goes. Of the way folks git strange when the rules get messed with. Like it's happenin' here. You really don't know, do you?"

Spear shook his head.

"I'll put it simple, sorta." Jebediah Jones' eyes glistened, then looked away, dredging from memory a time he rarely thought about. Recalling an era he'd left behind. "Years ago I was trapping with five other men north of the lakes. We'd built a cabin and spent the summer making out all right, fishing those shallow lakes and eating what deer we needed. Good men, each of them. Not that any of us liked working shoulder to shoulder, but there was a real comfort to the group.

"We'd each lay a loop of traps out from the home base, some twenty or so miles around. And each man walked his loop once a week, taking what he found and resetting the traps. The four or five-day walk, as I recall, was a pleasure. Each of us tracking our own markers, hoping we'd outdo the others, sorta taking our own time in the summer air.

"Anyway, we made out real good. And by fall we had a couple of silver fox, worth a whole lot to Eastern ladies, a sizable pile of ermine and more beaver and muskrat than you could count. The weather was getting ornery, though, winter headed our way, and sitting around the cabin we allowed as how one more loop should close us out. No sense in walking out of there in the snow. Only problem with the plan was that the youngest of us, fella named Zeke something, hadn't made it back to camp as yet.

"Not that we were worried about him. Man could run ten miles without breaking a sweat, knew his way around and was the meanest knife thrower I can recall. Nope, we didn't worry much about him. Still, if we left he was likely to make another loop on us without bringing in his traps. So we tacked a note on the door of the cabin, telling him to go around again and call it quits.

"I guess I got back first, lugging my traps on a sled with the furs. And I was surprised to find the note still sittin' there. Well, by nightfall of the next day we were all run home, waitin' on Zeke. We spent our time listening to Jim, the storyteller in the group, feed us nonsense about his summer. He could sure make up some tall ones. And we bundled the hides. The quietest guy among us shot a deer one morning, and I fished a bit. But it was getting colder and colder, the days shrinking so fast it seemed the sun never really warmed anything.

"Then Zeke came in, grinning and laughing. He'd done real well but not brought in his traps. Seems he couldn't read. Well, we told him to get out after the damn things right away and settled in for another week of sitting in that cabin.

" 'Course, it happened. Snowed like hell, for three days running. We kept having to dig out the door so we could open it at all.

"Now you have to understand the way these summers worked. A bunch like us teamed up and shared. The food was for whoever got hungry, the furs were divided even, the fun of trapping the most was just fun, not business. It got to be a close kinda thing, six men out there. We got to know each other real well. So while the five or us watched the snow make the woods quieter and quieter, making the trees shorter and shorter, we didn't talk much about Zeke. Now and then one of us would cuss him out for being slow. But there was a lot of worry there. And by the time the snow stopped, I was beginning to think he was in real trouble.

"Zeke was a kid, a strong, likable, dumb country kid. Nobody wanted to leave him in the woods. But it got to that, of course, after two weeks. Jim, I remember, figured it didn't matter anyway. Figured we could wait till spring. He'd be thawing out by then, Jim said.

"So we had six men's share and five men in the cabin. And we were waiting in the snow, wondering when the next go around would bury us for good, listening now and then for Zeke. It got so quiet in that cabin you could die from it. We stopped playing cards 'cause of the fights. Our snowshoes were made, the sleds loaded and covered, we were set to leave. It got real itchy, you might say.

"Naturally, we had it out one night. And it seemed that all of 'em 'cept me was ready to start walking south the next morning. I knew I couldn't make it through to spring in that cabin, but I knew I wouldn't die there either. I could wait.

"Damned if that didn't set it off. Jim didn't care a hoot if I froze stiff, he said. Just didn't like the idea that Zeke's furs would rot. It seemed to him that we ought to each take a slice of Zeke's goods and do what we wanted, leave or stay. And I allowed that if Zeke had caught his share, then his share ought to wait for him.

"Jim got nasty at that. Said I'd wait a day and make off with two shares. And I must of been a little cabin-sore myself 'cause I got plenty hot under the collar when he started carrying on that way. Before I knew it, I'd called him a thief, stealin' another man's hides. He was on me in a hurry then and to this day I can't say that I blame him. But it was him or me and I got to him first. Shot him with my rifle.

"Then the divvying got worse. Something broke up inside that cabin, it was like the summer dying on us, the warm drifting away. There wasn't a wit of kindness in any one of us, the two boys out of St. Paul being real scared of dying by then. Next morning they were gone, lugging only one of the three sleds piled up with furs.

"So it was just me and a likable guy named Bill. And he was scared of me more than of the snow. He just sat there, playing cards with himself. I tried to talk about it with him, but he wasn't having any of it. 'Zeke's dead,' was all he'd say. Three days later he told me we were all three dead, him and me and Zeke. And the next morning he was walking out the door, didn't care about the furs, he said.

"So I sat there wondering who it was that's crazy. It was more than likely we'd all got killed waiting for Zeke. And it was sure, by then, that at least some furs would rot. Shares sitting on a sled near a cabin, shares working their way south in the snow. Bits and pieces of that summer gone to waste. And Jim dead.

"I think, now, I probably was addled, or sick with a kind of sorrow I don't know the name of, but I kept on waiting. It was two more days of watching the sun sink lower, of looking at the spot where Jim was buried in the snow, before Zeke showed up. Hurt bad. Had a run-in with a bear that near killed him and it was sure two fingers at least were gone from the cold. Said he followed the smoke from the cabin for three days.

"We made it out, though, Zeke and I. He could walk pretty good, though slow. And the weather stayed clear for us. Never did see any of 'em again, never."

Jebediah Jones looked weary, some of the ginger gone from his face, the lids over his eyes seeming more wrinkled and low than they had before.

"What happened to the furs?" Brad asked.

"Can't recall."

Spear looked down at the empty mug in front of him.

"But I don't think I'll ever forget the dividin' up of

things. Like the carvin' up of land the railroad brings with it."

"The Land Grants," Spear said, wondering if they were the point of all this talk.

"That's right. The railroad's makin' one big, snow-bound cabin out of this country. They're chopping it up and making folks pay for it. And all the while good men with picks and shovels are trying as best they can to dig a living. And it isn't working. The smart ones and the rich are gonna own it all. What silver there is left, what gold there might be, all of it."

"Jeb, are you telling me there isn't enough to go around out here?" It seemed impossible to Brad.

"I'm telling you there's never enough to go around. There's always somebody lookin' for more than his share."

"And the land's the thing, at least to you, those chunks of ground the railroad peddles, those worthless squares of dry gulch and tumbleweed everyone's so anxious to get at."

"Some's worthless, some's not."

Spear sat at the rough table, watching Jeb eat his steak. His mind's eye conjured up a vision of men in a small room, cordoning it off, dividing the world around them as though their lives depended on it. And he pondered the mountain man, the buffalo hunter, the relic that sat across from him. Jebediah Jones was a stranger to boundaries, to fences. His life had been spent in the open and so, somehow, he more quickly and precisely detected the change that was occurring. Perhaps, Brad thought, he was overreacting, or perhaps he was a bellwether sensing the shift of winds before anyone else.

Alice Carter had aged. She sat rocking, an embroidery hoop on her lap, looking very much like an old woman. Brad had been told that she was well, as fit as could be expected, but he was not prepared for the almost shrunken creature that smiled at him as he entered her room.

She seemed to have settled into Lady Jane's home comfortably, mildly thrilled by the lavish appointments around her. A delicate spool bed, draped with a lace slipcover, stood in one corner, a low chest of drawers, a writing table and two chairs filled the rest of the room. Alice's face was nearly ashen, her hair less tended than Brad had ever seen it.

"Good afternoon, Miss Carter," he said, trying to conceal the catch he felt in his throat.

"Good afternoon, Bradley, if you don't mind my calling you by your Christian name."

"I don't mind at all, Miss Carter." Brad wondered how she could be so prim, after all, she had saved his life. And he was surprised she didn't ask him to call her Alice. Instead, she turned immediately, directing her attention to the floral design she was stitching almost as though she had forgotten he was there.

"Alice?"

"Yes, Bradley."

"Thank you. They told me what you did."

"You're welcome."

"I'm sorry I got you involved in all of this."

"It's all right, really. I'm fine."

"But Alice," Brad pleaded with her, trying to get through whatever shield she had erected, "your home was burned to the ground."

"It'll be all right, Bradley. Now stop fussing. Do you like my tulips?" She held her work up to him for Brad's approval.

"They're lovely." Alice Carter had disappeared in the flames and smoke of her home. The woman, Brad thought, had endured more than she was equipped to withstand, too much pain, too much terror. "The doctor tells me you're doing very well. Says you'll be back at the bank in no time."

"Doctor? Not that awful man. He's an awful man."

Brad was puzzled. The physician from the mine was very pleasant and courteous.

"No, Bradley," Alice said, almost lecturing him, "don't ever speak of that awful Dr. Brockington again. He's not the sort of gentleman a fine young man like you should associate with."

"Why don't you think so, Alice?"

"He wouldn't take us in. Don't you remember? They carried you to his door, bleeding and all. And I stood there in the shadows, reading that sign: 'Knock and Come In' over and over while they pounded on his door. But then he wouldn't let you in. He just said, 'Take Spear to the Silver Lady, they've got a doctor.' They yelled at him you were dying but he wouldn't take us in."

"It's not important now, Alice," Brad whispered. He noticed Lady Jane behind him, in the doorway. "I'm going to be fine."

"That's good, Bradley," Alice said, feeding her needle through the cloth.

Spear closed the door to the room as silently as he could. He was certain Alice wouldn't notice his departure just as she might not remember his visit. He turned and found Jane weeping into her hands.

"Oh Brad, what they've done to her . . ." was all she could manage.

# Chapter 10

Brad Spear stood in his room at the Nevada House Hotel, haunted by Alice Carter's vacant gaze. He dropped his bundle of newly purchased clothes on the bed and cut the twine that bound them. He saw her eyes staring at the hoop she held in one hand, picturing the mindless repetition of her work. Embroidery. A precious art, a delicate comfort. Spear lifted his carpetbag to the table beside him, wondering if Alice would ever reclaim the slow, predictable flow of her life. Or if she'd sit, stitching, forever.

Night was coming early to Silver City. The cloudless sky offered no reflected light and the sun had long since disappeared below the mountains. Brad's lone kerosene lamp smoked slightly and he lowered its wick, brightening the room.

Brad took the long, narrow folding knife from his bag, opened and locked its blade in position. A brass lever on the handle's side allowed it to be refolded. He put on a black shirt and buttoned it to the neck. The heavy wool jacket he had bought at the dry goods store was navy blue, but dark enough. A thin, black knitted cap covered his head, and the skintight leather gloves that always traveled with him darkened his hands to the wrist. Fifty feet of rope, tied to a grappling hook, hung over his shoulder but was concealed by his jacket.

The hotel's narrow stairway was dark, lit only by small lamps at each floor's landing. As he walked down toward the lobby, he considered the thin threads of evidence and implication that he'd gathered in this case. They led to a single source, he was sure. There was a pattern here, he just couldn't make it out. But even uncertain, he felt confident about this evening's work. Though as tedious as Alice Carter's pastime, following his hunch might make some things clear.

The desk clerk grinned, clapping his hands together. His grimy scarf and worn mittens were still in place but, to Brad's amusement, he'd added earmuffs. They clung to his gaunt face, fuzzy balls, making him look ridiculous. The man nervously shifted his weight from one foot to another.

"Too cold out there, mister," the clerk chattered. "Best stay in tonight."

"It is getting a bit raw," Brad noted. The agent felt peculiarly sympathetic toward the man. He seemed a harmless madman, pursued by a chill wind no one else felt. Not dangerous or mean. Like Alice, he thought.

"Too cold," was all the clerk said.

Brad shrugged as if to indicate he had no choice and the clerk mimicked him. Spear left the hotel and turned quickly to the alley beside it. He picked his way through the crates and discarded bedposts strewn there until he came to a narrow walkway that ran behind the buildings on the street. Jogging, he covered a hundred yards quickly, turned down another alley and walked back to the street. He knelt in the shadows and studied the buildings in front of him.

Dr. Brockington's home and office stood, incongruously residential, between two storefronts. Its small front yard and picket fence were out of place in the middle of Silver City. And as if to set it off from everything nearby, alleys flanked the property. While six or seven storefronts commonly butted one against another on this main street, Brockington's home sat like an island, untouched.

The harness shop next door was typical of the business district's establishments. A small, wood-frame building, it housed a modest retail operation on its first floor. Its large, paned-glass window at street level was dark. On the second floor, Brad assumed, the proprietor lived. Two small windows there were lit. Above those windows stood the false front of the building, extending three or four feet above the roof and bearing the words "Keo's Harness & Saddle."

Spear ran back to the walkway he'd just traveled, jogged farther down the street and then up another alley. He walked casually to Brockington's side of the road and then made his way to an alley five doors from the harness shop.

He slipped one arm from his jacket, releasing the rope from his shoulder. In a moment, the grappling hook whistled through the air, circling like a windmill. He let it fly and the iron hook clattered on the roof above. He pulled in rope, listening to the scrape of the hook and its handle above him. And then it lodged, biting into something. Spear tested the line, first tugging at it, then using it to support his weight.

Confident it would hold, he climbed silently, hand over hand, up the side of the building. He found toeholds on windowsills and the ornamental lathing that marked the first floor from the second. At the top he lifted himself over a low ridge and noted the precarious hold his hook had enjoyed.

The rooftops before him were black, only their perimeters illuminated by the glow of windows below. Gathering his line and hook, he made his way from roof to roof, half-crawling, half-running on all fours. He soon found himself atop the harness shop and inched his way to the false front sign that faced the street.

Huddled behind the sign, overlooking the alley and Brockington's home, Brad set his rope beside him. He sat, dressed in black, concealed by the night, and felt the swirling wind spill over the sign at his back like ice water over a flat rock. The empty sky sucked the warmth from the day. Brad brought his kness to his chest, waiting.

The roof was littered with broken shingles that had blown from nearby buildings. There was an abandoned bird's nest tucked in one far corner and shifting rivers of sand and dust, blown by the wind, curled across the tilted roof like the veins on the back of a hand.

Below, in the alley, he saw two barrels, their staves split, their hoops rusting. A case of empty bottles sat outside the door of Brockington's office and a discarded wad of paper blew in circles, trapped in a corner where a fence met the building. The faint, intermittent rustle of the paper reminded Brad of the sound made by a snake moving through dry leaves.

Spear waited, thinking about waiting. Stakeouts, he thought, were bad enough. But the stillness of a winter watch chilled him to the bone in a hurry. It might take hours, or days. And it was cold.

He thought about the odds, the patient longshot of sitting, anticipating where something might happen. This particular tool of his trade was hard on him. He was patient only with great effort, inaction gnawed at him.

Staring into the darkened alley, he remembered another stakeout. He had hidden in a recessed doorway and waited there for nearly twelve hours. Twenty feet away, another Pinkerton had watched as well, neither of them speaking or moving. It had been a hunch, a guess, that Spear hoped would explain an inexplicable situation. They had waited, and in the end been fooled by a woman propelled by jealousy. Undisguised, almost brazen in the early morning light, a wife had simply walked to the house they surveyed, entered without knocking and killed her husband's mistress. Spear's partner, stunned, had run to the sound of the shot and had taken a second shell in the chest.

Death and darkness had become his currency, Spear thought. He lived and worked in the places that brought fear to most men. That brought fear to him. Still, he worked there. Sitting on a rooftop, cold, he wondered why.

The minutes turned to hours, the agent marking the time by shifting his weight as the blood slowed in a leg or arm. He noticed that the streets quieted and then began to darken as one lamp after another was extinguished. Silver City was quitting for the night.

Below him, in the apartment above the harness shop, he heard a woman laughing. He could make out the mutter of conversation, but couldn't discern its meaning. Only the laughing made any sense. Then a window opened.

"You're crazy! It's cold!" the unseen woman shouted.

"Then get in bed and warm yourself," a man laughed.

The window closed again, not five feet from him, and within minutes Brad heard the steady thump of a bed's headboard pounding against a wall. The couple had clearly found the bed. After a while he heard the woman yowling and thought to himself he didn't deserve this sort of abuse.

He thought about Lady Jane. About the curl of her hair on her shoulders. About her smooth, warm arms. And about the stubborn integrity of the woman. She understands herself, he thought. She has somehow married her rugged, streetwise beginnings with her up-per-class life. He remembered her caring for him after the explosions at Alice Carter's. Remembered her fond-ly for allowing him hours of preoccupied thought. Jot-ting in his notebook, drawing arrows connecting names, concocting maps of possibilities. Trying to put together a puzzle without all the pieces. She had tolerated his ignoring her for two days.

Out of the corner of his eye, Spear saw a man cross the street two blocks away. He was short and thin, his hands alternately tugging at his collar and diving into his pockets. Leaning, Brad watched the man move furtively from alley to alley, pausing, ducking into shadows, his head turning from side to side with the kind of caution only fear brings. Two passers-by ap-proached him, talking, and he ducked into a doorway.

There was something about his unpredictable gait, something about the pent-up frenzy of the man, that was familiar to the agent. You've hunted too many ter-rified bastards, Spear, the agent told himself. They're starting to look like one another.

The little man moved down the street until he came to the alley beside Brockington's. He looked around briefly, searching the street, then walked to the doctor's office door. He knocked and it opened.

"Dufond, get in here," Brockington ordered.

Spear couldn't believe it. It was impossible. The des-perate, vicious little priest that had so plagued him in Cheyenne was in Silver City. And like filings to a mag-net, he'd found Brockington. Scum floats to the edge, Spear whispered to himself.

Dufond had worked a payoff scheme with a particu-larly sordid bunch of elected officials in Wyoming. He had raped Lady Jane, tried more than once to kill Spear, yet had managed to escape arrest. Dufond's sense of caution and his ruthless energies had served him well then. It would, Spear hoped, be different this time.

As Spear sat, recalling the bloody confrontations in Cheyenne, he felt himself grow angry. It was an emotion he rarely allowed himself. He had seen it distract and finally destroy too many men. But still, the thought of Dufond burned in him. The defrocked priest was the most senseless form of evil Brad knew: a man running, and in his retreat spreading cruelty behind him as a kind of delaying tactic. Spear thought of Dufond as more than an adversary, he was an enemy.

Fighting to dispel the image of Jane bloodied and afraid, bound to a bed by Dufond, Spear heard a noise from the back end of Brockington's alley. He squinted into the darkness, not sure he could believe his eyes.

Scrambling over the low, rough stockade fence that blocked the end of the alley came the desk clerk from the Nevada House Hotel. The pale, gaunt man stumbled as he fell to the ground and put a finger to his lips as though quieting himself. He wore his mittens and scarf, his earmuffs still perched on his head, but there was something different about the man. As he crawled along the side of the doctor's house and then crouched behind one of the deteriorating barrels in the alley, he seemed steady, almost calm. Unlike the skittish, constantly moving character from the hotel, he now looked as though he knew what he was doing. Brad thought, for a moment, the man in mittens looked like an expert card player considering his hand.

Within minutes another man crept down the alley from the street. Dressed in a gentlemanly overcoat, complete with felt collar, this latest guest was a man of stature. He stood at Brockington's side entrance, impatient to be admitted, rapping on the door with the silver top of his walking stick. He was welcomed without a word being spoken.

Brad pondered the meeting taking place. An odd group had assembled, to be sure. And judging from the resources that seemed to have gathered inside the house, he was faced with a powerful bunch. Spear looked down at the man with the mittens, still kneeling behind a barrel, and shook his head.

Somewhere, far up the street, two cats began to fight. The screech of their battle sent a shiver down the agent's spine. Then, the streets once again quiet, time wore on. Minutes, perhaps half an hour passed, as Spear and his unlikely companion below waited. Finally, a carriage came to a stop at the front of Brockington's home. Out of it strode Judge Thorpe, Lady Jane's long-winded dinner guest. Without pausing, he climbed the doctor's front stoop, knocked once and let himself in. The judge, Spear thought, was clever. His appearance had been so obvious, his presence so unconcealed that no one watching could think it suspicious.

If, as Brad thought, the conspirators below were behind the bank robbery, there was more to it than a simple theft. He had to move quickly. As quietly as his stiffened legs would allow, the agent walked from rooftop to rooftop, retracing his earlier steps, and climbed down his rope to the alley some distance from Brockington's.

Running, and warming with the effort, he circled the house. He felt comforted by the activity, blood at last pumping through his feet and hands. Taking some care not to alarm the mittened man at Brockington's back door, Spear moved down the alley on the other side of the house. The ground was freezing as the night wore on and it crackled beneath his feet.

Once hidden in the deep shadows of the narrow alley, Spear felt safe. It was unlikely that anyone in the brightly lit parlor would notice him. Or even look for him. No guards were posted, no shades drawn. Brockington was confident.

Figures moved past the illuminated frame of the parlor window as though they were characters on a distant stage. The yellow light of burning lamps inside was steady, but the men flickered past the thick, gathered drapes. Dufond stood warming his hands by the fireplace. Brockington paced, his hands clasped behind his back. And both the judge and the gentleman still wielding his cane circled a large table in the middle of the room. They were studying something, talking too quietly to be heard, nodding and taking notes.

Whatever animated conversation was taking place stopped as a man wearing a Stetson entered the room. Brad watched his cool blue eyes roam about the room. Brockington shook his head and pounded on the table with his fist. The Stetson nodded and then shouldered a gleaming, nickel-plated rifle. Spear smiled to himself. At this distance he recognized the weapon, more or less. It was a custom-made Colt, an extremely accurate rifle with a six-shell revolving chamber. Though it fired only .36 caliber shells, it made up in long-range capacity and rapid-fire ability what it lacked in raw punch. A gun meant for small game and humans, Brad thought.

Spear had seen enough. Before the festivities ended, he planned to be warming himself in his hotel room. As Brad moved, backing his way toward the street, he heard the sounds of an argument at Brockington's office door. Bewildered, he crossed the street and positioned himself in the alley facing the house. Incredibly, the mittened man stood at the back door, talking to a beautiful, dark-haired girl.

"Bunny, please," he shouted, trying nevertheless to hold his voice down.

"I can't, I just can't," Bunny answered him. "Now

take this double eagle and get out of here. He'll find us."

Slipping the coin into his pocket, the curious figure of a man walked away from the house, over the fence at the rear of the alley and into the darkness.

# Chapter 11

Pattie shifted on the bed, a sizable lump in its thin mattress pressing against her side. The bed creaked as she moved. The air around her was chill. She thought to herself that she must've fallen asleep for a while.

The girl sat up, gathering a blanket around her shoulders as she did so, and looked out the window. Silver City was nearly shuttered for the night. It occurred to her that it must be very late, even midnight, and it was likely Spear would never show up. Wrapping the rough, brown blanket around her like a shawl, Pattie crossed the small room and poured three fingers of whiskey into a tall glass. She then settled in a straight-backed wooden chair, pouting. A chill crept along her exposed legs as she held the drink in her hand.

"Tarnation," she said, almost sighing. As if toasting her complaint, she raised the glass and then took a healthy swallow of the warm liquor. Its bite surprised her, but the warmth that followed ran quickly and pleasantly down her throat.

"Whew, sippin' whiskey," she noted to herself and began to assault the drink cautiously, but steadily. "Might's well be warm," she muttered, climbing back into the bed.

When Spear walked into the room, she was sitting

sideways on the bed, leaning against the wall, grinning at him as he entered. His gun was drawn.

"Damn you, girl!" he shouted, throwing his rope across the room. "You have any idea how easily dead you are right now?" She shook her head, her eyelids drooping slightly, her smile lazy.

"It's as cold in here as it is out there. Fire's out in the lobby and that lamp isn't about to warm this room." Spear spoke rapidly, the shiver that ran through him rattling his nerves. He stripped off his cap and removed his gloves. "Pour me a drink," he ordered, pacing the room, rubbing his hands together.

Pattie headed, a little wobbly, to the bottle and poured three or four inches of whiskey into the glass she held. While walking back to him, her grip on the blanket failed and it slid off her. She stood in the middle of the room, naked, a blanket draped beside her, reaching toward him with a glass of whiskey.

"Thanks," he took the drink and waved her to the bed. He drank, rubbing the back of his neck with his hand, pacing, shaking his head.

"And what the hell are you doing here?" he asked, finally warming enough to pay attention to her.

"Usual," she replied, slurring the word a bit.

"Isn't it past your bedtime or something?"

"Yup," she grinned.

Spear pulled off his boots and rubbed his toes. At first there was no feeling in them, but a short massage and another swallow of whiskey brought them around. He looked at Pattie. Her short brown hair was tousled, locks flying in odd directions, the result of having slept on her side. Her smooth white skin seemed all the smoother for the rough wrapper she clutched and one well-turned calf peeked at him from beneath the blanket.

Spear shook off the thought. It was late, he was

tired. The city was filled with powerful men whose business it was to kill him. It seemed neither the time nor the place for this cute young thing.

"I heard about your accident, Bradley," Pattie offered. Her comment brought to mind that she had somehow discovered his identity the first day he was in Silver City. Her departing note, inquiring about his alias, had bothered him for a while. But it had since become clear that his real name was no secret and so he had dismissed her. Now he was curious as to how she knew his name.

"I'm better, much better. A few more days' rest and I'll be as good as new."

"I'm glad," she said without much conviction.

"Pattie?"

"Yes."

"Would you mind telling me how it is you know my name?"

"Oh, that. It's nothing, really. Don't pay it any mind."

"I'm curious, that's all. When we first met, you knew my room number and my name. Do you read minds or something?"

"No, silly," the girl laughed, as though that ended the conversation. Spear thought to himself that this particular interrogation was going to be difficult.

"Really, I'd like to know."

"Know?"

"How you knew my name."

"Oh, that." ·

"Yes."

"I can't tell. It's a secret."

"Pattie, I'm not in any humor to play twenty questions. Who told you my name is Spear?" Brad was growing angry. This was ridiculous.

"I can't tell. I really can't."

"Then get out of here. Beat it."

"Nope."

"What?"

"I said, nope. I'm not going anyplace. I've been waitin' for you for God knows how long and I'm not leavin' now. And anyway, it's too damn cold out there."

"Get the hell out of here!" Spear was too exhausted to follow a conversation quite so inane.

"You stop fussin' and come to bed. I'm wakin' up and it's gettin' warm in here."

Spear looked at the girl. She was fidgeting under the blanket, taunting him in the most obvious way, her hips rocking from one side to another. She raised herself on one arm and a soft, round breast came into view. Her audacity was matched only by the splendid curve of her shoulders and the gentle slopes that peaked at her small, dark nipples. It occurred to Spear that he might not be as tired as he thought. He raised his glass to his lips and emptied it. He was definitely warmer.

Pattie looked up at the tall, dark man through the gentle glow of three ounces of warm whiskey. She thought it much too late for talking and wondered to herself why he kept on with it. As she eased her head down onto the pillow, Pattie felt the chill of the room tighten the skin across her exposed shoulder and breast. The ripple of sensation ran like a finger down her belly and thighs, spreading into a longing that pressed her crossed legs against each other. Without thinking, she pulled the covering over her, small movements echoing through her hips and shoulders.

She watched him as he drained his glass. He set it on a table, locked the door and removed his heavy, dark jacket. Standing over her he seemed immense, the black of his shirt meeting his trim dark beard, and as he removed the shirt, his broad, tanned shoulders spread above her, larger than life.

Pattie rolled onto her back, the heavy blanket rough as it drew across her chest, and watched Spear hang his holster over the short bedpost. As he stood, not three feet from her, unbuckling his belt and unbuttoning his trousers, she put her hands behind her head, spreading her legs and stretching. In a moment he was naked, walking slowly toward the lamp. Hmmmm, she thought as his broad frame half-disappeared in the dimmed light.

Spear slid beside her on the bed, his weight rolling her toward him. Her arms were around his neck as though they had a life of their own. Her mouth went to his, open and hungry, and she shivered against his cool skin as her breasts flattened, brushing against him. Pattie noticed, out of the corner of her eye, that her small hands were dwarfed as she kneaded his shoulders and ran her fingers down his sides.

His thigh, broad and insistent, spread her legs as Spear rolled half onto her. She felt his tongue at her ear, then drawing down her neck and his hand slid surely across her breast. He was warming above her, a heat emanating from his body that drew her to him, her hips yearning to engulf him, her legs wrapping around his. She felt the flick of his finger teasing her hardened nipple.

Spear's hand trailed lightly up the inside of her thigh and she raised her knee, opening to him. She arched, his touch circling her, promising but withholding. She turned, his thigh sliding roughly across her leg. His fingers approached her center, the attentive tip of her yearning for him, and then retreated, sliding across her belly. One hand, dipping between her buttocks and racing down the back of her leg, inflamed Pattie. Impatience flowered in her, moist and waiting, and she forced herself toward him, mindlessly closing on him, surrounding herself with his body.

At last his touch danced along the core of her, sending her waves of relief that splashed back as further wanting. She felt his hardness against her leg as she spread, clawing at him, pulling him over her. Still he hovered, toying with the sensitive tip of her desire, his tongue burning across her lips.

Pattie buried her face in his chest as he moved over her, her eyes closed. She felt his tip taunt, slipping at once hard and liquid toward her. And she gasped as the weight of Spear's chest bore down on her, his hands slipping low on her hips, encircling her buttocks. He filled her with one, slow, sure, steady thrust that brought a moan to her lips and her knees into the air. She pressed up to him, her tiny hands still on his back, her concentration centered on his constant motion and her reply.

Finally thought disappeared as, deep within her, he urged her on with his relentless cadence. His rhythm constant, she gave in to it, flowing with him. Immobile, pinned below him, she pressed, the wave of warmth building in her, running from somewhere hidden to the edge of his touch. He drove into her, once, close, closer, then there, as she shuddered, a spasm of delight spreading through her body. Falling, turning, holding on as she met him over and over, she continued, uncontrolled, her pleasure as constant and enduring as his pounding. Then, caught between one wave and the next, she felt him change inside her, spilling, slower, deeper, more powerful than she thought possible. Locked together as the wave overtook him, they quivered, lingering, and were quiet.

Pattie lay buried beneath him. His warmth filled her, his body overpowering still and she kissed his chest lightly. Her hands felt the ridges of muscle crossing his back stiffen as he lifted himself. Her deep, quick breathing slowed and she rolled on her side to look at him. Brad gathered her in his arms, collected one pale leg between his legs and she slept.

Brad rolled over and the crisp, white light of early morning flashed across his face. Without opening his eyes he saw it burning red across his closed eyelids. He rolled to his belly, trying to count the few hours he'd been asleep.

Pattie, he knew, had long since gone. It was just as well. His mouth had a peculiar taste to it and there was a rumbling in his skull. Never drink whiskey neat or warm, he thought. With some effort, he raised his head. Finally, sitting on the edge of the bed, his eyes made a vain attempt to focus on the room. Catching a quick glimpse of the shambles before him, he closed them again. Somewhere in this room, he thought, there is a pitcher of cold water standing in a porcelain bowl. Peering through narrowed eyes, he found it and splashed water on his face. It frosted him awake.

Brad dressed, climbing into his chilled clothing quickly, trying to escape the room's cold air. He walked stiffly down the stairway into the lobby and felt the heat pouring from the stove.

"Mornin'," the man in mittens chimed.

"Yeah," Brad responded, moving steadily toward the door.

"Coffee's hot in the kitchen," the clerk called.

Spear stopped, looked at the tall, thin man and then walked to the desk. "Would you get me a cup, black?" he asked.

"Comin' right up." Mittens disappeared at a dead run through a door to his left. Almost instantly, he returned, a cup of coffee teetering on the saucer in his hand.

"Thanks," Spear managed, sipping.

"Pattie makes it fresh every morning," Mittens explained, his grin splitting his face in two.

"Amazing young woman. Amazing."

"Sure is."

"Know where I can get a short glass of warm beer for this head of mine?" Brad asked.

"Mammoth's open, I think," Mittens volunteered, pounding his sides for warmth.

Brad turned, warmed by the coffee and the red-hot stove, and headed for the street. One raw egg floating in a warm beer would help, he thought. If he could only make it from here to The Mammoth.

As Brad walked into the daylight, he pulled his Stetson low on his brow. He turned, set out up the street and saw a stranger approaching him. The agent instinctively looked over his shoulder. Two more men rose from chairs leaning against a storefront and fell in step a few yards behind him. His head cleared as he bore down on the lone man ahead, walking quickly.

As Brad passed the single, unarmed man, he looped an arm around the stranger's neck, wheeled and drew his side arm. Using the man as a shield, Brad leveled his weapon at the two approaching men.

"Tell your friends to stop where they are," Spear barked.

"Friends? What, hey, I don't know those guys," his shield croaked, a forearm digging into his windpipe. His breath reeked of cheap whiskey and he quivered in fear.

Spear prodded the man's kidney with his gun. "You tell 'em to hold up right where they are."

"Hold it!" the man screamed, both hands raised in front of him.

The pair stopped. "You talkin' to us?" the larger of the two asked.

"Damn right," Brad answered.

"What the hell you doin' pulling down on us?"

"I don't know these two guys, mister," the drunk whimpered.

"And we don't know that stumblebum," the large man added.

Spear studied the pair. They were rawboned, dirty and well-armed. "Beat it," he decided, waving his pistol down the street.

"Sure, sure," they nodded, shrugging, and walked away from him.

Brad released his shield, who dropped to his knees before scurrying away. You're getting jumpy, he thought, watching the two men wander down an alley several stores away. He turned on one heel and marched toward The Mammoth. Two doors down he realized his mistake as a .44 slug whistled past his ear. He spun, saw the two men standing with their guns leveled at him and dove to the street. Prone, he fired, catching one of them in the chest. The man tottered and fell forward, his forehead bouncing twice on the wooden sidewalk. The second man wheeled and ran.

Spear leapt after him, sprinting down the frozen street. The lumbering thug ducked into an alley and churned toward a fence that blocked its end. When Brad reached him, he had hoisted half his body over it and was kicking furiously to escape. The agent grabbed an ankle in both hands and pulled the gunman back to the ground. The man rolled once and then tore at Spear like a battering ram, his head down, his arms spread. Brad sidestepped him and sent a fist into the man's jaw as he barreled by. Rolling in the dust, the man reached for his gun.

"Don't touch it," Brad yelled. He stepped forward and drove his boot into the man's side just over his belt. A second kick caught the man in the groin

and he rolled into a ball, wailing. But the victory was
short-lived. No sooner had Spear stepped back than
the man reached for the .44 in his holster. Brad's boot
crashed into the man's wrist, bones cracking beneath
his toe.

"Had enough?" Spear asked.

The man let loose with an unholy howl, pain racking
him. He rolled to his seat, rocking, holding his shattered wrist with his healthy hand. "It's broke, you
bastard, it's broke."

"Should I put you down?" Spear inquired, his pistol
pointed between the man's eyes.

"Jesus!"

"What's your name?"

"Hudson, Sonny Hudson."

"Who hired you?"

"Don't know. It's the God's truth. Me and Jeremy
just got into town when this fella offers us two dollars
to bring you down the street and ten to bring you
dead."

"What'd the guy look like?"

"Tall, blond fella with shiny blue eyes. Had a dirty
little runt with him and a gleamin' kind of long gun under his arm. It's all I know. Jesus, that hurts somethin'
powerful."

"What's his name?" Spear asked again, his voice
even, measured.

"Don't know."

Spear pushed the unsteady man over with the heel
of his boot, took one step and quickly pinned the broken wrist beneath his foot. He shifted his weight
slightly, the ball of his foot pressing against the man's
injured wrist. The gunman screamed, a howl of raw agony. Spear eased the pressure.

"The name."

"Don't know, I swear I don't know. Don't, please

don't." The man lay on his back, tears running down his face.

"You get your two bucks for delivering me?"

"What?"

"Did you get paid in advance for walking me down the street?"

"Hell, no. Damn, I'm hurt bad."

Spear dropped two silver dollars at the man's side and walked away. At the mouth of the alley he glanced at Hudson's partner. The man still held his gun. He was dead. A two-dollar promise and he was dead. Spear watched the street, scanning it for Dufond or the gleam of a rifle. He saw nothing. The little priest knew enough not to stand and fight with Spear.

Two women, dressed in their Sunday morning best, walked quickly around the body lying in the street. Spear watched their bonnets turn aside, their gloved hands pressed to their mouths. A man ran from The Mammoth toward the undertaker's as a small crowd began to gather around the corpse.

"That one can wait," Spear shouted from the alley. "The guy back here needs the help."

The group stared at him, no one wanting very much to saunter down the alley. Spear stepped aside, headed back to the Nevada House. Adrenalin had cleared his head. It was time to get to work.

The desk clerk's mitten waved frantically at Brad when he entered the hotel. As the agent approached him, papers began to fly in all directions, the clerk searching for something buried in the disorder of his desk. Brad waited as the man fumbled with envelopes and struggled to leaf through sheets of paper while wearing mittens.

"Can I help?" Brad asked.

"Minute, minutē, it's here. Ah!" The man handed

Brad a familiar blue envelope, from Lady Jane. "Forgot to give it to you this morning."

Spear took the envelope, unopened, to his room. "Gala event scheduled for this evening, but we must dance first." Brad thought to himself that a pattern was developing, not only in the messages he received from Jane but in the nature of their meetings.

As he placed the note on the table beside his bed, he saw one of his business cards propped against the lamp. It had been taken from his carpetbag, undoubtedly by Pattie, and left for him to notice. He picked it up, annoyed once again with himself for having succumbed to late-night temptation. On the back of the card was written, in childlike block letters, "Worth the wait. Senator Rogers told me."

Brad thumbed the card absent-mindedly, wondering how a waitress in Silver City's cheapest hotel found herself conversing with a U.S. Senator. And how could his identity have possibly come up? The most plausible explanation involved Pattie's considerable talents while horizontal. But a senator? And Pattie? Perhaps he liked her coffee.

Senator Rogers and his wife were both at the door to greet Jane Harrington and her escort.

"Jane, darling," Mrs. Rogers gushed. "It's so good of you to come. And you brought a friend." Spear watched his handsome hostess assess him, noting the gilded tones of envy run through her voice.

"Rebecca, this is Brad Spear," Jane said, "an old family friend from Cheyenne. He's here working with Mr. Loftin at the bank."

Senator Rogers kissed Jane's hand and shook Brad's. "Ah, yes, Mr. Spear. I understand you're in town to help the bank with some of its problems. And from what I've heard, the task is proving hazardous."

"It is, indeed, Senator," Spear agreed. The evening had suddenly taken on a new complexion. The elegantly dressed and cordial host who stood pumping Brad's hand was the same man he'd seen enter Brockington's house carrying a silver-headed cane. Rogers knew Spear's whereabouts through Pattie, knew his identity from the moment he came to the city and was working with Brockington. Whatever motive stirred such a powerful and wealthy man to finance a bank burglary must be substantial.

Another couple approached the door and the senator turned his attention to them. Brad heard the effortlessly feigned enthusiasm of the hostess pour, once again, over the latest guests and watched Senator Rogers clasping another voter's hand. He wondered at the politician's self-control. He had treated Spear like anyone else. This was to be a delicate evening.

Brad and Jane found drinks and moved about the room. He was introduced to people she knew, but who meant nothing to him. There was a certain amount of insincere chatter, condolences to the widow, and plenty of sidelong glances at the tall, dark, handsome man on Jane's arm. Judge Roscoe Thorpe walked toward Brad, his cigar billowing smoke behind him. But before the agent had an opportunity to talk to the second conspirator at the party, Rebecca Rogers hooked an arm through his and dragged him away.

"There you are, sweet man. Let me steal him for a moment, won't you, Jane, dear?" Jane nearly laughed aloud at Brad's apparent distress, nodding her permission to Mrs. Rogers.

The senator's wife kept her hand on Brad's biceps, drawing him tightly against her side and breast as she walked. They made a circle of the room, Brad smiling and greeting people he would never recognize again.

Finally, they bumped into Dr. Brockington, who nodded to Spear.

"You two seem to have met," Rebecca Rogers observed.

"We have, though I'm afraid we haven't been formally introduced," the doctor smiled. For the record, at least, Brockington knew Spear as Streib.

"Brad Spear, Doctor. I'm with the Pinkerton office out of San Francisco." They shook hands and Rebecca turned her head toward Brad, studying him once again. Apparently his occupation had never been fully described to her.

"Well, Mr. Spear," Brockington probed, "are you making any progress at the bank?"

"Some. It seems Mr. Loftin will be able to recover the better part of his losses."

"That's wonderful."

"Yes, it is. The man deserves some relief." Spear glanced at Loftin, talking excitedly with a few of the less genteel guests.

"Will insurance cover the full amount of the theft?"

"No, I'm afraid it won't. But he has nearly twenty Land Grant Certificates that the bank purchased to aid the railroad, setting a value on them for future marketing. It turns out he will be able to sell them for substantially more than he paid."

Brockington's eyes wandered about the room, trying but not quite managing to conceal his interest in the certificates. He turned back, composed. "Ah, yes, Land Grants. There has been quite a flurry about them in this area for some time now. But the boom seems to have died down. I hope Lyn sells quickly, before his holdings erode further."

The doctor handled himself like an experienced horse trader, criticizing the merchandise even before expressing an interest in it.

"Well, Doctor, we hope to move all the certificates at once, selling to a single buyer. If you know of anyone . . ."

"Are the lots in adjoining sections?"

"No, not quite. They're scattered across this end of the state, a lot of them right here in Washington County."

"And what, if anyone should ask, would you like for them?"

"No definite price has been set, Dr. Brockington, no minimum, surely. Whatever is at the top of the scale these days would probably be fine, maybe a little less."

"Hmmmmm." The doctor looked pensive. "There might be some people here tonight who would be interested. Keep me in mind as well. In fact, why don't you stop by my office tomorrow morning with the locations and section numbers so I can look them over? Never can tell, I might see something I like."

"I'll do that," Brad said. He then followed Rebecca around, making his Land Grant Certificate pitch to Judge Thorpe, a wealthy miner at the party and one or two others who inquired.

Suddenly the small group of musicians that had sat so sullenly in the corner began to play. A piano carried them, the French horn struggling and the violin never quite right. Nevertheless, the tunes were pleasant. Brad searched the room for Jane and, not finding her, stood watching couples waltz about. The senator's tastes were lavish, the crystal chandeliers, wall sconces, elaborate picture frames and hand-carved furniture much more formal than the simple, polished beauty of Lady Jane's home. And there was a certain lack of color in the room, all its hues rich and dark, unrelieved by a spot of red or bright yellow.

As Spear observed the activity, he noticed a small, dark woman standing near the orchestra. She was simply and elegantly dressed, completely without jewelry. Her soft, dark hair hung freely about her shoulders, unlike the upswept styles of every other woman at the party. Brad was attracted to her and, feeling abandoned by Jane, he asked her to dance. She accepted with a nod. As they moved about the room, she nodded meekly or shook her head whenever he asked a question.

"You're a very good dancer," Brad lied as the music stopped.

"Thank you," she responded.

"Do you live here in town?"

She gave only a nod for an answer and then slipped back into her own world.

"Thank you for the dance. My name's Brad Spear."

"Bunny West," she replied and then walked away. Spear suddenly recognized her: the girl he'd seen talking to Mittens. This party grew more and more odd by the minute. During the remainder of the evening, Brad watched the beautiful, quiet girl by the orchestra. She was asked to dance several times, but never again accepted. She seemed not to be able to decide whether she belonged at the party at all.

Brad enjoyed a dance as much as the next man, but the company at the Rogers' made him uneasy. So as the party began to break up, he was relieved. And when Jane asked if they could leave with the first departing guests, he was even happier. They walked down the street to her home and she held his arm tightly, as if to make sure he wouldn't slip away.

"I noticed you met Bunny West," she remarked, not so offhandedly.

"I did. She's a quiet one."

"She's a beautiful girl."

"And a lousy dancer."

"You know," Jane said, "that's one thing I can

never understand. Men seem to constantly request the company of sexy young women, regardless of their skills on a dance floor."

"Amazing, isn't it," Brad agreed, Jane's playful jealousy amusing him.

As they approached her door, she turned to him. "Would you like to come in?" she asked, her eyes twinkling.

"Are you sure it's proper?" he needled her.

"Get in there, you son-of-a-bitch," Jane muttered. Brad chuckled and walked slowly up the stairs behind her. He climbed into her bed fully dressed and watched, bemused, as Jane unbuttoned her long blue gown. She wriggled now and then, twisting to free herself from the endless layers of clothing that remained. As she shed her corset and the chemise beneath it, Brad whistled appreciatively.

"You, sir," she declared, "have an annoying streak of arrogance in you."

"Self-confidence," he retorted, watching the light of a single lamp shade the contours of her body. He started to rise from the bed, unbuttoning his shirt.

"Stop," she nearly shouted at him. "Leave your clothes on. All of them."

"Even my boots?"

"Even your boots."

# Chapter 12

The next morning Spear and Lyn Loftin pored over the bank's records, searching for the section numbers and descriptions of Land Grants held by the bank. Loftin had purchased only six, not the twenty promised by the agent, and all were relatively worthless. It took some time to find them and longer still to be certain others weren't lying about, unrecorded.

Brad elected not to carry the actual documents with him during his tour of the town's land speculators. Folks didn't seem to last long when carrying Land Grant Certificates.

Spear wanted an official-looking envelope in which to transport his notes on the land holdings, so Loftin directed him to the back storage room. While searching for something to light the lamp in the tiny room, Brad heard the door close and felt something grab him. The touch lingered on him.

He relaxed. "Good morning, Wanda," he spoke into the darkness.

There was a giggle.

"Little girl, get your ass out of here before I tan it with the back of my hand."

Another giggle. Then she took his hand and slid it beneath her skirt. The soft fur and easy rocking motion startled him a bit.

"For God's sake, Wanda, stop it." He pulled his

hand from her, reached out and pushed harshly where he thought she must be. His palm found a soft, small breast. "Listen, young lady, you're too young for me, much too young." She didn't say anything and Brad didn't like talking into the room's blackness. "Hey, I mean it!" He was becoming annoyed. Just then he felt her hand groping around his groin. He backed up reflexively, tripped over a carton of something and fell to the floor. Before he knew it she was sitting on his lap.

"Stop wandering around in the dark, Bradley," she cooed.

"If you don't get off me, I'm going to tell your father."

Wanda laughed. "Daddy knows, he knows all right. He just tries not to notice." She reached for him again.

"What?"

"I said, Daddy and I have a little agreement."

"What?"

"Sure, he doesn't get in the way of my fun and I don't interrupt his."

Brad shoved the girl to the floor, stood and lit a match. He found the lamp and the room brightened.

"You know about . . ."

"Virginia? Sure."

"Oh, brother."

"I think most of the town knows," Wanda spoke casually. "Mama probably knows, too, but she doesn't talk about it. Just drinks a lot. How about a quick one standing up?"

Brad grabbed the first envelope he saw and slid past the girl out the door. As he left the bank, he wondered if Lyn really knew what a hellion his daughter was.

Brad made his first call on the senator, walking up into the best neighborhood in town. Rogers waved him into the library, a small room that smelled of leather and cigar smoke. The room was immaculate, though. Volumes of classics bound in leather stood on the shelves lining the walls. To one side stood the senator's desk, surrounded by plush, red-leather chairs.

"So, Mr. Spear, you've some land to sell."

"I do."

"Do you have the section numbers and legal descriptions of the parcels?"

"Not all of them, no. I have a few with me now and the balance will be released tomorrow, I believe."

"Let's have a look."

For the next twenty minutes, they read through the list and found the land sections in question on a large map of Nevada hanging on the library wall. Two sections were just outside of town and another two miles farther north. They lay near the railroad's right of way. The other three were sprinkled in the back country. Rogers seemed disinterested in each as it was located, quickly dismissing the sections as soon as he found them on his map.

"Hmmmph," the senator snorted. "Too bad. Nothing here that interests me. But when you've got the others, bring them around."

Brad thought to himself that the man was in search of a very specific piece of property. "Well, Senator, I'm aiming to sell the whole lot at once. If there's nothing here for you, then I guess that closes you out."

"Not necessarily," Rogers corrected. "I'd be willing to buy the lot for a good section or two."

"I'll remember that, sir," Brad said. They exchanged a few pleasantries, the agent commending Rogers on his party the night before, and Spear left the house. He marched straight to the center of town, across the street from Brockington's.

He fingered the knife in his pocket and checked the chambers of his revolver. Brad settled the weapon lightly into his holster, leaving his coat unbuttoned in case he had to retrieve it quickly. With a shrug, he crossed the street and knocked on Brockington's door. Not waiting for an answer, he walked into the front hallway.

Brockington stuck his head out of his office. "Good morning, Mr. Spear. Could you have a seat? I have a patient in my office." Brad sat, watching the landing at the head of the stairs above him and paying close attention to the doctor's office door. The house was quiet, except for the murmuring that came from Brockington's office, and Brad's anxiousness subsided.

"Come in, come in," Brockington waved with a smile. "Do you have the certificates with you?"

"No, just their descriptions, and only six have been released so far."

"What a shame. Ah well, let's see what you have . . ." Brockington unrolled a map essentially identical to the one Rogers had on his wall. The doctor's had large areas of the map shaded in red and blue, however, and one small portion near the railroad's right of way was colored yellow. As with the senator, none of the plots offered were of interest to Brockington. "These aren't the quality sections I'm looking for, really. I could make only a nominal bid on them. But I'm interested in any others you have."

Brad nodded as the doctor rolled up his map. "I'll remember," he said.

The scene repeated itself nearly everywhere Spear visited. One rancher scoffed at the offering, explaining what barren country was involved. "Gulches and riverbeds worth nothin'," he muttered. Judge Thorpe studied each certificate's identification carefully, if quickly, and sent Brad on his way. Absolutely no one made an offer on any of the land.

By noon, the agent was tired. His feet were sore. It

was cold. His neck hurt from resisting the urge to blow
holes in several of the men he'd talked to. Those that
were involved in the bank burglary were slick, frustratingly slick. And those that weren't treated him like a
peddler, a messenger sent from a troubled bank to
raise a few extra dollars. Both the oily graciousness of
one group and the condescending rejection of the other
wore on him.

Carlotta was furious. She stood in the open double
doors of The Mammoth Saloon, cold air pouring into
the room. Her tight fists planted firmly on her hips, the
woman's dark eyes flashed about, searching the upturned faces of the men eating and drinking inside. She
wore a black hat with a stiff, flat brim, a buckskin
jacket that had seen more than its share of foul
weather and chaps over worn corduroy slacks. Even
dressed in a man's clothing, she was a striking woman.
The bridge of her nose merged smoothly with her forehead, arching into dark, thin eyebrows above her piercing gaze. Her olive skin and long legs, the fine line of
her dark lips and thin wrists all suggested a delicate
woman. But her posture, the set of her jaw and the
natural way her .44 hung against her hip told a different tale. It seemed to those looking in surprise at Carlotta that she was the sort of woman one ought not to
anger.

"Hey! Close the door!" Sandy, the bartender, bellowed.

Ignoring him, Carlotta strode to the middle of the
room. One of the barmaids shut out the cold behind
her.

"Jebediah!" Carlotta called, her voice not loud but
filling the room.

Leaning against a wall at the far end of the bar,
Jebediah Jones was apparently concentrating on his

beer. His long fur coat hung on a hook behind his head, his rifle propped at his feet. The intricate bead-work across the front of his shirt and his long, white hair would have made him obvious were it not for the deep shadows at the back of the room.

"Girl, you making a fuss again?" he seemed to be identifying himself as much as asking a question. The fiery young woman marched the length of the bar, two miners who towered above her standing aside in mock terror as she bore down on Jeb.

"Want a beer?" Jeb asked, amused, intentionally prodding her.

"You bastard," she hissed.

"Now settle right here," Jeb patted the stool beside him, "and we'll talk this over." The old man then leaned and kissed the girl on the cheek.

"Bastard."

The clatter of lunch plates resumed shortly after Carlotta took a seat. And for a few minutes, Jeb's predicament became the topic of some speculation around the room. Most of the young men thought Jeb a little old to be horsing around with such a young girl, but the older miners disagreed. There was much shaking of heads, a little laughter and a general feeling of admiration for the old guy. Soon, steaming steaks and pitchers of beer turned the room's attention to other matters.

"Sandy," Jeb called down the bar, "two beers, one for me and one for the, uh, lady."

"If you think I'm about to cool off over a beer, Jebediah Jones, you got another thing coming."

"I'm only trying to slow the attack is all. Now sit still and be quiet." The beers arrived and Jeb slid two nickels across the bar.

Carlotta pursed her lips and took the hat from her head. As she did so, great black cascades of hair fell from under it. Straight and shining, it reached her waist. There was a single, gold loop piercing one ear lobe.

"Jeb," she sighed.

"Yup?"

"You damn near got me locked up this time."

"If you'd mind your own business, find some fella and stay off my trail, that sort of trouble would move around you."

"Shut up, old man."

Jeb sipped his beer awkwardly, his smile so insistent it made it difficult to swallow. "The son-of-a-bitch stole my horse," he muttered.

"The son-of-a-bitch was a Federal Marshal, Jeb, and he impounded it. All you had to do was pay for the busted chairs and window."

"I didn't start that brouhaha."

"Hardly matters, does it? Fact is, you're decidedly unwelcome in Eureka."

"Not much of a place anyway."

"And you owe me a rifle and a pair of boots."

"What?"

"Marshal took 'em to make good on the horse you stole."

"Stole? Goddamn! That's my horse we're talking about. How the hell can anybody accuse a man of stealing his own horse?"

"And, just so you know, the fella whose skull you creased won't be too pleased to see you next go around."

"Serves him right, he wouldn't give me my horse."

"Jebediah Jones," she'd nearly finished her beer, "you are the stupidest, cussedest old man I know."

"Want another beer?"

"Yup."

Their argument had apparently ended. And while neither seemed the slightest bit interested in the other's views, they had made a tentative kind of peace. It was as though they had rehearsed the conversation so many times before that the substance of it hardly mattered. Jeb put his arm around Carlotta and her head fell to his shoulder.

"Been all right, girl?"

"All right."

"Good."

They sat, neither speaking, neither knowing quite what to say, until the crusty prospector Elephant Osborne joined them. He was wearing a strange-looking fur hat that perched on his head, partly covering his ears. It made the scraggly locks that poked from under it look all the more disheveled.

"This that daughter of your'n you think so highly of?" he asked Jeb.

"This is her, Elephant. Carlotta, this is Elephant Osborne, a prospector who ended up with more stories than money." She shook his hand.

"Alls I want to know, Jeb," the prospector grinned, "is where she got the mean streak?"

"Jeb?" Carlotta looked at him, her eyes narrowed. "Have you been making trouble here, too?"

"Blew a hole in some guy just the other day, ma'am." Elephant seemed genuinely pleased with his contribution to the situation, as though he were stoking a fire, smiling at the sparks that cracked and hissed from green wood. Elephant liked Jebediah, not only because they were both older men, but because the railroad man never seemed to waste a movement or a word. Elephant, the world traveler, the storyteller, the lost soul and happy loser, radiated energy. A peppery sort, he could talk forever. His life, through the interesting eye of his memory, was filled with quirky, oddball, ridiculous stuff that it tickled him to recall. He'd spread his heat all over the place, squandering it relentlessly, but never running out. And so he liked Jebediah, a man whose words and actions were so sparse, so lean, they were almost invisible. Jebediah was remarkable to Elephant.

"Kill him?" she asked.

"Extremely dead, right over there," Elephant pointed.

"Why'd you go and do that, Jeb?" Carlotta's voice was mixed with anger and resignation.

"He knifed a perfectly harmless sort of fella. Then ran for it. Didn't seem right to me."

Elephant laughed heartily, his red cheeks nearly rising to his eyes. Someday, he thought, this would make a great story. He ordered himself a beer, took off his hat and settled onto the stool next to Carlotta. Sandwiched there between them, she thought herself as fortunate as any woman alive.

Carlotta Jones was Jebediah's only child. Her mother was a Mexican whom Jeb had married when he was forty. She'd made a home for them in Texas, investing Jeb's considerable pay in land and cows. An illiterate beauty from an impoverished family, she had seized the opportunity with extraordinary energy. During the first sixteen years of Carlotta's life, the ranch had grown and prospered. Jebediah, of course, was rarely there. He wintered at the ranch, enjoying his daughter's glee and his wife's love. Though twenty years his junior, she was devoted to him.

She died of pneumonia. And her loss twisted something inside Jones' middle. It took what he thought to be the shape of his life, its rounded, full dimensions and strung them out. There wasn't an end for him any longer, a stopping place had disappeared, and so he turned into a man who passed from one place to another, not wandering, but moving all the time. And, Carlotta followed him, everywhere. She dogged him, the image of her mother, as though she could protect him. He argued with her, naturally. Tried to convince her to move East, pleaded with her to settle down, find a man, let him go. But she wouldn't.

Spear entered The Mammoth sick to death of the little squares and numbers that covered maps, tired of getting nowhere in his search for an explanation to the Land Grant Certificate craze. He scanned the room briefly, out of habit searching for a suspicious stare or nervous hand near a side arm. But he didn't expect to find anyone hunting for him. He was easy to find.

Walking to the bar, he waved at Sandy. "Whiskey and a beer."

Elephant recognized Brad first and rapped on the bar with a nickel to get his attention.

"Well, don't you look hangdog today. You hung over or down on your luck?" he asked. Brad downed the shot of whiskey and picked up his beer. As he walked toward the storyteller, he noticed Jeb and then stopped short, literally stunned by the strikingly beautiful woman sitting between the old men.

"Sore feet, Elephant," Brad said. "Either of you two going to introduce me to this young lady?"

Though Jebediah had seen scores of men stand slightly awed by his daughter's beauty, it always made him feel good. "Carlotta, this is Brad Spear, a Pinkerton out of San Francisco," Jeb explained.

"Pleased to me you, Mr. Spear," her quick, sharp appraisal of the agent almost stinging him.

"This here fella saved your daddy a slug, I reckon," Elephant offered, still stirring sparks into the air.

"Your daughter, Jeb?" Spear asked.

"Sure is, and mean, too. Watch yourself," Jebediah nearly smiled, but thought better of it.

"You help Jeb out of a jam?" Carlotta asked.

"Maybe. It's hard to say. Seemed so at the time," Brad didn't want to make too much of the incident since he wasn't sure what Jeb had told his daughter. Elephant wasn't nearly so concerned. He went through the whole story, filling Carlotta's ear as she watched Brad drink his beer. At last, having embellished the tale to such an extent that neither Brad nor Jeb quite recognized it, he stopped.

Spear hadn't been paying much attention to the story and didn't acknowledge its end. He was stumped.

"Not getting very far, are ya?" Jeb suggested.

"Nope," Brad admitted, not wanting to describe his frustration.

"Mind if I ask?" Jeb probed as politely as he knew how.

"Ask away."

"You know who robbed the bank?"

"Yup."

"Then what's the problem?"

"Haven't any idea why, at least not a real idea."

"For a bright young fella, you're sorta stupid," Jeb said, expressionless. Brad was, at this point, inclined to agree. "Seems plain as the nose on your face that whoever done it wanted what was in there."

Brad smiled. True, he thought, or what they hoped was in there. What they thought was in there. He knew it had to do with the land, but what land and why?

"Elephant, what happens when the mines close down in this state?" Brad was wondering if state funds or federal subsidies or railroad money was somehow involved in the special interest being paid to land along the railroad's right of way.

"There'll be new mines." Elephant had lived so long on that faith it was impossible for him to abandon it. "If'n they're not here, they'll be somewhere else."

Brad wondered. If Jebediah was right, it all had to end sometime. Perhaps soon.

"There's plenty of ore left, Spear," Elephant continued. "Jest we ain't found it yet. But it's out there, mountains of it." His eyes took on a glazed appearance, as though he were reciting the terms of a contract that bound him forever. "Where it ain't thought to be, you'll find it, where you looked but didn't search, it's there, where folds never go, where they're stumbling as we talk, where there's stones that ain't been dug, it's there."

Jebediah shook his head. "You're a damn fool, old man," he said.

Elephant couldn't be dislodged. He considered undiscovered wealth an article of faith. He had been a prospector so long that the absolute truth of possible riches couldn't be denied.

Carlotta looked at Elephant, sorry for the old man. "And what if you never find it?"

"Can't do anything about that, miss. Discoverin' a strike just sorta happens, like an accident. All you can do is look."

For some reason, the baffling old man with a thousand stories made perfect sense to Brad. There must, of course, be more silver hidden in Nevada, or Utah or somewhere.

"Ya see, Miss Carlotta," Elephant went on, "ya just git ya a map and start in on the slopes. It takes . . ."

"What?" Brad interrupted.

"The slopes, ya walk 'em, one foot low and one foot high . . ."

"No, you said maps."

"Ya gotta have yourself a map, boy," Elephant explained to Brad as though surprised by the agent's ignorance.

All of a sudden it made perfect sense. The Land Grant Certificates made sense, the maps and the burglary and the poisonings, all of it. So obvious, he'd missed it. There *was* more silver, or gold, or something, in Nevada. And they'd found it. They'd made a strike, probably a big one, but didn't own the land it sat on. And unlike the early days of prospecting in Nevada, a lucky prospector couldn't simply claim his find. Huge stretches of the state had been subdivided by the railroad, the parcels were owned by someone. Almost certainly purchased for a few dollars, pennies an acre. Incredible. Somebody owned a silver mine and didn't know it. And those who knew where it was were trying to steal the Land Grant Certificates that would control the ore.

Brad reached across the bar and kissed Carlotta on the forehead. "Hot damn!" he shouted. Jebediah looked at the agent as though he'd lost his mind.

"Elephant, you lunatic, you hit on it."

"I did?"

"Yup."

"Hit on what?"

"The strike," Brad lowered his voice. The odd trio looked at him askance. "There's been a strike, a big one, and I know roughly where it is." Brad was rambling, talking to himself while picturing the yellow squares on Brockington's map. "Northwest, near the railroad's right of way, somewhere in the middle of four thousand acres of nothing."

"Are you out of your skull?" Jebediah asked.

Brad's mind raced. Pinpointing the location of the mine site would be difficult. It was unlikely he could follow Brockington or Dufond or anyone there without being seen. And he might look forever in the vast, barren hills to the north without wandering up the right canyon. Still, he had to locate the place, identify the serial number of the Land Grant in question and then see to it that the news was published. Whatever lucky son-of-a-bitch owned that hunk of nowhere was about to become a very rich man.

"Common ailment 'mongst newcomers to the business," Elephant remarked. "Gone loco thinkin' he's a-knowin' somethin' from a dream. Common ailment."

"Elephant, you want to take a few days' ride with me?" Brad asked.

"In this cold?"

"Elephant, Jebediah, listen to me. I need your help. The bank in town was robbed so that the deed to a bit of land north of here could be stolen. Silver's been discovered on that land, but I don't know exactly where. And I'm not sure how to look for it. I know roughly where it is, I can show you on a map . . ."

"You're asking us to wander around in the cold . . ."

"Yup," Brad responded quickly to Jebediah's unfinished question.

"You outfittin' the lot of us?" Elephant asked.

"I am."

"Gonna cost ya a bunch."

"Now hold up there, I ain't said nothing about going along with all this," Jeb was wondering if Elephant had somehow warped Spear's mind.

"I'll pay for everything, Pinkerton'll pay."

"I need new boots and a new rifle," Carlotta interrupted, a hard, determined stare bearing down on Jeb.

"Well?" Spear asked.

Jebediah thought the whole thing sounded a little foolish. But he owed Spear one, even if he wasn't about to admit it. "Best get started," he said, finishing his beer.

"Ha!" Elephant fairly exploded.

"Good boots," Carlotta added.

Spear had given Jebediah a hundred dollars, more than enough to buy what they needed. There had been some conversation about Carlotta not really needing boots, but Brad had insisted. He'd given her fifty dollars for shoes and a rifle. Jebediah swore at him, complaining about the wastefulness of getting fancy boots muddy on the trail. But his protest hadn't been particularly sincere, or long-lived. Carlotta was tickled with the windfall and Spear didn't seem to mind, so Jeb went along.

As Brad approached his room at the Nevada House, he noticed once again that the door was ajar. Pattie, he thought. This was getting ridiculous. He had work to do. He entered the room and found it empty. The agent stood puzzled, scratching his beard and then heard a footstep behind him. His quick turn was interrupted by a jarring tackle from behind. Brad was propelled forward, one set of arms wrapped around his knees, another circling his shoulders. As he was hurled to the floor he thought, "Mistake." Then the butt of a .44 slammed against his head, just behind his ear, and everything went black.

Brad came to briefly when the buggy that carried him lurched across a small log. The harsh daylight pained his eyes, and when he reached up to shield them, he realized he was trussed like a calf. His head hurt. The buggy bounced again and he rolled against the hard floor of the buckboard. He closed his eyes and was soon unconscious again. The next time he awoke he was being half-carried and half-dragged through a large, wooden gate.

He was deposited on the ground and heard the creak of old hinges and the rattle of a steel latch closing. Brad struggled against the ropes that tied him, but couldn't move.

As he lay on the ground, trying to focus his eyes, several figures approached and began picking at his jacket. Brad sorted out the bodies and realized that the hands poking and scratching him belonged to a crew of haggard old women. Still groggy, he was unable to dis-

cern just what they were trying to do. But he soon felt
his hands being untied, then felt his jacket disappear.
In a moment a half-dozen hands were prying at the
buttons of his shirt. What the devil was going on?

A bearded man sauntered up, shooed the women
away and squatted beside Spear. "Can you stand?" he
said. "We better move you away from here before
them vultures pick you clean. What's your name, young
fella?"

Brad stared at the man as intently as his fogged
brain would allow. He was unwashed and unshaved,
wore a dirty work shirt and, like Brad, had no coat
against the Nevada cold. Brad tried to stand but, his
feet still tied, couldn't. The man bent and loosened his
bonds. He would have to trust this guy, Brad thought.
At this point it was clear that he had little choice.

"Welcome to Fetterman's Asylum," the man said.

Brad groaned and rolled to his seat, his head in his
hands. When he looked up, he had an audience of
nearly two dozen half-clothed men and women. Most
were pale and thin. Many sported vacuous expressions,
the result of starvation or dementia or both. The unwashed man who had helped him seemed healthy and
sane by comparison.

"I don't belong here," Brad spoke wearily.

The man laughed. "That may be, but you sure as
hell ain't going anywhere in a hurry."

Brad looked at the man, his features distinct at last.
He was a little wild-eyed, but seemed controlled,
stable. "How long have you been here?" the agent inquired.

"Now that's a pretty personal question coming from
a guy who won't even give out his name, isn't it?"

"Sorry," he replied. "Spear, Brad Spear."

"Pleased to meet you, Mr. Spear, although I'm not

too happy with the circumstances. My name is Big John."

"John," Brad said, shaking his hand.

"You sure don't look crazy."

"I'm not."

"Then you musta got somebody with some clout mighty sore at ya. Him?" The man pointed to the top of the barricade. Towering over Brad, expressionless, stood Pierre Dufond. Spear wondered why he hadn't simply been killed. Was this the work of Dufond's twisted mind, the most bitter revenge the defrocked priest could concoct?

"I used to work for a man with power, the governor of this fine state, as a matter of fact. But I did my job too well." Spear listened, watching Dufond's motionless stare. "I tracked some missing state money to the governor's right-hand man, to his pocket to be exact. Three weeks later I was here. Committed by a doctor, real legal and all."

"Doctor," Brad could imagine who.

"Doc Brockington's his name. Comes around here now and then to see what he can pick from this dung heap. That's about the only way anybody ever gets out alive."

"Brockington," Brad muttered, still watching Dufond.

"You know the good sawbones?"

Brad nodded and examined the long log wall that closed in the box canyon. He looked at the buildings, at the men and women wandering around aimlessly and then back at the cliff face. "Anybody ever climb out?"

"Not that I know of. The guards may be drunk most of the time, but they got plenty of time to reload while folks are trying to inch their way up those rocks. Those that don't get shot fall anyway."

"What about the cave?" Brad asked, pointing to the mine shaft.

Big John snorted. "That's what's left of the old silver mine. Not a big layout, really. They closed off all the old shafts except one, so it's just the tunnels and drifts on one level. Hell of a good place to get lost in. If anyone ever found a way out through there, they sure didn't come back to tell us about it."

Brad felt his head throb. "How long you been here, Big John?"

"I'm coming up on my third winter. Most folks don't last that long, but I've managed to put together a kind of group. It's the only way to make a go of it. We're sane, most of us, leastwise we were when we got here . . ."

Brad and Big John took a slow tour of the compound, passing the barracks to the far end of the wooden fence where it butted against a sheer facing wall thirty feet high and as smooth as glass. A knife blade wouldn't fit between the timbers and the rock.

"Somebody planned this place pretty well," Spear remarked. "You want out?"

"Everybody wants out. I'm for a bottle and a woman more than you can think."

"Have you tried?"

"Not me. There's no logical way to go about it . . . 'course that hasn't stopped folks in here from trying." Big John pointed out the three guards spread across the top of the fence. Dufond was gone. "And there's three roving around in here all the time."

"Anybody ever grab a gun from one of 'em?"

"Once or twice, that I know about. Never came to anything."

They heard a horrible screeching behind them. A woman sat on the ground, howling for no apparent reason. A guard walked over and yelled at her to shut off the noise. She continued to shriek and clutched the startled guard around his knees. He tried to kick her away at first and, failing that, panicked. In an effort to his shotgun. It went off, blasting away half her head.

"Goddamn bitch wouldn't let go," the man screamed as two other guards ran up, their weapons leveled at the onlookers. People gawked, riveted to the bloody scene. "Move it!" one of the guards shouted with a menacing wave of his shotgun. "Scatter!"

As they were dispersing, Brad felt a rough hand on his shoulder. "You, come over here," the guard ordered. "We need a big one to tote this mess." Big John offered Brad a subtle nod, telling him he'd better do as he was told. "Pick her up and follow me." Spear lifted the woman's lifeless body and threw it over his shoulder. She didn't weigh eighty pounds.

At the mouth of the mine, the three guards held a conference. One remained at the mine entrance and the two others escorted Brad into the darkness, a small coal oil lantern leading the way. After about five minutes of plodding, half-tripping most of the way, the path came to a halt next to a shaft that dropped into blackness. A small railing barred the way. "Pitch the be rid of her, he butted the woman with the barrel of old hag over the side," one man ordered.

Spear lifted the body over the railing and let it fall. He suspected it was as good a burial as most folks got around Fetterman's. He waited and then spoke to the guard holding the lantern. "I didn't hear the body hit bottom. It must have hung up on the side of the shaft."

"Naaah," the guard answered, "that's four hundred feet down. Listen now, soon she'll hit . . ." There was a faint, distant thud. The three men turned, one preceding Spear with the light, the other behind him with a shotgun, and retraced their route.

"God, I hate it in here," one muttered.

"Yeah," his coworker agreed.

Night fell on Fetterman's in a way different from any Brad had ever known. The raucous sounds of drunks in bars, the music and laughter of parties and the bustle of a day coming to an end often filled a city at dusk. But the steady movement of an evening quiets the world. However gradually, night brings silence. But the cries and whispers, the interrupted nightmares and brutal assaults of Fetterman's grew constantly louder as darkness fell. This weird corner of the world erupted at night into a battle ground of fear and violence.

Brad sat near the compound's only working stove, trying to keep warm. Big John and two other disheveled men huddled nearby, shoulder to shoulder, eating their spare rations of bread. All drank from a barrel of water in the middle of the barracks that had two ladles chained to it.

A woman wrapped in a heavy shawl entered the room. She nodded to Big John and grinned, her mouth almost toothless. The man stood, stuffing the last of his meal into his mouth and walked toward the door.

"What's up?" Spear asked.

"Quiet," John glared at him, his dark eyes filled with a kind of desperate warning Brad had never seen before. The agent walked quickly to him, grabbing his arm before the inmate could escape into the night. Big John looked at the powerful agent and pulled his arm free. "Be very quiet, friend. I'll kill you if we're discovered."

The two men slipped from the room and crept along the side of the building like field mice hugging walls in the dark. In the shadow at one side of the canyon John stopped, peering at the silhouetted figures at the stockade's guard stations. The night sky was bright and the men were easy to see. Then John stole away, almost losing Spear in the darkness. The agent barely managed to follow, perplexed, lost.

At the back of the canyon, at a point farthest from the guards, John stood, looking up at the rim of their prison's crater. They waited there, hidden behind a boulder, for what seemed hours. Finally, a pebble fell from above. Spear looked up, amazed. Twenty-five feet above, his head craning over the side of the canyon's walls, grinned the desk clerk from the Nevada House Hotel. His earmuffs stood away from his head, his scarf dangled and his mittens held a package. The carefully wrapped bundle fell, drifting toward them, and John stood quickly. He caught the package and disappeared behind the boulder again. Brad's eyes flew to the top of the canyon wall, a cry for help forming on his lips. But Mittens had withdrawn, retreated into the night even before his gift found John's waiting arms.

Hunkered around the stove once again, Brad watched the men open their bundle as though it contained fine crystal. Slowly, as though they feared they might destroy it with a single rough movement, they unwrapped the brown paper and burned both it and the string in the stove. Inside they found cheese, dried slices of apple, beef jerky and strips of fried bacon. Like a priest at an alter, John divided the food into two precisely equal piles. He then wrapped one portion in a rag, handed it to a companion and turned to Brad.

"Half to the other barracks." Brad understood. The few who were strong and sane maintained themselves with the extra food that fell from the sky at the back end of the canyon. The women's group in one building, the men in another. He also soon understood that the cruel necessities of the place meant that the weak or insane went hungry.

Brad chewed the small square of cheese slowly, tasting it. "I know the man in mittens," he said simply.

"And he knows you," John handed him a tiny square of paper. On it was written "I will help, Spear. Jebediah knows."

# Chapter 13

Jebediah crouched behind an outcropping of sandstone. The moon was full, shedding its pale white light all along the rim of the canyon. Below, he could see smoke trailing from a chimney and hear the moans and screams of men and women whose torment made his stomach churn. The strange, thin man in mittens whose mind had been captured by the cold knelt behind Jeb, shivering, breathing on his neck.

Jeb didn't like the situation. Spear had been held in the compound for a day and a half. The Pinkerton might well be dead by now. Jeb had the advantage of high ground and the element of surprise on his side. But he had come to Fetterman's with a broken-down prospector, a lunatic who wore mittens indoors, and a girl. His daughter, a crack shot, but a girl nonetheless. Jeb cradled his buffalo rifle in his hands. Soon, he thought.

Consarned if'n this wasn't the peculiarest fix he'd seen in a spell, Elephant thought. He was nervous, his palms sweating. The miner was positioned no more than forty feet from a shotgun-toting guard atop the stockade. The guard was drunk and cold, stamping his feet to stay warm. And he had that shotgun. Damned peculiar, he thought.

"Least I'm packing a punch," Elephant mumbled to himself. "Two six-guns and a rifle." He glanced down at the pistols once again, reassured by them. And he aimed carefully, slowly, at the guard, drawing a bead on him for the sixth time in as many minutes. "Pretty soon," he said to himself.

Carlotta was ready. She lay on her belly squinting into the hole below, listening to the suffering it held. Worse than death, she thought. She fingered the two bottles in her hand, listening to the kerosene in them slosh from side to side. She could smell the rag wicks and feel the kerosene slippery on her fingers. Her pistol lay on the ground nearby.

The cabin which stood just outside the stockade was directly below her. Sparks blew from its stovepipe and men laughed inside. A man walked out the front door of the place, took a few strides and then urinated on the ground. Liquor, she thought. Good. She watched patiently as the man fumbled with his trousers and then, still buttoning them, returned to the cabin. She'd decided. The first bottle would fly unlit. Maybe she could hit the stovepipe with it. If not, the second would follow, burning.

Watching for it, Jebediah saw the black object arch through the air. He heard the sound of breaking glass, but saw no flames. His heart pounded. What was that girl doing? Then the second bottle flew, flames pouring from it. It hit the cabin and exploded, black smoke billowing into the air.

The rim of the canyon roared gunfire. Jeb unloaded his buffalo rifle's only shell into the guard at the center of the log wall, then picked up a .44 and leveled it at the stockade. He was aiming at the guard that Elephant was assigned when the man flew from his perch, tumbling in the air. Then the prospector seemed to go berserk. Two six-guns flashed from his position, the bright yellow flame of each shot following rapidly one after another. His fire was relentless, withering. And Carlotta was shooting, her pistol more controlled, each shot aimed, but there was a frenzy to her as well.

One guard still stood on the stockade. His silhouette turned toward Elephant and two thunderous explosions echoed down the canyon. Jeb emptied his pistol in the general direction of the man, knowing his weapon was nearly useless at such a range. Then he turned to his buffalo gun and began the slow process of reloading.

Looking up, he saw Elephant standing in the moonlight at the edge of the canyon. His hat was gone and blood ran down one side of his head. The old man stood bellowing, a wordless, furious cry of anger and pain, both pistols blazing in his hands. The last guard fell under his fire, lying doubled across the top of the stockade, and still Elephant fired on him. Then, his guns emptied into the corpse, the prospector disappeared from sight. Dead or reloading, Jeb thought.

Carlotta continued her steady barrage. Jeb couldn't see her and hoped that no one else could, either. The cabin burned, its flames licking the stockade, brightening the scene as though it were noon. Inside the asylum men and women ran about aimlessly, hiding, screaming, confused. Some scrambled toward the mine shaft, seeking shelter. Others huddled together in open spaces, transfixed by the flames. A few beat on the still-locked gate, trying to open it.

Jebediah turned his rifle on the stockade wall. While his daughter kept firing on targets concealed from Jeb by the stockade, he searched the compound for signs of Spear. Then Elephant opened fire again.

Jeb watched, stunned, as the gate opened. Through it raced a man carrying a shotgun, his clothes burning. The guard turned, raised the weapon and fired both barrels into the air near Elephant. Carlotta shot him and he managed two crippled strides before falling to the ground. He lay there, motionless, burning.

Through the open gate Jeb saw men running from the burning cabin, some with their clothes aflame, others shooting randomly toward the rim of the canyon. Even burning, those who were able to fired into the air, searching for their tormentors. And all the while, the prospector and his daughter kept up their assault, killing one man after another with their hail of bullets.

Two men crouched beside the gate, their backs to each other, pumping shells into the night. Jeb aimed slowly, squeezed the trigger, heard the hiss of powder and then the sudden explosion of his rifle. The force of the shell sent one of the two rolling across the ground. His partner turned, stunned by the fire from an unexpected source and then ran from the compound. Carlotta's single shot caught him in the back. He fell, wounded, and kicked senselessly on the ground.

Jeb reloaded his rifle yet again. But before he had done so, Carlotta appeared at his side. Her face gleamed with perspiration, a few long, dark locks of her hair clinging to her brow.

"Elephant's hit," she screamed.

"Get down," Jeb ordered, pulling her to the ground beside him. Jebediah looked toward the prospector's position. He neither saw nor heard a thing. And it seemed that all the drunken wardens had been killed or wounded. Only the sound of crackling wooden shingles and logs splitting in the heat came from beyond the stockade.

But the tumult in the compound was reaching a kind of inhuman crescendo. Two women, their arms raised

over their heads, raced through the open gate. Ten
yards beyond it one tripped and fell, the other stopping
to lift her. And a rifle shot cracked, killing the standing
figure. At least one crazed guard remained, hidden
somewhere, barring the exit.

Jeb heard the stumbling run of an injured man and
then saw Elephant approaching through the weird,
flickering light of the fire. He held a bandana to the
side of his head, his hand and wrist coated with blood.

"Lost the ear," he said.

"Oh, God!" Carlotta ran to him.

An inmate, hunchbacked and limping, ran to the
open gate. The unseen rifleman felled him instantly.

Carlotta pulled the bandana from Elephant's head,
turned and vomited. Wiping her mouth with a sleeve,
she returned to him, dabbing gently at the torn flesh at
the side of his head.

Jebediah stood, enraged by the madness around him,
and roared into the compound. "Spear!" For all the
force of his voice, it was clear that he couldn't be
heard above the bedlam below. Spear was dead, or hiding, or held somewhere, but he surely couldn't hear
Jeb.

Out of nowhere, the tall, thin man in mittens appeared at Jeb's side. His eyes were wide in panic, his
mouth forming words without sound. Jeb had forgotten
about him, but now he stood, a long, thick rope cradled
like a child in his arms. Jeb took it from him, wound it
around a huge rock nearby and tossed the free end into
the compound. They'd come this far, there was no al-
ternative, he had to go down into the place. Jeb moved
toward the rim of the canyon, dazed by the prospect of
walking through the melee below.

"F-f-forget it, old, old, old man," Mittens stam-
mered. And before Jeb could move to stop him, the
pale figure slipped like a spider over the edge, skim-

ming hand over hand down the sheer rock cliff. Once on the ground he bolted, zigzagging through the asylum, bumping into men who wandered, looking at the fire and women who ran screaming in every direction. Finally, Mittens disappeared into one of the barracks.

"Jesus," Jeb muttered, his rifle trained on the open gate. "Where is that son-of-a-bitch?"

"Ah!" Elephant yelled.

"Sorry," Carlotta said. "But the bleeding's stopping, I think."

"Smarts, jest the same," Elephant almost laughed.

"I see him!" Jeb shouted to them. Spear was running behind Mittens, slowing his pace so as not to run up the man's back. Jeb concentrated on the gate, certain that whoever remained alive outside it would try to kill the agent. But no shots were fired, there was no movement he could detect.

At the base of the cliff Mittens climbed on Brad's back, his arms wrapped around the agent's neck, his knees clinging to his waist. Then, slowly, Spear climbed, his feet searching for toeholds. He inched his way up the rock while Jeb looked first at the opening in the burning log wall and then at the frustratingly slow progress the climber was making. After what seemed like hours, Brad approached the top and yelled to Jeb. "Pull him over," Spear demanded.

Jeb grabbed the frail man and pulled at him, but he wouldn't let go of Spear.

"Pull him," Brad shouted.

"He won't let go!"

"Then pull on me, for Christ's sake."

Jeb grabbed the agent's hand, clasped it in both of his own and hauled for all he was worth. The two men rolled to the ground above, Mittens still holding onto

Spear. They lay there, exhausted. Brad patted the man's arm for a moment and was released.

"Where the hell were you?" Jeb asked.

"They wanted to rush the gate," Brad replied, catching his breath. "I had to hold them, there was no way."

"There's one still out there, I figure," Jeb said.

"I saw."

"What do you think?"

"Don't know." They sat silently for a moment, no one certain what should happen next. Mittens stood, watching the group.

"It's worth a try," Brad said, half to himself. He put his hand on Jebediah's rifle and glanced at the old man's face. Jeb nodded.

Spear ran along the rim of the canyon until he was even with the stockade, then disappeared, retreating into the darkness. Elephant groaned as Carlotta wrapped his head, tying a strip of shirt around his forehead to hold a makeshift bandage in place. Finished, finally, she leaned against a rock, staring into the sky. The sounds from the compound rang in her ears, still frenzied, pained, chaotic. But there was a dullness to the cries as the inmates grew tired below her.

The great, full blast of the buffalo gun rang through the night. There was no other sound, no shot or cry, nothing.

Minutes later Spear appeared, walking in full view only feet from the edge of the canyon. A filthy, bearded man climbed onto the roof of one barracks building and waved frantically at Brad, who returned the wave by raising Jebediah Jones' buffalo rifle over his head.

Lyn Loftin hated this. He paced outside the Silver Lady mine's main office while the doctor worked to mend what was left of Elephant Osborne's ear. The sun was beginning to throw the faintest blush of pale red along the horizon as he walked back and forth, his hands clasped behind him. He watched the dim light spread through the cloudless sky and turned to see it reflected bright and clear off the peaks of mountains to the west. It was early morning, the first hint of the day to come glowing like embers in the distance. Loftin hated this.

Men were dead, more would surely die, and an aged prospector, a good-humored drinking companion from The Mammoth Saloon had somehow found himself in the middle. The sight of his head, raw with buckshot wounds, filled the banker with loathing. It wasn't worth all this, he thought.

Jebediah sat on a bench, cleaning his rifle. Carlotta picked at the mud which caked her new boots. And Spear stood, caged fury building in him. The agent imagined the healthy inmates traveling away from Silver City, headed in small groups toward worlds where they might be anonymous. And he saw the sick, the demented and the weak lost in the hills, dying there. None in the small group spoke.

Lady Jane came through the door with a smile on her face. Not happy, but pleased. "He hears just fine out of it," she reported. "It isn't pretty, but he hears perfectly."

No one spoke.

Elephant walked through the door grinning like a ninny. Half his head had been shaved and then wrapped, the white gauze of sterile bandages circling his skull.

"Mornin', folks," he greeted the quiet group.

"Mornin', Elephant," Brad answered, his voice thick with regret. Elephant looked at them, puzzled by their melancholy attitude, thinking to himself that they certainly looked like a sorry bunch, considering how well they'd done.

"Hey," he shouted at them, "what's with you?"

Heads turned his way but no one looked at him for long, their eyes falling to the guns they held, their boots or the sunrise glowing in the distance.

"Hey, I'd a-thought we'd celebrate a bit. I mean, we musta kilt a hundred of 'em."

Jeb shook his head, the old liar still pumping stories by the gallon.

"Yeah, a hundred, easy," Elephant continued, agreeing with himself since no one else would. "But I guess we don't have time for a proper kind of blow-out party, right?"

"What?" Carlotta asked, looking at him and then turning away.

"We gotta git to it, right? We got some prospectin' to do." Elephant's eyes twinkled, cheerful but desperately trying to stir his audience.

"No, old-timer," Jeb said, his tone quiet and tired.

Elephant Osborne furrowed his brow. He thought for a moment that they were giving up, quitting. Then it occurred to him that they thought of him as damn near dead. Useless, a hindrance, an old man in the way. They meant to leave him behind! The thought stung him.

"You mean *I'm* not goin', right you old man?" the prospector stared hard at Jeb.

"You'd best mend for a while," Jebediah persisted.

"Bullshit."

"You got half your head blowed off, you old fool. You can't go riding to hell and back like that."

"Bullshit."

Loftin couldn't believe what he was hearing. It was insane enough for a professional like Spear to go in search of clearly dangerous men, but to invite an old man, a girl and a wounded prospector was inconceivable to him. He looked at Brad, his eyes pleading with the agent to take control of the situation.

"You're pretty shot up, Elephant," Brad said. "You take it easy for a while."

"I'll rest and you pack the animals."

"Don't think so." Brad meant it, they couldn't take him.

"If'n you folks take off without me, and God knows you won't know what you're doing that way, and then you go and get real lucky, you just might find the bastards what started all this, right?"

Spear nodded to Elephant.

"Then I'm gonna be there."

It was hard to argue with his reasoning, Brad thought. In fact, it was impossible. "Guess that's right," Brad figured. "You sleep, we'll get the horses ready."

"Hah!" Elephant laughed, kicking his heels and noticing that he shouldn't do that, his head swimming with the leap.

The sun still hadn't risen as Spear tried the rear door leading to Brockington's office. It was locked. He fished through his vest-pocket and pulled a long, thin length of tempered steel from it. It looked like a simple latch mechanism, one common in Western towns, and Brad knew he could pick it quickly. In moments the lock clicked, the door open. The house was quiet, everyone in it apparently asleep. Brad lit a match and put it to the lamp on the doctor's desk.

It took a few minutes to find the rolled map Spear had watched Brockington so carefully study. But it contained the information he sought. All the land grant sections surrounding Silver City were blocked off in one of three colors. He counted forty-two red sections, twelve blue ones and six that were yellow. Which were which? What did it mean? The yellow sections were all in a small area, adjacent to one another. The others alternated, random blotches of red and blue spreading across the paper.

Suddenly, the door behind the agent opened. He whirled, drawing his pistol, instantly afraid he was too late. But it was the beautiful young woman he'd met at the dance, Bunny West. She wore only a thin nightgown that dropped to her knees. She stared straight ahead as though she didn't see him.

"Please don't hurt me anymore," she pleaded. Tears filled her eyes. "I promise to be good, I'll do anything you say, honest . . ."

Just as Brad made the assumption she was sleepwalking, Bunny pulled at the thin nightgown, lifting it over her head. She stood in the middle of the room, naked, weeping.

"I'll do it, anything, *anything*." She walked up to Brad and put her arms around his neck, pressing her body against his. He looked down at her, the weird, mechanical hold she had on him startling the agent. "I won't go back to that place. Please don't make me go." She pushed herself away from Brad. "Please don't send me back to Fetterman's . . ."

Spear led the girl to the door, picking her thin chemise from the floor. She was in a daze, sleepwalking, possibly out of her mind. Brockington had control of her, that was clear, a refugee from Fetterman's who would do what she was told to stay free of the place. Brad handed her the nightgown, somewhat regretfully. She was a magnificent creature.

"Put your nightgown on, Bunny," he intoned. "And go back to your bed. You'll never see Fetterman's again. It's gone, you're free."

As the girl disappeared, Brad wondered how much

time he had before someone else wandered into the office. He opened the desk drawer in search of a pen and paper. In it he found a pile of Land Grant Certificates and a dozen bundles of newly printed United States currency. He checked the serial numbers of the bills: they were in sequence. He took ten of them from the middle of one bundle and slid them into his shirt pocket. They wouldn't be missed, not for a while at least. He could check the bank's records to learn whether they were part of the money stolen during the burglary. He looked at the map, wishing he could steal it, too. But that would tip them off. Quickly, he wrote down the plot numbers of the yellow land grant sections, rolled and replaced the map. He nearly left without blowing out the lamp, but remembered it.

As he walked away from Brockington's, Brad wondered if he selected the right color. The thought was amusing. It came down to that.

Lyn Loftin leaned back in his chair, his hands behind his head. "Brockington and Rogers I can understand," he mused, "but I thought the judge to be an honest sort. Oh well, can't ever tell. Let's have a look at those land grant section numbers."

The bank's survey maps showed the area in greater detail than any Brad had previously seen. Loftin had made personal notes on several of the grids, commenting on whether they looked like good grazing land, or whether they were too rocky to put roads through.

"Yup, that's what I thought," the banker continued. "Right in the middle of Broken Leg Gulch. We thought we had a mother lode of silver in there about ten years ago. Three of us prospected it for a while after some fella found a vein and got us all worked up. But the lode ran out after six or seven feet. I heard news of interesting ground elsewhere, so I left. Good thing, too. Nothing ever came of that place."

Loftin then reached the obvious conclusion. It was as though he'd been hit over the head with it. "Brockington must have found some silver out there!"

Brad nodded. "That's right, Lyn, and he's trying to corner all the land around it so he can set up a mine, free and clear of other possible claims. Seems he's missing a couple of Land Grant Certificates, though."

"That could be," Loftin agreed, "that might be."

"Well, then, how about we start a rumor? We talk about a strike and there'll be five hundred men up there within a few days. That ought to stir the pot."

"It would at that, Brad, but what about the doctor?"

"He's nailed," Brad handed Lyn the bills he'd taken from Brockington's desk.

"Why, these are in sequence!" Loftin exclaimed. "Fresh bills! Where'd you get these?"

"I borrowed them from a bank robber. You keep track of the new bills that come into the bank?"

Loftin's answer was to unlock his desk drawer and pull out several sheets of paper covered with neat figures, Alice Carter's handwriting. "Alice had, I mean has, the delightful task of inventorying bills we get straight from the government . . . and, no surprise to you I guess, these bills were taken from my vault." The banker looked up from the sheet of paper. "You think Brockington, Thorpe and Rogers were in on the bank burglary?"

"Well, you can be sure they weren't in here breaking down doors, but I think they put the whole thing together. Obviously hired someone to do the dirty work."

"Damn!" Loftin slammed his hand on the desk. "That really grates on me. I can handle a dirty Jasper with a gun in his hand, but when the likes of them sends hired help while my back is turned, that's more than I can stomach."

"If we're going to wrap this up, I guess I better go have a look at their strike. My fun-loving troupe and I will take a ride out to Broken Leg Gulch and see what we find."

"And while you're out there riding around," the banker said, "we let Brockington strut around town like he owns it?"

"Yes, until we get some solid evidence."

"What about these?" Loftin waved the bills in the air.

"They don't implicate Rogers or Thorpe. You want them too, don't you?"

"You bet." Loftin sighed wearily.

A half hour later, Lyn had drawn Brad a map of Broken Leg Gulch, pinpointing a few areas that he thought might contain silver. Brad wondered to himself how Elephant would take to Lyn's advice.

# Chapter 14

Tucker McGee slid two fingers under the bridle, checking it. Firm enough, he thought. He ran his hand across the horse's flank and down its hind leg. The animal turned its great black head, watching the man as he inspected the shoe. McGee nodded to himself and the horse snorted, apparently agreeing with the liveryman's appraisal.

McGee's livery was a modest establishment. Four stalls and a smithy, with a shed out back for oats and hay. Tucker owned a wagon and occasionally hauled lumber on consignment. He sold horses, shod them and now and then tended to a sick or lame animal. But his real love was in training them. And Diamond, the immense creature that now occupied his attention, was his pride and joy.

He'd taken him in trade from a farmer down on his luck. The animal, not suited to the work, was thin and weak from pulling a small wagon out of Texas. His hooves had split on the trail and had been ignored until the great black horse had become useless, barely able to walk. Tucker had swapped a mule for Diamond. Had fed and cared for him and had brought him back. Now, with top dollar offered by the Pinkerton agent, Tucker was about to let Diamond go. He was satisfied with the price and pleased with his work with the animal. But he regretted the loss.

So Tucker McGee was lingering over Diamond. He'd fed and groomed him. The horse was saddled and ready. There was nothing more to do. And still he walked around Diamond, admiring him.

Out of the corner of his eye, Tucker saw the young girl pulling the boy by the hand, running into the stall. Kids, he thought. Always lookin' for a pile of hay to mess in. Children, almost, pawin' at each other. Tucker shook his head, half-pleased with the thought of teenagers necking in his livery. He backed Diamond into a stall and walked toward his small office. No sense interruptin' 'em, he figured.

Timothy Ryan was a gangly sort of sixteen-year-old who had grown a full eight inches in less than a year. He was confused by his new-found awkwardness and perplexed by the changes that were happening to his body. He was almost a man, but not quite. Old enough, certainly big enough, but still a boy. And this crazy girl was all over him, talking much too fast.

"Hush now, Tim," Wanda whispered. "Don't want an audience, do we?"

Tim sat back in the empty stall, settling into the hay, shaking his head. In an instant she was beside him, her arms wrapped around his neck, her lips pressing his. Not quite sure what to do with his hands, he hugged her as best he could and kissed back. She wriggled, mewing to herself. God, he hoped no one found them.

Wanda moved one hand down Tim's chest to his groin. He was hard but stunned by the move, and he stopped kissing her as soon as he felt her touch. He was all knees and elbows, but she didn't care. She stroked, amazed at the size of him. He fidgeted, trying desperately to imagine what he was supposed to do.

"Damn hay's not so soft," he said to her, backing farther into the stall.

"Hmmmm," her answer wasn't very helpful and she

pursued him through the hay. She kissed him again, her mouth open, and it occurred to him that he was truly lost. He reached for her breast and it filled his hand, softer and bigger than he had imagined. "Wait," she halted him.

Wanda stood over Tim, smiling down at him. He felt embarrassed by the bulge in his trousers, but couldn't think of a way to conceal it. Then she stepped back from him, suddenly calmer, moving more slowly.

She unbuttoned her blouse deftly, moving without the impatience of the overwrought girl she had been only moments before. She seemed feline, poised, moving with the ease of a child and the grace of a cat. Sunlight slanted through the small louvered windows high in the stall and cast turning, swaying lines across her body. Her small shoulders and taut breasts seemed out of place among the rough textures of scarred wood and old tools. But however delicate, this young animal was perfectly comfortable undressing as Tim watched her.

Wanda removed her skirt quickly, pulling her bloomers to her ankles with it and then stood. Naked, she walked to the back of the stall and threw her clothes into a corner. Her firm hips and buttocks mesmerized Tim, the muscles of her thighs flexing surely, smooth and tight as she walked. He wanted to touch her, not hold her. Feel the small, tight curves of her breasts and the long, wandering shapes of her legs.

Wanda knelt beside him, took his hand and placed it on her breast. He stroked her gently, tentative, and he lingered there, fondling her. She lay down next to him as his other hand moved across her. Wanda closed her eyes and concentrated on his touch, feeling the light brush of his fingers and the chill in the air send shivers through her. She arched her back, twisted to one side, turned her hips toward him, basking in the sensation, moving without thought.

She felt the ache grow deep within her, taking hold and pulling her. She looked up at him, his eyes wide, hands wandering faster and faster across her belly, down her thighs, skirting the dark triangle she offered. Wanda's legs spread slowly, inviting him, and she felt his fingers inching up her inner thigh. She shuddered and hummed softly to herself. It felt so good, she thought. Too good, she wanted more.

She sat up quickly, startling the panting young man, her breasts bouncing in front of him. "Jesus," Tim swore. Without a word, Wanda unbuttoned his trousers as he watched, horrified, amazed, mindlessly thrilled. As she tugged at his belt, slipping his heavy woolen slacks to his knees, he sprang at her, hard and throbbing. She wrapped the fingers of one small hand around him, overwhelmed with her success.

With a deep-throated groan he rolled, climbing on her. Strong, much stronger than he looked, he pressed down, his rough shirt scratching her skin, his belt buckle dragging across her thigh. Then she felt him pushing at her, huge, blunt and impatient. Before she could gather her senses, he was in her, the pain of his haste mingling with the strange, wonderful sensation of his strong body pounding against her. She felt him tense, hurry and drive at her just as she began to settle on the feeling, just as she sensed it growing better. He was groaning, panting, holding onto her as though she might escape and moving in her quickly, too quickly.

Then he nearly stopped, suspended over her, a sound coming from him unlike anything she had ever heard. His moan frightened her and for a moment she thought he was in pain. But she felt it, the hurried surge of his release pouring into her and she knew it was over. He collapsed on her, heavy enough to make breathing difficult, and lay still.

Wanda pushed on his shoulder, not strong enough to

move him, and he eased himself off her. The combination of a deep, hidden ache, her frustration and the satisfaction of having managed it bewildered her. She felt like crying, or laughing. There was panic, an uneasy sensation that unsettled her. She looked at the boy, his forearm covering his eyes, his organ drooping, and wondered how she was going to make all this work better.

"Fix yourself, quick," she whispered.

"Oh, yeah, yeah." Tim opened his eyes, blinking at the shafts of sunlight that fell on his face.

Wanda scurried about the stall, ignoring him as she dressed. There was straw in everything. She brushed hard at her dress with the palm of her hand, angry at it for clinging to the dust of the stall. When she turned around he was gone. "Lord," she muttered.

The standard .44 caliber Colt that Jebediah had bought for Brad felt oddly light on his hip as he walked into the livery office. He wondered if he'd ever see his pistol again, remembering its heft, pondering its future. That speculation was cut short, however, by the incredibly cramped quarters of Tucker McGee's office. There wasn't enough room to stand, much less think in the space.

"Diamond's saddled and set to go," McGee reported, not looking up at the agent.

"Good," preoccupied, Brad fumbled in his pocket for the cash he owed McGee.

"You're late."

"Sorry." Spear still couldn't find his billfold.

"Fine animal you bought there. Treat him good, will ya?"

Brad looked at Tucker, noting the sorry kind of tilt to his eyes. "I will, don't worry," he reassured, handing the man sixty dollars. "All goes well, I'll sell him back to you, cheap."

"Good luck, then," Tucker said, wondering if Spear meant it.

Brad turned and strode over to the horse. He ran his hand down the animal's nose and then stroked its neck. Diamond was strong, he thought. Probably fast, too. Brad lay his saddlebags across his back and tied them in place. Time to go.

Two miles outside Silver City, the bitter cold wind bit into Spear's back. It swirled through the ragged gulches, churning sand and grit into the air so viciously that the motley group had to cover their mouths with bandanas. The wind's sting caused the horses to prance, skittish in the cold.

Elephant's mule plodded in front of them, an aged, determined animal that seemed resigned to the abuse being heaped upon him. The old man sat atop the creature like a frog on a rock. Mile after mile he croaked his complaint at the weather, the terrain, the blister forming on his backside. Step after weary step he mumbled into the wind. Elephant's mule, called Henry, turned his ears around whenever the old man spoke, listening patiently to him. While all those who traveled behind slumped in their saddles, ducking the cold, Elephant and Henry clopped along erect, indignant, feisty in the chill. Spear thought to himself that the man had a gift for moaning and bitching. And he was grateful for the drone of his voice.

Jeb, riding beside Spear, was relentless. He moved above his animal with a grace Brad thought impossible. Anticipating the misstep, watching for the rut that might trip his horse, rocking easily with the animal's gait, Jeb rode along, alert and relaxed. He had settled into his stride, Brad thought. Comfortable with that rifle cradled in his arms.

"Weather comin'," Jeb muttered.

"I see it," Brad agreed, looking at the grey clouds bearing down on them.

"You see clouds, young man. My bones feel rain, cold, driving rain."

"Great news, old-timer. Seems I keep you folks along for luck." Carlotta laughed, Brad's sarcasm mirroring her own.

They wandered through switchbacks, their animals turning into and out of the wind reluctantly, and began to climb the scrub-forested foothills, a territory littered with pines and struggling shrubs. The ground rose before them constantly, barren and dry. A land more ruined than the desert, Spear thought.

Elephant led them up the washed-out gullies of dry riverbeds that hurried down the hills. Now sandy avenues, the spring thaw would fill them with roaring water, sending foam down the side of these mountains. Brad could see, at the debris-strewn edges of these riverbeds, the evidence of spring's violence. Uprooted trees struggled to endure, their limbs bending toward the sky, their trunks leaning into the gullies. Broken rock, shattered into shards, lay at the riverbed's perimeter. Worn and broken tree limbs rested alongside the rippled sand of another season's flood. Everything seemed frozen, still, dead.

Carlotta's horse minced away the miles. A small, quick animal, it pieced its way through the rough terrain, devouring the journey tidbit by tidbit. Spear watched Carlotta, alive on the horse's back, ready, measured, patient. Though Jeb and Elephant badgered one another occasionally, Carlotta never spoke. She seemed completely absorbed by her horse's work.

The weather blew overhead quickly, dampening the

wind, giving it a cutting edge. And though there were two hours to sunset, it seemed to Brad they ought to search for shelter.

"Elephant!" he yelled into the wind. "Got a hole nearby we can put up in?"

"Think so," the old man replied, turning Henry aside. "This way."

The rest of the troupe followed Elephant over rough terrain, Spear dismounting to save Diamond the awkward load on such uneven ground. And then it started to rain. Jebediah hung a slicker over his long fur coat and Carlotta slipped a poncho over her head. The rain rattled on the cloth, loud and driving. Brad felt the wet working toward his skin. Terrific, he thought. Maybe it'll snow soon.

A mile or so from the riverbed, the group came upon an abandoned mine. Its timbers were askew, tilting broken at the tunnel's entrance.

"Safe, you think?" Spear asked.

"Beats the rain," Elephant answered.

Brad walked into the black hole, lit a match and peered about. The space opened into a large, circular room with a flat floor extending well beyond his view. He heard the trickle of water somewhere out of sight and noted the heavy timbers and posts that supported the mine's ceiling. There was a musty smell to the place, but it was dry.

They unsaddled the horses and tied them at the rear of the mine's entrance. The animals quieted slowly, uneasy in the dark and spooked by the lightning that flashed through the mine's opening. They unrolled their bedding, set their saddles aside to dry and began to settle in.

Jeb and Carlotta fetched wood from the hillside. They returned bearing armloads of twigs and broken tree limbs. As the girl busied herself with a fire, Brad and Elephant rubbed down the animals, drying them. Their quiet, steady work settling the horses, calming them.

"Two men went loco here," Elephant recalled, loud enough for all to hear. "They say those two dug together in California and Utah for years before they started in on this hole. Worked it steady for near six months, I heard. Diggin' and shorin' like they meant to live here forever. And findin' nothin', not a damn thing.

"No explainin' why they kept at it, considerin'. But they did. Stubborn, I reckon. Or crazy. Found 'em outside that door, right there, dead, each with a knife in his hand."

"Anybody know what happened?" Brad asked.

"Nope," Elephant replied. "These mountains soak up·a lot of that there stuff."

The fire was roaring, smoke wandering across the ceiling and creeping into the rain-soaked sky outside. Its light flickered around the mine, giving it shape. And its warmth spread slowly, gradually filling the room.

It was nearly black outside by the time they'd finished the simple meal Carlotta prepared. She fried bacon and heated coffee for them and each, in his own way, stretched out on the dirt floor to linger over a tin cup of the dark liquid. It was hot and the cups even hotter in their hands as they stared into the fire.

"Reminds me of Paree," Elephant began. "Not the coffee, jest the rain. Rains like this in France, ya know. Steady-like and cold as steel. But leastwise they got places to hide in, warm and bright, places make you forget the rain."

Brad smiled at the old man, as warmed by his voice as by the drying clothes on his back.

"Now mind ya, missy," Elephant eyed Carlotta, "I don't mean to be talkin' like some barroom slob down at his mouth, but France is really somethin'. 'Specially in the rain. Cold and wet, you kin sit for a nickel beer and watch 'em dance damn near naked. Ladies so amazin' you can't near believe it, kickin' high enough to stop your heart, singin' and wavin' their arms to end it all. They wear them lacy kinda garter things around their legs 'case the fellas that's watchin' don't know where to look. And they prance around for hours on end. Amazin', really, when it's rainin'.''

Carlotta smiled to let him know she didn't mind his story.

Encouraged, he went on. "And that talk of theirs, criminy! It wheedles in your head, oozin' and groanin' a thousand sounds that seem to be directin' ya somewhere, somewhere strange. It's enough to drive ya nutty, listenin' to them French ladies with all that classy talk.''

Brad watched Elephant shake his head, thrilled by his memory of women from another time. The agent marveled at the prospector, his head wrapped in gauze, his clothes soaked, telling stories in an abandoned mine. He tried to imagine the Paris bistros he'd read about, tried to picture the cabarets that newspapers occasionally pictured, but couldn't. Brad's whole conception of France had suddenly been reduced to a vision of a woman wearing a garter dancing on a stage. Elephant was amazing.

"Have you really been to France, Elephant?" Carlotta asked.

"Sure enough have, missy."

"And Rome and Egypt, too, like they say?"

"You bet."

"Why'd you come back here? Seems like those places are a whole lot more exciting than sitting in a cold mine, breathing smoke." Carlotta turned a log in the fire, flames quickly lapping over the unburned wood. The light glowed in the enclosure, illuminating the walls so that for a moment Brad felt the cold stone pressing all around him.

"Don't know. Ran out of money. And I guess I got to missin' this country some. Course ya know, the lady I was with died. Jest seemed the time to turn around."

"You got tired, then, of strange lands and foods, their foreign languages, the wandering around?"

"Nope, can't say I minded any of it."

"You're a strange one, Elephant. Not like most men I know."

The old man shrugged, a smile on his face. He wrapped his blanket more tightly around his shoulders and stared into the fire. It was the kind of company he most enjoyed, the sort of evening he'd shared a hundred times before, never growing tired of it.

"Give a man like this old coot ten dollars and a mule and he's like to turn up anywhere," Jeb laughed.

"It's not the wandering that strikes me, Jebediah," Carlotta said, poking at the fire. "Lots wander. It's the being happy with it, the not regretting or looking forward that makes this old man different from most I've known."

Elephant was pleased with himself. Now that he thought about it, he did mostly enjoy his travels. For a young woman, this here one was no fool.

"In the past few years, since Mama died, I've seen all manner of peculiar goings on among men. I met 'em creeping out from under rocks. I've seen men senseless, raging mad over almost nothing. Unhappy and proud. I've watched men run scared of dying and seen others walk straight into it. I've watched 'em chase after money and run from power, terrified of even being near the stuff. And as far as I can tell, there's a lot of moving around going on and not much comfort anywhere."

Jebediah didn't want to think about the years since his wife had died.

"But you, Elephant, take the cake. You're sitting in a hole, a dead mine, listening to the rain, staring at a fire that barely takes the chill out of the air, wet and tired and cold as any of us, with your head partly blown away, and you grin, spinning some fool story, happy, eating up the minutes. Thinking about young legs on women far away."

Elephant slapped his knee, biting hard on the stogy between his lips. The smoke from it rose, wafting around him, mingling with the mist of blowing rain. He beamed. Nothing as pretty had paid so much attention to him in years.

"Not like this one," she said almost solemnly, glancing at Brad. "Not careful and gloomy." Spear didn't say anything. What she saw and what he felt had nothing to do with each other.

"Being quiet ain't the same as being low-down miserable, girl." Jeb was annoyed with his daughter, she was out of line. "You watch your tongue."

"I'm riding in the rain just like you and Elephant, getting cold and tired right along with you, following this man to God knows where. I'll say what I damn well please." She sparkled, fierce and angry, the most beautiful woman alive, Brad thought.

"Young lady's got a little vinegar in her veins, Jeb," Brad said. "But she sure has a right to wonder what we're up to."

"I know what we're up to. It's *you* that spooks me."

"Don't ask about it, woman. It's just something you don't want or need to know." He hated her, this beauty who had helped save his life.

"I'm not a child. And I want to know what it is about this trip that's eating at you."

"It's not this trip, in particular."

"Then what?" She wouldn't let go.

"It's the air I breathe, woman. Don't ask about it."

"You breathe the same air we all breathe."

"No, I don't. Mine is filled with death."

"Horseshit."

Brad felt edgy, as though Carlotta were goading him into a corner. He felt a strange affection for the unlikely trio that had pulled him out of Fetterman's. They were a peculiar lot, to be sure, but for reasons he couldn't quite understand they were helping. He owed them and it bothered him. He was putting them in danger, more perhaps than they imagined, and he was beginning to think they should know.

"Lady, don't kid yourself." Spear's mind turned, he'd finished backing up. "You say you've seen a lot of foolishness and greed. Well, you catch a glimpse of it, that's all. I live with it. I live with desperate, frightened men, with sordid, ugly creatures like those you watch crawl out from under rocks. I live with them. I crawl in after them."

"And survive?" her voice incredulous.

"Shut up, girl," Jeb nearly shouted at her.

"It's all right, Jebediah," Brad calmed him. "And kind of survive. Between times, I watch the girls and their garters just like anyone else."

"It makes no sense to me," she was quiet, surprised and a bit afraid of what she had uncovered.

"That doesn't make it complicated," Brad was feeling more comfortable.

"It makes no sense."

Nothing that Spear remembered ever looked as perfect as the dark, clear eyes that Carlotta bore down on him. He'd never seen anything so lovely, so alive, as her insistent stare. He listened to the rain drip from the walls of the mine and watched the smoke trailing along the roof into the night sky.

"You squash bugs for a living, then?"

"Sometimes."

"The men that created that hellhole we pulled you out of are insects, or worse. They are disgusting bugs."

"Carlotta," Brad said, startling her with the gentleness in his voice. "The men who built the place aren't weak or stupid. They're not bugs. They're strong, evil men who know what they're doing. They may kill us all."

"Then let them be."

"I can't. You can, I can't."

"Why not? To hell with them."

"Ease up, girl," Jeb seemed inclined to interrupt her, but from his expression it was clear to Brad he wanted to understand.

"It's all right, Jeb, really." Spear welcomed it. Her lights shining on him, threatening. She'd come close, too close.

"You'll kill them?" Carlotta asked.

"If I can."

"And that's all?"

"And then I'll stop, for a while, and feel sick. I'll walk through some town, looking at the goods behind the windows, listening to the miners grouse, watching the lazy men stroll, the women shop, the people eating at tables and drinking in bars. I'll just watch."

"Some part of you is missing, Spear." Brad couldn't answer, he didn't know.

Elephant ground his stogy into the dirt beside him. "I think I'm a-might scared by all this talk."

"Good," Brad said.

"There gonna be a fight?"

"I think so. I hope not, but I think so." It was the best Brad could offer them.

Loftin's map was vague, drawn from recollections

far too old. But Elephant followed it, more or less, working his way through the hills, ticking off familiar sights one at a time. They rode down scores of narrow valleys, crisscrossing wildly for the better part of the next day until the old man led them onto a particularly forbidding stretch of ground.

The hills that spilled onto the flat area of sand and rock were scored with gullies. Water poured down these slopes during wet weather and spring thaws, dragging silt into the basin below. And there were pockets of salt, long white smears of packed powder where the water's minerals had been left behind on the soil surface as the moisture disappeared into the dry air. Farther off, Spear saw spires of jagged rock, the chimneys noted on Loftin's map. These columns of granite and basalt were less susceptible to erosion than the soft ground that once surrounded them. And so they stood, strange obelisks as much as twelve feet high, natural monuments on the flat land. They marked the entrance to Broken Leg Gulch.

The four riders dismounted, gazing on the desolate world before them, its lifeless spaces unrelieved by greenery or motion.

"Incredible," Carlotta exclaimed breathlessly.

"I take it we're here, Elephant," Brad's complaint obvious in his tone.

"The spot you think we're looking for is over there, a mile or so off," the prospector pointed past the rock chimneys to the north. "But there's signs of quartz all along these hills, on both sides, so there could be a strike made anywhere."

"Let's walk the animals a while." Brad suggested, leading Diamond down the short slope and onto the hard, flat ground that stretched ahead of them.

They walked like sightseers, heads turning constantly, pointing out unusual twists of rock to one another. They plodded through a surreal world, a cathedral of jagged, infertile ground and cliffs. But Spear ignored the spectacular sights around him, intent upon the area that lay directly ahead.

The flash gave them away. A mile or so ahead, halfway up a hill to their left, a spur or coffeepot or gun reflected a bit of sunlight. Brad stopped. They'd found them.

"There." Brad pointed. There was a second flash.

"I see it," Carlotta cried.

They moved behind an outcropping of sandstone.

"I'll walk along the ridge, above them. Keep quiet and out of sight, I won't be long," Brad instructed.

"Want comapny?" Jebediah asked.

"Easier alone, Jeb." And he was gone.

Brad scrambled on foot up the slope, dodging the boulders that lay strewn everywhere. Loose ground made the going slow, his feet sliding out from under him periodically. But finally he made his way up and over the hillside, then headed north.

He jogged easily on hard ground past weathered pines and clumps of dry grass. The sun warmed his back. He could feel the quickened pulse of anticipation and concentrated on remaining calm. One false move could give away his position.

Slowing, he heard voices. Over the ridge, halfway down the other side into Broken Leg Gulch, men were talking casually to one another, relaxed. He inched his way up the slope to the crest and then crawled behind a boulder the size of a small house. He couldn't tell exactly how far below him they were, nor could he distinguish their voices clearly enough to count the men accurately. Two or three? Probably three.

Sitting with his back to the boulder, his head craned, listening, Brad felt something move across his boot. Some instinct froze him. As his head turned, he saw the small, steady eyes of a rattlesnake staring back at him. Its tongue tested the air.

The snake wasn't coiled and made no sound, but it didn't need to be attacking him to be dangerous. The broad, triangular head was only inches from his leg. Spear's first reaction to the thing was to kick it away, but he controlled the thought. Excited, the snake might attack and he'd have to shoot it. Any gunfire would expose him.

The rattler was probably dulled by the winter chill and pleased with the warm leg it had come upon. Spear felt a shiver run down his spine as the scaly head turned slowly, looking up his pant leg. The head weaved and then lowered, the snake moving away from his boot across his left calf. As the thin tongue bristled in the air, directed toward his thigh, Brad began to wonder how important remaining concealed really was. Then the snake vanished between his legs.

Spear could no longer see his sleek adversary. He struggled for control, trying to breathe evenly, slowly. He felt nothing. The rattler wasn't touching him anywhere. Down a hole? Had it crept away? He felt the cool trickle of sweat down the side of his head.

Suddenly there was a smooth, even scraping under his knee. He looked and saw the five rattles at the reptile's tail disappearing under his leg, its head moving steadily away from him. The snake crawled sluggishly, its full length now visible to him. Spear smiled. Halfway down the creature's side there was a lump that made the snake appear to have been tied in a knot. It had just found dinner, probably a desert rat, and was simply looking for a warm place to curl up and sleep. In no condition for combat, the snake had to hide from its predators and soon disappeared between two rocks.

Brad reholstered his .44 and listened. The men below still talked, idly it seemed, but he couldn't make out their conversation. As silently as he could, he worked his way farther down the slope until he was no more than thirty feet from them.

The camp was a simple affair. The men slept in a large, green tent that was pitched far below, at the floor of the gulch. Six horses stood tied to a rock. Brad wondered where the other men were. The two that he could see were sitting halfway up the slope in front of a newly-worked mine entrance.

He heard shots and the two men rose quickly, reaching for their weapons. The gunfire came from the mouth of the gulch, in the vicinity of his friends. Brad turned quickly and ran up the hill, ignoring the men below.

"Hey!" one of them yelled at Brad.

"What the hell is this?"

"Get him!"

Shots ricocheted off boulders and slapped into the sand at Brad's feet. From the sound he knew they were firing at him with pistols and that he'd soon be out of range. So he didn't return their fire but kept running, trying to keep as many large rocks behind him as possible. At the top of the hill he turned and looked below. The two guards had abandoned him and were riding hard toward the gunfire they heard.

Spear sprinted toward the sound. Panic filled him, adrenalin pumping through his veins. This was supposed to be the easy part. What was wrong?

At the crest of the ridge that overlooked the barren salt flat below, Spear saw them. Jebediah and Carlotta lay flat on the ground, their backs to the sandstone outcropping that he had thought would hide them. Both their horses lay dead, felled carefully to provide the pair with shelter on their exposed side. Carlotta was reloading, hidden behind the belly of her horse.

Brad couldn't see Diamond, Elephant's mule Henry, or Elephant, for that matter.

Jebediah sighted down the long barrel of his buffalo gun. Brad saw the cowboy that was in the old man's view, saw too the flash of powder from Jeb's weapon and watched as his target fell, rolling down the hillside. As soon as Jeb fired, he rolled to his back and began reloading the weapon. At the same instant Carlotta rose, a .44 in each hand, and fired two shots toward a large, granite spire. Bullets sent stone chips from the column whistling through the air.

Father and daughter held the low ground. They were trapped, circled by as many as half a dozen men. They'd killed at least one. But where were the others? Had Jeb spotted them? Where was Elephant? Dead?

Brad's mind churned. A professional, he surveyed the scene before him methodically, quickly reviewing the bits and pieces of the puzzle that confronted him. But there was a frenzy to him. He was outraged. He'd been cornered before, outnumbered more times than he cared to recall. He'd been attacked in the night, bush-whacked, tricked, before. But this was different. The sight of Jeb's long white hair pressed against his dead horse, the vision of Carlotta pinned down and desperate on the canyon floor burned through him. The coordination of Jeb's and Carlotta's efforts, the simple beauty of their defense against such odds, filled the agent with a fury that troubled him, disoriented him. He rocked, sitting on his heels, looking for a man to kill.

Two men squatted high on a ridge opposite him. A hundred yards away, they apparently hadn't spotted Spear, but he knew at least one of them. The tall, thin blond with a nickel-plated rifle studied the floor of the canyon. While shots rang below them, the two talked, calm. They hold the cards, Spear conceded.

But dislodging Jeb and Carlotta was clearly a problem for the men. Positions that would afford a clear shot at them easily could be defended by Jeb's remarkable rifle. And they'd watched him handle it so their timidity was well-founded. An old man and a girl had them stumped, Brad thought. He tried to imagine how they would attack. Watching them discuss the situation, he couldn't decide. Unless someone were willing to die in order to get at Brad's pinned-down friends, it was going to be difficult to end this siege.

Then the shooting stopped. Brad watched as a runner from the ridge beyond scurried away from the blond rifleman. Spear studied the man as he circled the canyon, keeping low. He stopped near a boulder and Brad saw another cowboy who had been hiding there listen intently to the news that was carried to him. Then the runner moved on, explaining whatever strategy they had decided upon to each of the men around Jeb and Carlotta. In so doing, of course, Brad learned the exact position of each. But their next move remained a mystery to him.

Then, after nearly a half hour of deadly silence, it became clear. They would wait until nightfall. Under the cover of darkness they could get close enough to end it.

Carlotta moved away from the dead animal, sliding on her hip to her father.

"You all right?"

"So far," he replied. "And you?"

"Okay."

"Kinda quiet."

"Sure is."

"How many of them do you think there are?"

"Too many," her answer was simple and calm, but made it clear to Jebediah that she understood the situation all too well. They were surrounded. Brockington's men had somehow spotted them as they waited for Brad to return. And the gunmen had positioned themselves well before opening fire. Only Jeb's quick instincts had saved them. "You think Spear's dead?" Carlotta asked.

"Doubt it," Jeb answered.

"He better not be. I have a few things to say to that man."

Jebediah Jones laughed at his daughter. There was a white frosting of mineral salt across her cheek and he wiped it away with his thumb.

Spear made up his mind while watching the shadows lengthen across the gulch. The setting sun stood the rocks and spires of the barren valley in high relief, giving it the appearance of a garden strewn with rocks. He realized that Brockington's men could work their way through those rocks, hidden by them and the darkness, and close in on Jeb and Carlotta before they could see their enemies. Brad's only hope was to turn their strategy in his favor.

The cowboy-guard nearest Brad was alone. His rifle leaned against a rock. His hands were buried deep in his long coat and he jogged in place, trying to keep warm. It was dusk, the half-light disappearing in the winter sky.

Brad was no more than twelve feet from the man. It had taken him nearly an hour to crawl only a hundred yards. But the deathly quiet of the gulch and the random placement of the boulders that concealed him made the going slow. It was essential he move carefully, creeping down the hillside unheard. As the agent opened his long, black, folding knife, it clicked into position. He winced at the sound, but the puffing guard didn't hear him.

Holding the knife by its blade, Brad stared at the man. It was impossible to move closer without the risk of being seen. He stood, the heft of the weapon comforting, and threw the knife. It hissed through the air, turning once and lodged deep in the cowboy's back. The blade sank in to the handle, high, over the heart. The cowboy turned toward the pain, but by the time he faced Spear he was dead, still standing, but dead. He never saw his attacker, never uttered a word. He collapsed without making a sound.

Brad pulled the knife from the dead man's back, grunting with the effort it took. He had thrown the knife harder than was necessary; he was more nervous than he thought. Brad wiped the blade on the man's collar, folded it and headed for his second target.

As it grew darker he moved more quickly, walking not crawling, along the floor of the gulch. He heard Jeb laugh in the distance. The old man's steely patience overwhelmed the agent. Then Brad heard the two men he had to deal with next whispering to one another. They'd heard Jeb, too. A ragged-looking pair, they seemed to be nervous, frightened men. Like children afraid of the dark, they stood close to one another.

Spear circled the boulder that concealed them. It was a jutting, flat rock eight feet tall and twice as wide. He climbed onto it easily, wondering if he were visible to others as he moved on all fours to its edge, just above them.

"Wish that bastard would stop laughing," one man muttered.

"Shut up about it, will ya?"

"Hate that laughing. It's like he ain't a-scared of nothin'."

"He's scared."

"Well, maybe so. But alls I know is that he's laughing and I ain't. He's got that damn buffalo gun and I ain't. He's hidin' and I'm gonna be walkin' at him. Shit, he's got good reason to laugh."

"They ain't got a chance, dummy. Can't see ya, can't shoot ya."

"Maybe."

"Absolutely. I'm just hopin' we don't have to kill the girl. Three months out here, not bein' able to even go to town and I could use a little time with her."

"You're the dummy, for Christ's sake. Some guy's gonna do his level best to blow a hole in you in a few minutes and alls you think about is what hangs between your legs."

"Gotta keep your perspective." He chuckled.

"Jesus."

The miner who was so adverse to Jebediah's laughter fidgeted in the moonlight, shaking his head. Their breath clouded around them and the man with thoughts about Carlotta paced back and forth. Spear jumped from the rock onto the standing miner, his feet landing squarely on the unsuspecting man's shoulders. There was the snap of collarbones and a piercing scream as the man collapsed to the ground. Spear rolled away from the helpless guard and turned on his companion.

The scream had frozen the second guard. He stood with his mouth open, his eyes wide in disbelief as Brad lunged for him. The knife drove deep into his chest, blood running down Brad's hand as the dead man doubled over and fell. The agent went immediately to the groaning body that writhed on the ground, took his pistol from its holster and slammed its butt into the man's skull. He was instantly silent.

Spear ran from the scene. The noise of the suffering cowboy almost certainly drew someone's attention and he wanted to be far away if reinforcements arrived.

Brad worked his way among the boulders, squinting into the darkness. Three of the six men he'd spotted earlier were dead or unconscious. The odds were improving all the time. But those that remained had been alerted; he'd have to be careful.

Brad fell to his belly and crawled through the shadows. If he hadn't lost his bearings, there ought to be another man not far ahead. But he couldn't see him. And there was no noise.

Spear moved slower and slower as he approached the granite column he was sure concealed another guard. Still nothing. He eased his .44 from its holster and cocked it.

At the sight of the sitting cowboy, Brad rolled reflexively to one side, aiming as he did so. But he didn't fire. The grinning face that seemed so luminescent in the moonlight was that of a dead man. Propped against the carcass of an old pine tree, eyes askew in the night, the guard looked like a demented theatergoer. Comfortable, just dead. As Brad crawled up to him, the sight of his face sent a shudder through Spear, taking his breath away.

The man's head had been crushed by a blow from behind. But the smiling corpse told another tale. The man's ear had been cut from his head.

"Elephant," Brad muttered to himself.

Shots cracked in the distance, flares of yellow light spurting into the darkness. Spear stood, alarmed. The gunfire erupted, frenzied, the unmistakable sound of handguns firing. He was too late.

Brad ran across the salt flat, a battle raging before him whose combatants he couldn't identify. Still, he ran into it, his gun drawn, looking for Jeb and Carlotta. Instead, he found a hired gun peering over a rock. The man steadied his pistol on the stone shield in front of him and fired into the night with an even, methodical cadence. It was impossible for the man to see what he was shooting at. He just knew roughly where they were. Spear never broke stride. Racing by the man, he brought his pistol down on the gunman's head, just behind the ear. No further shots would be heard from him for a while.

High up the slope to his left, Brad saw a rifle firing. To his right, a pistol. Straight ahead at ground level, nothing. He couldn't return the fire for fear one of the gunmen was Elephant. And he still didn't know where Jeb and Carlotta were. He stopped, genuinely panicked.

"Jebediah!" he bellowed into the night. "Jebediah!"

Nothing.

"Jebediah!"

Still nothing.

He moved forward, a man lost in a strange, darkened room, stumbling into things. The steady crack of a rifle continued, but the sound of handguns had disappeared.

Spear raced past a boulder, fending it off with one hand, and turned onto the scene. It was as though he hadn't approached it so much as it exploded at his feet. Jebediah sat on the ground, his back leaning into the belly of a dead horse. His beaded shirt was open, red with blood, his hair brilliant in the moonlight. Elephant stood near him, his bandaged head filthy, a strip of gauze hanging nearly to his waist. A rifle drooped in one hand. For the first time that Brad could recall, the prospector looked old.

Carlotta knelt beside her father, holding one of his huge, thin hands between hers.

Jeb opened his eyes as Brad lowered himself next to the man.

"Doesn't hurt at all, I'm afraid," Jeb said. Brad parted his ornate and bloody shirt, then closed it.

"How many were there?" Jeb seemed to really want to know.

"Six or seven, I think," Brad answered.

"Too many," Carlotta added.

"Easy, daughter."

Jebediah Jones lowered his chin slowly to his chest, the bright white hair of his beard flowing across his coat. His eyes closed and he died.

Carlotta placed the hand she held against her cheek and then settled it gently on the ground beside her father. She stood, took his buffalo rifle in one hand and walked into the darkness. Those who had tried so hard to kill Jebediah had fled, the few survivors far from the place in minutes.

Spear knew no words and Elephant felt like offering none. So they stood over the simple grave, staring at it. The slender spire that marked Jebediah's resting place caught the morning sun, reflecting it onto the ground. Elephant stood ramrod straight, waiting for Carlotta to return.

Brad left, walking among the bodies that lay on the hillside, propped against rocks, splayed across boulders. All were dead, the man whose collarbones Brad had broken had succumbed to some inner injury, the others shot or knifed.

The agent approached the abandoned tent, the great green barracks that had housed the secret mine's guards, knowing it was empty. A quick look inside revealed lamps, picks, assay equipment, cots and clothes everywhere. But no men. He climbed the hillside toward the mine.

Just inside the entrance to the tunnel, he pulled a stinker from his pocket. The heavy match sparkled as he struck it and then steadied to provide an even glow.

He looked around briefly and whistled in spite of himself. The flame wasn't all that glittered in this hole.

The vein was silver, he was sure. In some places it stood a foot-and-a-half wide, three different slashes of it running along the tunnel wall. It was argentite, he thought, three rich veins of it! He touched the black luster with his knife and it cut easily. Brad carved a fist-sized sample and slipped it into his pocket.

"Never seen nothing like it," Elephant declared, startling Brad with his presence.

"Rich."

"Eighty percent pure, I'd reckon."

"Carlotta show up?"

"She's below, with Henry and your horse," Elephant replied.

"Let's get out of here."

Carlotta rode behind Brad, her arms wrapped tightly around him. The side of her head pressed against his back but only once, all morning, did he think he heard her weeping.

# Chapter 15

Lady Jane looked like a whore, a painted lady in the truest sense. Her sequined gown plunged halfway to her navel, revealing nearly as much of her as it concealed. Her eyelids were darkly colored and painted the same bright blue as her dress. Arching eyebrows made her face a rivèting sight. Black patent-leather shoes glistened on her feet. Mesh stockings wrapped tightly around her calves as they peeked through the open slit at the front of her dress.

"Perfect," she appraised, admiring herself in the full-length mirror that stood near her bed.

Lady Jane had had enough. The gruesome sight of Elephant's shattered ear and Brad's bitter silence as he waited for the doctor to finish with him had proven too much for her resolve. The quiet widow, the efficient businesswoman, the patient nursemaid to her injured Pinkerton, had snapped. The frustration of waiting and the fury that had grown in her daily as Alice Carter sat rocking in her room overwhelmed Lady Jane. She knew only one way to immerse herself in this struggle, only one way to affect its outcome. She was going to make a scene.

She dipped a finger into the brandy snifter that sat beside her. With a smirk she dabbed a bit of it behind each ear and then patted a drop on one breast. She lifted the glass, filled her mouth with the rich liquid and then spat it back. She retreated from the mirror and turned to view her profile. Her shoulders and breasts gleamed white, the corset narrowing her waist to almost nothing. "Perfect," she repeated.

Lady Jane picked up her purse and counted the cash: three thousand dollars. Then she slid three Land Grant Certificates into a brown envelope and folded it next to the bills. On a carved walnut bureau she found a felt-covered case and carried it to the bed. Inside were two small holsters containing derringers. Strapped just above her knee, they looked to all the world like lace garters. Lady Jane had to laugh. This was wonderful.

She walked into the Sundown Saloon, stumbling as she approached the bar. The bartender looked at her, aghast.

"Mrs. Harrington?" Though he'd seen her hundreds of times, it struck him as impossible that the drunken woman before him was the owner of the Silver Lady mine.

"Whiskey, straight up," she ordered with a slur, clapping a coin down in front of him.

"Are you all right, ma'am?"

"Yup. Right as rain."

The bartender couldn't take his eyes off the round globes that seemed to be struggling out of her dress.

"Where's my drink!"

"Comin' up," he said, incredulous.

She emptied the shot glass with a quick swallow, her head held back. Lady Jane tottered once, holding onto the bar and then swung wildly around, apparently surveying the place.

"A drink for the man who'll point me to a card game," she announced to the room. "And a beer for anybody smart enough not to play."

The barkeep glided over to her. "I might be able to

find you a game. But are you sure? I mean, the stakes get high in here."

"I got me three sections of ground somewhere in the boondocks, three useless Land Grant things and I'm looking for a card game to lose 'em at. Stake enough?"

The bartender whispered something to a man at the bar and the messenger raced from the room.

A half-hour later, in a dingy back room, the game was under way. Three men and one apparently drunk woman sat around a table, studying their cards. The game got off to a slow start, the first pots going for twenty or thirty dollars. One man dropped out when he hauled in a fifty-dollar prize and a new man slid in, announcing that he had five hundred dollars in his pocket. Lady Jane laughed loudly. "Big deal!" she remarked.

The new man in the group was dressed well and moved with confidence. A gambler, Lady Jane decided. He laid down five one-hundred dollar bills so that everyone could see them and then tucked his bankroll into his vest. He introduced himself as Wyoming Jones, settling himself into a chair.

The third hand after Jones' arrival was won on a pair of aces and a pair of jacks. Forty dollars changed hands on the pot and the new man won. It was his deal.

Lady Jane leaned over the table, counting what was left of the cash she had originally placed there. Her breasts hung before her audience as she counted the bills in front of her. No sense taking any chances, she thought.

Wyoming called his game, seven-toed Pete, and the players whistled as he threw in a five-dollar ante. He then won the hand easily and two players dropped out. A new man, clearly drunk, sat in. He said his name was Johnson and that he'd just sold his ranch. He didn't want his wife to get her hands on any of the money he had left. He mumbled, only half-conscious of his words.

The stakes climbed higher. Within an hour, four-hundred-dollar pots had become common and only Johnson, Wyoming and Lady Jane remained at the table. The woman continued to bob above her cards, feigning intoxication and pretending to be indifferent to the five or six hundred dollars she had lost.

"You fellas gonna nibble at me till there's nothin' left?" Lady Jane asked. "Can't let that go on." She pulled the brown envelope from her purse and set it on the table in front of her.

"I tried to sell one of these things early today for $2,500 and had no takers. Seems like this is the place to unload 'em. How 'bout two thousand each . . . ?"

Johnson picked up a certificate. "Looks like just a fancy piece of paper to me," he guffawed. "What the hell is it?"

Jane explained, briefly, stumbling over her words. Johnson picked up the thick sheet of paper again, squinted at it and looked across at Wyoming. "What ya figger this thing's worth?" he asked.

"Fifteen hundred, tops," Wyoming responded, obviously unenthused by the Land Grant.

Lady Jane watched Wyoming Jones carefully. His grey eyes were alert and constantly moving, his hands working the pasteboards like a true card-room mechanic. The man had been cheating steadily and Jane knew it, but no large pots had come to him as a result. It seemed he was trying to keep the betting close, keep Lady Jane in the running for a while. He was good, feeding his mark winners in order to build confidence.

Jane shrugged, "Ah, what the hell, fifteen hundred is

fine with me. I don't plan to lose the things anyway. Who's buying?" She peered across the table.

"If you stay in the game," Wyoming said.

"I ain't going anywhere," she replied, sipping at the whiskey her shot glass held.

Wyoming counted out fifteen hundred dollars and handed them to Jane. The game continued. Two hands later Johnson dropped out. He'd lost his last eight hundred in one deal. It seemed to Jane that things were about to get serious.

Wyoming dealt, five card draw. The lady, recently the owner of Cheyenne's most prosperous saloon, knew that the game was the easiest of all to misdeal. Looking at her cards, she found two aces and so opened the betting at two hundred dollars. Wordless increases brought the pot to over a thousand dollars before either requested their new cards. Lady Jane patted her cheek, a clumsy gesture from a drunken woman. She wanted Jones to think she was in over her head.

"Powerful card playin'," she observed. "No fiddlin' around with small bills when a real man's playin'." She looked longingly at Jones. He threw down three cards and watched her do the same. Jane watched her replacements arrive, carefully noting the dip Jones' index finger took as he handed her each card. Very professional, she thought.

Three queens. And two aces. A damn good hand and a winner ninety-nine times out of a hundred. Jane knew she was being set up. She bet an additional hundred dollars, paused and increased it to two hundred.

Wyoming looked at her over the tops of his cards. "Two hundred to me, right?"

"Right."

"Hell, you must be loaded," he laughed. "But I got to take a shot. I'm looking at too much to lose the trail on the hard rocks. I'll see your two hundred," he continued, "and jump you three hundred."

He put the money in the pot, five one-hundred-dollar bills, and looked back at Jane.

She counted the cash that still sat before her and looked at Jones. "You're too sweet to take this way," she cooed and threw in her hand, face-side down on the table. Wyoming looked surprised but gathered in the pot without a word.

The cards were cut, two small stacks before her. She fumbled with them briefly while her adversary counted his winnings. Jane knew her previous hand was a loser, good enough to be interesting, but not a winner. She'd been set up, carefully, slickly, but set up. She dropped the cards, offered an "Oops" and asked Jones to cut the deck again. Her head rocking back and forth, she prepared to deal.

Lady Jane had spent years watching cheats. During the cold, lonely nights that Cheyenne so often had brought her, she had practiced the quick shuffle and clumsy deal that so frequently had graced her tables. A kind of solitaire, the style and grace of a fast move, a properly set-up mark, intrigued her. While she ran an honest table, a decent saloon, she never forgot the beauty of a truly professional thief. The craft that had so long ago propelled her past poverty still had its appeal, she couldn't deny it. And so, when the snow was piled high in the streets of Cheyenne, she had practiced in her rooms, shuffling and dealing endlessly.

She opened with a two hundred dollar ante. Two men at the edge of the room sucked in their breath when they saw the size of the unstarted hand's pot. Jane glanced at them, angry.

"Out!" she snarled. "I've lost enough cash already, no distractions from you yahoos!" The men left quickly, closing the door behind them.

Wyoming slid two one-hundred-dollar bills to the middle of the table. Jane dealt. Jones looked at his cards briefly and added three hundred dollars to the pot. Jane studied her hand as nervously as she could. Perhaps it was time to seem indecisive, she thought.

"Three hundred?"

"Yup."

"Golly."

"It's a man's game, lady."

Jane shook her head, trying desperately to control her impulse to find the situation hilarious. Jones was grinning, sort of. She saw his raise and selected two cards in her hand to discard, keeping a pair of aces and a king. Then she put down her hand and picked up the deck.

Jones cast three cards aside and Jane dealt him three more as fast as she could. If the gambler suspected anything, it didn't register on his face.

"Three and two," she said.

Jane didn't look at her cards. She knew what her hand contained, two aces and three kings. And she was certain of Jones' hand. Good, but not quite good enough. As she sat there staring at him, her body the perfect distraction, lulling him with her drunken behavior, she wondered at his arrogance. He peered into his hand and did his best to look concerned.

Jones bet five hundred with a straight face. She met it and raised him one hundred more.

"Your hundred and a thousand more," he said.

She frowned and examined her cards. Looking nervous was difficult now, but she managed it. "I've only nine hundred on the table. Will you take my note?" she asked.

"No chance," he stated flatly. He looked thoughtful. "But if you got more of them certificate things, I'll take 'em."

Jane nodded as though she had forgotten about the bits of paper in her purse, rummaging through it frantically for the documents. "Fifteen hundred still?" she asked, innocently.

"Sounds fair," Jones responded.

She hesitated. "Hell, I don't know . . . a raise of a thousand . . ." She let the words hang in the air and then slowly took a broad, stiff certificate and let it drop to the table. She counted five hundred dollars in the pot and pulled the cash into her hands. "Look right?" she questioned, almost sheepishly.

Jones nodded.

"And a 'nother hundred," she said, a silly, drunken flourish to her gesture.

Jones was cool and unconcerned. He dropped a hundred dollar bill in the pot and then pulled out the Land Grant Certificate he'd won earlier. "Your hundred and I raise you another fifteen hundred." He looked at Jane without expression.

She stood up, fanning her forehead with one hand. This was truly wonderful, she thought. Then she sat down and chugged the dregs of a shot glass, looked at her cards and sighed. "What the hell, the damn things didn't cost me much in the first place." She reached into her purse and deposited her last certificate on the table. "I'm seein' your fifteen hundred and addin' some of my own." She put three hundred dollars in the pot. This last was salt in his wound, but she couldn't resist. He'd call either way and the last three bills made her feel so much better.

"Three hundred to me," Jones said. He was nonchalant. He threw the bills onto the table and said, "I call."

Jones peeled his cards from his hand one at a time. The agonizingly slow pace of his gesture grated on Lady Jane's nerves, his superiority, his smug attitude annoying her. A jack of diamonds appeared, a jack of clubs and a jack of hearts. Then he lay down his two aces and smiled. "Full house, aces over jacks." He reached for the pot.

"Well, lordy be," she declared. "Seems I beat you." Jane smiled, her hard, crisp look piercing him. Two aces and three kings appeared on the table.

Jones stood up, knocking over his chair in his haste. "You cheat!" he shouted.

"Your arrogance clouds your vision, sir," Jane spoke curtly.

"You cheated," he roared as he reached for a gun hidden in his coat. Leveled at her, the thing was enormous.

"I beg your pardon," she said, prim, controlled.

"You cheated!" He'd been conned and hated it.

"Sir, what do you propose to do about it?"

"Hand over that pot or I'll kill you."

"Indeed," she responded.

"Now."

Jane pulled the trigger of her derringer. A small red hole appeared on Jones' forehead. His gun clattered on the table and he slumped to the floor. A crowd pushed its way into the small room to see what had happened.

"Who staked him?" she asked to no one in particular.

"Don't know," the bartender answered.

"You must think me a fool," she remarked, almost imperiously.

"We send for the bloke, or sent for him anyway, at Doc Brockington's. That's all I know."

"That's enough," Jane revealed, gathering her winnings and walking from the room.

It was nearly ten o'clock that evening when Lady Jane headed for Dr. Brockington's front door. She was carrying over $11,000 worth of Land Grant Certificates and cash in the middle of one of Nevada's roughest cities. And she was dressed like a drunken whore. But no one approached her, or even spoke as she marched down the wooden sidewalk to Brockington's. While she couldn't unravel the mystery surrounding the burglary and murders that had plagued the city of late, she had solid evidence that the doctor was backing a cardsharp. She'd begin with Wyoming Jones and see where the conversation took her.

As Lady Jane's small fist hovered, about to knock on Brockington's front door, she heard an argument going on inside.

"Listen, Young. We can't wait any longer! That mine has to go out on strike tomorrow."

Brockington was screaming at her night foreman, Dick Young.

"Engle says he can't, he doesn't have enough men signed up yet for the walkout to work."

Jeb Engle, the slimy little union organizer and Dick Young were working for Brockington.

"Shoot those that don't walk, you idiot. Close that mine tomorrow."

"Jesus. This ain't what we bargained for."

"But it's what you've got."

"If the walkout fails, we've had it, Brockington. We'll never close the place down if we miss on our first try."

"Mr. Young, the Silver Lady will close, a devastating explosion sealing off a good part of it. I simply want the strike to add a little chaos to the scene. Do you understand?"

"Oh, yeah . . ."

"Mr. Dufond, here, will accompany you below. He'll help with the charges."

Jane reeled. She was certain she had heard the

name, but couldn't believe it. Dufond. The priest. The murderer. The filthy little man who had raped her so many months before. She backed from the front porch, staring at the house. It contained so much that she hated. She had to think.

Jane raced up the street, her earlier composure and self-assurance having disappeared. She had to get home.

Riding two-up it was impossible, even for Diamond, to make the journey back to Silver City in one day. After three hours the great black horse slackened its pace almost imperceptibly, tiring, and then recovered. But each step was labored, the animal consuming something of itself in order to proceed. Spear brought Diamond to a halt and with one arm eased Carlotta to the ground. Brad knew that the spectacular horse would walk itself into the ground if asked, that it would plod endlessly until it dropped. They had to stop.

"Whoa, Elephant," he yelled ahead.

The old man turned his mule on a dime, looking back at them. His face was cherry-red in the cold wind as he rubbed the mule between its ears.

"Stoppin'?"

"Yup," Brad said as he climbed from Diamond.

Elephant hated to stop. He didn't want to look into Carlotta's huge, sad eyes. He didn't want to talk about it. He didn't want to express his sorrow, his regret, his mourning. Elephant accepted death. Not as the inevitable end to any man's time, but as a thing he'd seen a lot of. It was a wretched, black moment of silence, the instant a man stopped talking, an end. But he'd seen so much of it, one quick exit barely touched him. He'd seen people die while they still walked around, numbed by failure, beaten into silence. And he'd known a few whose vision was so filled with hate that death circled them like clouds around a mountain. Elephant had seen old men quit, he'd seen women stop hoping, he'd seen lots of death.

But as he rode through Nevada's foothills, listening to the clop of Henry's hooves, he and his mule had discussed Jebediah. Had anyone overheard them, Elephant would have seemed a cruel and indifferent man. For he and Henry decided that Jebediah bought the farm pretty well, all things considered. He went a bit too quietly, but that was his way. At least he didn't linger over it, bubbling helplessly or moaning complaint into the sky. Jebediah had stopped, there was no sense wondering over it, or grieving. At least he'd had the good sense not to grow sullen or useless in his old age. Better to stop before that death came over you.

"Mind if I don't wait up?"

Brad looked up at the old man, wondering what thoughts whirled through his head. The agent decided that the moving made Elephant feel better and that he and Henry ought to go on. They could make Silver City before nightfall.

"Don't mind. Tell Loftin we found it, but don't tell him where. We'll be in early tomorrow."

Henry turned and walked on. Brad could hear the old man talking to the mule, his voice low and hoarse. In minutes they had gone out of sight.

As the day wore on, the sun warmed them. By midday Brad and Carlotta came upon an area littered with clear pools of rainwater, collected in broad stone basins two nights before. Lizards, brown and wrinkled, darted from the water's edge as Diamond approached. Birds came and went from such places, their small, quick wings fluttering above Brad's head.

At times they walked beside Diamond, making slow, easy progress, stretching their legs. In one deep valley they rested in a stand of white birch, Carlotta idly peeling thin white strips of bark from a fallen tree limb. It was a long day that went by without a dozen words passing between them. Brad was grateful for the quiet.

As the sun dropped behind them, the wind seemed to rise colder. The sky before them grew black, stars appearing here and there. They were four or five hours from Silver City. It was time to gather wood for a fire before night made the chore nearly impossible.

As Diamond chewed on the oats Brad carried, Spear rigged a lean-to from a tarpaulin he had taken from the mine. Carlotta built a fire two feet from its raised, open end and stacked broken brush nearby. Spear soaked dried beans and they cooked them in water and brown sugar over the flames. The winter camp chilled the agent. Though the bright fire warmed them, no insects chirped at one another, no wolves howled.

Spear walked to his saddlebags, tied to a tree out of harm's way, and pulled a small silver flask from it. The screw cap chained to the side of the bottle clinked as Brad handed the liquor to Carlotta. She offered him a half-smile and took a deep swig.

"Thanks," she acknowledged, handing the bottle to him.

He nodded and drank.

"I sure will miss that old man," she said.

Spear couldn't imagine her grief. He'd been a young boy when his father died. He could only think that the loss of someone so long loved must eat at your middle.

"Your father alive?" she asked.

He shook his head.

"I'm sorry."

"He died long ago, I barely remember him."

"That's really a sorrowful thing," she whispered, reaching for the flask. "Do you think I'm supposed to cry?" Her question surprised him. The striking dark

woman who sat across the fire had, from the moment
he first met her, seemed bound tightly, some hidden
sinew holding her together more rigidly than any
woman he knew. There seemed no flex to her, no give.
Unlike a sapling, which bends with the weight of fallen
snow, she would resist until she broke. But now she
asked him, of all people, if she should cry. There was
something of a little girl about her.

"I don't know."

"I don't either, Spear, and it sorta bothers me."

"Why?"

"I walked all night, last night. Up and down that
gulch, hiding so you and Elephant wouldn't know I
didn't cry."

"You don't owe either of us a thing, especially
tears."

"I know."

"Then rest easy with it."

"It's not Jebediah being dead. It's not that." Her
eyes bore into him, searching his face for some tenderness he hoped she'd find there. Her eyes glistened in
the firelight. "It's not having him around to follow. I
don't know where to go now."

Carlotta stood, her worn chaps flapping once against
her legs, and took off her hat. Her hair spilled across
her shoulders and she shook her head, unraveling the
last tangled locks of ink-black and shining fibers. It
hung straight, to her waist, making her look smaller
and more beautiful than before.

"You said you look in storefront windows when the
killing's over with." He was surprised she recalled his
remark. He nodded.

"And it makes you feel better?"

"Sometimes it does."

"And women?"

"They help, sometimes."

"Spear, I need a man filled with life to make me feel alive. Lie down with me."

She was a kind of jewel, hard and precious. It seemed to him he could hold her in one hand, tiny and turning, someone remarkable just to behold. She was magnificent, too difficult to get close to, too compelling to avoid. If nothing else, he had to trust her.

He stood and took her in his arms, lifting her from the ground as he did so. Carlotta wrapped her arms around his neck and pulled him to her, their mouths open, greedy for one another, propelled not so much by urgency as longing. They kissed, deeply and long, her small body pressing against his. Brad set her down and she took his hand, walking toward the crude tent he'd made.

Lying there beside her, the light of the fire banked off the slanted ceiling of their shelter. She slipped from her clothes quickly, never taking her eyes from his. Held by them, he shed his clothes along with her and they stopped, not touching, naked and utterly alone in the night.

Her hair fell across her shoulder and trailed over one breast, its small, round contours etched in black. Brad's hand eased behind her ear and he drew those dark strands away. He moved to her, bending, reaching, and his lips found hers once again. She touched his arms, hungry and quick as his fingers traced her side, inching along her chest, feeling her ribs rise and fall with each hurried breath. She sighed as his hand found her firm breast, surrounding it, and she cried out as his lips met her dark, stiff nipple. Her hands took his head, pushing him against her.

"Oh, God," Carlotta murmured as she raked her fingernails down his back. He felt her passion growing, lust obvious in her arms and lips, her back arching toward him. He pulled slowly away from her and watched his hands as the shiver they brought closed her eyes. She lay back, her small breasts flattened against her chest as he touched them slowly, lightly, the dark buds that tipped each hardening in the cold air.

His lips brushed across her belly, his fingers dancing down her dark, firm thighs. She seemed tiny to him, her hips rocking, small and trim. Her dark triangle moving toward him, then away. He parted her legs gently, his lips on her shoulder, and touched the yearning tip of her. Carlotta gasped, opening wider.

His mouth on hers, their tongues exploring each other, Brad's hand teased across her mound, then dipped into her.

"Oh, God," her voice rising now, she pushed up at him.

His finger slipped deeply into her and then withdrew, its exit drawing slowly across her. And then again he moved into her, slower still. And withdrew. And then again, her body finally arching and twisting, moving steadily around his touch. He drew his free hand to her breast and rolled her nipple between his thumb and finger. His lips found her ear, whispering "Yes."

Her still-growing passion thrilled Brad, her body arching before him, her hips rising to his touch. Then, as his hand teased and entered her over and over, Carlotta's eyes opened, fierce, and her lips spread, oval. "More, more, more," she repeated in time to his touch until she suddenly slowed, her body rigid, consumed at its core. She moaned, churning against him, her delicate body racked below him. And then she lay quietly, her chest rising and falling as she calmed.

Brad kissed her lips as he pulled the rough blanket over them. Below it, his fingers stroked her and she cried out, tortured by his gentle touch. But his hand continued across her, bringing a quickness to her breath. She turned her head from side to side, confused, overwhelmed, too quickly spurred again. She moaned up at him, her body wriggling, half-trying to escape, half-greeting his delicate prodding.

He knelt between her legs, his hands sliding down her small sides, brushing across her hips and cupping her buttocks. Her dark eyes opened once again, boring into him. She reached but couldn't find him, bewildered under his touch. And then he lifted her, his huge, strong hands grasping her buttocks roughly as he drove himself between her legs. He eased over Carlotta, his face buried in the soft, black hair that lay behind her. Brad moved steadily in her, each thrust deep and searching, the feel of her hands at his sides driving him.

He felt his need building slowly, distracted, delayed by the frenzy he sensed in her. She arched at him and pushed, her legs rose and fell around him, her hands raced over his body and she grew louder and louder, almost wailing into the night. He was inflamed, almost desperate, his wish to thrill her into exhaustion, torture her into sleep, merging with his own deep lust. He surged into her, a mindless wave driving against Carlotta, into Carlotta, wanting Carlotta. And then he felt it in her again, the deeper rocking, the buried flowering of her passion that went on and on.

He saw her eyes then, wild, and burst into her. He was seized with it, unsure whose passion he most keenly felt, feeling her still bucking below him and meeting her. It was colossal and then over.

Brad awoke to the sound of a bird in the morning light. Carlotta's dark hair covered his chest and arms, her small body warm against him.

# Chapter 16

With the arrogance that only a weary man can muster, he slumped into the crushed velour chair, smearing mineral salt and dirt across it. The toe of his grimy boot hooked the leg of another chair and pulled it to him. Exhaling deeply, tired, he propped both boots on the delicate fabric. The tall blond man whose shining rifle was for hire seemed to have reached the limit of his tolerance, the edge of his professional calm.

With one hand he lobbed his rifle into the air and it clattered across the huge, polished table in the middle of Dr. Brockington's parlor. The physician winced as a long, white scratch appeared on the wood.

"That bastard is a goddamn butcher!" the gunman exploded. "He killed them all around me and I never heard a thing. Not a thing. We opened fire and there wasn't anybody shooting. Me and one other, out of seven for Christ's sake. I never heard a goddamn thing!"

"Calm yourself, Henderson." Brockington was uneasy in the presence of such emotion. It made planning difficult.

"Shove it, Doc. You weren't there. What the hell do you know?"

"He's good, but Spear can be handled."

"Good? Good?" Henderson was disgusted. He kicked over the chair which supported his feet and stood. "He's inhuman. Get it straight, Doc, inhuman." Henderson's professional admiration for his target had grown steadily, but he had always regarded Spear as quick, tough and experienced, nothing more. The bloody night at Broken Leg Gulch had changed all that. He struggled to make the clean, calm doctor in ruffled cuffs understand.

"Do you know what it's like to kill a man with a knife, Doc? To stalk him in the night and run a blade through him, standing close enough to feel his breath on your face and his blood on your hands? Do you know?"

Brockington stood mute, the nearly hysterical gunman ranting in the middle of his parlor.

"And to kill another and another and another without a sound? Of all the men he butchered, only one even screamed. Inhuman." Henderson shook his head. "He was all around me and I didn't even know it." It was his nightmare, his private terror.

Dufond entered the room, hurried. One look at the beleaguered expression, the panic on Henderson's face, and he froze.

"The mine?" he asked Brockington.

"They found it. Everyone's dead."

"It's worse than that," Dufond muttered.

"What?" Brockington barked.

"And Fetterman's. Burned. Gone. Fetterman himself blown in two with a buffalo rifle."

Henderson smiled. "That thing gets around."

Brockington knew from Henderson's first, incoherent report of the disaster at Broken Leg Gulch that Spear had somehow escaped from the asylum. But there had been no news from the place until this moment. His intricate conspiracy was collapsing, bits and pieces of it being shed like the leaves from a tree.

Bunny stood in the doorway holding a tray with

coffee and biscuits on it. The cups rattled, the news from Fetterman's having thrilled her. The trace of a smile crossed her lips as she tried to bury her glee, conceal it from Brockington to avoid being punished. He could never send her back, she thought, the words repeating themselves over and over in her mind.

"Stop Spear," Brockington said to Dufond, the drunk recoiling from the order as though he were burned by it. "I don't care how, just do it."

Henderson looked at Dufond, Brad's huge .45 strapped to the little man's waist. He looked like a dwarf in king's clothing, the weapon's holster reaching nearly to his knee.

"You're crazy, Doc. That weasel ain't about to finish Spear."

"Do it, Dufond. Now."

The priest ran from the room as though it were on fire. He raced up the front stairs of the home and scurried up the simple wooden ladder that led to the attic and his cot. He took a twenty-dollar gold piece from its hiding place below a louvered window and slid a sawed-off shotgun under his coat. He left Brockington's at a dead run, closing no doors behind him.

At the hardware store Dufond purchased a ball of thick cord, six screw eyes, a hammer and a fistful of nails. The clerk looked at the retreating little man, amazed that he hadn't waited for change from his twenty dollars.

Dufond raced down alleys, scampering over two fences, until he came to the back door of the Nevada House Hotel. He climbed the backstairs to the third floor and checked the hallway, then picked feverishly at the lock to room 312. It took what seemed an eternity to open the door. Inside he found Spear's carpetbag and his banker's suit, still bloody, hanging in a closet. The agent would be back. It was all he needed to know.

Dufond studied the room quickly and then went to work. He took several nails from his pocket and drove them into the legs of the wooden, straight-backed chair he found. He pounded nervously, hurried, until the chair was nailed to the floor, six feet from the door.

On the inside of the door, three feet from the floor, Dufond pushed a screw eye into the soft wood and twisted it tight. Checking the angle, he fastened another screw eye to the bedpost, this one only eighteen inches from the floor. A second screw eye in another bedpost brought a grin to the man's face. Good work, he thought. Very clever.

The two pillows from the bed found their way to the chair and cradled the double-barreled shotgun. After a few adjustments, Dufond had positioned the weapon so that it was angled upward, chest-high at the door. Then he tied the gun in place, lashing it with the ball of twine. Once it was secure, he cut the cord and tied the end of what remained to the screw eye in the door. He then threaded the twine through both screw eyes on the bedposts and finished off the route by wrapping the string around both triggers of the shotgun. Dufond made sure the gun wasn't loaded and cocked its hammers. He opened the door to the room slowly. At first the string went slack as the door swung inward, but as it moved through its arc the string tightened. When the door was open about two feet, the shotgun's hammers clicked.

Dufond nodded, closed the door and locked it again. More and more nervous, he quickly loaded the shotgun and checked its position. Satisfied, he gathered up his hammer and the ball of twine that sat on the floor. Carefully, he unlocked the door, took one last look and then opened the only exit from room 312 a crack.

Sweat beaded on his forehead as he watched the twine slacken. With the door barely a foot open, he edged past it into the hall. A grunt of relief came from him as he closed the door and locked it. He was out, safe. Dufond ran down the backstairs taking them two at a time.

Pattie saw Brad ride into town a little before noon. She ran from the dining room of the Nevada House into the lobby and leaned against the front window so she could study the young woman behind him on the great black horse. She turned and, folding her arms with a "Humph," looked absently at Mittens. He was working quietly, his scarf trailing behind him. The dining room was still empty, but would soon start to fill. She'd have to hurry.

She ran up the stairs as quickly as she could, holding the silly white hat the cook made her wear with one hand while she pulled at the railing with the other. As she skipped down the third-floor hall, Pattie fingered her passkey. She giggled.

The two blasts rocked the building, deafening in the confined space of the hallway, pouring down the stairwell and filling the lobby. The desk clerk Mittens ran toward the sound, listening for further shots. There were none and his brow furrowed. Pausing at the second-floor landing, he strained for the sound of footsteps. Again, nothing.

His long, thin nose and one eye edged around the corner and glanced down the hall. One quick look and he withdrew. The meaning of the glimpse took a moment to sink in and as he stood, leaning against the wall, his mouth dropped. Mittens staggered forward and then dropped to his knees beside the girl. The two shots had nearly cut her in half. A bloody horror, she'd died instantly.

Mittens looked into the room and saw the still-smoking shotgun tied to the chair. The shivering, gaunt man wondered what kind of cold-blooded coward rigged such a thing. He ran for the sheriff.

Karl Oppenheimer never sat down in Mrs. Harrington's office unless she asked him to do so. A rough-hewn man, a miner accustomed to the boisterous, hands-on discipline below ground, he put aside his swagger and bellowing voice when he entered her office. Quite simply, he was awed by her. She had managed what few men and no woman he knew would even attempt. She had not only taken control of the mine, but had improved its operations. And so, in that one room on earth, the loud and powerful manager listened more than he spoke. And, like a nervous choirboy, stood until invited to sit.

As Karl stood in Lady Jane's office this morning, waiting for her, he recalled the endless meetings they had held when she first took over. He had questioned whether even her concentration and determination would allow her to succeed. But he had avoided condemning the effort to failure. Karl had waited to see. And now he remembered the time with a smile. For during so many of those long days, he had been forced to stand for hours on end simply because Jane had not noticed he wasn't sitting.

Good friends, finally, it had become a joke between them. She complained about his formality and he promised to become more relaxed. He never kept his promise, as she knew he never would.

So he stood, hat in hand, looking at the mementos on the wall. Bits and pieces of his past, the years spent working with Randolph Harrington. The reminiscence they evoked in him felt good this particular morning. He had news for his boss.

She blew through the door like a horse from a gate.

"Morning, Karl," Jane greeted, not looking at him.

"Morning, ma'am," his voice bright, cheerful.

Jane was dressed peculiarly. She wore rough woolen slacks and heavy boots, a leather jacket and a hat more fitting to a cowpoke than a wealthy woman. Karl was confused by her garb, but didn't comment on it.

"Good news this mornin' I think." He was uneasy, all of a sudden. Her soft features and graceful movements were twisted by her angry look and erratic, hurried gestures.

"What?" She wasn't listening.

"Good news. My man in the union says they're stalled. Can't get enough men to shut us down, it's that simple. Those that see what good you've done around here won't mess with 'em and those too dumb to notice won't pay the twenty-five cents dues. They're beat."

She snorted, a rough sound that dismissed his information, somehow. Karl was irritated. Didn't she understand?

" 'Scuse me, ma'am, but didn't ya hear?"

"I heard you Karl. I'm sorry, but you're wrong."

"What?"

Lady Jane stood behind her desk, shuffling papers there. She stopped and looked at him.

"They're not beat yet, Karl. Not yet."

After overhearing Brockington's plans for her mine the night before, Jane had panicked. She'd run to her home and stewed, first afraid; then angry. After a sleepless night of concocting and discarding plans, she had settled on the one flaw in their scheme that would allow her to foil it: Dufond. They intended to get him in the mine to help with its demolition. And she knew him. He would be the red flag, the notice that they had begun. Since well before dawn, she had sat in the cold, watching the mine's main entrance. Jane saw Dick

Young drinking in his shack, observed Jeb Engle's hasty comings and goings, and peered into the gloom for some sign of Dufond. But he hadn't arrived. He wasn't there yet.

Jane had since told Karl's assistant that no new men were to be admitted to the mine without Oppenheimer's approval. The myriad shafts and tunnels were sealed off. She now controlled them.

"Ma'am?"

"The walkout is today, Karl."

"What?"

"Today. I know it for a fact. And I know that those men that don't walk will be killed. They plan to turn the Silver Lady into a bloody hole. And then blow it."

"Blow it? That's crazy."

"Not if I die down there. The courts would sell the mine cheap after a strike and an explosion."

"God." Karl wasn't sure he could believe her. It was fantastic, incredible. "God."

Lady Jane stooped and pulled open the bottom drawer of her desk. From it she retrieved her husband's handgun, a weapon he had cherished for years. It was a Remington army revolver with ivory grips. Its metal was blued, but the silver cone sight shined brightly and the brass trigger guard was obviously polished regularly. A substantial weapon, it weighed nearly three pounds. Jane loaded it without speaking.

"Mrs. Harrington, you sure?"

"Yes," she answered, holding the weapon in both hands, sighting down its barrel.

"Then you'd best be out of here."

"Not on your life, Karl."

"It's not my life we're discussin' here. Unless you want me to hogtie and carry you, you'd best go home without a fuss."

"Shut up and listen," she retorted, edgy. Hearing her

own words, Jane realized her exhaustion and anger were getting the best of her. She sat heavily in her chair. "I'm sorry, Karl."

He disregarded the apology. "Lady, I've got some good men here. We can handle it, just don't get in the way."

Jane decided not to be offended by his implication. An argument wouldn't help anything.

"Karl, please listen. There's a man, a wretched little man I knew in Cheyenne who's with them. He's desperate and ruthless and a coward. But like a small snake in tall grass, he's damn near invisible until he strikes. You'd miss him, never know him. He'd slip by you. And he's the one that's going to be behind the explosion."

"Is he down the hole now?" Oppenheimer was visibly shaken. Once below it would be virtually impossible to find someone who wished to hide. The mine was too large, too sprawling.

"No. I stood guard most of the night."

"Jesus."

"And I told Bob not to let any new men below without checking with you."

Karl's confidence in the woman returned in a rush. She was hard as nails and quick as a whip, he thought. But he didn't like the ugly tone to her voice when she spoke about the man who was being sent to do them in. There was something there that bothered him, but he didn't want to ask.

"Will you sit down, for Christ's sake," Jane barked, a smile spreading across her face. "A new man or two will arrive today. Probably sent by Dick Young, but maybe by Engle . . ."

"Young in on this?"

Jane nodded. "Anyway, the men will be sent to you. They'll have good credentials and will be anxious to work. Just the sort you're always looking for. When they show up, you'll take them below for a sort of tour, a nice, warm, get-acquainted tour. And then bring them out again."

"I'm listenin', I don't like it, but I'm listenin'."

"Then there's going to be a problem of some kind that requires my attention. The strike or an injury or something will demand my immediate presence. That's when I'll need to know exactly where the new man is, where Dufond is."

"Can I ask a stupid question, ma'am?"

She chuckled.

"Wouldn't it be much easier for you to finger this guy so I can blow a hole in him?"

"That, my friend, would make me feel wonderful. But I doubt that it would stop the mine from being blown to smithereens."

Karl Oppenheimer thought for a moment. So far she had outlined a kind of attack, but one that left her vulnerable. There had to be another way.

"Mrs. Harrington, you can't stop a riot in that hole with one pistol. If there's a strike, or any shooting or an explosion, even the rumor of a blow down there, all hell's gonna break loose. And you won't be able to do anything about it."

"That's right, Karl, I won't."

"Then what in the name of blazes do you think you're doin'?"

"Pulling their teeth."

"I don't follow."

"You will, just be sure to keep tabs on the new man, Dufond."

Careening down the stairwell, Mittens missed a step. He tumbled, his head bouncing off walls and risers, to the landing below and then rose, still running at full tilt. Two alarmed guests at the hotel gazed up at him from below but he slipped by them without a word, the blood-soaked body behind him driving the strange, thin clerk forward. In the lobby, he barged past a group of men working their way toward the dining room. They growled at him, impatient and hungry.

He felt his stomach rising to his throat. His disgust overwhelmed him and he ran, gagging, struggling for air. As Mittens burst from the building and reached the crisp noon breeze that swirled up Silver City's dusty streets, he stopped and sat on the splintered steps that led from the hotel to the street. Overcome, breathless, he couldn't move.

The man who wore mittens thought of himself in the third person, like a strange, uncontrollable object to be observed. Sitting on the hotel's stoop he thought, "He died six years ago. Listening to the water, that cold, slow water, he died." Hearing its drip in his ears, a shiver whirled through Mittens. The tap of a metronome, the tick of a clock, the sure, cold, even sound of doom haunted him. The sound of that water told him that he'd died.

Mittens' head filled his hands, tears streaming down his nose and falling to the sidewalk. He sobbed, mourning himself, his shoulders bobbing at the memory of Pattie's body on the hallway floor.

The strange, sad lunatic who sat on the steps of the Nevada House Hotel hadn't always been a quiet, shivering man. Mittens, in fact, had left San Francisco a lighthearted sort of fool in search of his fortune. It had been a time for such young men, bound for paths of glory, headed out on expeditions into the yawning expanse of the American wilderness. Hordes of men were invited. And they'd accepted the invitation. It had been an era of good humor, of travel, of shiftlessness disguised as ambition, a moment in the West when all things seemed possible. And Mittens had ventured into it all, young, educated, a man-child with high hopes.

He had barely begun to shave, yet he found himself in the company of bearded men. And, somehow, his optimism had endured those first few years. The hearty men who moved through the bitter country called "the West" seemed wonderful to him. Often violent, sometimes vicious, nearly always struggling, he admired their strength and courage. Their will to survive. And so the frail young man from San Francisco had adopted their momentum, had thrown in his lot with theirs. Caught up in the thrill of the world in which he found himself, Mittens had accepted the life of a man in search of luck.

He dreamed right along with them. In the mining towns, waiting for word of new strikes. In the hills, searching for signs of ore and in the streams, panning for flakes of gold and silver. He'd done it all, kept up with the brutal strength, the inexplainable discipline and energy of the men he found all around him.

And, still young, still jotting notes in his diary of the romantic world he'd discovered, still believing in the fortune that his future held, Mittens got lucky. He'd studied the guesswork called geology and had mastered the basics of surveying. He had read and had learned. At the same time he had listened to the older, most experienced men that came out of California's dwindling mines. He heard them talking over fires, spinning yarns in the night, and absorbed much of what they had to say. It was a slow process, even withering to him, but he assembled the fragments of understanding, the suggestions, the experiences into a body of knowledge that made sense. Eventually, he thought he knew what he was doing.

One night, in a drafty shed that called itself a saloon, he'd convinced a pair of prospectors that he could help them. Tired of digging in other men's holes, he wanted to look for himself. He deeply wished to discover if what he knew made any difference. And, against all odds, they'd bought it. They heard his desperate yammering about rock formations, mica deposits and trace minerals like men stumbling onto a miracle. The grisly pair of prospectors had accepted him. They had heard his spiel and made him one of them.

They searched the hills together for three months before settling on a site. They'd followed the flow of silver up insignificant streams for weeks. They'd watched the silt pour down crevices, peered at the run-off from showers and drawn a conclusion. They'd decided upon the even trickle of water that came from one, weird cleft in a sheer rock wall. Steeled for the task, they started to dig.

The work was brutal. Harder and longer and more frustrating than anything he'd ever known. The trio never spoke. Not working. Not eating. Never. Exhaustion consumed them, the even pattern of work and sleep their only routine. The hopefulness, the giddy anticipation that he'd expected wasn't there. It was work, pure and simple. And his tough, strong partners never spoke.

The silence, of course, became numbing. The ache of muscles disappeared, the blisters borne of pick handles healed, but the silence beat on him. Mittens became a man whose only desire was not to quit.

The hole was deep, branching twice and wandering down into the mountain. Countless barrels of rock were strewn on the hillside outside the mine and endless dark possibilities lay below. But Mittens knew it was a dead hole. Though they followed the drip of water through the ground, it would never end. They'd been wrong, he thought. It was a bad site.

Still, he dug beside them, determined to pay whatever dues were necessary to enter into their company.

Then it happened. Picking mindlessly in a hole they'd sunk, he heard the roar far above him. Knee-deep in the chill of mountain water, he'd heard the rumble of ground collapsing. His ear tilted, straining to hear. It went black around Mittens.

Hours, perhaps days later, the water startled him awake. It invaded his lungs, soaked his clothes, chilled him into consciousness. He stood up, banging his head on the rock above, and felt the cold water lapping at his knees. Everything was black. He was entombed.

Within minutes he knew he was in a cavity the size of a small closet. Rock surrounded him. And the water kept trickling, dripping from some crack he could not see. He listened for his fellow workers, rapped on the rock above his head. He waited. But the only sound he heard in that chamber was the drip of cold water falling around him.

Mittens lived three days in that cell. The low ceiling forced him to kneel, so he slept leaning, doubled over against a wall. He felt each crack around him, palming the contours of his prison. And he shivered uncontrollably in the cold mountain water that surrounded him.

Then it came again. That rumbling. The mountain's indignant roar coming closer all the time. He knew he was a dead man, that it was over. He pressed himself against one wall and waited for it, for the warmth he imagined death must be. But instead it came at him bright, not dark. A hole, barely a crack, above his head sent a shaft of light that opened in the rock overhead. So he shouted, screaming for help in the bitter cold water. But nothing answered except the tap of cold water falling, drop by drop, around him. His fellow prospectors were still silent.

For three more days he dug at the glittering hole

above him. Pebbles fell and stones came unlodged. The shaft widened, gradually, as he worked. And the sound of water continued, the biting cold all around him as he worked. Desperate and delirious with hunger, he clawed at the rock.

Now, sitting on the steps of the Nevada House Hotel, Mittens felt the pain of pulling through that opening. He remembered with vivid certainty the light above, the death below and the numbness everywhere. And he recalled dragging his body, trying to escape the sound of that cold water splashing into his coffin below. He remembered it as though those seven days were the most real in his life.

They were gone, of course. His hearty, hard-working partners had departed. They took his mule and left no food. They had abandoned the mine and the dead man in it.

Mittens remembered nothing much beyond his escape. Time had passed thereafter, but there was nothing in it he could recall until Fetterman's. There, no one seemed to know what had happened. And as hard as he tried, he couldn't stop the quaking his chill brought on. He looked into their faces and saw nothing. He ate and slept and waited, a man moved from one cold hole into another. Until Bunny West came and warmed him.

The gaunt young man who never spoke was tended to by a beautiful young woman who hated men. It was a dream. She wrapped him, she warmed the gruel that was offered on the fires they made, she kept the scavengers from his boots. And so, Mittens survived. A madman, mute, uncontrollably cold, he survived.

In the end, she took him with her, leading him by the hand as he jerked from side to side, trying to hold a steady course. She'd brought him to Silver City and nursed him back to health. She'd protected him and found him work in the hotel. She'd saved his life, for what it was worth. And now he had to decide what to do with it.

The banker scratched his head, waiting anxiously for some news of the expedition. He had spent hours sitting and thinking about the unlikely crew that had gone in search of the hidden mine at Broken Leg Gulch, worrying about them. For a day and a half he'd thumbed the pages of ledgers, stared at columns of numbers without seeing them and had repeatedly concluded he was a fool. Two relics and a girl had ridden with Spear out of Silver City and he'd stayed behind. They'd risked, perhaps lost, their lives while he sat at his desk. They had gone and he had stayed. It ate at him.

Lyn Loftin looked at himself in the mirror on his wall. The sight sent a shiver down his spine. The banker thought of himself as a young, strong miner. A tough customer. A man one gave way to on the street. But this particular day he saw an aging banker in a crisp blue suit, a man who could do nothing more than sit and think about Spear and his cohorts. He shook his head, worrying for the thousandth time that they were dead. And he was alive in his suit. He wished he had a spot somewhere at the side of a mountain where he could go to dig.

Lyn Loftin was usually a tidy man. His keen mind found disorder intolerable and so his world was well organized. But in the last forty-eight hours, his office had become a shambles. A disaster. His random, nervous work had produced piles of papers, mounds of files, open ledgers spread everywhere. And so, when the banker saw Elephant stride into the bank, he had to zig and zag through the debris that surrounded him to greet the old man.

Elephant didn't look himself. The scruffy, tangled hair that invariably hung at his shoulders was clean and combed. His worn shirt was replaced by a starched white one, complete with a straight black tie. His trousers were pressed and his boots polished. Most remarkable, the red-cheeked, almost cherubic face that constantly bobbed above his shoulders had been replaced by a wrinkled and serious visage.

As Lyn Loftin sat wishing he were dressed in working clothes, prospecting, digging, doing almost anything with his hands, Elephant stood before him, his spit and polish complete.

"We found it," Elephant stated quietly.

"The mine?"

"Of course."

"Wonderful! Wonderful!" The banker was thrilled. He spun like a gleeful boy in his bank's lobby. They were safe, they'd discovered the glittering dream that had caused so much trouble. It was over. "And you're celebrating! I love it. You're duded up in your Sunday best for a wild kinda party. Terrific!"

Elephant shook his head. Loftin looked at him, puzzled, and then saw the pain in Elephant's clear eyes. The banker blanched. He looked around at his employees, men and women disturbed by his strange behavior over the last few days, and ushered Elephant into his office.

"What happened?"

"There was a fight."

"And? For God's sake, what happened?" The banker ranted, running his fingers through his thinning hair. A nightmare, he thought.

"Jebediah's dead."

Loftin sank back into his chair. It was true, he was getting old and cowardly. He'd let them go alone and now one old man with nothing to gain was dead and he was safe.

"And Spear?" Loftin managed to whisper.

"Bringin' Carlotta in."

Lyn didn't want to think about the young woman.

Elephant strode up and down the room, his pent-up energy shining from his eyes.

"What? I mean, what are you doing that for? Why are you walking around like that?" Loftin was annoyed with himself and so striking out at the least irritation.

"Gettin' set."

"Set?"

"For some serious killin'."

"Oh no." Loftin understood. The fight wasn't over yet and he was excluded. The anger of men assaulted was something he knew about but, at least in this instance, couldn't feel simply because he hadn't been there. Hadn't felt it. He was the banker who'd stayed behind. And while he waited, it had begun. He couldn't stop it, or change it, or even participate.

"Fittin'?" Elephant asked, his thumbs behind the lapels of his coat. The old man glanced at Loftin with a special kind of sympathy. Elephant knew Loftin was feeling rattled and pushed aside. He didn't belong in this tussle. Still, the old prospector admired the banker. He was a good, tough man who had earned his good fortune. He just hadn't earned his way into this fight.

"Well, fittin'?" Elephant repeated.

"Oh God . . ." the banker moaned, feeling lost.

A bell rang. The sound of noon. It interrupted both men's thoughts, the clang insistent, lasting longer than either wished. Then Mittens ran into the bank, looking like a crazed messenger running from some conflagration. Since the strange man almost never spoke, he was greeted with indifference by Loftin. Whatever the little lunatic wanted could wait, he thought. But Elephant went to Mittens immediately, as though he held some secret. Loftin followed, stunned, frustrated, feeling old.

"They keep coming at him!" the desk clerk shouted.

"What now?" Elephant asked, his voice a pick shattering through rock.

"Th-th-they set up a sh-sh-shotgun. Booby trap. Killed Pattie, the waitress at the hotel."

Elephant turned, a smile across his face, and looked at Loftin. It was starting early. "Come on, Shivers, let's go." Elephant led Mittens from the bank.

"We gotta find that blasted Pinkerton," Elephant said almost idly as he stared up the street. But Mittens shook his head, mute again.

"He's gotta be back in town by now." Mittens nodded and pointed down the road toward the livery.

"Let's go!" Elephant took off at the best run his old legs allowed, then stopped. Mittens hadn't moved. He was looking north, in a trance. "Come on!" the old man screamed, impatient. But Mittens didn't seem to have heard the order. He just stood there, clapping his wrapped hands against his quaking upper arms.

"Good horse," Spear remarked as Tucker McGee drifted around the animal, his hand always on it. Brad watched the man, noticed the rapport between the great black and his keeper, and decided.

"Ten bucks?" the agent asked. Carlotta glowered at him.

"Huh?" McGee wondered aloud.

"Ten bucks. Will you give me ten dollars for this horse?"

Tucker still didn't understand, blithered at seeing his horse again and confused by the amount offered.

"Come on, man," Spear shouted. "Give me ten bucks so we can go get cleaned up."

Tucker disappeared into his tiny office, so bewildered he didn't seem to know what he was doing. Carlotta looked profoundly irritated, her eyes filled with the vacant, angry stare of a woman whose criticism runs deep. Brad dismissed it. Diamond was his horse and he wanted to sell him to Tucker McGee.

"Animal's worth more." She studied him.

"Yup."

"Then get more."

"I'm getting enough. Aren't you a little tired to be arguing?"

She pouted away, her clear, consistent, unchangeable disapproval something he didn't want to bother with. Not now.

Elephant came at him, churning up the street in the clumsiest sort of way, looking uncomfortable in his fancy clothes. When he skidded to a halt in front of Brad, the old man leaned over, his hands on his knees, and tried to catch his breath. The cold air had numbed his lungs and the sprint had completely exhausted him, so it took quite a while for Elephant to speak.

"Whew," he finally muttered.

"You all right?" Carlotta asked, her arms wrapped around the old man's shoulders.

"Sure. Sure. But it's startin' up already. Them sons-of-bitches tried to bushwhack Spear here with a shotgun rigged in his room. Blew some waitress to pieces."

Brad knew it must be Pattie.

"Jesus," Carlotta murmured, the unknown woman somehow important to her.

Tucker McGee walked from his office, counting the bills he held in his hands. The man was obviously delighted to buy back Diamond and in a hurry to complete the transaction before Spear changed his mind about it. That fiery little woman with him clearly thought the agent was a fool to part with the horse so cheaply and Tucker didn't want to take any chances on her convincing Brad to keep the animal.

Brad saw the glint of shining metal up the street and recognized the cool, sure posture of the man with the nickel-plated rifle. He pushed Carlotta roughly to the ground and shouted, "Down," to Elephant. In an instant, all three of them lay on the ground, Elephant griping about the dirt on his jacket. Tucker McGee stood among them, looking at the trio as though they were mad. First these folks buy his horse for more than its worth, then sell it back for next to nothing and now they're rolling around in the dirt. Lord, he thought, strange folks. Then the slap of lead pounding into wood startled him and the sound of gunfire scared him out of his wits. The rifleman had opened fire, at midday on a busy street. There would be no more sneaking around. Tucker lay on the ground next to Spear.

"What the . . ." the liveryman arched his brow at the agent, a pathetic, plaintive expression dominating his face.

Spear rolled away from Tucker quickly, but the liveryman followed, mimicking his every move.

"Hey, you," he called, "here's your ten bucks, okay?"

Brad laughed, took the bills and crammed them in his coat pocket. Then he saw Carlotta racing behind Diamond and heard the crack of another round being fired through the cold air. Men and women were screaming, running from the street between the livery and the hired killer. And still the blond man held his ground, aiming and firing a third time.

"Spear!" Carlotta barked at him. He turned to her and saw Jebediah's buffalo rifle drifting through the air at him. He caught the weapon and rolled to his belly, prepared to fire. But the rifleman had disappeared again.

Brad rose and hurried up the street, the ponderous rifle in one hand. People poked their heads through doors and peered from behind windows as he passed.

Brad turned down an alley, guessing at his adversary's escape route. He saw nothing but wooden crates thrown into a pile. Flattening himself against the side of a building, he inched down the alley. It was deadly quiet. Then he heard the click of a hammer being drawn back, ready to fall onto a shell meant for the agent. He strained, trying to pinpoint the source of the noise, but couldn't.

The rifleman handled his weapon as deftly as a pistol. The gleaming, lightweight rifle spun, glistening into the alley and rattled off three shots in hurried succession, the first two splintering the wood above Brad's head, the third grazing his shoulder. The burning pain twisted him and the buffalo rifle fell from his hand, but he was down for it only a moment later. Picking it up, he realized that the thing was essentially useless now that one arm was wounded and so he tossed it against the crates.

The blond rifleman was running, turning out of sight around a building at the back of the alley. It was a warehouse, a huge, ugly building that stood nearly empty during the slow days of winter. Brad followed, his pistol in one hand, and heard the heavy door of the warehouse creak closed as he pursued.

Inside the great, dark room, Spear could see that a few crates and dozens of barrels littered the floor. The storage building, nearly empty, offered scores of hiding places. Brad listened to the wind whistling through the cracks in the building's roof and noticed the loft which hung over half the enclosed space. The high ground, Brad thought. This one likes being above the fray. Spear remembered the sight of the man as he contrived his strategy at Broken Leg Gulch. He stood out of range, high on the opposite ridge, waiting for a safe moment to strike.

Spear walked among the heavy oak barrels, certain his target had climbed into the loft. He moved silently, waiting for the telltale rustle of a man on the move and fingered the trigger of his .44. Nothing, for the longest time, not a sound. Had he lost him? Brad turned his back to the loft, took two steps and then hurled himself behind a barrel. As he rolled on his injured shoulder, the pain of the flesh wound ran down his arm, but he caught a glimpse of the blond as he hurried behind cover above.

It was a stand-off. Each knew where the other waited, neither able to escape or get off a clear shot. Then the agent saw it, the line of five-gallon tins on a shelf in the loft. "Lamp Oil" was printed on their sides.

"Mister!" Brad shouted. "Better climb down out of there."

"Go to hell, butcher!"

"It's you that'll be doing the burning. Better climb down out of there."

"Go to hell!"

Brad almost enjoyed the conversation, a card player who knew his opponent's hand, the agent wasn't in any hurry. He sat for a moment, trying to decide on a safe exit once the fire started. He concluded it would be tricky to get out of the warehouse until he was sure the rifleman was dead.

"Hey, buster," Brad shouted. "Take a quick look over your shoulder. Seems you're sitting in the middle of some flammables."

"Shit," the man cursed to himself.

"Mind if I take a shot at one of those tins?"

Without answering, the blond rolled to the loft floor above, the barrel of his rifle spitting shells into the oak in front of Brad. Spear fired back, his first shot digging into the beam which supported the loft. His second grazed the man's skull and his head ducked out of sight. Brad waited. But heard nothing. Just as the agent was considering the possibility that the hired gun was unconscious, the man stood up.

The side of his head bloody, he shouldered his rifle and began firing it. The warehouse's dirt floor spat sand as shells hit it and the barrel in front of Brad sent slivers of wood twisting through the air. Four or five shots were fired from the loft with methodical accuracy and without haste. Then Brad rolled, firing at the blurred target above, squeezing off rounds as quickly as he could. Before the agent came to a stop, he saw the blond man buckle above him and then tumble from the loft. He landed on his back, a dull thud echoing in the hollow room.

Spear approached cautiously, trying to detect even the slightest sign of life in the man. There was none. Holstering his six-gun, Brad stooped and pulled the magnificent .36 caliber rifle from the killer's death grip. He turned and saw Carlotta, kneeling in the entrance to the building, the buffalo rifle in her hands.

# Chapter 17

The sheriff was duly impressed. Sitting on the bed in the Nevada House Hotel's room 312, he fingered Brad's vest. The garment was lined with thin steel plate, capable of stopping a small caliber bullet. Tricky stuff, he thought. The man stood and poked his nose awkwardly into the agent's carpetbag. There were three shotgun shells inside, each with two dozen tenpenny nails taped to it and a steel ball fastened to its firing cap. The sheriff picked up one of them, curious, and studied it. Then the grenade's purpose came to him and he gingerly replaced it.

The sheriff justified his snooping by telling himself he was looking for evidence. In fact, though, he was fascinated by the paraphernalia the Pinkerton had in his room. And rummaging through it all allowed him to ignore the bloody scene in the hall. Sheriff Wadkins hated blood. It unsettled his stomach. So while his two deputies wrapped Pattie's body in canvas and carted her away, he walked around the room, trying to imagine what a detective would look for in it.

Going through the pockets in Spear's suit, the sheriff was alarmed when Mittens walked in. He backed away from the coat, embarrassed.

"Yeah, what?" he asked.

Mittens shook his head. The desk clerk simply wanted to look at the sawed-off shotgun strapped to the chair. He looked at the string, the screw eyes, the pellet holes in the door and wall. Mittens went to the window and looked out. A three-story drop and the window was locked from the inside. He scratched his chin, the rough fabric of his mittens scraping across his skin. Mittens couldn't figure out how the man who had rigged the trap left the room. Had he been sitting in it when Pattie opened the door? Then why such an elaborate mechanism? It didn't make sense.

The idea that death waited in an empty room frightened Mittens. His nerves were on edge, his joints ached.

The sound of gunfire from the street visibly shook the strange, thin clerk. He froze, trembling. The sheriff listened to the noise, the sound of a rifle he thought.

"Now what?" Wadkins muttered, annoyed by the inconvenience all this killing was causing. And the gore, the disgusting gore that seemed to be plaguing the city. He walked slowly from the room, not really anxious to find out what awaited him on the street.

Alone, Mittens pushed the chair which cradled the shotgun. He tilted his head and considered the nails that held it to the floor. Then calmly, as though he were a janitor straightening up the room, he took a pocketknife from his trousers and cut the twine which bound the weapon. He untied the string from the shotgun's triggers and cracked the barrels open. Two spent shells dropped to the floor. He snapped the barrels back in place and groped for the trigger. His mittens were in the way so he took one off, cocked one hammer and pulled the trigger. It rapped home with a clear, metallic click. Replacing his mitten, the desk clerk wandered from the room, the shortened gun in one hand.

As Mittens crossed the street, the sound of a gunfight came from the freight company warehouse three blocks away. But the desk clerk ignored the battle. Some connection had short-circuited in his mind. The intricate pattern of greed, violence and anger that had built up around Spear had finally overwhelmed Mittens. He couldn't hope to unravel its mysteries. There were far too many inexplicable, yawning black holes involved. And so he trudged across the street, indifferent to Spear's battle.

Men and women still scurried on the road, curious about the gunfire and frightened by it. Several peered down the alley that led to the warehouse. And as Mittens walked among them, slow and apparently deaf to the furor nearby, people ran from him. The ghostly figure with a sawed-off shotgun walked patiently away from the battle, a perplexing sight, almost eerie.

Mittens clopped down the sidewalk at a steady pace. A man who was reporting to a friend on the sight of the rifleman standing in the middle of the city's main street pulled his companion into a store when he saw the clerk approaching. The desk clerk didn't notice them. The single spark that lit his mind tunneled his vision, moving him like a pallbearer down the street.

Brockington's front door was unlocked. Mittens walked through it without knocking and, standing in the hallway, removed the mitten from his right hand. He had never been in the building and now found himself in a place he feared, holding an unloaded shotgun.

Halfway up the stairs, Mittens heard Bunny West's voice. At first she seemed to be talking to herself, her tone even, almost mumbled. But as he climbed farther, he could make out her words and stopped.

"I don't understand, I don't understand," she repeated over and over.

Brockington's voice suddenly boomed over her protest. "Shut up, you bitch!" Bunny began sobbing, the sound of hopelessness she made one that Mittens knew all too well. He edged to the top of the stairs and looked down the hall. At its end he saw the girl, naked, tied to a chair. Her arms were crossed behind her head and strapped to the chair back, her legs spread and bound at the ankles to the ornately carved claws of the chair's legs.

Mittens had seen scores of naked women at Fetterman's. Old and young, the addled, the weak and those few attractive women that the guards abused often wandered about with few, if any, clothes. And before his struggle to survive the collapsed mine, he had explored the delights offered by the women who followed mining booms. But the sight of Bunny took his breath away.

Her breasts were perfect orbs, high and taut. Her sides trim, heaving with each moan and her hips flared soft and smooth before him.

Brockington stood beside her in shirt sleeves and black trousers. He ran one finger down her cheek, following the path of a tear to her neck. His hand cupped her face and then stroked her neck and breast. Bunny moaned and sobbed uncontrollably as her head thrashed from side to side. Brockington tugged at a nipple, grinning, and she screamed. Then his hand slipped between her thighs and his fingers disappeared in the soft, black hair.

"God, no, no!" Bunny screamed, her voice piercing.

He withdrew his touch and slapped her. "Bitch, I'll fix you," he snapped, marching through a door. In an instant he returned with a bit of cloth and gagged her mouth. A look of true terror filled Bunny's eyes.

Brockington then pawed her breasts with both hands, his touch brutal, and sank to his knees, prying at her thighs. Bunny's muted cries rang in Mittens' ears, her agony tearing at him. As the doctor parted

Bunny, she twisted, struggling in the chair and Mittens stepped silently into the hallway.

He stood there for a moment and then slammed the barrel of his weapon against the wall. Bunny stared at him and Brockington turned, surprised. The doctor scrambled to his feet and watched the shotgun bang against the wall, over and over, until bits of plaster littered the floor.

"Stop," the doctor pleaded, but Mittens continued pounding the wall as he walked toward the frightened man. The desk clerk stood, anger shaking through him as his eyes darted from the doctor to the sobbing woman. Bunny looked at him, incredulous, mumbling something, shaking her head. Mittens waved the barrel of his gun at Brockington, motioning him aside. The doctor moved quickly, his eyes locked on the gaping barrels of the shotgun, and pressed his back against a wall.

"You're not going to kill me?" Brockington asked, not sure if the chalk-white face of a madman that glared at him could even understand his words. Mittens nodded to the doctor.

"No, for God's sake, no," Brockington raised his hands, his palms facing Mittens as if to stop him. "Listen, I can pay you, lots, set you up with anything, give her to you, buy a hotel, I can . . ." Brockington was interrupted by a single, thundering crash of the gun barrel against the wall. He shivered and fell silent.

Mittens' thumb reached across the hammer of one barrel of the gun and cocked it with a snap.

"God, no . . ." Brockington seemed to be trying to back up farther, to melt into the wall behind him.

The clerk cocked the second hammer. Brockington's hands flew up again, begging Mittens and barring his way at the same time. Then Mittens lifted the gun, aimed it at the doctor's head and pulled both triggers.

Brockington screamed, his hands flying to his face and then fell to his knees. Bunny's eyes closed and her body tensed, waiting for the sound. But there was only the click of the hammers falling on empty chambers.

The kneeling doctor looked at Mittens just as the desk clerk brought the barrel of the shotgun down across his head. Brockington's elbows flew up but were little use, the steel crashing against his skull. The doctor grunted, slumping, and Mittens struck again, this time opening a wide, rough gash in the man's temple. Brockington turned his head, barely conscious as the third blow fell toward him and closed his eyes just before he died. The last, crushing assault shattered his skull, bits of bone killing him instantly.

Mittens dropped the shotgun across the fallen doctor's body and stood looking at the corpse. The gruesome sight of blood spreading on the floorboards somehow took control of the man, transfixing him. Mittens stood there, staring, feeling absolutely nothing. Suddenly Bunny's cries, muffled and distant, crept into his mind. Hearing her, he wondered for a moment where she was, then turned and looked down at her. Red blotches had begun to appear where Brockington had pulled at her body and scratches grew crimson along her thighs. But all Mittens could see were Bunny's dark eyes pleading with him to help her, tears streaming down her face. With his fingers he wiped the drops from her cheek and then untied the gag from her mouth.

"Oh, help me, help me," she begged.

"I will," Mittens stated, his voice clear and direct. The man then cut the cords that bound her hands and legs and gathered Bunny in his arms. She held him, sobbing, grasping him as tightly as she could.

"We've got to run," Bunny urged. "Get out of here before they come back."

"Get dressed first," Mittens ordered her. Suddenly, she was embarrassed. She sprinted to a room for clothes and the tall, thin man from the Nevada House Hotel walked down the stairway to the front hall.

The doctor at the Silver Lady mine had been sent for, so Spear sat at a corner table in The Mammoth Saloon, idly sipping a beer. The magnificent rifle in front of him occupied his attention completely as he dabbed with a napkin at bits of dirt on it and polished the rifle's barrel. The thing fascinated him. Old, engraved "By Special Order of Samuel Colt, 1855," it had obviously been cared for meticulously. While there were fine scratches in its finish and its black lacquered stock was worn, the rifle was in perfect condition.

It had the heft of an oversized pistol. Its barrel was nearly eight inches shorter than Jebediah's buffalo gun and its stock equally diminutive. Spear could easily lift and hold it in one hand. Empty, he squeezed off three quick pulls at the trigger.

"Beautiful," he admired.

"Looks like a toy," Carlotta interrupted.

"It's for killing people and damn good at it." The agent was annoyed by her remark. The sharp pain in his shoulder had been put there by the gleaming weapon in his hand, so he knew how well it functioned. But more important, it was an extraordinary piece of equipment. The kind of tool Spear sought constantly. The sort of aid that might, one day, make all the difference. He resented the belittling of it.

"Arm okay?" Elephant asked. Brad looked at the bandana that had been tied around his arm. No blood seeped through it.

"A scratch, mostly," he replied.

"Lucky."

"Every once in a while, I'm due."

Elephant chuckled at the agent. The man never seemed to rattle, he thought. Glib as a hawker, just quieter.

"I wish you'd put that thing away," Loftin said to Brad. "It's a gorgeous hunk of iron, but I'm not real fond of it." Brad leaned the rifle against the wall, checking to see that the black leather belt holding several dozen .36 caliber shells still sat coiled at his feet.

"What next?" Loftin wanted to know.

"Well," Brad exhaled deeply, "seems like we know where to look, at least. Brockington's gotta have the Land Grant Certificates stolen from the bank. We know he's got cash taken in the burglary. Only problem seems to be nailing the good judge and the senator."

"Maybe they've got some of the cash," the banker suggested.

Spear shook his head. "Doubtful. Fact is, it's doubtful they've got anything that might connect either of them to the burglary."

"Damn," the banker muttered.

"Don't quit on them, though," Brad wasn't finished. "If we can't jail that pair, at least we can hurt them a bit."

"You're nuts," Elephant noted, an obvious compliment.

Brad liked the old man's sense of gamesmanship. He seemed to be the only one among them who saw this as sport. As a form of maneuvering so desperate and dangerous that it had to be taken lightly in order to be endured. Only Elephant seemed to know that they played a game without rules, without boundaries and for high stakes, but still a game. Only Elephant seemed to understand Brad's playfulness.

"We can't finish those guys, but we can mess them up some, I think." Brad was talking to Elephant.

"What ya got in that head of your'n?"

"Don't know, what do you think?"

"Welp . . ." the old man was in seventh heaven. He stared at the smoke that churned toward paddle fans in the bar. "Seems to me that ol' Doc Brockington is the ringleader of the bunch. 'Pears like he's runnin' this show. Probably pushin' and pullin' at those other two all the way. Strikes me like they'd be real nervous if'n something were to spook 'em. Sorta like boys playin' where they ought not to play."

"The man's a senator, you old fool!" Loftin was stunned by Elephant's rambling.

"This ain't Washington."

"What in blazes can we do to scare a senator and a judge?" Loftin asked sarcastically. He was feeling useless and resenting it.

"Got a thought?" Brad was trying to provoke Elephant. Get him spinning a yarn. Making things up. His question was essentially a challenge.

"Yep," Elephant nearly erupted.

"You cat, have out with it." Brad was amused.

"What we need here is something real spooky. Sorta scary, ya know?" A question directed at no one. "What we gotta do is aim the gun at some heads and see who flinches."

"Have any idea how?" Brad asked.

"Nope."

"Hmmmmm."

"But then I'm not gettin' paid for all this fancy thinkin'." Elephant grinned at Spear.

"Tell you what, old man," Brad offered. "You wander out to the judge's place and tell him a man with five thousand votes wants to talk to him. Tell him that this guy stumbled on those votes in Broken Leg Gulch and wants to sell them. Then head over to the senator's and tell him a cardsharp's in town. Some guy who has nothing but Broken Leg Gulch Land Grant Certificates to play with. Let both of them know that your friend will be available here at six o'clock tonight."

Elephant cackled, slapped his knee and went on cackling.

Loftin scowled. Carlotta looked down into her empty beer mug. Everything was perfect, Brad thought.

The doctor came through the door like an animal searching vainly for a place to hide. His head twitched, looking around the room.

"Spear?" It was a desperate croak, breathless.

"Here."

The man hurried to the agent. "There's a strike at the Silver Lady. Damn fools won't work."

Brad wasn't surprised. Jane had known something like this was coming and he was confident she could handle it.

"And Mrs. Harrington's headed into that hole. Going in there! Dressed up like some man who's headed out to dig rock." Brad looked up at the doctor, his mouth tight.

"You know what to do, Elephant?" Brad asked.

"Yep, see ya at six."

Spear nodded to the group, picked up his cherished rifle and headed for the Silver Lady mine.

# Chapter 18

Dufond arrived at the mine fifteen minutes before the day shift was to begin. He came alone, his rendezvous with Jeb Engle and Dick Young scheduled for noon. Karl Oppenheimer knew he was the troublemaker Mrs. Harrington expected the moment he saw Dufond walking across the yard in front of the mine. The ex-priest was small and walked stooped at the shoulders, leaning forward as though each step were difficult. His thin shoulders had never hauled rock and his frail hands had never worked a pick for very long.

Nevertheless, Karl listened carefully to the tale Dufond offered. He presented the general manager with forged documents attesting to his good service in Utah and California mines. Karl feigned enthusiasm for his new employee, described the pay and medical services available to workers and cautioned Dufond about the union that seemed to be forming on some work crews. Pierre Dufond lied brilliantly, explaining to Karl that he'd never teamed with workers and never would. Didn't like the idea of being told when and where he could work and couldn't tolerate having somebody else doing his negotiating for him. No, Karl had nothing to worry about from Dufond.

Karl asked Dufond to wait for him while he checked some records at the main office. He then headed for Jane.

Through the large window in her office, she watched the day crew straggle in. Men clapped their hands in the cold, their breath visible in the morning air as they greeted one another. Jane watched the sea of bright-red caps, plaid jackets and heavy coats mill about. She noticed several workers holding their hands over a small fire, laughing and watched a few miners puffing deeply on their last cigars of the morning. There was no smoking underground.

Oppenheimer knocked and entered, not waiting for Jane's permission.

"He's here, I think. Dirty-lookin' little man with thin fingers and no handshake."

"Sounds like Dufond, all right."

"That's the name he's usin', ma'am."

"I'm surprised. An alias would have been easy enough. I guess he's sure he can get in and out in a hurry."

Karl shrugged. He still had no idea how Lady Jane planned to avoid real trouble once the man got into the mine and he had a healthy fear of Young and Engle. But having met Dufond, his natural reaction was not to be concerned about him. The little weasel simply didn't seem dangerous. Tricky perhaps, but not the kind of obvious physical threat Karl had expected.

"Well, Karl, I guess you better walk him through the operation. Show him everything. And take your time. We can't know when they'll make their move, but it will probably be soon. Stall, make them nervous. Understand?"

"That much I understand. As to the rest, I'm still sorta baffled, ma'am."

"Don't worry, just don't let him out of your sight."

"I won't."

As the shift whistle blew across the yard and men begrudgingly ambled toward their day's work, Jane watched Karl and Dufond head into the mine. She shivered at the sight of him, her hatred burning through her imagination. She had never put the memory of his sordid assault on her out of her mind. The recollection of it haunted her, a moment of powerlessness and disgust so profound that it was indelibly imprinted on her. The mere sight of Dufond brought back the smell of whiskey on his breath and clothes as he raped her. . . .

Jane quickly turned away from the window. She would kill him. This time she would kill him.

The mouth of the Silver Lady mine was covered by a huge building. In it carpenters, machinists and engineers worked to supply the men below with everything from tools to cool air. The main room's ceiling was nearly thirty-five feet high, the space above the men's heads filled with pulleys and cables. In the floor were three large openings that belched steam year-round.

Karl walked Dufond to one end of the building and introduced him to Dan Frogle, an engineer about to begin his shift. Dan's job was to operate a hoisting engine that ran a car up and down one of the shafts. A small bell by his ear signaled him to lift or lower the car in accordance with the orders of a foreman far below. The engineer's job was a demanding one, his attention to his work crucial to the safety of the men digging below. So Karl checked often with his engineers to get word of the day's progress.

"Set for the day?" he asked.

"Yep," Dan chirped.

"Go slow with the first bucket, okay? I'm taking this new man down in the car and want to show him the layout."

"Slow it's to be then," Dan confirmed.

They walked past the pump, which brought thousands of gallons of water a day out of the mine, and stood in a car. As it dropped, they plummeted in total darkness past hundreds of feet of rock. The heat of the ground below rose toward them, an eerie, churning mist. Then, after only a few moments, a huge room appeared. Several men stood around, holding candles, preparing for the day's work. And then they were gone, the car dropping still lower into the earth.

"Not much coming out of here above 900 feet anymore, but we keep a crew at the upper levels to watch the timbers."

Dufond nodded. He'd never been so far below the surface of the earth before and the darkness chilled him.

At the 1200 foot level, the car came to a stop. Before them opened a huge room, supported from its floor to its upper levels, nearly 120 feet, by a honeycomb of massive wooden beams. In some areas each cell was floored with planks, in others one could see from the top to the bottom of the mine's space. The main drift, or horizontal tunnel, stretched black into the distance on either side of them.

Dufond was terrified and Karl could feel it. Hundreds of feet from daylight, the mine's great open belly was almost completely dark. Only the weird flicker of candles marked each worker. And the air was stifling, over 100 degrees and incredibly humid. The men who had shivered above only minutes before now stood naked to the waist, sweat pouring off them.

Karl walked Dufond down a crosscut to a small team of men. All three wore felt caps and heavy boots, and were picking at the soft black ore at the end of the tunnel.

"How's it?" Karl asked one of them.

"Clay, lots of it. Soft and spreading. We're gonna need us some timbers here soon." The porous, soft soil present in far too many sections of the mine posed a real threat to the men who dug in it. Even the massive posts and interlocking cells of their supports often buckled under the pressure of shifting clay.

"What of the rats?" Oppenheimer knew that hundreds of rats lived in the hole, eating the scraps from the men's lunches. And he also knew they were quick to disappear from a portion of the mine that was unsafe.

"Still got plenty of 'em 'round here," one man replied, smiling.

"That's the truth."

"Good." Karl felt better.

Karl felt hot and moved to a bucket of ice nearby, grabbing a chunk to chew on. Dufond lifted a large piece and pressed it against his neck. A rough rock wall near the ice bucket glimmered in the darkness, bits of quartz crystal shining in the light of candles. Dufond touched the rock and pulled back his hand, surprised. It was hot. Everything was hot.

They crossed a kind of bridge, a long, wooden maze of timbers that led from one area of the room to another. In the middle of the bridge, Dufond looked down. Two pipes, one nearly two feet in diameter for pumping air, the other six inches or so across, rose from the darkness below into the darkness above.

"Water," Karl explained, pointing to the smaller pipe. "At 1600 feet we've got lots of it." He pointed down. "That's where the steam's comin' from. Real hot water down there. Boiled a man in it three months ago. Killed instantly."

This was hell, Dufond thought. The dark, ugly world that hell must be.

Pale, huge men worked all around them. Their candles stuck in small holes in the mine's walls, their picks clanging in the darkness. Cars and wheelbarrows moved about, taking ore to the buckets that ran up and

down the three main shafts. There was little or no talking, the heat overcoming everyone's ability to be
pleasant, and men worked bored and weary in the
hole. An explosion here would kill fifty men, Dufond
thought.

"Stay away from the shafts," Karl warned. "If a
bucket hits you, it'll rip your arm off. You fall and
you're dead."

Dufond was ready to leave the place, it terrified him.
They returned to the car that had brought them down
and stepped into it. A man stationed nearby then
pulled hard on a cord and Karl knew the small bell at
Dan Frogle's ear was ringing. In an instant they were
hurtling upward, the engineer pulling them to the surface. Dufond felt his head swim as the cold air poured
down on them from above. He wobbled and Karl
steadied him.

"You get used to that," he said, smiling at the little
man's obvious fear.

The light in the huge building covering the mine entrance was blinding as they emerged. But the cool,
drier air was welcomed by Dufond. He felt as though
he'd escaped the most oppressive place imaginable.
Having seen the world the miners endured, he was
overwhelmed by their ability to work there. The heat
and darkness, the maze of timbers and the pitch-black
distances that spread in all directions convinced him
that the men who went into those holes were insane.
For four dollars a day they sweated in a huge grave.
Insane.

He pondered his scheduled meeting with Engle below. Noon on the great bridge. He remembered the
trestled span with a shudder. Everything on one side of
it would disappear in the explosion, buried in the
crumbly, soft soil that made the region so difficult to
mine. It would appear to have been an explosion of

natural gas, set off by a candle. But it would close the hole, at least for a while.

"Get a hat from the shed, and let Bob outfit you," Karl ordered Dufond. "And then come back here. I'll assign you."

Dufond slouched into the yard and watched the great ten-mule teams pulling ore to the railroad. The clear sky and fresh air felt good to him.

A few minutes before noon, the hoist crew walked to a car and had themselves brought to the surface. There were a dozen men walking off the job with Engle, most of them simply happy to be out of the mine, regardless of their reason. Another dozen that walked with them responded to the derringers in their ribs. But the effect was the same. The ore stopped moving.

Dan Frogle brought them up in three loads, operating his engine with the sort of skill that took years to develop. When he'd finished, the last carful of men brought up and his bell quiet at his ear, Dan strode across the hardwood floor of the building and grabbed Engle by the lapels.

"You dumb bastard!" he screamed. Men stood watching the confrontation, their universally high regard for the engineer making him untouchable, no matter what he did.

"Get off it, Dan. We're walking." Engle didn't want a scene.

"You're gonna ruin this mine, the best mine in Nevada."

"Gonna make it better," Engle said, walking away from an argument he couldn't win.

Frogle sprinted past him, headed for Mrs. Harrington. Along the way he joined Karl, headed in the same direction. Together, they stormed into the woman's office, Dan visibly agitated.

"They're walkin'," he snorted, furious.

"Quiet, Dan," Karl said calmly, baffling the loyal engineer.

"Where's Dufond?" Jane asked.

"Up in the shed with Bob, gettin' outfitted," Karl reported.

"Good, keep him there until Engle's out of the way." Jane paced the room. "Now, empty the hole. Get everyone out, quickly. But send Engle to me before you give the order." Karl grinned. She was a fox.

Karl kept telling Dan to shut up and do as he was told as they ran back to the building over the mine entrance. By the time they'd arrived, the ore had stopped moving, the two other engineers standing idly by their huge machines. One checked the massive spool overhead for cable wear, not really expecting to find any.

"Engle!" Karl bellowed across the room. The organizer walked, very slowly, to the general manager. "The lady wants to see you."

"Good. I'm gonna tell her about it." Engle seemed agitated all of a sudden, a man playing his role unconvincingly. "The creakin' and the runnin' rats. It ain't safe down there. Somethin's wrong, and we ain't gonna keep workin' in it . . ."

"You tell her. Go on." Karl pointed to the exit.

"I'll *show* her. She can look for herself."

Karl thought that she'd been right again. Engle wanted her in the hole. She wouldn't go. She couldn't go. They'd kill her.

The union man left, the door slamming behind him. "Go," Karl hollered at Dan. In minutes they'd spread the word and the mine emptied. Only a few minutes thereafter, all eighty-seven miners stood, filthy and bewildered, in the main room above ground. Then Bob walked in with Dufond, the little priest looking like a fool in his brimless felt hat and heavy boots. His huge coat, containing a half-dozen sticks of dynamite, hung heavily from his shoulders under the weight.

"Lunch break," Karl explained nonchalantly to Dufond, sure the man didn't know that miners always eat below.

"Ah!" Dufond exclaimed, wondering to himself how he would keep his appointment with Engle on the bridge.

"You hungry?" Karl asked.

"No. In fact, I think I'll ride down and get a feel for the place. That okay?"

"Sure," Karl nodded. "Dan, run the new man down, will ya?"

As Dufond plummeted down the shaft, his stomach rising as he fell, the miners began to snicker, laughing and talking in small groups. The strikers had left, headed for a drink, they said. And those that remained were happily off the picks and wheelbarrows, welcoming the chill of open air. There was speculation about the new little man. Eager, some said. Stupid, noted the majority. The idea of lunch above was hilarious to most. They were amused that the little guy had accepted such nonsense. And the yammering about the union grew. What the hell were they up to? Best mine in Nevada, a rotten, hot hole to be sure, but the best. What's to gripe about, the men wondered.

Still, the shutdown was a holiday. They relaxed. Swapped stories, asked questions about women and the last night's drinking. They were up and safe, so whatever it was all about didn't worry them very much.

Engle, meanwhile, stood in Lady Jane's office trying not to be intimidated by the powerful woman. She was grilling him. Asking about the expanding clay he complained of and querying him as to the sounds of strain in the mine. He was surprised by her expertise and

taken aback by the relentlessness of her cross-exam-
ination.

"Listen, lady, just come see it. That'll tell ya what ya
need to know." This wasn't working the way he'd
thought it would.

"All right," she said, giving in to his request precipi-
tously. She strapped her husband's six-gun around her
waist while Engle looked on, amazed. "Let's go."

As they entered the huge room over the mine, Engle
froze. Every man in the hole was standing in front of
him. He didn't understand. Couldn't figure it out. What
was going on?

"Figured we better clear the place, ma'am," Karl reported, his face serious. "What with all that creakin'
timber below."

"Well done." She didn't look at him. "Run us down
to the 1200 foot level, please."

"Ah, Mrs. Harrington, might not be safe there now.
Only the new man below." Karl hadn't even contemplated the real possibility of her going into the mine
with these snakes.

"It'll be fine, Karl. Just checking on the timbers with
Mr. Engle here. Send us down, right now." She wasn't
about to continue the conversation. He'd been dismissed.

Lady Jane had been in the mine on countless occasions, checking progress, safety conditions or merely
overseeing changes in pumping or ventilation equipment. But she knew and understood the immense operation best above ground, looking at her charts. The
interlocking system of timbers that made up the mine's
support was meticulously charted in her office. Each
hollow cube, called a square set, was recorded as it
went up. So Jane knew the precise size and shape of
the mine's huge cavities, their direction, winces, shafts,

ledges, bridges and stations. The whole tangled web of wood and rock.

Still, the heat and darkness of the mine's lowest levels always disoriented her. When walking through them with Karl, she was constantly amazed he knew every inch of the place while she caught her bearings only periodically, when something recognizably unique appeared. Now, with the mine cleared of men, few candles flickered in the darkness and so it was especially difficult to get around.

Jane and Jeb Engle walked from the shaft car without saying a word. The man was visibly unnerved by the quiet in the hole. He commonly prowled among the miners, but with all of them topside, the only noise in the place was the steady slosh of the pumps pulling hot water from the sump nearly 600 feet below. Steam rose through the shafts and rock water dripped somewhere in the distance, but the mine was unnaturally silent.

"Can't hear that creak of beams you talked about," Lady Jane muttered to Engle, trying to follow the charade until its direction became clear.

"Gotta go over the bridge to the south wince, ma'am." The spot he referred to was familiar to Jane. The men had been working a ledge in the area and had come upon a large block of clay. It was unstable, expanding whenever air struck it and so moving and growing even as they worked on it.

Engle led Jane on what seemed to be a circuitous route. He wandered the mine, taking cutoffs and detours that she was sure weren't necessary. She tried to memorize their path on a map in her mind, but couldn't. Then the great bridge appeared ahead of them and she knew where she was. Dufond stood on it, three candles lit around him.

Jane stopped in her tracks. It really *was* him.

"My guide first," she gestured to Engle to precede

her across the bridge. The moment he stepped in front
of her she drew her pistol, struggling with its great
weight.

"Dufond!" she shouted. He looked up, his anxiety
from being alone in the hole instantly replaced by the
fear his recognition of her brought with it.

"*Mon dieu!*"

"We meet again."

"Where did she come from?" Dufond piped to
Engle, his voice squeaking with confusion.

"Mrs. Harrington?"

"*She* is Mrs. Harrington?"

"Yeah. Hey, what's with the gun, ma'am?"

Dufond understood the situation. With one arm he
swept the candles around him from their perches and
backed up, disappearing into the darkness. Jane fired
where he'd stood, but the little man had slipped away.

"Jesus!" the shot had just missed Engle.

"I'm afraid you've run out of time, Mr. Engle. Your
plan was clumsy to begin with and now hasn't a
chance." She shook with anger, both hands gripping
her husband's pistol.

"Plan?" He was trapped on the bridge, darkness on
one side, Lady Jane on the other. "What's this all
about?" As she cracked a smile, he dove away from
her and rolled across the bridge. Her pistol spit fire and
recoiled in her hands. The now-invisible union organizer howled somewhere out of sight and she heard
his clumsy footsteps clopping on the wooden floor of
the square sets beyond.

Jane knelt behind a timber. They were trapped, almost. She need only wait for them to come at her. But
the heat and darkness of the place had her soaking
now, muddling her concentration. Then two tiny black
eyes glistened nearby, a rat studying her. She picked up

a rock and hurled it toward the stare and the rodent vanished.

Jane propped her candle on the post next to the bridge and retreated slightly. She didn't want to be seen by either of the two men. Standing, wiping sweat from her brow, she saw a match being struck some thirty feet away. There was nothing to shoot at. Then the telltale glitter of a fuse burst in the distance and Jane saw a stick of dynamite rolling toward her. It skittered across the bridge as though it had a life of its own and then raced past her. She dove for the stick, saw that its fuse had only seconds to burn and threw the thing into the darkness.

The explosion rocked the place, timbers shattering in the distance, beams and floorboards falling toward the sump below. There was the sound of rock and sand clattering, bouncing, raining into the bottom of the mine, and an aching creak in the timbers all around her.

As the sand, rock and beams settled under the blow, quiet returned slowly to the mine. But it took several minutes for the huge quantities of shattered structure to creak still. When there was nothing but deadly silence around her, Jane heard the most terrifying noise imaginable. Out of the darkness beyond came a laugh, the high, giddy cackle of a man terrified and bent on vengeance. Of a soul so twisted that no caution or reason could be found in the tone of its scream.

It was Dufond. "We die in this hellhole!" he blared. "I swear it!"

"Jesus, don't!" It was Engle, wounded and hiding, out of touch with Dufond.

"Get out!" Dufond ordered.

"She'll kill me!"

Jane listened, unable to locate them from the sound of their voices.

"Get out!" Dufond screamed, his voice cracking again.

Jane heard the hurried run of a man fleeing, but not knowing where to go. Then it stopped and Engle lit a match. She saw the candle burn and his face loomed in the darkness. She aimed, steadying the pistol on a diagonal beam, and fired. He yelled again, hit, and the candle fell. It was black once again and he was moaning, then crawling away from her.

Dufond laughed, that horrible laugh.

Jane's mind raced to the diagrams on her office wall. She tried to place herself, position the two men and gauge their distances. She imagined the damage that the blast had caused, then dismissed it. Engle could circle her and escape. He knew the mine and, if he could walk and see where he was going, he might make it to an auxiliary shaft sixty feet to his left. But he'd have to move carefully. Between him and an exit lay one of the broad, open holes that carried water from the sump to the surface. It fell 600 feet into the 160-degree water below.

Jane watched for another match, knowing he'd have to light one. There was nothing. She could barely detect the scuffling of a man along the floorboards, but couldn't be sure that the sound didn't come from a rat. Either way, she thought to herself, a rat.

Timber settled, crashing in the distance and a billow of steam rushed from the bowels of the mine, completely covering the bridge.

Dufond lit another match. She froze. Then the glitter of the fuse appeared and the thing clattered toward her. It stopped short, just across the bridge. She ran for it, this time stepping on the fuse and pulling at the orange stick. The hissing string came free. Then a shot rang out. She fell to her belly and heard another. It was Dufond. She watched for a third flash of a muzzle, but none came.

Then he laughed that piercing, shrill laugh again and she fired blindly at it. The sound infuriating her. But the futile gesture seemed only to amuse the man and he continued. She hated it.

Suddenly she heard Engle running, his feet heavy and irregular on the floor. The hollow, clumsy cadence of the sound told her he had panicked, he was sprinting for the shaft ahead.

His body ricocheted off beams and crossmembers as he fell, his terrified cry lasting only a moment before he was knocked unconscious by one of the blows. Engle's body twisted in the air, his bones breaking as he clattered down the hole. By the time his corpse reached the water below, it was mauled beyond recognition, one leg having been removed and his head having been bashed into a bloody pulp. Lady Jane was alone with Dufond.

It was black. The texture of the darkness moving around her, patternless, empty. The hiss of steam, the clank of pumps and the creaking of the timbers in the distance were all the more disorienting in the black around her. The pure, absolute darkness of the place dominated Jane's thoughts. For one terrifying moment she thought that Dufond must surely be more comfortable than she in such a deathlike environment. Then she shook it off, too warm, too wet, too terrified, she tried to concentrate.

The three great stacks that reached far above the Silver Lady's main building belched smoke into the winter air as Spear ran up the hill toward it. The loose rubble of spent diggings made his going slow until he hit the path and only then could he concentrate on the sight ahead. The ore shoots that normally would be spilling rock into wagons waiting on the road were empty. No mule-drawn wagons were there. No hollering men hurrying the silver ore away.

Spear knew a strike would slow the mine, but he was surprised to see it halted altogether. There was something odd going on.

As Brad ran up the narrow wooden steps to the main floor level, he heard the blast, the rumble of deep and distant explosions. Throwing the door open he saw scores of men running away from the great open shafts of the mine, steam and smoke gushing from the broad holes in the floor. Miners tripped over one another, crawled and flattened themselves against the outer walls of the building. Some stood still, their mouths agape, their hands frozen at their sides, the simple horror of an explosion in the hole paralyzing them.

Spear searched the crowd for Karl Oppenheimer, asking several stunned men if Mrs. Harrington was in the mine. All nodded to him, unable to tear their eyes from the billows of dust and smoke that rose into the room. Windows high in the building were opened so that fumes might escape, doors latched wide to clear the air. But Brad ignored it all, looking for Oppenheimer.

He found him near the number two engine, the central hoist that led into the hole. Its cable disengaged, he and Dan Frogle were testing it. The thing worked, but they didn't dare lift the car below. To do so without a signal might easily kill Lady Jane. And the bell's cord, Karl figured, was as likely broken in the blast as not. They were stuck.

"There another way down?" Spear asked the distracted general manager.

"I shouldn't have let her go," he said.

"There another way down?"

Karl looked at Spear, his shoulder bleeding from the

long run to the mine, his rifle hanging in one hand. "Take half a day to walk the ladders," Karl responded, shaking his head.

"Who's in there with her?" Spear grabbed the shaken Oppenheimer by the shoulders, forcing him to his senses.

"The union man, Engle, and the new guy, Dufond."

The faces all around him told Brad that those in the mine were dead. The smell of burning timber and the dust that spewed into the room with it indicated to the miners that anyone below must be buried. There was nothing to do but wait for the calm and then go in after their bodies. Even Oppenheimer seemed beaten.

Brad put his one good hand behind Karl and pushed him toward the steam and smoke still drifting from the ground.

"We're going down," he ordered.

As Karl shuffled forward he turned to Brad, "You don't understand, man, the shaft is burning. The collapse is here, below us. We won't get to 'em even if they're breathing."

"Let's go," Spear shoved Karl onto a waiting car. Brad looked at the engineer who controlled the bucket. The man shook his head. A responsible, decent sort of guy, he couldn't drop Karl to his death. Brad lifted his rifle, gently raising its muzzle until it was under Oppenheimer's chin. "Tell him," he whispered to the general manager.

"Take it slow. Any slack in the cable, stop her. We'll rap on the cable if we want up, so keep a hand on it."

The car descended, smoke and steam surrounding them immediately. And then there was the darkness, not even the sheer rock of the shaft's walls visible.

"She's dead." Oppenheimer was certain, at least in his heart. His guilt made optimism impossible.

"Maybe. I doubt it. She's one tough bitch, Karl."

Oppenheimer listened to Brad, surprised by his language. He'd never heard anyone refer to Mrs. Harrington that way.

The floor of the car crashed into something and tilted, upsetting both men. But they held to it. In a moment, Brad saw the light of a match and Karl groping about for a candle. He found one, lit it and turned to the agent.

"We're as low as this thing'll be goin' today. 'Bout sixty feet above the spot she headed for."

"Come on," Brad pulled himself out of the car, up and over the beam that shone before them. "The ladders from here."

"This way." Oppenheimer was there now and the devastation wasn't nearly as great as the smoke at the surface implied. She could be alive, it was possible, he thought.

There was gunfire, sudden and brief, from below. Both men stopped and listened. "Tough bitch," Brad muttered. They raced, Karl running from pure memory through the treacherous mine, hurling himself through the pitch-black hole, and Brad held onto him, his fist filled with the man's coat. Soon they were descending, the simple ladder tricky to maneuver, and then descending again. After three or four levels had been passed, Brad heard shots again, but there was nothing to be seen below them so the pair struggled on.

Then there was the laughter. And a scream. And gunfire. And that piercing laugh. "Mother of God," Oppenheimer sighed.

One hand carrying the small rifle and his other only half-effective as a result of his wound, Brad found the going tough on the ladders. He stumbled on them occasionally, losing his bearings in the darkness. But the pump of his blood and the echo of that laugh drove him on and eventually, when he came to the bottom of yet another flight, Karl was standing waiting for him.

The smell of something burning lingered in the air. Not the odor of wood or coal, but a gagging stink he'd never experienced before.

"Afterdamp," Karl muttered. "But not bad."

"What?"

"That smell. Bad enough and it'll kill ya. This ain't bad."

"Where are they?"

"Don't know. How 'bout you shut up and let me listen to my mine." It was his mine, in every sense. Though his arrangement with Mr. Harrington, and thereafter with his widow, had involved only a profit-sharing deal, he owned the place the way an athlete owns a track. Because he lived with it, knew it better than anyone, it belonged to Karl.

The creak of timbers continued, the irregular settling of stone against wood sounding weird to Spear. He couldn't judge distances in the darkness and was confused by the vast, erratically creaking and shuddering space around him. Though he stood no more than a foot from Karl, he could barely make him out. Incredible, he thought.

There was another shot and Karl froze. "The bridge, or thereabouts, I think. Go slow now. Whole hunks of what used to be here ain't no more."

They walked carefully into the perpetual night of the mine, Karl moving much more cautiously than he had before. They found one candle burning in an upright, but no one was nearby. Then there was the flash of a match and the bright light of a dynamite fuse.

"Shit!" Karl exclaimed.

The thing clattered along the floor and came to a stop no more than thirty feet from them. Brad watched it spin, out of reach, a fistful of explosive that would surely kill them all. Then Jane leapt into view, grabbing it, and threw the candle-sized stick of death into the darkness.

"Down," Karl pushed Brad to the floor.

This second blast sent splintered timbers hailing down around them. Rock rattled everywhere and the entire structure of the lower level shuddered, not moving so much as straining to keep from coming unglued. It went on for two or three minutes, the crash of further damage coming slower and slower, unpredictable showers of wet clay and rock falling on them. But eventually there was a temporary stillness to the mine. Not silence, but a fragile truce agreed to by rock and wood.

"Jane!" Brad shouted into the blackness.

"Brad!" she answered. "Where are you?"

"Stay where you are, we're coming."

Karl led Brad to her, feeling his way among the stones and timbers that lay at odd angles, tilted. She stood as they approached and held Brad in the darkness for a moment.

"It's Dufond," she finally spoke.

"I know, Karl told me."

"He's across the bridge, somewhere, laughing and tossing those damn sticks our way."

"He has a gun?"

"Yes."

"Karl, move off there, maybe ten feet or so. Get well behind a timber and then light a match. Let's draw some fire."

Oppenheimer moved away, the sound of his shuffling feet receding only inches at a time. Brad eased Jane down, leaning her back against a still-solid upright timber. Then he lifted his rifle, its stock against his shoulder, his cheek pressed into the weapon. His finger slid up and down the trigger as he peered in the general direction of the source of the last stick of dynamite.

Karl's match flashed, a glow twenty feet away.

"Spear?" Dufond shouted from the darkness. But the agent said nothing. "Spear?"

Karl lit a second match when the first had gone and a shot rang out. Brad saw the yellow stripe reaching into the darkness, saw the source and turned, aiming quickly. He emptied all six shells in his shoulder arm's cylinder, firing at the memory of that one bright light. There was a screech. A hollow, almost feminine yell, and then silence.

"He's not dead, Brad."

"I think you're right."

"Let's get out of here."

"Right again." He stopped whispering. "Hey, Karl."

"Yeah."

"Gonna lead us out of here?"

"Yeah, why not?"

"Don't light a match, though. The rat may not be dead."

Oppenheimer arrived quickly, startling them both. Then, carrying Brad's empty rifle, he led them up the ladders to the car above. Karl lifted Jane to the floor of the car, embarrassing himself as he groped in the darkness to find and hold her. Then he lent Brad a hand into the bucket, giving him back his rifle as he did so.

Without a word, Karl scampered like a child up the side of the car's cage and perched on its roof. With a rock he began pounding on the broad, flat, braided cable that hung limp above him. In seconds it tightened and then lifted them, Brad and Jane sitting on the car floor as it righted itself, Karl standing on its roof as they climbed. The smoke and smell of burning gases fell below them, the cool air above falling like a shower on their sweat-soaked clothes.

"Chilly place, don't you think?" Jane asked.

# Chapter 19

Mittens found Spear's remarkable .45 hanging on a chair in Brockington's office. He pulled it from its holster and spun the beautifully machined cylinder. It made an even, whirling sound, perfectly balanced, immaculately cleaned and lubricated. The weight of the thing impressed Mittens: it was very light. Then, while considering the workmanship that went into the side arm, he noticed that neither of his hands were covered.

Still drained by the wrenching emotions that overcame him in the hallway, the tall, thin man looked at his fingers as though they belonged to someone else. Pale and delicate, he turned them over, pondering their steadiness. He wondered if the stillness that had overcome him meant he had lost or gained something in those furious moments with Brockington. But in the quiet of the house he couldn't focus his thoughts, couldn't establish a starting point. He was drifting.

Bunny walked into the room calmly, a robe covering her, its thick rope belt cinched tightly around her thin waist. Mittens replaced the weapon in its holster without realizing she stood behind him. As he turned, gazing at the books which lined the shelves of the small office, she moved toward him.

Mittens looked down at Bunny as though she were a child approaching him on the street with a foolish question. He didn't seem to recognize her. Instead, he had the look of a man who might indulge an infant's playfulness, who might stand and talk to a six-year-old for hours. It felt like patience, but he couldn't be sure.

"This room is very small," he observed. "I'd always thought it would be much bigger."

Bunny looked up at him. Clearly, she couldn't understand. He'd seen the room from the doorway many times, on those countless occasions when she'd slipped him money for the inmates at Fetterman's, whenever she had a message for them, or news. He knew that Brockington's lair was small.

"And I always thought it would frighten me to be in here." He turned his back to her, looking around. He was a child himself, a boy who had at last made his way into the candy factory only to discover it was largely machinery and crates with very little sugar to be seen. The only truly powerful man Mittens had ever known was dead and his office seemed very, very small.

Mittens sat at the doctor's desk and began opening the small drawers and doors it contained. He found several thousand dollars in cash, stacks of old prescriptions, ledgers, bankbooks, stock certificates of every kind, note paper, the extraordinary and ordinary junk that had built up around Brockington. Neither the cash nor the piles of random doodles had any impact on him.

The desk clerk was disappointed and Bunny could see it in his face. His hands fell to his knees and he leaned back, the chair creaking.

"What?" she asked, frustrated and perplexed by his sullen behavior.

"Nothing. Absolutely nothing."

"But what's the matter? He's . . . gone. It's over. What's the matter?" Her voice rose and fell as she struggled to control herself, yet probed as keenly as she could.

"There's nothing here. The man who dealt in so much suffering had a desk filled with trash. Not a secret anywhere." Mittens stood, a flood of disgust rushing through him. Brockington had been an animal, a vicious, cunning animal, but nothing more. The silence he left behind proved it.

Bunny watched his gentle hand slip a blank pad onto the piles of papers in front of him. Whatever search had been going on was complete.

"It is just over, he's dead. It's over."

Bunny recoiled from him. She hadn't realized it until that moment. They were alone, uncontrolled, unsupported, with neither the loathsome guidance or the comforting command that Brockington had supplied. He was dead, like her father, he was absolutely gone.

She took Mittens' hand, entwining her fingers desperately with his.

"Cold?" she asked, pulling him to her.

"No."

"Come with me."

He followed her, no longer dazed so much as directionless. As eager to walk behind the little girl that tugged at his arm as stand and wonder about the little office. In a moment they were in a small, spare room, Bunny's room.

The bed was pine, the crude writing table beside it too worn and stained to identify. Pale curtains hung in the single window and a braided rag rug was centered on the floor. There was a picture of Lincoln on the wall and a sketch of a boat. The doorless closet contained two or three stunning gowns and scores of ragtag dresses. Mittens thought to himself that it looked very much like the tiny cell in which he lived off the hotel's lobby.

Bunny reached up to him and carefully removed his scarf. It slipped from his neck quickly, no hint of protest showing in his eyes. She then wrapped her arms around his neck and pulled his pale, thin lips to hers.

As Mittens' eyes closed, the house evaporated around him. His hands felt the cloth of her robe as he held Bunny and his mouth opened, surprised by her darting tongue. They rocked, bound together by the simplest of embraces.

Slowly, she peeled away from him. His hands still on her waist, she unbuttoned his long, grey coat and then opened his shirt. Taking his wrists, she removed his hands from her and stripped him to his baggy trousers. Mittens stared at her, unalarmed. From some hidden pit within, he found a distant memory of the scene, but didn't acknowledge it. He was following her, letting her proceed. Then he looked into her eyes and was caught breathless by the dark, narrowed gaze she offered. It was lust, or love, or something. But it gleamed at him.

Mittens reached out for her, parting her robe and reaching behind Bunny to the smooth, warm skin of her back. As she came to him, her hardened nipples brushed across his chest and then pressed against him.

Her warmth rose around him, her hands and arms holding him tightly, as though reaching for something that might at any moment escape. And, responding, he surrounded her with his broad shoulders and long arms, enveloping her.

Bunny withdrew and kissed him, her robe falling to the floor. She stood bruised and scratched, but Brockington's violence seemed not to have touched her beauty. Her small, round shoulders caught the light spreading through the window and her hips, trim and soft, shimmered below his gaze. She was at once a child, looking up at him, unsure of his approval, and a spectacularly sensuous woman, certain of her allure.

He unbuckled his belt almost methodically, as though by rote, and the laughable trousers that hung around his waist disappeared. She walked to him and they fell to the bed, her face diving to his chest, seeking him with a kind of eagerness that at first frightened and then thrilled him. She was alive with motion, her touch and warmth overwhelming his quieter, calmer enjoyment of the beautiful woman that held him.

He touched her breast, fearful of his own clumsiness, his fingers barely grazing her skin, gentle, too gentle. She arched, pulling back, and Mittens' pale, smooth caress explored the lift of her ribs, the fall of her navel, the twin ridges that ran along her hips. She touched his side, his leg, his throbbing, growing member and he followed, his palm covering her mound.

Her eyes asked, her legs spread and he eased his touch along the moist edge of her. He brushed her glowing tip and she moaned once, quietly, the sound of satisfaction warming him. And then her tongue dove across his ear, the sound of her hurried breathing and the frenzy of the touch inflaming him. His hand dove to her deeply and she gasped. She rocked and moaned, pressing up at him, responding now, not leading. She hung on him, pulled and pushed, rapt below his hands.

Desperate for him, Bunny reached, searching for the hardened yearning that she'd awakened. Discovering him huge below her touch brought her a smile, the question gone. She pulled, leading him, and her knees rose around his hips. There was one tentative touch and then she guided him deep into her. Bunny's sudden sense of being filled, overcome, was startlingly intense, stronger and more compelling than anything she thought possible.

Mittens moved above her, steadily and slowly, reaching a new depth with each thrust. She opened to him, straining, the sweet pain of growing torment urging her on until the wave of wanting him overcame her in a rush. Below his powerful, continuing drive against her, Bunny arched, pinned and shuddering as the spark raced and spread into flames that consumed her. Then, as the warmth of her slowing, tantalizing pleasure evened across her skin, she felt him rise and fall, suddenly urgent and hurried. His eyes opened, his lips spread and the churning tip of him exploded in her, driving deeper, steadier, the full and tender expression of his lust, or love, or something.

The table, set in the center of a private room at The Mammoth Saloon, was a five-sided affair normally used for poker. But, since Brad's arm was in a sling, he couldn't sort his cards. His solution to the problem was to peer mischievously over Carlotta's shoulder, bidding from the hand she held for him.

Brad had arranged the game so that Lady Jane's more possessive instincts would be fully aroused. She and Brad, with the strikingly beautiful Carlotta's assistance, were teamed against Elephant and Lyn Loftin in a friendly game of pinochle. Lady Jane hated the game. "Stupid," she called it. And Brad wryly pointed out to his opponents that it would be wise of them not to let Mrs. Harrington deal as she was very quick with her cards. "Whose side are you on?" she asked.

For all the jealous banter that went on between Brad and Jane, there was little real seriousness to the situation. Everyone, even Carlotta, felt playful. They'd all survived and it was coming to an end. Only Judge Thorpe and Senator Rogers needed to be dealt with. Brockington was dead and Dufond had either died in the mine or would soon be captured. Eight armed men now waited at the top of the hole for him.

Loftin peered over his cards at Elephant as he gathered in a trick. For some reason the banker was playing the game with rigid concentration. "Elephant, for heaven's sake, drop points on my winners."

"Huh?" Elephant was tired, had several beers under his belt and could never keep the rules to this game straight.

"Points, lay points on my winners!"

"You're an antsy sorta fella, ain't ya?"

Loftin shook his head.

"I think the buckshot addled his mind," Jane chuckled.

"Or the beer." Loftin wasn't amused.

Brad pointed at the card he wished Carlotta to play, brushing against her shoulder as he did so. Jane thought he was transparent. Being silly. And worse, it was getting on her nerves. Carlotta shook her head, turned and whispered in Brad's ear.

"Oh, for God's sake, just play your card," Jane spat. "The beauty of this game is that it takes absolutely no mental ability whatever, so I see no good reason for your constant delays. All these conferences, really!"

Carlotta spun away from Brad and sat like a choir-girl, prim and proper except for the smirk that flashed across her face. She was fully aware of Brad's feelings toward Lady Jane. She had no illusions about their night together. And it was kind of fun, playing cat and mouse over a card table.

"Sorry, Mrs. Harrington," Brad oozed in his most sarcastic tone.

"Just play a card," Jane clapped her hand against her forehead. The card skidded across the table. "Oh, no." Jane was disappointed.

"Wrong, huh?" Brad asked.

"Jesus . . ." Jane was awed by his ability to perform brilliantly at one moment and then behave like a dolt the next. It was incredible to her that the man made it through life on his own. Brad shrugged. Loftin grinned and raked in another trick.

Ben, the barkeep, appeared at the door. "There's a gentleman here to see you, Mr. Spear. Judge Thorpe."

"Thanks, would you show him in?"

As the nervous banker began gathering in the cards, Elephant protested. "Hey, can't we finish the hand? We're gonna set you guys."

"I don't believe this," Jane exclaimed, throwing her unplayed cards on the table. It was Elephant's turn to shrug.

Thorpe was punctual. It was precisely six. And from his demeanor Brad knew that his invitation had unsettled the man. His pointed reference to Broken Leg Gulch had been effective and the news of Brockington's death must have panicked Thorpe. The rich and powerful group of conspirators was now a turtle turned on its back, vulnerable and lost.

Carlotta stood as the judge entered and moved quietly to a corner of the room. The man stood, squinting through his steel-rimmed spectacles into the darkened room.

"Mr. Spear?" not seeing the agent.

"Have a seat, sir, please," Brad gestured toward the empty chair beside him.

Thorpe was introduced to Elephant, who snorted at him, and Carlotta, who simply stared, grim. The nervous guest made a pathetic effort to chat with Mrs. Harrington, offering his regrets about the damage to her mine. He blamed the unions, she let it pass. Loftin shuffled the cards over and over, the clack of their stiff, varnished sides drawing a fidgeting glance from Thorpe every time he did so.

"Well, sir," Thorpe began, "shall we discuss this matter in private?"

"I don't think so," Brad replied. "In fact, there's one

more member of the group yet to arrive. Would you care for a drink while we wait?"

Before Thorpe could respond, a staggering Senator Rogers walked into the room. He was drunk, leaning on his silver-capped walking stick with each step.

"Ted!" the judge gasped.

Rogers didn't seem to hear him. He stumbled around the table searching for an empty chair and, having completed one full tour, stopped. Elephant stood, took the man's elbow and sat him down.

"Now then," Brad spoke confidently. "It seems we can begin."

"Exactly what's this all about, Spear?" Thorpe's tone of pompous interrogation was the best he could muster.

"I think you know, Judge. It seems that there's been a recent discovery of silver in these parts and I thought it would be a good idea if we all sat down and discussed our interests in the find. Since we all appear to be so involved, I mean."

"Involved?" Thorpe was determined to resist. He looked across the table at Rogers, but saw a weaving head unable to right itself and a pair of drooping eyelids that threatened to shut altogether at any moment.

"Shut up, Thorpe." Brad didn't feel like spending a lot of time dancing with the man. "You and Rogers and Brockington engineered the burglary of Mr. Loftin's bank, you killed God only knows how many men stealing Land Grant Certificates and you made an earnest effort to kill Mrs. Harrington here. I'm not guessing, I know it."

"But you can't prove it." The judge was right, the two were tied into the scheme only because Brad had seen them with Brockington's hired killer in his parlor. Hardly evidence.

"There is a chance that I might be able to, if I can find Mr. Fritsch."

Senator Rogers' head jerked as though he were a marionette yanked on by Brad's mention of the name. All of a sudden he looked fairly sober.

"I'm not familiar with Mr. Fritsch, never met the man," Thorpe said.

"Sure ya did, we all did," Rogers' words were slurred, a little garbled by his haste and drunkenness, but they were clear.

"Shut up, Ted. Let me do the talking."

"Ah, come on, Judge, who ya kiddin'?" Rogers certainly wasn't at his best, but he could discern their predicament well enough.

"Should you locate Mr. Fritsch, I'd be happy to meet him in a court of law." Thorpe felt certain he could win such a fight.

"Well, Judge, there's a problem with your suggestion. You see, I *will* find Fritsch and I can assure you that he will tell me everything he knows, that is unless he wants me to peel the skin from him strip by strip. So there's no question that we'll be able to prove your guilt, both your guilt. The real difficulty then becomes that young lady in the corner." Brad turned his head to Carlotta, almost impossible to see in the half-light of the room.

The young woman took a step forward and the large overhead lamp spread its glow across Jebediah's buffalo gun held firmly in her hands.

"Carlotta, you see, lost her father to your men in Broken Leg Gulch. I doubt that she would be satisfied if a court of law let you off, scot-free."

Thorpe, frozen at the sight of the broad, black muzzle of the monstrous weapon directed his way, tried to think. "Young woman, um, we didn't get involved in the gulch business. I mean, Brockington handled all of it. We didn't order, or, I should say, expect anybody to get killed. We just weren't in on any of that."

"I think, sir, that's probably horseshit," Brad said. Tears started to slip down Senator Rogers' cheeks.

"No, really, the Doc was in charge of all that stuff."

"If I may speak for Carlotta, it won't matter much once I find Mr. Fritsch."

Carlotta stood fixed in her corner, the ponderous weight of the rifle in her hands reminding her of Jebediah's strength. She'd thought about him endlessly during the last day. She'd considered how she would feel about the men that now sat in front of her. And their presence was as she'd expected. She didn't hate either of them. Both were greedy little creatures to her, men who tried for an easy fortune, guided by a truly loathsome man. All the resources, the skills, the courage and the strength that she valued in people were absent in them. They were pathetic.

She understood the kind of grim determination and strength that moved both good and bad men. She even had a certain respect for it. Brockington, in his way, was a force. A wretched power, but a power. The rifleman sent after Spear was at least strong, resourceful. But these men were different. Some deep conviction in her made it impossible to accept that a weasel like Thorpe or a slob like Rogers could kill her father. They were incapable of it. Still she stood, apparently ready to kill them, waiting for Spear.

"It seems to me we ought to try to find some other solution to this, ah, problem." Brad wondered just how frightened Thorpe was.

"Go on," the judge's note of resignation obvious.

"To be sporting, I think you two ought to be given a fair chance. So I propose a kind of wager."

"What?" Thorpe was being toyed with and he knew it.

"Shhhhh," Carlotta hushed him delicately.

"We will cut cards. If you take the cut, we call it a day. If you lose, you turn over all the Land Grant Certificates you own to Mr. Loftin here. He'll return those that were stolen. Any that you bought on speculation, he'll give to Carlotta and Elephant here, to sorta ease their pain. Fair enough?"

"And that's all there is to it?" Thorpe couldn't believe Spear wanted nothing more.

"Oh, well, in either case, win or lose, both you and Mr. Rogers must retire from, I hate to say 'public service', so let's say 'office'."

"Retire?"

"Immediately. Tonight."

Thorpe wiped his mouth, beads of sweat having formed on his upper lip. Elephant shuffled the cards once again.

"Who cuts first?" the judge asked.

"Senator?" Brad invited, sliding the deck to Rogers.

Fumbling slightly, Rogers cut the deck. A nine of diamonds. He chortled, sort of, and put the card down. "May I have a drink?" he asked.

"Soon." Brad slid the deck to Thorpe. A queen of spades. "Now then, would the lady do the honors?" Brad smiled at Jane.

"Beats pinochle," she answered. The ace of hearts. She looked at Brad, pleased with her selection. "I'm sentimental that way, sweetheart," she cooed to him.

"Well, I guess that about settles the issue," the agent beamed. So easy, he thought. "Elephant, would you and Lyn escort these gentlemen to their homes so we can collect our winnings?"

"Winnings? Humph!" Thorpe was angry, beaten.

"Now, now. Easy, Judge," Brad tipped his head toward Carlotta. "Perhaps the lady should go along, sort of as a safety precaution."

Thorpe grabbed Rogers and lifted him from his chair. The senator, much bigger than the judge, pushed him aside and staggered to the door. "Forget the drink," he mumbled.

Lady Jane shuffled the cards, her eyes rising now and then to Brad. The room had emptied and the two of them sat opposite each other across the card table. The agent sipped his beer but the warm liquid tasted terrible to him, so he replaced the mug on the table. She shuffled the cards once again, frowning at him. Jane was puzzled. She cut the deck to the ace of hearts, shuffled it and cut it once more to the ace of hearts.

"What's your problem?" she asked, her voice testy.

"You."

"I know the feeling."

"The hell you do," he almost laughed at her. "You don't have any idea."

She was startled, he wasn't jousting. Instead, she could see him wrestling with something, the puckish good humor of the past few minutes gone now, replaced by an almost leaden seriousness. She had intended to infuriate him with jibes and innuendo, veiled criticisms of his flirtation with Carlotta at the card table. But the jealousy Brad stirred in her didn't seem very important all of a sudden.

"Are you sure?" she pressed.

"Yes."

"Can I ask? I'd really like to know."

Her sincerity cut through him, the tenderness in Jane's voice whispering to him. It was that gentleness, that softness about her that so confused him. She was a tough bitch, to be sure. But at the same time, a vulnerable woman for whom he felt responsible.

"You frightened me in the mine." It was a simple

statement, one that any other man might easily make with no special significance assigned to it.

"I'm sorry." Jane wasn't sure what was going on.

"Don't apologize, it's not that. It's just that I was afraid something had happened to you, that you'd been killed in that hole. I panicked. I couldn't help it."

"It worked out all right."

"For no good reason, it just happened to work out. The problem is that I can't afford to lose my head while I'm working. Mistakes like that kill people, especially Pinkerton agents."

She couldn't stop playing with the cards, she wanted to, but the things kept fanning and shuffling under her touch. Here she was, with the most remarkable man she'd ever met, fiddling with a deck of cards like a nervous schoolgirl. Brad was, in his way, telling Jane that he was in love with her and that he hated it. And she kept shuffling her cards. She wished he didn't hate it.

"I'm sorry," she replied. "I love you, too."

"Bitch."

"Thank you."

"You're welcome." He grinned and she felt better.

Mittens stood in the doorway. " 'Scuse me, folks," he said, one arm wrapped tightly around Bunny. "Forgot to give you this, Mr. Spear." Mittens handed Brad his .45.

"Hot damn!" The agent bolted to his feet, pulling the pistol from the holster Mittens held. "Where was it?"

"Brockington's. Guess they figured it was a little conspicuous to be toting around the mine."

"Fantastic. Thought for sure this thing was buried somewhere in that blasted hole. Fantastic!" The familiar heft and balance of the weapon thrilled Spear, the thing a part of him. He nearly giggled with delight.

"So, good evening to you." Mittens tossed the empty holster to Spear.

"What are you two up to?" Brad asked, his question stopping them as they turned to leave. He felt like having a celebration.

"Packing. In a few days we'll be headed out of here."

"Where to?" Jane asked.

Bunny shrugged, happily indifferent to their destination.

"Probably Utah. They're opening new mines there all the time."

"They'll be opening a new one right here, soon enough," Jane offered. "Why not wait for it?"

"Nah. Too much bad baggage in this town for our tastes. We're gonna start over someplace. See what comes of it."

Spear liked the idea. Might even work. If ever there were a couple meant for one another, these two semireformed lunatics were it. "So long then, and good luck," he wished them.

Once they'd left, Jane cut the cards to the ace of hearts, took Spear by the hand and led him from the room. All the way up the hill to her home he fingered the pistol, reassuring himself it still hung by his side.

Dufond's side burned, two .36 caliber slugs having ripped through his flesh. He bled slowly in the darkness, huddled in a corner. After several hours men's voices filled the distance. There was the slow, muted sound of cautious digging, timbers were righted and hauled away. The clank of a lift, hurrying up and down the mine's main shaft, went endlessly on through the night. And still the man crouched, hidden well beyond the armed men searching for him and the frantic work crews that were busy repairing the damage done by Dufond's two sticks of dynamite.

Toward the end of the second day, the work in the hole became much more relaxed. The most threatening sections of the lower level were shored up, not permanently, but well. The men knew that real danger had passed simply because Karl Oppenheimer, who had labored steadily for nearly two days, left the mine and went home. No ore would be removed from the Silver Lady for weeks, but the work had settled into an even routine of digging out and propping up. The terrifying disaster in the hole had passed.

Dufond groped in the darkness, fleeing the sound of their voices, the rattle of picks and shovels. And after what seemed to be an eternity, he stumbled upon a sloping shaft, an airway running down to the lowest level of the mine, far below the work then going on.

He removed two of the three fuses that remained on the sticks of dynamite in his pockets and carefully tied them together. Two minutes, maybe three, he thought. He was filthy and delirious with the heat, the hunger and his loss of blood. But just as a dog holds a bone in his jaws, defying all comers, Dufond clung to the thought of escape. It fueled him, a stubborn refusal to die or give up forcing him to think.

He waited for the sound of men preparing to change shifts, the telltale clatter of lunch pails displacing the bang of picks. Then he lit the fuse and slipped one stick of dynamite into the airway. As the sparkling explosive slid down, out of sight, Dufond walked toward the voices ahead as quickly as he could. He followed the lazily retreating miners to the main shaft and then hid, only yards away, as they piled into the car.

The explosion rocked the place, a dull, distant turbulence spreading through the timbers with growing fury. As rock and sand fell all around them, miners screamed, scurrying for the cars that led to safety. Each cubicle normally brought a dozen men at a time topside, but in moments the two which stood waiting contained forty men. They were piled on one another, a crush of legs and arms completely filling the tiny space.

And, as timbers began to split around them, the screams of men left behind echoing below, thirty-nine miners and Pierre Dufond rose from the shuddering hole to the surface.

In the chaos above he escaped, sliding down an ore shoot to the street below.